IMM JOURNEY:

RISE OF REBELLION

VOLUME THREE

Ruth A. Souther

This book is a work of fiction loosely based upon Greek mythology and the magic of times past. All character interpretations, both mortal and divine, and the events described within are products of the author's imagination. Any resemblance to real people or incidents is purely coincidental.

IMMORTAL JOURNEY SERIES:

Death of Innocence, Volume One
Surrender of Ego, Volume Two
Rise of Rebellion, Volume Three

Crystal Heart Imprints
Immortal Journey: Rise of Rebellion
Copyright © 2015 by Ruth A. Souther

Cover Design by Chad Adelhardt
C.A. Photo & Design Studio
Cover Photo: Sabrina Trowbridge
Editing by Michaeleen McDonald

ISBN: 978-0-9721003-4-2

First Edition, 2015
First Printing, 2015

DEDICATION

To Jacqueline Grubbs - a goddess amongst us mortal writers, she fed my dreams and helped manifest them in the real world. We laughed until we cried at our own jokes, especially about our writing. Without her, this series would not be possible.

To Yvonne Salay Tyson - a cosmic dancer, a young woman of grace and beauty who swept into my heart with such joy. She encouraged me to be a better everything just by her very presence.

To Brad Collins - a fearless shaman who led the way for so many with generosity and kindness, who never blinked at the darkness, he just lit a candle. He brought me back to this story with two simple words: Claim it.

And so I have laughed, danced and claimed my story, thanks to these three amazing people. Love and honor to you always.

Though they have transitioned from this Earthly Realm, may they continue to shine their light from beyond the Veil.

Until we meet again, my friends. Until we meet again.

ACKNOWLEDGMENTS

I respectfully thank my family and many friends who supported me in the writing of this story. I could not have done it without you. Your love inspires me to be a better wordsmith and a better person.

A special thanks my editor, Michaeleen McDonald, who has the patience of a saint, to my designer, Chad Adelhardt, who created beautiful covers in spite of the many challenges, and to both Writing Rituals, senior and junior, for their focus and support during this process. An extra special thank you to Terri Woodliff, who saw me through 15 versions of this book and always stayed with it. She kept the characters and plot true to the storyline - I could not have done it without her.

RISE
OF
REBELLION

VOLUME THREE
OF THE
IMMORTAL JOURNEY
SERIES

RUTH A. SOUTHER

PROLOGUE

Rebellion begins from within, for only then will you find the courage to cast off the bondage and riot against those who would beat you down. Rise up, I say. Rebel!

My name is Deimos, I am son of Ares the Destroyer; I am known across the realms as Terror. Because I meddled in the affairs of the mortal world, a village was destroyed and the only woman for whom I have ever felt now lies dead.

On the night of the Summer Solstice, Niala Aaminah gave birth to her child. Born into my hands, I entrusted the babe into the care of my brother, Eris, he who is called Strife. Eris has hidden away the girl, for she must be kept safe - the child of a god without guardian would be in great danger.

The village of Najahmara remains in chaos, under the rule of their new king, Hattusilis. Will they find the strength to rebel against this regime? I know not, for I stay clear of their mortal woes. My own misery consumes all that is in my path. I can look no further than the smallest aspect of violence.

My father, Ares - Endless War, and my mother, Aphrodite - Eternal Love, being indiscreet were therefore caught and punished in a most terrible way. Hephaestos - God of the Forge Fires - trapped them beneath a web of gold chain while Cedalion - his loyal servant - put a poisoned dagger into the heart of Ares. His intention was to kill my father. Instead, Ares sank into a deep sleep and has not awakened. In grief, my mother abandoned her realm, leaving my twin brother, Anteros, to keep order.

Rebellion lies within the heart of each being, whether Immortal or Mortal, but can any find the courage to take action? I cannot answer other than for myself: I have no choice, for insurrection belongs to me. I wear the Mantle of Ares' Realm in expectation of his awakening. Until then, I am Endless War.

ONE

Deimos propped his elbow on one arm of the massive throne and closed his eyes. He was weary to the bone, too tired to strip away the remnants of battle or wash the blood and grime from his skin. Slack-jawed, he slumped further into the monument to War desiring only sleep. His body was pushed beyond limit. His mind was numbed by the staggering weight of his father's mantle. His voice was hoarse from the roar of War, and yet, rest was impossible.

He who held bitter fault with Ares now found himself ensconced in the same treacherous circle. Sleep would not visit. The god of Good Rest, Hypnos, shunned Deimos, unwilling or unable to reach him since the Hordes of War began to feed upon him.

This was the first silence he was allowed since Ares fell to the poisoned dagger of Cedalion.

Deafening silence.

Quiet torment.

A moment alone but without peace. His thoughts would not cease long enough for oblivion to take hold. Deimos' mind endlessly churned, returning to his last moments at Najahmara, a small village nestled in a fertile valley. A village bordering on near destruction from the invasion of an army assisted by Deimos before he understood that Gaea, Mother of All, watched over the land.

Over half of Najahmara's inhabitants, along with much of the invading army, died in the battle for control of the valley. Upon the night of the Summer Solstice, Deimos returned to the village, called by Gaea herself for a night of celebration. It was meant to ease the pain of the invasion by the Steppelands soldiers and their king, Hattusilis.

It was to be a festival of healing to unite the people in peace. Gentle Niala Aaminah, she who served as a priestess to the Great Mother, Gaea, led the festivities. Niala Aaminah held the power to invoke Earth and allow the spirit of the goddess to have a physical presence in the world she created. As Niala brought forth Gaea, Gaea summoned Deimos.

He had no choice but to respond.

The call was too strong to ignore and Deimos did not struggle against Gaea's command. He was overjoyed to go to Niala Aaminah under whatever guise, for he had fallen in love with her, knowing she was destined to become consort to Ares the Destroyer. Deimos had already crossed a forbidden line by stealing Niala from Athos and returning her to her people.

In doing so, Deimos caused Niala's death.

That moment of agony returned to him and once again brought the assault of images into his presence. Niala called Gaea into her so that Gaea could dance amongst her people, but Gaea was not content. She longed to settle an argument between herself and her mate, Kulika. To do so, Gaea needed a strong viable male to hold the spirit of the Sky God and who better than the son of War?

Deimos still vibrated to the depths of his soul. He still felt the fierce joy as Kulika's immortal soul flooded into his body, pushing Deimos' own essence down until Kulika had control. Once they settled their argument, Gaea and Kulika came together in a furious coupling, one that Deimos felt in his body but could not touch with his mind.

Their riotous sex caused a pregnant Niala to birth early. As the blood streamed from her body, the essence of the Sky God abandoned Deimos. At the same moment, Gaea receded from Niala, leaving her to die.

Deimos would not forgive either of them for such cowardice.

Sweating, Deimos brought his hands in front of him as if he once again held the tiny babe. He felt again the sting of jealousy that this child was fathered by Ares and not himself. The overwhelming grief enveloped Deimos as he relived the moment Niala lay bleeding to death while he could do nothing to stop her life seeping from her.

And then the final, all-consuming rage followed by madness that descended without warning. Deimos could not decipher the exact moment when the Mantle of War became his, but it had crashed down upon him that same night.

He remembered the tension as it coiled inside his body when Jahmed tried to take Niala's child from his hands. He had dim recollection of backing away, holding the babe so tight she cried, and then taking her without thought of what he would do with this fragile female. He was aware only that the babe was that of Niala and a daughter of War.

The child was special. She belonged to the immortals. Still, he had no plan in mind when he stole the child. By instinct, he returned to the place that had been his home for eons. He returned to the very room in which he sat, the altar chamber of War.

When the whirling shrieking hordes that claimed War as their master descended upon him, all was lost. There was a faint memory of commanding Eris to take the child, to hide her, to keep her safe. Then everything went black.

Deimos remained in that darkness for months, caught up in the brutality consuming the mortal world. He now had a far better understanding of his father. Oh, how much more compassionate, more understanding was Deimos of Ares' life, for all the good it did. Deimos regretted that he did not pay more attention to Ares' woes, and more, how Ares handled the pain of his existence.

Deimos could only wonder at the righteous disgust he voiced at Ares' display of raw sexuality, of the hours spent seducing mortal and immortal alike. Deimos shook his head at his own self-involved pity, and his escape into the earthly world.

He did not journey into the Mortal Realm as a seducer, but as one who was seduced by the many mysteries of being human. He was fascinated by those folk whose lives were so very short, whose deaths were often violent and without grace. Yet mortals lived with great passion and pleasure. This he wanted to understand. How they accepted such a fate without complaint. How they lived to life to the fullest, regardless of time.

His meandering thoughts brought him back to Niala's child. In his rare lucid moments, he questioned Eris on the whereabouts of the babe.

"Where have you hidden her?"

The young man's reply was always the same.

"I will tell you later, when you are less preoccupied, when you are able to shield yourself from this onslaught of blood and bone. Trust me, she is safe."

Deimos recognized the truth as he looked into the flinty gaze of his half-brother. He could fully trust Eris to have his back. This was a new revelation, one that took time to sink into Deimos' fevered brain.

Eris had been so long locked into youthful misbehavior - and perhaps even encouraged by Ares to keep his childlike delight in the vicious bloodletting of battle - it was difficult for Deimos to view him any other way. Mischievous Eris, unfit to lead, unfit to stand close to the throne of War, rather, left in the background with the rest of the minions.

Eris, son of Ares. Eris, he of fierce and brutal loyalty who followed War's command without question. The Eris who feared only his father, while at the same time found delicious delight in tormenting his brother, Deimos.

That youth became a man when the Mantle descended. A very different Eris charged forth during the chaotic, bleak moment when Deimos was engulfed by the hounds and hordes of War. Eris was now the right hand of War; he kept Deimos sane during the worst of it. He was the only one Deimos trusted.

There were small opportunities that allowed Deimos to barricade himself against the assault of War. These times lasted no more than a flick of an eyelash, and then the hordes were on him again and again and again.

But with each surge, Deimos discovered new strength to push back. Minutes became hours, hours became days. When he finally found the ability to banish War's minions from his sight, triumph belonged to him - until the time came that he was forced to call the hordes back. With each act of violence in the mortal realm, his unshakeable connection to human bloodlust resurfaced, Deimos lost control all over again and the vicious cycle resumed.

Exhaustion brought Deimos' thoughts back to the present moment. He rubbed a roughened palm across his bearded face and squeezed shut bleary eyes. He should go to his quarters, bathe and rest while he had the chance, for soon War's blitz would return.

Instead, he stared at the barren dais before him. Stripped of its grotesque garnishment of blood and bone - the sacrifices of both animal and human a thousand years gone - the altar stood in mute testimony to the absence of Ares, the Destroyer.

The black marble was draped in a pristine white cloth with gilt thread woven around the edges. A vase of fresh flowers stood in the center, flowers that most certainly did not come from Athos. There was only one who would dare and that was Deimos' twin brother, Anteros.

He who represented Love's Response, belonging to the House of Love, to their mother, Aphrodite. Anteros thought to sacrifice himself upon the altar of War to save Aphrodite from making a huge mistake. Once he laid eyes upon the horror of rotted carcasses, he simply could not abide the sight.

He did not believe it was appropriate in a place of worship. He could not help his response to violence for his nature dictated that beauty and harmony were the solutions to all matters. Therefore, he cleansed the entire area and transformed the ugliness into splendor.

At the thought of Ares seeing his precious altar with an embroidered cloth and flowers bedecking the marble, Deimos chuckled. The sound echoed into the length of the great chamber, startling himself, for Deimos had not laughed since Ares passed into the Realm of Sleep.

Not a single offering was made during Deimos' short reign as War. The adjoining hall was once filled with warriors waiting to honor their god. The stockyard was filled with animals waiting to be sacrificed, but no more. Those who sought Ares abandoned Athos, sent away by Love's Response. Not intentionally, but again, because Anteros was who he was, and there was not a single human who could refuse to honor Love when he was near.

All save for Ares, who would destroy Anteros precisely because of his innate nature.

Deimos could find humor in it all now. His twin invoked the gentler side of the hardened soldiers with his fine touch. They all filed down the mountain, taking their beasts with them, never to return. This action, this response spread as a single drop upon a pond, and Athos receded into the mist.

The face of War was forever changed. No longer was this god sought out upon a distant mountaintop and extolled fortune in battle begged. The fires still burned across the countryside, stretching into faraway lands, but the stench did not cover Athos.

Deimos detested the thought that the responsibility was now his and would always be so. He held hope that Ares would awaken someday, yet in the same breath thought of the burden if he did not. If Ares did awaken, he would despise it all.

And when Ares realized Niala was dead, there would be no end to his fury.

Niala.

Dead.

Deimos had seen the life fade from her eyes.

Her blood had covered him.

Grief fought for a hold, tried to overcome him, but he would not allow such emotion to bubble up and boil over. Deimos could not face his loss. He could not afford a moment of weakness.

War's minions were slaves only to the one who held the power. They had already attempted to destroy him, and would try again. All but Eris and Phobos.

Phobos, the latest addition to War's entourage. Phobos, the sweet lad who was wrenched from his mother and thrown into horrors he could never have imagined. Instead of grieving for the soft life at Aphrodite's knee, Phobos embraced his strength. He stepped into the role meant for him from birth: the god of Panic.

Eris and Phobos were inseparable now. Where Eris went, Phobos followed. They were nowhere in sight and Deimos supposed the two youth were most likely settled in somewhere for the night. Whether forest or seaside, or one of the many chambers within the fortress, Deimos was uncertain.

He did not lie claim upon their every breath. He allowed them certain freedoms, unlike Ares, who maintained control of all aspects of their existence.

Deimos, too, should seek his bed, a useless gesture, for he could not sleep. The moment he closed his eyes, he was devoured by the mortal world's aggression. He refused to sink into the mire that eased and abated Ares, that of sexual indulgence. Bodily gratification that drove away all else and eventually led to blessed rest.

He now understood how movement could overtake the mind. It was the rush that swept him forward during battle, the force of his body moving toward its destiny. With the blood-thirsty sword Amason held high, slashing bone and flesh, crushing everyone without regard to which side they hailed. Another discovery Deimos made about the Mantle of War - there was no discernment during battle.

How he wished he had listened to his father, though Ares spoke little of his trials. Deimos regretted that he had not asked his father what had transpired when War descended and his age when the mantle was bestowed.

What rites of passage had ushered Ares' into his power?

Deimos was never told; he had never asked. He was too bitter about the pain of his own passage and cared not what befell his father. At times he imagined Ares' ritual was worse than death and was glad for it.

Yet, now that he sat on the throne of War without guidance save his own experience in the mortal world, he bemoaned that decision. Had he paid attention, would the transition been easier?

This was the state of his thoughts these days. Constantly turning, constantly questioning, constantly finding no answer, no rest. Not even in the silence. His thoughts thundered and rattled as if a thousand hooves struck against the stone floors. Alone but not alone. Never to be truly alone again was almost too much to bear.

Ares must recover.

He must.

Deimos could not carry this burden into eternity.

But what if there was no choice?

Cursing, Deimos rose from the throne, impelled to action. He loathed the thought of seeking yet another skirmish, another hate-filled battle that was not his own. He refused to find gratification based only on the driving need to give himself over to the corporal.

There was not a soul about upon which to release his anger, no one to hear his rant but himself. Restless, Deimos circled the room, with a single glance cast at the hulking chair that served War. Deimos saw his brother's touch in the embroidered cloth that draped the throne, the brother who had been so long absent from Deimos' life, and now thrust violently back into it during the storm surrounding their parents.

Aphrodite, their mother, held the Mantle of Love just as Ares had once held the Mantle of War. Aphrodite, who, in a fit of madness, destroyed the bonds of her marriage to Ares, took a new consort in the form of Hephaestos, god of the Forge. Aphrodite, who bore a daughter named Harmonia, now refused to speak of her father.

Was it Ares or was it Hephaestos?

One could not tell by looking at the child. Harmonia was a pretty pink-cheeked babe with golden curls that lay against her round head and a sweet forgiving smile. The little girl, content to be in the arms of one of the Graces, did not seem to mind that her mother ignored her. Like all immortal beings, though she was so very young, she was already cognizant of her surroundings. Harmonia was like a tiny shining shadow, her wide blue gaze always steady in what appeared to be deep contemplation of Love's Realm.

As the months passed, and Ares remained locked within his slumber, Aphrodite receded. After Ares fell, Aphrodite shunned her duties and withdrew into a morbid silence, leaving Anteros to hold Love in check. Anteros became parent to both Harmonia and Eros.

The Realm of Love became Anteros' burden. Though not entirely, as Aphrodite was aware, unlike Ares who lay between the worlds. Yet both brothers faced the same dilemmas - the struggle crushing to keep balance between mortal and immortal. Though the brothers served different purposes, they lived parallel challenges.

Deimos turned to stare at the dark recesses of the chamber. A place that once echoed with the ribaldry of battle-hardened warriors waiting to plead for good fortune with sacrifices to their god. It no longer reflected Ares, nor did it match the violence of their existence.

How long could Deimos sustain this change? Was he doomed to repeat the patterns of his father? Yet Ares did not create the chaos, he merely represented it. Was it possible War could evolve?

There were no answers. Deimos could not find stable footing though he knew it could be done. Ares had achieved the balance.

But Ares was wedded with Aphrodite which brought the counterweight necessary to maintain both realms.

Deimos had no one.

Aphrodite told him to find love. Until he did, he would be a restless soul without an anchor.

Love brings purpose into disorder and without it, madness ensues.

"And yet, I have seen as much madness on the side of Love as I have War. Is one worse than the other?" Deimos' voice echoed throughout the vast and lonely hall. "I loved someone and now she is dead. How does that balance my soul, Mother?"

The reply was swift yet quiet, a voice within Deimos or was it Love's Response who hears all devotional yearnings?

Are you better for having had this love within your reach?

"Yes, but she is gone and I am alone."

You will know love again if you remain open to the possibility. If you refuse, you will continue to struggle. War needs Love.

"I am not my father." Deimos strode into the center of chamber as he made his declaration. "I am not Ares, and I refuse to walk in his footsteps. I will not resort to raw passion to keep the House of War in order."

Even if it is someone who can alter the course of War? Someone who can help hold the balance and bring forth a new alliance that will awaken Peace?

"And what would Peace do for War?" Deimos gave a harsh bark of laughter. "No one truly wins. Defeat and death repeat over and over again. There is no honor in Peace."

With this truth spoken aloud, Deimos felt different, as if those words somehow changed the fabric of War's Mantle. Indeed, the power shifted, lost some of the awkwardness and settled upon Deimos with intimate faith in his control.

Deimos twitched and a shudder ran down his spine as he accepted that which he could not change. The Mantle of War was his and he must wear it well. No longer would the energies of War suckle at him.

He was their master.

So be it.

TWO

Anteros smiled to himself as he overheard his twin's rant *no one truly wins* and decided there was no good response to Deimos and his anger. With a flick of his fingers, Anteros released the wisp of conversation.

The fury of War did not belong on Cos, the Isle of Love. Anteros stood in Aphrodite's temple, empty save for himself. It was a place of respite from the grief permeating every corner of the palace. From his place upon the grassy hill, beneath the roof of an open-air pavilion, Anteros could see the sprawling structure where everyone who dwelled upon the Isle of Cos resided. Aphrodite insisted everyone live together under one roof, as family who honored each other.

He could see the white sandy beach where the children played and count the women who watched over them as they lined the turquoise water's edge. It was a peaceful scene. Peace that he was in sore need of to quiet his own thoughts.

So many hearts were vying for an answer to their lovelorn secrets that Anteros could scarce keep track. It was his fate as Love's Response to give hope when there was none, for to have hope, created the possibility of love.

Most of the time Anteros sent these waves of faith throughout the realms without a second thought. Nevertheless, when he heard Deimos' lament, he could not resist listening with a closer ear.

"And it is true, Brother, there is someone waiting for you to notice. Iris pines for you but it is not my place to point in that direction. Either you will see her affection or you will not."

Deimos' longing reflected Anteros' own battles, though his were magnified by the fact that the Mantle of Love could not decide where to settle. Aphrodite was not insensible to the world as was Ares - she simply refused to be part of it.

The Mantle discerned her withdrawal yet could not leave her unless she was rendered incapable of holding the power. That was not the case. There was naught Anteros could do for she would neither rule the Realm of Love, nor would she release it.

Even if she could.

No one had ever before witnessed a Mantle passing from one immortal to another. No one had ever abdicated their power.

Anteros sighed and stared up at the domed ceiling. Fat cherubs and demure young maidens played amongst flowing fountains and flowering flora. The scene was cast in shimmering chips of pastel-colored stone and appeared to move in a game of hide and seek. He knew if he stared at the ceiling long enough, he would see the satyrs and lusty young men hidden within the foliage.

In times when mortals were allowed to pay homage to Aphrodite at Cos, the erotic nature of Aphrodite's temple came to life. All manner of sexual behavior ensued. These festivals continued for weeks, much to Aphrodite's delight and everyone else's vexation.

In the past months since Ares had fallen, Cos was quiet - the island's breathtaking beauty left unsullied by riotous crowds. The only sounds were Aphrodite's laments, and in sharp contrast, the children's shouts of laughter.

Anteros felt a twinge of jealousy as he paced about the gazebo. He wove around the tall white pillars that held up the roof, his sandaled feet traced the pattern of an underwater landscape laid into the marble floor.

Turquoise water with shades of aqua and cobalt blue, exotic fish in bright colors of yellow, orange, green and red, lush sea grass waving in the gentle waves and, at the center, the open pink clamshell that brought Aphrodite to the surface, as a fully formed goddess representing Love.

He circled the silver-wrought chaise with its myriad of bright pillows and jeweled feathered fans then crossed over to the raised pool overlooking the azure sea.

Sweetly scented steam rose from within the marble sides of the spa, just waiting for Aphrodite to immerse herself in the luxury of her watery birthright. Small blue and green tiles were inlaid in a soothing pattern that mimicked the swell of waves on high tide.

Aphrodite's favorite place on Cos.

Nothing could amuse her, not even the beauty of this pavilion since Aphrodite was in mourning for Ares, her beloved mate. Anteros felt a twinge of jealousy, for he, too, longed for true love. He prayed for the one that would complete him, the one who would sacrifice everything for him to be happy.

"Sad that I cannot see my own future." Anteros shook his head and his long golden hair slid across his tanned shoulders.

"What is it you want to see?"

Fingers stroked through and caught in his fine strands, causing Anteros to jerk away.

"Euphrosyne, what are you doing here? I thought you were to care for Harmonia."

"As I am." Euphrosyne gestured at the silver couch, now host to a sleeping babe. The multi-colored fans were now on a small table and a myriad of pillows laid round the little girl as a pretty barrier to keep Harmonia safe. "The babe needed fresh air, so we came here. A happy coincidence, I think."

Euphrosyne smiled in delight as she reached for him again, this time to place a kiss on Anteros' cheek.

"Humph." Anteros did not believe it was a coincidence at

all, but rather a design on Euphrosyne's part. "I came here to be alone for a short moment. Perhaps you could find another place for the babe to reap the rewards of a sunny day."

"You sound lonely, Anteros. What future do you seek? Your vision is cast upon all the realms, scattered like so many stars. It would seem you could see close to home as well."

Catching Euphrosyne's hands in his own, Anteros pressed her away. He could feel Euphrosyne straining against his grip, wanting nothing more than to be caressed, but he was the stronger one. He put her aside with a firm though gentle touch.

"It is a pity I cannot envision the future for my own household and yet, who does not enjoy a surprise or two?"

"I would like to surprise you," Euphrosyne whispered. "And you promised me."

Anteros heaved a great sigh and looked upon the youngest Grace with kindness. She was lovely in appearance, with blonde curls pinned atop her head and round pink cheeks, her blue eyes earnest with passion. Euphrosyne yearned for him, nay, fair quivered with the desire to possess him, this Anteros knew well.

But it was not to be.

"You did as I asked and brought Ares to Hephaestos' isle. And he did, indeed, reconcile with Aphrodite."

They both glanced at Harmonia. "Though it did not turn out the way I expected."

"No one could have foreseen such a turn of events," Euphrosyne was quick to respond. "Such an awful thing as Cedalion poisoning Lord Ares. I would not have thought it possible."

"There is not one soul who would have thought the great Ares would succumb to a poison dagger, except Hephaestos. He has done the impossible. I hope he suffers greatly in his banishment and I never have to look upon that hateful visage ever again." Anteros gritted his teeth.

"I can scarce stand to see my mother languish in sorrow. Each time there is no word of Ares, Aphrodite turns away, her gaze void of interest. She lives only to hear of her beloved. She takes no interest in the daughter she so longed to birth. It hurts my heart."

Anteros paused for a breath, and waved at the sleeping babe. "She knows nothing of their troubles. Or what mischief Eros causes. Or how I must deal with the mortal slings and arrows flung at Love that I must intercept on her behalf. The Mantle will not shift and I am left with little power to change any part of this predicament."

"I am sorry, my Darling." Euphrosyne stroked Anteros' bare arm with warm fingers anxious to feel more. "Come, Anteros, let me soothe you with scented oils in a bath."

"Euphrosyne, I cannot."

"But you promised."

"Of that I am aware. Now is not the time."

"When? I long for you. Anteros, I love you."

Euphrosyne's heart-wrenching gaze left Anteros shamed and red-faced. He did not know why he withheld his favors from one so lovely and there was no more perfect a place for a liaison than one that overlooked the birthplace of Aphrodite.

Yet he could not bring himself to it.

"I am sorry, Euphrosyne, but I must see to a few matters."

With that, Anteros left her alone in the Temple of Love.

Aphrodite dreamed.

She dreamed of her life before she became Eternal Love, for she did, indeed, have an existence that was safe and free. It was long before she rose from the sea and accepted what she was to become, a fully formed goddess.

She dreamed of an instance before the death of her innocence. A brief moment when she was the cherished daughter of Poseidon and Amphitrite, nothing more and nothing less. In a time before time began, she thought only of when she would awaken to the next wondrous day, what she would feast upon, who she would play with and when she would retire for the night into a rewarding slumber.

Truly an oceanic princess, Aphrodite was adored by her

parents and all creatures that swam beneath the surface. She was carefree and joyful, filled with grace and a glorious love for all living things.

She did not know the truth of her birth, for it was hidden with great care from her turquoise gaze. She did not know that her free spirit would be captured and imprisoned. She did not know she was destined to become the one who held Love's Realm within her heart or how heavy the Mantle of Love would become.

There was no memory of how she arrived or anything prior to her pleasant life beneath the waves. There was no memory of that fateful day when she rose from the sea to assume her duties, still filled with the innocence of a simple and protected childhood. She did not know grief or sorrow. She did not recognize jealousy or revenge. She did not recall the darkest side of love that awaited her like a monster willing to consume her soul for the mere sake of pleasure.

Aphrodite dreamed, and as she did, she drifted further and further away from the pain. She did not want to return. She wanted to glide through the buoyant salted water, hair streaming behind her, tail pushing her faster than any beast, dual fins propelling her forward with agile elegance.

The dolphins that swam at her side chattered in loyal companionship while the swarms of bright fishes came to circle about her in awe. All other sea nymphs wanted only to be in her company, to amuse her with their antics. Nothing was more beautiful to her than the land beneath the waves.

Her dream held no worry, no fear, and no sadness. Here she was unafflicted by remembering to hold the balance between Mortal and Immortal Realms.

THREE

Just before dawn, Ajah made her way across the plateau overlooking Najahmara. The ground was barren save for the tangled brown grasses and scrub bushes growing wild around the edges. Her skirt snapped about her legs while her shawl threatened to tie a loop around her neck. Strong winds yanked at her braid and blew dust into her eyes as if to threaten her presence upon the ridge.

It was six short months since Niala Aaminah passed from life into death. Six short months since hope fled their midst. The seasons turned from summer to winter, from light into darkness. It was the bleakest Ajah had ever felt.

She sighed and closed her eyes, remembering the joyous rituals held on the plateau in honor of their goddess, Gaea. Such celebrations, such radiant life! She could still hear the drums and feel the rhythm in her body as she danced, calling to the mysteries of Earth and Sky to bless Najahmara.

She was just beginning her seventeenth year when all she loved was destroyed by the invasion of foreign warriors. She was preparing for initiation, working in the gardens and learning to mix medicines, happy to serve her elders. She studied hard and spent much time in deep reflection over her path.

Once admitted into the Sisterhood, one would remain there until the last breath escaped. There was no doubt in her heart she wanted to become a Priestess of Gaea.

Until she failed miserably. First at the Spring celebration, when she abandoned her post, when she did not stay by Jahmed's side and help her hold Gaea's energy during the ritual. Second, at the Summer celebration when she did naught to stop Niala's death.

Ajah was consumed by shame and guilt. She did not deserve to become a sacred priestess. It was why she made the trip up to the top of the plateau early each morning before the daily work began. She did her best to atone for her mistakes yet there was no peace, only a sickened heart.

Jahmed disagreed and continued to train her as if she would take her vows when the moment was right, but Jahmed did not know the truth. Jahmed did not know Ajah dishonored the path of priestess by refusing to accept Gaea's mark.

A tear slid down Ajah's cheek and was immediately dried by the relentless wind. She failed to uphold her duty and now it was too late.

Months prior to the invasion, Ajah had happily immersed herself in the elements, into the instinctual presence of all seen and unseen beings of their world. To become a true priestess, a name must be given that reflected her path. For this, a totem must first choose her.

She yearned night and day to have a spirit guardian who would protect and help her as she made her way through life. This totem would give her strength, support and guidance when she became a priestess.

She waited long and prayed hard to Gaea for this gift. Nothing happened until one night she dreamed of a giant bird of prey. He was fierce with a great spiked ruff about his neck he could flare out in a most frightening way and with wings that folded tight to his body. His eyes were ringed with red and glowed with inner fire.

He was a ferocious beast and an admirable spirit guide. He

chose Ajah. In her dream the magnificent bird whispered his name, Sagittariidae, the Snake Eater, and marked her with his fiery tongue. Upon rising in the morning, she found the brand upon her shoulder. She was certain it was not a dream. It was real.

Each night, the vision reoccurred. The longer she delayed, the more violent he became. Stamping and howling, Sagittariidae demanded she accept his gift. Though smoke and fire consumed her, strangled her, terrified her, still she resisted.

A necessary part of the initiation was to have the spirit's totem indelibly drawn upon her body, to remain a permanent reflection of her loyalty and acceptance. Ajah prayed for the strength and courage to accept this offering of her totem. She wanted to fulfill her role within the tribe, she knew in her heart if she had just a bit more time, she could go through with the rites of passage.

But she was terrified to undergo the ceremony.

Ajah had witnessed the rites of passage only once, when Pallin endured the ritual in the sacred cavern, the womb of Gaea. There had been much smoke as the blessed herbs were scattered onto the fire while the priestesses chanted. She remembered how the deep resonance of drums echoed off the stone walls.

Ajah was young when Pallin accepted the ocean spirit as a totem but she still recalled in great detail the blood, the painful grunts and Pallin's tears. Ajah remembered how the sound of the bone needle squeaked against Pallin's skin as the image of the Cetacea, her spirit animal, was etched onto her back. Though Pallin held tight to the hands of her sisters and bit down on a damp cloth to keep from screaming, her face was tormented.

At one point, Pallin passed out and had to be revived. To fully accept the gift from spirit, one had to be awake to receive the totem's power. Ajah wanted more than anything to accept the gift, yet she simply could not bring herself to do it.

Now she felt she did not have the right to serve as a full priestess. She had refused the protection of the Sagittariidae with horrifying consequences.

On the night Najahmara was invaded, the flames became real. The serpent that burst from the skin of Niala Aaminah destroyed everything in sight. The smoke grew thick as the town burned, as the streets ran with blood and death was everywhere.

Ajah believed it was all her fault. If she had embraced Sagittariidae, the Snake Eater, and accepted his guidance, she was certain none of it would have happened. Sagittariidae would not have allowed those she loved to die and her beloved home would not have been destroyed. For this, Ajah could never forgive herself.

Every moment, she lived with this disgrace. Her penance was to serve without complaint: clean until her fingers bled, work the gardens until her back nearly broke and care for the sickest without concern for her own well-being.

All this and more. Since the night of Niala Aaminah's death, Ajah had withdrawn from any personal comfort.

Guilt lay upon her as thick as wool upon sheep. She could not bear the grief, the shame, the anguish of her inability to embrace that which was meant to be. All she could do was work, scarce sleeping or eating. Work and more work. No matter how long or hard she scrubbed the floors, Ajah could never erase her sins. She could only try to atone, and pray that someday she would be strong enough to accept her guardian's gift.

Until then, before anyone else rose from their sleep, she climbed up the long overgrown path to the plateau and knelt in front of a single white obelisk pointing to the sky. The stone was smooth from constant wind. It had stood sentry over Najahmara for hundreds of years. The name etched upon the stone was barely legible and in a language Ajah did not speak, yet she knew well what it meant.

It was the name of Niala Aaminah. The ground below was destined to be Niala's final resting place. Until the invasion. Until a god found Niala and claimed her as his own. Until Niala Aaminah died giving birth to that god's child.

Ajah wept at the memory. She touched the stone, tracing the name written on its face before falling to her knees in grief.

"Ahh," Ajah moaned, "Ahh."

The wind tore the keening wail from her lips and tossed it aside like the dust that swirled over the sacred ground. It whistled through the sad remains of the four shattered monuments, their jagged edges beseeching the sky.

Ajah looked at the pieces of stone, broken by a jealous god, and wept harder.

Gone. It was all gone.

All that was left was the ruins of what once was. All that Ajah could do was journey to the top of the plateau before the temple work began and care for the area around the stones. Ajah owed her this respect. Niala had been like a mother to Ajah, a mother, a teacher and a friend.

The hardest to accept was that the body of their priestess did not lie in the consecrated ground of the goddess Gaea because the leader of the invaders had forbidden it.

A curse on Hattusilis.

She would never call him king. She would never bow to him. She would rather cut his heart out and feed it to the fishes in the lake.

Their cherished Niala Aaminah was entombed in the cavern below her feet, the holy cave of the Mother, where they had once held the blessed rites of the harvest. Jahmed cautioned the women to keep silent, to voice no resistance, even when the cave entrance was sealed. She feared for their safety for they had seen firsthand how irrational and violent the king could become.

Hattusilis was frightened of the caverns. In his cowardice, when the Blue Serpent destroyed his troops, he hid in the caves. He claimed he could not find his way out and instead fought against ghosts. These spirits attacked until a heavy storage urn fell on Hattusilis' legs, crushing one and nearly ripping the foot off the other.

Unable to free himself, he lay on the ground for several days beneath the urn. He believed he would die there. When found, he was hot with fever, babbling about a giant serpent who tried to kill him.

Jahmed said Hattusilis spoke of Kulika, the Blue Serpent, he who encircles Earth and holds his beloved Gaea under his protection. Kulika had not returned to his Sky Realm as he should have after the fighting ceased. He stayed only to cause havoc amongst them all, without discernment.

Guilt reared its ugly head once again and Ajah felt ill. Her belly rolled and threatened to release upon the ground. Breathing hard, she sat back on her heels and watched the stars fade as the sun began to rise.

She wondered what life would have been like had Hattusilis perished in the caverns. Instead, he gained control of Najahmara. The remaining townsfolk left were too beaten to protest when the soldiers took over.

This, too, Ajah felt was her fault.

If she had accepted the Sagittariidae, she could have saved them. Ajah wept into her hands until there were no more tears. Only then was she able to stand and move to the edge of the plateau and look down upon the village.

There were few priestesses left after the invasion.

Pallin chose to leave them and align herself with Hattusilis. She wed the foreign king, birthing his son on the day after the Summer ritual.

Seire, the eldest of the women, died the night of the invasion, brutally murdered by the king's nephew.

Inni, midwife, healer and teacher, went mad after being raped and abused.

Her spirit crushed, Jahmed was left hollow and broken-hearted, struggling to hold Najahmara together with each day a constant grind of work and worry.

After the fire, Jahmed sent the surviving girls home to their relatives. There was nowhere for Ajah to go as she had been abandoned as a child and held the temple priestesses as her family. She stayed and she worked and no one disagreed.

It was a time of great sorrow and confusion as grief laid like a blanket across the entire valley. So many injured, so many dead. Ajah went about ministering to those in need without drawing attention.

In the aftermath of the invasion, the women moved into the small and cramped medicinal hut as Hattusilis took up residence in the ruined temple. The former dining area behind the healing quarters was blocked off and retained as a place to sleep, but always with someone standing watch. Fear was at its peak during those times.

There was no trust between Hattusilis and the women. He was not forgiven for his rude treatment, casting them out of their own home after Niala died. It was clear he cared nothing about their well-being. Even now, if Hattusilis could entirely disband them, Ajah knew he would, yet their deep belief in the Earth goddess would not allow them to hate.

During those dark days, the priestesses, led by Jahmed, trudged along with unswerving belief in Gaea's love yet refused forgiveness of the invaders. Every priestess avoided Hattusilis and his fervent supporters as much as possible, although they dutifully cared for the ills and injuries of the soldiers and their women.

The only one of the intruders that bore any connection with the women was Zan, for they saw the gentle side of the rough warrior. He assisted them when he was not at Hattusilis' side and appeared to be winning Jahmed's trust.

Ajah smiled through her tears at the thought of Zan and Jahmed becoming friends.

"Gaea, perhaps there is hope, if that should happen. It would certainly be a miracle."

The wind picked up as if the Earth goddess agreed with Ajah's thoughts.

"Still, there is so much misery even though Pallin labors to bridge the differences between what was and what is now. I do not believe their king will ever accept us as we are."

There was no bigger relief than when Hattusilis declared the temple haunted and found another residence. He moved his wife and tiny son past the lake shore and beyond the foot of the plateau into a deserted home.

Those who had built the little house were dead and could not argue. Once Hattusilis abandon the chambers, the women were left to complete the repairs he started. The process was slow and painful, bringing up many heartaches, but the priestesses persevered and soon they would return to their former quarters.

Months later, Hattusilis would not leave them in peace.

It was not enough that after Niala Aaminah died, Hattusilis forced the women to place her body into the cave grotto of the goddess and seal it shut. He forbid any offerings to Gaea and kept a soldier stationed within their midst to force compliance. Hattusilis believed he had thwarted their rituals and undermined their goddess. He believed he was in control of their destiny.

What a fool.

Outwardly, the priestesses were kind to the soldiers, providing food and drink to those who stood watch. Unbeknownst to the men, the food or drink was oft times salted with a sleeping powder.

This happened each month when the moon cycle waned into darkness, when a ritual to Gaea was held. The sentry was given the customary refreshment and whomever was on duty gladly accepted. Soon after, he was fast asleep and did not awaken for several hours.

The women would climb the path behind the temple to a rear entrance into the caves. The entry was hidden by heavy undergrowth and the many vines that grew across the opening. By the time the sentry awakened, they were back in the temple going about their nightly duties. A smile and a nod at the guard gave false confidence to the soldier and all was well for yet another moon cycle.

The priestesses went on to hold their sacred rites within the Mother's womb with only a handful of survivors. Jahmed did not trust anyone else and would not invite others to join them. No more collective celebrations, no dancing or singing, no communing with Gaea.

So many changes, so much grief and naught to be done about it. All Ajah could do was work and pray to Gaea that normalcy would return to their valley.

With a sigh, Ajah rubbed the tears from her eyes and took a deep breath to steady herself. It was time to begin the day's work and there was much to do. This very evening marked a new moon and the women would gather for ritual.

As the night deepened, Ajah brought a supper of cheese, bread and dates along with a cup of dark honey-sweetened tea to the guard. She bowed her head as Razi thanked her in the trade language that had become the common means of communicating with the local folk.

"You are welcome," Ajah murmured. "Please enjoy."

Though she spoke with politeness, she would not look into Razi's intense gaze. She feared he remembered their liaison during the Spring celebration, the ritual led by Jahmed before Niala's return and subsequent death, when the Great Mother's energy brought everyone into a frenzy of blind lovemaking. Just the thought of his hands upon her body brought a flush to her cheeks and she was grateful dusk was upon them.

The Spring ritual was to heal the grief of loss and unite the people into a common bond - instead, it brought more anguish and cemented the separation between invaders and Najahmaran folk.

Jahmed did her best to create a safe harbor for Gaea to bring Najahmara together in peace. Jahmed called the Great Mother into her body, hosting her energy for the benefit of all gathered. Gaea came to them with great joy for it had been a long while since she was invited into their midst. She wanted coupling. Ancient spirit that she is, lovemaking is her every response to human needs.

She sent her power throughout the amassed folk causing

much merriment. Everywhere, invaders and locals paired off, eyes blinded to their differences. Ajah, herself, fell under Gaea's spell though she was supposed to watch over Jahmed, to make certain no harm came to her. Instead, Ajah found herself seduced by a handsome soldier.

Razi.

All had been well until Kulika emerged from the shadows and took hold of King Hattusilis. He wanted his mate in the most carnal sense but Gaea was angry with him.

A dreadful brawl between them ensued; Jahmed was injured. Ajah could not forgive herself for allowing it to happen, though somewhere deep inside, she knew she could not have prevented the deities from fighting. It was their way.

She understood that the immortal beings, Gaea and Kulika, Earth and Sky, do not look upon life the same as humans. They do not see the fragility of a mortal body nor the complexity of human interactions. They see only themselves in whatever form they possess at the moment.

Still, Ajah felt responsible.

Worse, even, was the moment she recognized the young soldier upon his first assignment at the temple. Their coupling had been tender and sweet, not the frantic sweaty revelry that held sway on the rest of the folk. She had felt safe in his arms, lost in his kisses. To see him again under the divisive terms of Hattusilis united with her shame. She could not bear to face him.

She kept her gaze averted and spoke as little as possible, in spite of his efforts to engage her in conversation.

"It is a beautiful evening, is it not?" Razi touched Ajah's hand, hoping she would linger for a moment longer. He winced when she jerked away as if he had burned her skin.

He was saddened by her distrust and yet he understood the tension between his King and the priestesses.

Razi liked the quiet hardworking women, especially Ajah. There was something familiar and comforting about her though he could not place why. She was unlike any female he had ever seen.

He thought her to be the most beautiful amongst the women of Najahmara.

In the evenings, after a long day, he prayed she would be the one who brought his meal. When the setting sun caressed her face, her copper skin glowed and set afire the fine mist of curls that had pulled from her braid.

It was a curious thing. Her hair was dark, nearly black, and yet with the sun rays piercing the tendrils, Ajah's hair turned red, like a crown of embers. Her eyes, also dark brown, would light up from the inside when the sun kissed her face.

She appeared to Razi as a goddess. Her gentleness only enhanced his desire. He knew he loved her. If he was home, in the Steppelands where he was born, he could take her as his wife without question. Here, in this foreign land, he was afraid to speak of it.

There was no doubt King Hattusilis would arrange a marriage between them, if Razi spoke of his desires. Nothing would make Razi happier but he did not want Ajah on those terms. He would not have that for the one he loved.

And beside his quest for her affection was the question of the priestess order that Ajah served. Did they even allow the women to marry?

It was true King Hattusilis had taken one of the priestesses to his bed and she had given him a fine son, but only then did the King wed her. Was it a forced union? Razi did not know. The one called Pallin seemed to care for King Hattusilis, but Razi overheard many arguments about the arrangement from within the temple.

"Thank you, Priestess. I am pleased that it is you who brought me food and drink. Perhaps we could..."

"You are welcome."

Ducking her head, Ajah cut off his words and hurried back into the depths of the temple, leaving Razi to settle down upon the bench to eat.

Sighing, he bit into a piece of tart cheese and wished the

beautiful priestess would allow him to court her, for he would like very much to wed her. As he started to say to her, perhaps in time. Perhaps.

He watched the sun sink below the outline of the plateau and thought how peaceful life had been since the bloody invasion. Thankfully, he had been a foot soldier and one of the second wave to gain entry to Najahmara. He was no stranger to battles but the depth of the destruction had been disturbing, particular for him, the amount of soldiers who had died in an explosion of fire.

"And yet," he murmured between bites, "Had they not perished, I would not have gained this station."

He relished his role as a guard, splitting his time between the temple and at a post before his king's home. He favored temple duty over the pathway near the lake, mainly because of his growing affection for Ajah but also because the priestesses treated him with kindness.

Savoring the last bite of fresh bread smeared with fruit paste, he swallowed the dregs of his tea and soon began to drowse. He struggled to keep his eyes open but the temptation to close them was too strong to resist. Within moments, he began to snore in soft little bursts.

Just inside the doorway, Jahmed signaled the four women to wrap their dark cloaks about them and hurry along through the gardens. Ajah led the way with Tulane, Deniz and Inni following close behind. They moved in silence along the path to the ridge with a swiftness that belied the day-to-day shuffle.

Everything they did was meant to throw Hattusilis and his men off the real trail. So far, their subterfuge had worked.

Though for how long? Jahmed thought as she took up the rear. With a last glance over her shoulder to make certain they were not observed or followed, Jahmed hurried to catch up with her sisters. Guilt gnawed at her heart for not inviting Pallin to join them, but Jahmed could not risk it.

Pallin professed to love Hattusilis and therein lay the danger. Add a child between them and Jahmed could no longer trust Pallin would honor her priestess vows.

Even though she carries out her duties day after day. I dare not let her attend our rituals.

And the babe, Mursilis. Pallin would never be able to slip out at night without the child and both would bring undue questions from Hattusilis. It was difficult enough for her to attend to her duties during the daylight hours, though she managed, in spite of her husband's disagreement.

What if the babe were to cry out and call attention to our stealth?

Jahmed shook her head and the many beads on her long braids clicked together. With a quick hand, she silenced her hair and gave a wry smile into the shadows, concerned she, herself, might cause someone to look upward toward path.

Inni whispered over her shoulder, "Who do you mumble to, Jahmed? Is someone behind us?"

"Shhh, I speak only to myself." Jahmed flushed. She did not realize she had spoken aloud. With her lips clamped shut, her thoughts would not escape. *Am I going mad? I do not even know when words come from my own mouth?*

She urged the women into the cave hidden behind a thick wall of vines. They formed a circle around what once was a fire pit but now contained a small altar with a statue of Gaea in the center. Together they invoked the elemental protectors.

"Winds that cool us, Breezes that bring change and offer new truths, please come among us as the voice of Gaea to guide us." Jahmed laid a feather upon the altar to represent the bird's eye view as it soared in the sky.

"Flames that warm us, Fire that feeds us and offer new beginnings through release, please come among us so that may we see the possibility of peace." Ajah lit a small candle that set on the small altar.

"Waters that deliver life, Rivers that flow and offer healing for our bodies and our hearts, please come among us so that we may survive." Deniz filled a small chalice with water from the lake.

"Soils that sustain us, Earth that holds us in her arms, please come among us so that we may find the strength and courage to rebuild." Tulane laid a smooth rock shaped into a female figure upon the altar.

"Come, Great Mother Gaea, be among us."

They spoke the last phrase together. As they did, a cool breeze blew through the cavern from the tunnel behind them. A shiver crossed each women's shoulders as if passed from one to the other. They took hands. Jahmed lowered her head and prayed that Gaea would once again speak to them.

It was the same prayer repeated month after month since Niala Aaminah died, yet Gaea had refused her presence during their rituals.

No matter how much they beseeched and honored the goddess, it appeared the Great Mother had abandoned them. With tears in her eyes, Jahmed called the circle to closure, thanked the elemental guardians for their help and bade the women return to temple.

The priestesses hesitated, reluctant to leave. They waited for Jahmed in an uncomfortable silence, still feeling the chill as it seeped from the tunnel and swirled about their feet.

Tulane and Deniz huddled together, seeking warmth as Inni moved closer to the opening that led into the heart of the plateau.

"Gaea is angry that Niala is dead. She will no longer come to us," Jahmed mourned, face buried in her hands. She was unable to stand, too worn out to continue.

Ajah put aside her own fears and squatted next to Jahmed. "Zahava, my teacher, I do not believe our Great Mother would forsake us in this manner."

"Then where is she? How are we to survive these changes if Gaea will not lead us?"

"Perhaps she wishes us to call upon our own reserves and find our way through."

"And how do we do that?" Jahmed's head snapped upward, appearing cadaverous in the flickering candle light. "I have failed."

Ajah took in a startled breath and prayed it was not a death mask that she saw laid over Jahmed's features. Since the serpent had blown fire all throughout Najahmara, since that horrifying night, Ajah had seen far too many omens of loss on the faces of those she loved. She feared there was much more to come and all the healing they did may be for naught.

"Or perhaps you simply do not hear Gaea when she speaks," Inni whispered.

"I hear the grief of our people, is that not enough to bring Gaea to our aid?" Jahmed scrubbed at her face with her sleeve, self-recrimination glinting in her eyes. She knew she must summon the strength to go, if not for herself, then for Inni and the young women who looked to her for guidance.

"Do you not hear Gaea's voice within the caves?" Inni lifted her chin, cocking her head to one side.

"I hear nothing." Wobbling a bit, Jahmed stood with Ajah's help. "You hear nothing. It is the wind as it moves through the caverns, crying for us."

"Jahmed, you are wrong." Inni crept closer to the tunnel entrance. "She speaks to me. Listen…."

All the women froze in a moment of silence, listening for the voice of a distant goddess.

"There, did you hear that?" Inni turned to others with a wide smile on her face. "Gaea speaks!"

Every face grew sadder as the women watched Inni's excitement. Though her body mended, her mind did not. She regressed to near-childlike behavior, appearing as if Telio's brutal attack or the invasion had never occurred.

When Inni wondered aloud where all the strange men came from, Jahmed, Ajah, Tulane and Deniz said they were visitors. When she wandered the streets looking for Niala, one of them retrieved her, explaining Niala had passed into the Shadowland. Her tears were dried and she was set about on some small task that made her smile.

When she heard voices - which she frequently did - the

women could only reassure her no one was there. Inni never believed them.

"Did you not hear the words of the Great Mother? She says that our Zahava, our Niala is not truly dead. Gaea says that Niala will help us."

They heard nothing but the slightest hiss from the candle as it was extinguished. The cave fell into the blackest of black night but still, no one moved to leave as Inni's disconnected voice echoed around them.

"Ahh, Inni," Jahmed's sigh echoed eerily within the stone walls. "Niala is gone. What you hear is only in your mind."

"No, my Love, Niala is not dead. She lives and we must find her."

Inni would that minute have gone into the tunnel in search of Niala if Ajah had not grabbed her arm and guided her toward the exit.

"Stop, Ajah, let go. I must find Niala." Slapping at Ajah's hands, Inni fought to be released.

"Tulane, Deniz, help Jahmed down the mount."

As the younger woman did as they were told, supporting a wretched Jahmed out into the night, Ajah held tight to Inni in spite of the stinging blows. She held on until Inni gave up and fell weakly within Ajah's arms.

"Niala lives," Inni mumbled. "Why will you not believe me? Gaea has spoken, Niala is alive and we must help her."

"We will. We will help her, I promise." Ajah felt the weight of the other woman on her body as well as in her heart as she guided Inni from the cave.

"We will find Niala? You swear?"

"Yes, Inni." Ajah closed her eyes and prayed to be forgiven for her lie. "I swear."

*****

Pallin held her cloak a bit closer as the chilly north wind picked up and swept across the dried grasses at her feet. In a rare moment,

Pallin found a chance to be alone. The babe, Mursilis, slept in his cradle and Hattusilis drowsed in his chair beside the fire, allowing her to slip out the rear entry of her new home.

She stared with great longing towards the outline of the plateau, knowing her sisters trekked upward and filed into the sacred cave to honor Gaea on the eve of a dark moon. She very much wanted to be with them, though she was not welcome.

Jahmed had made that very clear.

Behind the ridge's absolute darkness was the sky, now void of sunlight but sparkling with the brilliance of a vast array of stars. With the moon hiding behind her veil, the rest of the heavens were able to show off the bounty of the constellations.

"He is afraid, that is why. That is all," Pallin whispered into the night, referring to Hattusilis. If not for him, she would be honoring Gaea along with her sisters.

"Who is afraid?"

"Zan, you startled me." Pallin whipped around to face her husband's second in command.

The grizzled warrior, who sported many battle scars and a limp to mark his courage, took a step backward from the ire of his Queen. Though he wondered why Pallin was so quick to admonish him, Zan was ready with a polite bow.

"I am sorry, my Queen, I only want to ensure your safety."

"Why would I not be safe? And please do not call me your queen." Pallin eyed the large man with suspicion knowing her safety was not his main concern. He checked her whereabouts to be certain she did not go to the temple.

"You are the consort of my King, therefore you are my Queen." Zan gave a slight bow in her direction.

Shoulders stiff and squared, Pallin walked with deliberate firmness around the ever-growing house. When would Hattusilis be satisfied with the size of his 'palace'?

This Pallin could not answer but she tired of the constant changes taking place on the former farmer's dwelling. She had known the folk who once lived there and it grieved her to know they were dead while her husband reveled in creating a structure that suited his royal status.

To be followed from dawn to dusk, and now, even into the night was an insult to her integrity. That anyone could believe she would leave her babe and disappear was inexcusable.

Pallin stopped short and scarce noticed Zan very nearly stumbled over her slender frame. She knew in her heart it was not his wife Hattusilis was concerned with - it was his son. Her daily trip to the temple irked him to no end, though it was worry that drove his behavior. He did not want Pallin to take Mursilis away.

"Where would I go?"

"Pardon, my Queen?"

"Nothing." Pallin drew Zan away from the view of the plateau and the possibility he would notice movement amongst the bushes and scrub trees. They now faced the lakeshore and the soothing waves that brushed against the pebbles.

To Pallin's right was the path that would lead across a bridge into Najahmara and to the front door of the temple where she once lived. To her left, the land continued in a narrow swath until it opened into a vast meadow. It was the place Niala Aaminah had described to the women as her first sight of the valley, the place where the five founding mothers had decided to stay.

Herd animals had always roamed the meadows with their keepers but now there was a large dirty encampment of soldiers spread across the once beautiful pasture.

Pallin sniffed and turned away from the sight of campfires and the scent of singed meat.

"A wise decision." Zan moved to block the view. "That is a dangerous path."

"I would not go amongst those filthy men save for the life of my son." Pallin flicked her fingers in the air. "I wish they would all go away."

"They will not, my Queen, not as long as Hattusilis remains."

There was no response to that for Pallin knew Hattusilis had grand plans for their lovely valley, plans she would not share with

Jahmed for fear it would be the final break between them.

"I suppose you are right."

"Yes, my Queen."

Pallin sighed and thought further before she could respond with curtness to the man beside her. Zan did many things to assist the folk of Najahmara after the invasion. Even now he helped the priestesses with difficult tasks that would be impossible to complete if he was not present.

True, he was part of the horrifying events that brought about the fall of Najahmara. Yet, without fail, Zan continued to heal the wounds, as much as could be done. Pallin could hear Niala's voice speaking to her from the past.

Be kind, Pallin, for kindness is rewarded in all manner of ways. Cruelty will only gain more grief.

"It is a beautiful evening, is it not, Zan?"

"Why, yes it is."

Zan's tone was pleased though Pallin could not see his face.

"May I ask a question?"

"Of course, my Queen."

Pallin bit back her irritation in the continued reference to queen and went on in a mild voice. "Does it seem to you that Hattusilis is not as well as he should be?"

"What do you mean?"

"He seems distracted."

"King Hattusilis is involved in decisions greater than himself."

"Do you mean the construction of our home?"

"I do."

Pallin hesitated. "That is part of my confusion. Since he has expanded the space," flushing under cover of the darkness, she continued, "Hattusilis insists I sleep in a separate room with Mursilis."

"Is that all?" Zan was glad Pallin could not see the relief on his rugged face. "It is a Steppelands custom to have mother and children in separate chambers."

"I see. But is it custom for your king to have conversations with no one? I hear him through the wall between our sleeping quarters."

"I do not understand." Zan claimed ignorance but he also heard Hattusilis carry on a speech without another soul present. Zan feared it had to do with Hattusilis' injuries but did not want to further alarm Pallin.

With a slight shake of her head, Pallin shrugged. "It is of no consequence. Let us go back inside before I am chilled all the way through."

"Yes, my Queen."

FOUR

Just before dawn, Iris of the Shimmering Rainbow, whose opaque hair and skin mirrored the soft colors of water and sky with every movement, stood outside the great walls of Athos.

In spite of her delightful and innocent appearance, Iris was both feared and admired, for she was Hera's messenger. Her duty was to bring forth the commands of her Queen. On this day, Iris sought out Deimos, whom she was hopelessly in love with, though he paid little attention to her.

Iris sighed. Though she had many years, hundreds, in fact, to profess her feelings, her courage had just emerged when the Mantle of War descended upon Deimos. He succumbed to such pain that no one could break through, least of all the beauty of the Rainbow.

Still, Iris' heart beat a bit harder at the thought of entering Athos, perhaps finding herself alone with the one she longed to have by her side. Squinting at gray shadows, Iris wondered how any soul could survive within the dismal fortress. It hunkered near the peak of the mountain, dark and foreboding and all but deserted.

Not a flicker of life appeared in the flagstone courtyard or any of the multitude of shuttered windows above her. The sunrise had not yet touched the mountain top and Athos was in the grips of bitter cold.

Iris sought Deimos with a message from Hera, but where to start in this monstrous pile of rocks? She stood in the eerie silence and searched for him with her mind, preferring such ways over checking every chamber in person. Deimos was present. She knew that much. To find him, however, was proving difficult.

With hands on lean hips, Iris pursed her lips and stared upward, gauging each floor for possibilities. Would Deimos most likely be in the bowels of his prison or at the pinnacle?

Iris seldom visited Athos in her service to Hera but on the rare occasion she was sent to give Ares a message, she found him in his private quarters. In the early hours of dawn, would she also find Deimos at rest?

The thought of Deimos lying abed gave Iris a little shiver of delight.

"I shall start in the uppermost of Athos," Iris said to herself. "And if I am wrong, no harm."

"No harm?"

A chuckle brought Iris whirling about to face a green-tinged youth who crouched near the base of a fir tree.

"Eris. You startled me. Have you been here all this time?"

The young man rose to his feet and twitched his pointed ears. He was the same height as she, yet wiry with a sense of swirling pent up energy around him. Grinning, he approached her.

"If you mean to speak to Deimos, you might want to have patience until he is fully awake."

"I am here at Hera's command." Iris eyed the youth with suspicion. "Why should I wait?"

Eris shrugged, "Do as you please, but Deimos has been in an ill mood since Ares fell. He rarely rests with ease, but for once, he has slept well."

"I am undoubtedly aware of the shift that occurred when Ares was struck down, but Mistress wishes to speak with Deimos. That he might be out of sorts is not mine to consider."

"Then go to him." Laughter glinted in Eris' brown eyes, "But do not shout for help when you anger him."

"It sounds as if you speak of Ares, not Deimos."

"Their dispositions are not far apart these days."

Hesitating for only a moment, Iris straightened her shoulders. "He is in his chambers, then?"

"Ahh, yes, he is indeed in his chambers."

Lifting her hand, Iris pointed with one finger. "Up there?" She stared at the shuttered windows just below the turreted crown of Athos.

Eris touched the back of her hand, pressing down until her finger was level with the next line of blank windows. "You will find Deimos there, on the far side of Athos. His quarters face the sea."

"Hmmm." Iris bit her bottom lip, a slight frown creasing her forehead. "Will you announce me, Green One?"

"I think not." Eris quirked one eyebrow upward. "What of you, my Brother? Will you announce Iris of the Shimmering Rainbow?"

Iris gave another startled whuff as Phobos leaped from his hiding place within the tree branches. He landed next to Eris, pleased at her irritation. He was taller than Eris, and skinny, all knobby elbows and knees, with a most dirty face. Iris frowned at his appearance but made no comment.

"If you must speak with Deimos, go to him yourself. We have seen enough of his bad temper." Phobos jabbed Eris in the ribs and they both doubled over in laughter.

"That is altogether impolite. One of you should escort me to your master."

Eris shook his head, his mop of curly brown hair bouncing with his glee. "He is not my master. Deimos is our brother. We are in service with him, not to him."

"There is a difference?"

"Yes." Eris threw a sly glance between Iris and the upper floors of Athos. Her gaze followed his. "A monstrous difference. Enjoy your visit."

"But…." Iris wished for Eris to play guide, instead, she discovered the two boys gone. Returned to the scraggly stand of fir trees, she supposed.

"How rude," she called after them. "I only asked for a little assistance."

Which she did not need. With an aggrieved sigh, Iris began to make her way to the entrance before thinking better of it. There was no need to walk through the dismal and dark corridors of War's fortress when she could move from ground to the top of Athos in a blink. She had only to will herself somewhere and there she would be.

Of course, it helped to know where she was going. According to Eris, Deimos was not in the uppermost reaches but on the floor beneath what had been Ares' private quarters. Though Deimos assumed the Mantel of War, he did not take the personal effects of Ares.

Interesting tidbit of knowledge.

But did Deimos not carry Amason, the wicked blade of War? And did not those who once feared Ares still inwardly cower at the sight of Ares' son? Iris heard tales of his brutality as did everyone else.

Curious, now, and more than a little excited to see the dark brooding grandson of her mistress, Iris moved to the narrow balcony that encircled the top floor of Athos and followed it around until she faced the vast ocean. Here the winds stirred her long hair and, at the same time, lifted the petals of her skirt to tickle her nether regions.

Iris took a deep breath and peered over the side of the railing. Far below were jagged rocks, broken by thousands of years of pounding tide. A frightening view and quite appropriate for War's haven, yet Iris was more concerned with the row of secured windows.

With closed eyes, she sought the energy of a sleeping immortal. Quiet energy, but hot, like coals banked against the cold night, in need of a few twigs to ignite once more into flame. Fire that licked at the fuel, dissolving the wood into ash as it fed on the sacrifice placed within its embrace.

Iris blinked as a sharp brine-filled breeze stung her face, bringing her back to herself. She smoothed her hair and her skirt. With a calming inhale, she went inside. Her first guess was right.

She amused herself with games of intuiting those she sought. Sink into their energy and hone in on their whereabouts. She rarely missed her mark.

There before her was an unassuming bedchamber with very little to bring comfort to its owner. Stark walls bearing no decoration, a black reflecting floor resembling mysterious water broken by a single rug, and the hulk of a bedstand, all washed in the shadows of early morning.

A hint of light seeped in from the cracks in the shutters, weak streams of predawn gray. Iris was tempted to set a fire in the arched hearth at the far end of the room, or at the very least, turn up one of the oil lamps that hung against the walls. Anything to illuminate the depths and add warmth.

She decided on a rack of candles near the bedside. As the small flames grew, a pool of golden light spread over Deimos. Iris stared at the man sprawled in front of her, naked except for a blanket draped over his hips. She had never seen Deimos unclothed, or even in the short tunic favored by Ares when in attendance at Council. Deimos always wore the heavy clothing of a warrior, as if the layers of cloth could protect him from the verbal slings of the elders.

With a sharp inhale, she drank in the sight of his long, finely shaped, nearly smooth legs stretched out beyond the edge of the coverlet. Her eager gaze rose to the powerful angles of his chest and shoulders and along each arm where even in repose she could see the strength in his hands. Though his body lay still, Deimos grimaced in his sleep, twisting his lips into a snarl, as if he fought a battle in his dreams.

Iris yearned to stroke the black curls on his forehead, to run her fingers along the short coarse beard covering his chin and upper lip, to touch his mouth and nose and the dark fringe of lashes lying on his flushed cheeks.

How could he be overly warm in a room that made Iris shrink with cold?

With a little shiver, she laid one finger on his shoulder, her index finger, lightly, carefully so she would not awaken him, and traced the hard corded line to his forearm.

Deimos groaned and shifted onto his side. Clapping a hand to her mouth to stifle a burst of delighted giggles, she gazed at the valley running from hipbone to below his flat belly in a teasing hint of what delights might be hidden from her. Iris circled the bed to better view his newly exposed flesh.

One hip was bared along with his backside, but the blanket stubbornly clung to his skin, covering his manhood. Desire made her body heavy and the tingling of her nether regions made her throw caution to the wind. With care, Iris climbed onto the bed, glad that it was solid and not jiggling as she sat crossed-legged on one corner.

She contemplated the idea of making love with Deimos, imagining hot wet kisses, and caresses that would make her wild. She thought of their bodies sweating with the effort, moving together until that exquisite peak of blinding pleasure. Afterward, they would lie together, entwined in each other's arms, exchanging gentle feather-light kisses until their passion rose again.

"Ahh, Deimos. Wake up, for I want you so very much."

Deimos made no response.

"If you would only turn toward me," Iris pleaded, knowing this would cause the blanket to slide away. She wanted to see all of him.

Playfully, she straightened her leg and nudged the firm flesh of one buttock with her foot, to no avail. Deimos lay in deep sleep, oblivious to her presence.

She prodded him again, curling her toes around the edge of the blanket. She began to pull the blanket away, hoping the sensation would bring him to an erection.

Her lips watered to taste him, to take him in her mouth and roll him about with her tongue. She wanted to feel him grow bigger and bigger until he was close to bursting. Just as a plum would split its skin as the sun beat down on it, his juice would run down her chin the same way. More, she wanted to press her body to his, to explore every angle, to merge with him.

With closed eyes, Iris gave a soft moan of anticipation only to have the sound turn into a screech as calloused fingers latched on to her foot. She was yanked forward without ceremony, throwing her torso backwards and striking her head on the footboard as she came to rest next to Deimos.

"Owww. That hurt." Iris rubbed the injured part of her head.

All thoughts of lovemaking evaporated as she stared at an awakened Deimos. He sat upright, his heavy-lidded eyes black as the night and filled with a lust that frightened her. To no avail, she tried to pull free from the unwavering bone-crushing grip on her ankle.

"Deimos, release me. I come bearing a message from your grandmother."

Again, Iris struggled against his hold only to find it grow tighter. He pulled her closer as his hand slid to her calf, his long fingers kneading her flesh.

"What message?" His voice was hoarse.

"That…that…."

His hand moved upward to her knee, his burning gaze never leaving hers.

"That you are…that you should…." Iris swallowed, running her tongue around her lips.

Deimos now had his hand on her thigh. The warmth of his palm sent quakes through her nether region and she could not help that her legs parted as his fingers explored further. The heaviness at her peak was unbearable. She writhed as his touch slowly trailed upward, reaching her tenderest of places.

Iris gasped.

"Should what?" Deimos rose up over her, keeping his hand in place.

"Hera bids you...to...visit...her."

Deimos' fingers left her as he grasped both her hips and pulled her flat onto her back. Her skirt slid up past her waist exposing her nakedness to his hungry gaze.

Still holding her in such a manner that later would cause bruises, Deimos thrust into her. Iris cried out, and though she was ready, he was immense and he did not enter with affection.

He plunged in as if she were an ocean that could take him all, swallow him into the depths, but she was not made of water. She was air. She needed time to breathe him in.

"Wait...." she pleaded. "Wait!"

Deimos ignored her entreaty as he lay on top of her, his body heavy and awkward against her slender form. His mouth covered hers with a kiss that made her lip split.

Blood mingled with sweat on her tongue for only a moment before he sucked it away. She was pinned beneath him, his hips grinding into hers. She could do nothing more than ride with him.

When she reached that brilliant point of ecstasy, it burst over her in torrents of color and swirling light. Iris could not help the shrill scream that tore from her, or the shuddering twitches of her body, or that when her breath finally calmed, she was ready to lay quietly in his arms.

Yet Deimos kept on in a near mindless assault upon her body. When he gave one final lurch and fell away, Iris straightened her bent knees and brought her legs together. With trembling fingers, she smoothed her skirt over her thighs and then lay still, staring up at the streaks of dawn painted upon the ceiling.

She was angry at him. She was wounded that their lovemaking was violent, that Deimos would be so coarse with her when she offered sweet affection. In turn, she was distressed that he brought her to a quaking gasping pitch with such coldhearted intent.

Did he enjoy such games?

That he would not touch her now was worse. He rolled to his side, his back to her. She could hear his breath had not yet slowed but he did not reach for her, and sadly, did not want the closeness she craved.

Tears threatened to spill into her hairline. Furious maddening tears. Taking care not to brush against Deimos, Iris sat up.

"Well, that was entertaining." Her tone held forced lightness.

"You are in War's bed, what did you expect?" Deimos responded without looking at her.

Iris clamped her teeth together and fought to regain her composure. Deimos was changed. He was no longer the youth with hidden sensitivities who sometimes brought her a small gift. He was not the reserved and seemingly shy man who visited Olympus or the one who offered a quiet smile at her appearance. He was not the one who rejected Ares' way of life, preferring to be amongst fragile mortals.

This Deimos was an indifferent brutal beast who cared nothing for her. This Deimos was not the one she loved.

"Expectations are for fools. Your grandmother bids you come to Olympus immediately."

"What does she want?"

"It is not my place to ask."

"And if I do not go?"

"That is between you and Hera. I am, after all, only the messenger."

In a blink of the eye, Iris fled Athos.

Deimos lay still awhile longer as fury mounted within him. That he should be summoned with curious abruptness when, as a normal course of events, he was not welcome in Olympus?

Fury that his grandmother had sent Iris rather than Hermes.

Fury that he had treated Iris of the Shimmering Rainbow

with such harsh disregard. Was this yet another aspect of War taking hold? Now that he had gained control of the violent and murderous energies of his father's realm, was he to bear the burden of a cold heart as well?

Should he answer his grandmother's call?

If he ignored Hera, might he might lose his only ally in the Council? If he followed through on the immediacy of her request, might he appear weak? How many knew she summoned him to her side?

And then a dreaded thought occurred: was Ares dead? Iris had given no indication. But then, she would not. As she said, it was not her place.

Was it possible that Ares had succumbed to his wounds?

Sickened, Deimos leaped from his bed.

"Eris." Clothed and ready to depart, Deimos called to his brother, demanding he appear at once.

The green-tinged youth was beside Deimos before he could draw in another breath.

"I must go to Olympus. Look after Phobos."

"Of course." Eris ducked his head, letting his curly locks fall across his face so that Deimos would not see his sly smile. "Yes, of course."

FIVE

Eris waited a bit to be certain that Deimos would not return then shouted for Phobos. A few moments later, the youth ran into Deimos' quarters, panting and red-faced. Phobos had not yet mastered the art of transference - moving self through space at will - which forced him to run up the many staircases.

"Could you not have taken me with you when our brother summoned," Phobos demanded.

"He did not call you, only me."

"There are no secrets between us. What would have been the harm?"

"It matters not as he has gone off on an errand."

"What errand? And why did he need you?" Phobos pushed strands of black hair from his sweating forehead.

"It does not matter where or why he went. Only that he is gone." Eris arched an eyebrow at the younger boy.

"He tells you everything and me nothing. I am tired of being the only one who does not know battle plans."

"There is no battle, Brother and you miss my reason for calling you. Deimos is not *here*." He jabbed a finger at the floor and made a circle to illustrate his words. "But we are. Alone. Without Deimos. To do what we want."

"Ahh!" Phobos leapt into the air and came down with a whoop. "We can do as we please without Deimos becoming angry. What should we do?"

"I thought perhaps...."

"I know, let us trick that old hag Enyo into coming here, lock her in a cage and torment her until she cries," Phobos shouted.

Convulsing with disgust, Eris held up a hand, palm out. "No, I do not want that one anywhere near me. There is no cage that can hold her and she is wicked enough to devour the both of us, then claim it is not true."

"You are afraid of Enyo." Phobos was delighted and clapped his hands together.

"I am afraid of her, and you should be, too, Brother. She is an elemental creature, and to her nothing is sacred. It took Ares a very long time to control her and we dare not upset that balance." Eris grimaced. "And if she could not succeed, Deimos would."

"Then let us seek out an encampment of warriors and appear as specters. We can scare them so much they will either run away or attack their enemy. I know of a war starting on the outer range of...."

"No, Brother, contain yourself."

Phobos kicked at the edge of the rug. "Can we at least go to the village at the bottom of this mount and drink with the townspeople?"

"We are forbidden since the last time we found revelry amongst the mortals."

"Never mind," groaned Phobos. "Why did you call me if we are not to amuse ourselves?"

"Because there is something I must do, and it is something Deimos need not know about."

"Do we plot against him? I love a plot."

"Not a plot. You are such a child." Eris flicked his fingers in dismissal. "We are going to my homeland."

"Oh, no, not that." Phobos covered his face with his hands, voice muffled. "I do not want to go to Ellopia."

"It matters not. It is what we are doing."

"You cannot make me." With arms crossed over his chest, Phobos did his best to appear menacing.

With a slight shake of his head, Eris moved with lightning speed to stand behind his brother, capturing Phobos with an elbow around his neck.

"I *can* make you."

Moments later, they stood on the floor of an ancient forest. The trees were thick enough to block out the sun, creating a canopy of fragrant green to shield the Sylphs who lived in the boughs of the old trees. Phobos could not remove himself as he did not yet know how. Eris grinned at the pouting boy.

"Mind your manners, Phobos, these are my people and you are to do nothing to cause trouble. Understand?"

Phobos lifted one shoulder in return, glaring daggers at Eris. "I feel too contained here. We cannot even see the mountain range or the sea while stuck within this ghastly timber."

"This *ghastly* timber is my homeland. Do not cause panic amongst these folk, or I will beat you silly. Swear to me that you will not."

Phobos was the budding god of Inspired Fright. He loved nothing more than to bring unsuspecting folks into a confused terrified state that involved bloodshed. Eris was so well aware of this tendency that he held his brother's gaze with his own threatening one until he received a response.

With an exaggerated exhale, Phobos muttered, "I swear, but only because you force me to take such an oath."

"If you are good, I will take you to a battle and let you cause as much mayhem as you wish." Eris winked at his brother.

Phobos grinned and nodded, his attention already focused on a young Dryad maiden who peered from behind a tree in curious question.

"Do not go far, Brother."

"Of course," Phobos answered over his shoulder as he

danced toward the lichen-hued girl who now offered a timid smile and a certain willing gleam in one eye. The other eye was hidden behind a sheet of straight dark-gray hair that fell to her waist.

"I will regret this, I am sure," Eris mumbled but turned away. His interest was with his mother, Aglauros, and that of the child Alcippe. Eris came as often as he could. Of late, it had been long months since his last visit and he was anxious to check on Alcippe's well-being.

The last time he paid a visit, Aglauros hinted at an arising problem, but Eris was called away before he learned more. He prayed the issue was not about the babe for if he had to remove Alcippe from amongst the Sylphs, he did not know where he could safely take her.

With nimble grace, Eris climbed the nearest giant tree and swung onto a large limb. He crouched there for a moment, surveying his old home. As he sniffed the air, expecting the fresh scent of leaves, he smelled a strange mixture of smoke and ash.

The whiff was faint but obvious. As Eris stepped onto the extended platform hidden high within the branches, he scoured the area for something charred.

The forest folk lived in great terror of fire. On occasion, lightning would strike one of the great trees and untold grief resulted from the loss of one of their own. The tree spirit was mourned with a ritual that went on for days and left a permanent mark on all those who inhabited the ancient forest.

Their entire village was built into the upper levels of the giant oaks, held tight by the strong boughs and dense foliage. The Sylph people shared the Sacred Grove with the Dryadic folk who made their homes within the wide trunks of the trees. On occasion, the species mingled and children born of these two parentages were easy to spot. They would appear an interesting mix of green and gray and have an affinity for wild dives from high to low ground.

The last Eris remembered of Alcippe, she was developing into her father's child. She no longer carried the pale green hue brought about by the breast milk from her foster mother, Aglauros. Instead,

Alcippe's skin was a pretty bronze unlike any other child in the Sacred Grove. She was also growing much faster than the children of either species.

This remained in his mind and had caused Aglauros much concern. It was now the reason Eris returned. Alcippe was brought to the Sacred Grove to hide her from Ares' enemies. Once word spread of this entirely different child, there would be those who sought her, intending harm. As she carried many other features of her father, one glance would reveal her true identity.

Where might the influence of her mother come in? Eris thought. *Something that might help disguise her?*

So far, he had seen none of Niala's gifts. Not unusual, Eris mused, as Niala had been human and the inherent immortal appearance would overtake any mortal features.

Outwardly, he did not speak of these things. He kept her location secret, even from Deimos, never breathing a word of her to anyone save Phobos. He was the only other who came to the Sacred Grove with Eris, but the boy had never laid eyes upon Alcippe. Phobos was always sent to play with the Sylph children when they visited.

Eris arrived at his mother's hut only to find it was deserted. A layer of dust lay upon the table and dried leaves littered the floor. Belongings were scattered, as if the hut had been abandoned in a hurry. As he stood inside the small arched doorway, worry knotted his brow.

"She would not just leave without sending word." Eris turned about, squinting toward the nearest rope ladder. "Where would she go?"

"Indeed, where would she go?" A voice spoke behind Eris, a voice made of the summer breeze creaking through old wood. He turned to see the ancient Chieftess of the Sylph tribe standing in bent silhouette.

"Son of Aglauros, welcome." The Chieftess leaned on a cane, her withered face solemn.

Word traveled fast in the Sacred Grove.

"Pehun, greetings." Eris bowed low to the honored leader and then kissed her gnarled fingers. "Where can I find Aglauros?"

"You cannot, for she has gone away from the Sacred Grove, Grandson."

"Why? Why has she left?" Eris stared at Pehun with disbelief. "What of her child?"

"She, too, is gone."

Fear rose up at the flicker in the old woman's gaze. "Where did they go?"

"I do not know. They disappeared into the Great Forest."

Eris paled. The Great Forest was vast and dangerous. No one left the tribe and went out into the wilderness alone, for they did not survive. He could not imagine his inexperienced mother with his baby sister fighting the beasts that inhabited the Great Forest without help. Did they have food and water? Weapons? Shelter?

What if they were already dead?

"Why? Why would my mother take such a risk, and with my sister?"

The old Chieftess dipped her chin in thought. When she spoke, it was with careful intonation. "The child has brought bad fortune unto Aglauros, and all her folk as well. She will not say who she bred with to bring such a threat into our midst, but it has been written in the stars that Alcippe is our downfall."

"That is lunacy. Alcippe is the daughter of...." Eris pressed his lips together so that 'Ares' would not come out.

He was not certain announcing the girl's father was the god of War would lighten this ominous moment. The pronouncement would cause further disturbance.

"This is dreadful, just dreadful. How could you allow this?" Eris clutched his belly, feeling as though he might heave. How could he explain this to Deimos? Or Ares, should he wake up from his slumber?

"Why would you allow your own daughter to leave the safety of this tribe, let alone your infant granddaughter?"

Pehun frowned and cast a tight-lipped, disapproving expression at Eris. "You forget your place, Grandson. Living away from your tribe does not suit you."

"Ahh, Grandmother, I apologize." Eris went to one knee and bowed his head. "It is just unbelievable that my beloved mother and sister were released to their fate in the Great Forest. I am overcome with grief."

Pehun nodded and placed one knotted hand upon Eris' head. Her voice was soft. "I understand. It deeply pained me to see them go but it was necessary for all our folk to survive."

With a wretched expression, Eris lifted his gaze to meet Pehun. The warrior fled and in his place was a frightened boy, caught between the wrath of War and the honor of his birth tribe.

"Come, Eris. I will show you what happened, and then you will understand."

He rose and followed Pehun as she moved with a slow and aged gait across the swaying bridges that connected the village. As they passed huts, Eris expected to be greeted with joy, as he always was when he returned home. Instead, not a soul emerged. Those who were outside retreated within their shelters.

As they reached the far side of the aerial village, the smoke and ash odor became stronger. Gut churning, Eris could not, at first, bear to look when Pehun came to a halt and pointed outward. With eyes closed, Eris inhaled a full breath and felt as well as smelled the stench of a deadly fire. He could taste it upon his tongue.

Not just the ancient oaks that was their home, but the stink of burned flesh. With his senses wide open, he could hear the screams and wails of those lost and knew their spirits had not left their beloved forest. He could see the ghostly shapes of destroyed trees, gray specters looming over them with those who died trying to save them entwined in the branches.

Eris opened his eyes to see the sickening reality - over a

dozen charred oaks, their branches bare and blackened, still reaching toward the sky. There was nothing left of any of the huts that had been tucked beneath the once-thick protective canopy of leaves.

"How many?" Words could not escape his lips at first but Eris finally pushed them out. He saw innumerable battles and Death was not a stranger, but those were warriors and these were his blood kin. He knew every single inhabitant of his village, knew them from birth.

And now, unto their death.

"Thirty-one."

"Ahh. Ahh. Ahh." Eris could not ask who. He could not bear to know.

"The fires that destroyed our folk and our forest were set by those who hoped to capture Aglauros and her babe. We would have lost everything save that it began to rain."

"Who? Who attacked you? I will bring the wrath of War down upon their heads."

"I do not know, Grandson. They came in the dark, flying through the air on the backs of great horses. There were only two, but two were more than enough to cause this." Pehun gestured at the ruined stand of trees and the dangling pieces of bridge with her cane.

"They would burn the entire grove if not for the bravery of Aglauros. She taunted them and then she ran. I do not know if they found her or the babe but she saved the rest of her people."

"Ahh, Pehun, I am so sorry." Eris wept, his fear so strong he believed his heart would burst. "I must find them, if they are still alive."

"It is not your fault, Grandson."

"But I brought Alcippe here. I brought her here."

Pehun turned away from the carnage to face Eris. "What do you mean, you brought her here? She was born to Aglauros."

Eris shook his head, "No, Grandmother, she was born to another. I brought Alcippe here to keep her safe. I begged my mother to take her and make others believe she had birthed the babe. It was to keep her safe."

He stared out over the destruction and wept harder.

"You brought the child here without permission?"

"I am sorry, Grandmother. How could I have known this would happen? How could I have known?"

"Is she yours?"

"No, not mine." Eris raised his tear-stained face to meet his grandmother's bewildered gaze. "But she is my true sister."

Stunned, Pehun could not speak for a moment. When words would come, she gasped, "You brought a child of War here, to our village? How dare you?"

"I am also a child of War, Grandmother, and you love me." Eris stood a bit taller, the green tinge on his cheeks becoming darker.

"You were born to Aglauros. This is not the same."

"Please forgive me. I brought her here because I feared for my sister. Ares has succumbed to a poisoned dagger and lies between the worlds. He cannot protect her. Deimos bade me save the babe from the Hordes of War. I had nowhere else to turn."

"Eris, you deeply grieve me. We have lost many because of your rash actions."

"Grandmother, please, I did not know what else to do but bring her to my people."

Pehun stared at her grandson for long moments before speaking. "Then you must find them. And if they are dead, then you must uphold the honor of the Sylph and seek revenge against those who would destroy your folk."

The grief for his people, for his mother and sister, began to spark into a dark rage. Eris lifted his face to the heavens and released a howl so great it resonated across the tops of the giant trees. The branches rustled as frightened birds took flight and small animals scurried to safety. Those of the Sylph nation froze in place as the battle cry echoed in wave after wave around them.

On the ground beneath the canopy of ancient trees, the

howl did more than raise an alarm - it called Phobos away from his Dryad playmate. With a quick kiss to the girl's cheek, Phobos left her and followed the summons. With proficient agility, he scrambled up the branches of the nearest tree and ran along the walkway until he found Eris.

"What has happened?"

With a shaking hand, Eris pointed at the ruined trees. "The Sylph were attacked. My mother and our sister fled into the Great Forest to divert the monsters and save the Sacred Grove. Pehun does not know if they were captured. If they are dead or alive."

"We must go after them." Phobos danced from one foot to the other, already aching for a fight.

"Yes, Brother, we must go after them. If they live, we will rescue them. If they are dead." Eris' brown eyes grew as hard as that of the oldest wood. "We will kill every last one of the monsters."

Phobos hesitated in his excitement. "What of Deimos? If he calls to us and we do not answer he will punish us."

"I do not care what punishment I might receive. I will find my mother and our sister and reap havoc upon those who would dare touch them."

"Agreed." Phobos spoke without hesitation.

The two boys sealed their pact with hands to each other's arms, eyes locked, and gave a brief nod.

"Grandmother, I swear we will not return until our people have been avenged."

Tears glistened in Pehun's eyes. "Return to us that which is ours, Grandson."

Without any further words, Eris and Phobos set off into the Great Forest. They had no need to carry food or blankets. They could take care of themselves and, if necessary, call upon the Hordes of War to fight with them.

They went in search of Aglauros and Alcippe, praying mother and babe were still alive.

SIX

Olympus seemed deserted save for the three old women dressed in white who hovered near the giant hearth at the far end of the chamber. They were the Moerae, Keepers of Fate, and daughters of Moros - Destiny.

Was it Ares' destiny to lie between the worlds for the rest of eternity? Zeus commanded the Moerae to work day and night to return Ares to health, yet naught had come of their ministrations. They huddled together by the warmth of the hearth flames, shaking their collective heads and muttering between themselves.

It was unclear as to how much power the Moerae held, under the circumstances. The fate they controlled did not harbor an immortal struck down by another immortal. Such a thing had not been written within their fabled weaving, thus the constant fussing which consumed their every moment.

Deimos turned his attention away from the women to look at his father, lying cold and gray upon the ornate bier, lifeless save for the slightest rise and fall of his chest. The grievous wound inflicted by Cedalion's poisoned dagger oozed dark matter from Ares' exposed side, staining the white linen cloth folded beneath his ribs.

Shorn of his long hair, beard and mustache, the once-great warrior appeared too youthful to have led vast armies into battle, too innocent to have caused major upheaval in dual realms, and too tender to have left a void that could scarce be filled.

Touching his bearded chin, Deimos just that moment realized what compelled him to alter his own appearance. Father and son exchanged lives and therefore manifested the opposite aspect. Deimos chose to remain clean-shaven his entire existence in an act of rebellion against Ares. Now he was his father, beard and all.

The irony was not lost, yet he could see no humor in the switch. Though Ares was difficult, he did not deserve to lie between the worlds in such a vulnerable condition.

"They have applied hundreds of remedies, all to no avail." Sorrow thickened Hera's voice. "There is no cure for the poison."

She entered the room on quiet feet, approaching Deimos as drifting snow would overtake a traveler. Her grief enveloped him and brought a choking cough to his throat.

"Hephaestos should be made to find one." Deimos coughed again and waved one hand before his face to clear the air. His grandmother paid no attention, her gaze fixed on her once-invincible, now fallen son.

"He refuses."

"Demand it."

"We have had these words before, Grandson. How does one enforce such a demand? Hephaestos would rather suffer imprisonment alone, forever, than see Ares awaken."

"Such hatred."

"Indeed." Hera touched fingertips to her breast. "And in the name of Love."

"It is not her fault."

"Aphrodite is not innocent in all this. She is the most devious of all. I curse the day she rose from the sea." Hera's face twisted with an ugliness that startled Deimos.

"She is my mother. Never forget that." His tone rose with an implied threat.

Hera's features settled into an implacable smooth mask and the tension eased as she patted his hand. "For that I am grateful. If not, I would not have you. Ares was not inclined to take a wife until Aphrodite was born into our world. I am certain he has many offspring on the mortal plane, but not within our ranks. He refused until Aphrodite was in our midst. She brought him into a balance, of sorts."

"It is her nature to love. She cannot help she loved them both."

"It is her nature, but she used Hephaestos to punish Ares. Now Hephaestos suffers and I cannot bear it. Ares lies here, neither dead nor alive, while Hephaestos has been stripped of all ability to create.

"His reason for living has been taken from him. He is a gentle soul who lived only to make beautiful things for others. He did not deserve this."

"Do you imply that both my father and mother have received just rewards for their actions?" Deimos' face flushed with rising indignation.

Hera ignored his ire. "I say Hephaestos was caught up in their web of deceit and had no other thought in mind than to love Aphrodite."

"You truly believe he had no intention to cause Ares' pain?"

Hera shrugged, her silken chiton rustling with the movement. "I believe Ares will awaken and Aphrodite will regain her strength. At the same time, Hephaestos has been diminished for all eternity. Once he has served his sentence, he will shrink from the world and barricade himself in his palace.

"His cavern is already sealed and his fires dampened. He is alone, so very, very alone in his pain. He has not even Cedalion as companion. For he, too, is banished for his crime."

"Though it is a sad ending to all, do not fault my mother. She meant none of this to happen. She could not have known what would befall those she loved. Aphrodite suffers endlessly in her grief. She has become a recluse, exiled by her own will. She has withdrawn from everything."

"What of the daughter she bore Ares? Or is it Hephaestos? A grandchild whom I may never see. One whose father remains a mystery."

"You must ask Anteros in regards to the babe, Harmonia." Deimos glanced toward the Moerae, who had moved around Ares and begun to chant as they scattered herbs over his body.

"War is upon me, and Love is failing. The weight of the Realm of Love falls to Anteros."

"Anteros will not speak to me. He is angry I shun his mother, and he cares not for his father."

"He cares more than you think, more than he would have you believe. His loyalty is to the House of Love, just as mine is to the House of War. He steps up to take charge now that Aphrodite languishes."

Once again facing Hera, Deimos felt the prickle of warning that always ran along the back of his neck while at Olympus. He must be very careful.

"And you divert the conversation." Hera glanced at Deimos with shrewd eyes. "You have seen this little one - does she take after Ares or Hephaestos?"

"Harmonia has her mother's blonde locks and turquoise eyes. There is no way to tell who might be her sire."

"You think not? I see both your mother and father in you and Anteros. I see your mother in Phobos, a dear sweet child, who suffers mightily at his father's hand. I see the tender edges of love etched on his face though he wends his way toward War. I see War's mark on Eros in the clever way he observes others."

"It is true we who are a blending of War and Love display a part of each. Since it is not written upon this new one's face, then perhaps it will be shown upon the soul as she matures."

"I am caught between despair and hope. I plead endlessly with Hypnos to release my son from his grip. I beg Moros to change his destiny and let him live." A sob caught in Hera's throat. She held a fist to her chest, sighing before she spoke again.

"If Ares lives, then it is possible to forgive, but if he dies." The threat of retaliation hung in the air with Deimos' words.

"Alive or dead, Ares would prefer, but not this. This unholy sleep that robs him of his place in the world. Sleep that drains his vitality and gives false hope that he may once more open his eyes. False hope that Hephaestos will survive his punishment and be allowed entry into Council chambers with respect."

"Hephaestos never had respect." Deimos made a rude sound.

"But he will, Poseidon swore it. There will be no further cruelty." Hera turned away. "It was the only way Hephaestos would release Aphrodite and Ares from imprisonment at his fortress in Lemnos."

"He would leave them forever constrained together beneath a gold-link net? Aphrodite would be bound to Ares' near-lifeless body for an eternity? And you speak of cruelty. Hephaestos does not deserve forgiveness."

"I would expect you to speak so, but you do not fully understand the consequences."

"I do not understand?" Disbelief curled Deimos' lip. "I bear the Mantle of War, thrust upon me by the actions of others, and you claim I do not know the importance of what has befallen my parents?"

With an impatient flick of one hand, Deimos continued. "It is you, Grandmother, who does not understand what has befallen both Realms. Ares was right when he said those who reside at Olympus have too long been separated from truth."

"I see you have adopted your father's contemptuous views of the Greater Realm. He continually mocked us. Yet who is to say what the truth is? Mine represents what I am. His represented what he was. It is sad to think there was no compromise."

"Grandfather has no interest in compromise. Zeus hates Ares."

"There is no hatred here." Hera spoke with gentleness. "Distrust was born with Ares."

"Again, you blame one who cannot defend himself."

"Perhaps. I wish Ares would rise and take issue with this purported insult." Hera paused to wipe away a tear. "I fear Ares will never recover. With that grief hanging over my head, I request you bring me his child."

"His child." Deimos' thoughts went to the babe Niala birthed, the girl Eris hid away for safety's sake. "I do not know...."

He was about to voice that he did not know where she was but brought himself up short as Hera continued.

"Harmonia deserves a proper upbringing and it will not be so on Cos. With her mother languishing away in a stupor, all the while uncaring as to what becomes of the little one. I want the child here, where I can provide for her. I request that you bring Harmonia to me."

"She is well and happy on Cos. Though Aphrodite is still in the grips of sorrow, she loves the child and would allow no harm to come to her."

"No harm, but who will help her with her gifts?"

"She is too young to be concerned about her balance of power."

"Is she? You came to influence at a very young age, as did your brother Anteros. And need I remind you of Phobos and his trials? He, too was younger than anyone would expect to discover how Panic would shape him."

"Females are different."

Hera laughed, a mirthless sound. "And your experience with females coming into their own authority has been how vast? Not quite, Grandson. Harmonia needs direction and Aphrodite is not up to the challenge."

"Harmonia is no more than a babe in arms. Her need for instruction is a long time coming. If Aphrodite has not recovered by then, Harmonia will have Anteros to help her."

"Again, your brother has had practice in the ways of a young girl coming into her own?"

"No, but he adores her and will care for her in every way possible. And further, Anteros has the Graces, particularly Thaleia, to help with the babe."

"I am not questioning his affection, nor the care Thaleia gives the child. I am questioning what is right for Harmonia. Until Aphrodite regains her senses, it would be best for the babe to abide here with me."

"If you truly believe this, I advise you to fetch the babe yourself. Or have Anteros bring Harmonia here. Why do you insist on placing me in the middle of this quarrel?"

"Ahh, and so there it is: Anteros will not respond to me. Love's Response will not acknowledge his own grandmother. He refuses to discuss this matter. I ask that you go to Cos and talk sense into him, make him see there is more harm in keeping Harmonia close to a mother that ignores her than allowing the child to reside here."

"He will refuse me as well."

"No, he will not. You are the only one Anteros will listen to these days. Please, Deimos, you must convince your brother to let Harmonia come here. Even if it is temporary, until Aphrodite has recovered. That is all I ask."

Deimos gave no further argument. It was quite possible Hera was correct about the girl needing a strong female bond. Would Aphrodite's servants, Thaleia, Aglaia, and Euphrosyne, provide enough? There were other women on Cos, other children, would not Harmonia receive their care as well? What was the correct thing to do? Who could know?

Certainly not the son of War.

"I will consider your request under one condition: both I and Anteros will be received with respect in Council. We will be full members. Just as our parents, our voices will be heard. If you cannot agree to that, then you will have to retrieve the child yourself."

As Deimos turned away, he caught sight of another behind him, close enough that had he taken a second step he would have trod upon her. "Iris, do not approach me with such stealth."

"Or what, great warrior?" Iris lifted her chin in a subtle challenge. Instead, her breath caught as their gazes met and an onset of sudden desire rushed through her. "Will you ravish me once again?"

Deimos stared at the rapid rise and fall of Iris' breast beneath the pale blue tunic. The gown was short and without sleeves, draped so that Deimos had ample view of her supple skin. Iris' finely molded arms and legs glowed with swirls of colored light.

"You caught me unawares on your visit to Athos. It is not my way to be so callous."

With a tinkling laugh, Iris held up one hand, palm out. "Peace, My Lord, I accept your apology. I bear some blame for our tumble."

"Apology?" Eyes locked with that of the Shimmering Rainbow, Deimos' lips quirked upward for a second. "I do not regret the moment."

"Nor I, War god. I meant for placing you in that position."

The brilliance of white teeth against pink lips and glow in her rainbow eyes made Deimos' heart lurch within his chest. The expansion of heat was more than lust and appeared foreign amidst the ravages of War. It was the first true sentiment he held, besides loathing, since the Mantle fell upon his shoulders.

As Iris slipped past Deimos, the top of her head reached his chin and her delicious scent rose from her hair. Her breath warmed the flesh at his neck, spreading desire to his belly.

Carnal images sprang upon Deimos, pushing aside the gentler response that took him hostage only moments before. Sweat wet his brow as he fought to regain control.

He had treated Iris badly at Athos. He did not want to repeat his uncouth behavior in front of Hera.

"Lord Deimos?"

Iris' melodious voice called him back to sanity. As Deimos met her gaze, now deep violet, he let Iris see the hunger reflected in his eyes. She touched his arm and whispered, "Later."

Iris turned away from Deimos, to Hera. "Mistress, I come bearing a message and I must speak to you alone." She nodded toward Deimos.

"Well enough," Hera responded, eyes narrowed as she split her suspicious gaze between the two. "Deimos, do as I bid, return with the child and I will grant the favors you request."

Hera drew her messenger away to confer in private. With their murmurings trailing behind as they left the chamber, Deimos buried a desire that bordered on something more disturbing and went back to stare at his father's body.

There was no change.

Deimos glanced toward the high vaulted hearth flickering with orange flame and watched the Moerae. One of the old women tossed a small bundle onto the logs. Stifling a gag as the cloying smoke filled his nose and mouth with the flavor of burnt amber, Deimos shook his head.

There was not a twitch from the silent gray figure lying on the raised dais. He watched for a sign to show Ares held awareness. Deimos waited for a deeper breath to be drawn, a muttered word or two, a shifting of body position, but there was no change, though the old crones continued their rituals every waking hour.

The other two women circled the bier that held Ares' prone body. One shook a rattle to awaken the spirit; another waved a thin stick of incense, smoke curling from the lit end, to cleanse and prepare the body. The third crone joined them and lifted her arms up, mumbling mystical incantations, imploring Ares to hear them. They appeared to pray for his wandering soul to return to his body.

Deimos let them continue their work, knowing the ritual would not bring Ares back. And just as his grandmother was aware, so was he that if the Moerae could not change Ares' path, he was doomed.

In a barely breathing shell, Hephaestos' revenge held Ares between the worlds, neither among the living nor the dead. Deimos could not weep for his father, or even for himself, for just as Ares was gone, so was the old Deimos. He was irrevocably changed. The insidious power of War had eaten through his armor, and transformed him from reckless youth to the Destroyer.

Even though Hera refused to give up and charged the Moerae to awaken Ares, Deimos was aware of the significance of the burning of amber. It signaled that Ares would not recover. Amber was reserved for the rites of the dead, for safe passage to the Shadowland. The crones secretly strove to release his soul rather than call him back.

Sly witches.

Hera would punish them in the most horrible manner if she realized what they did.

Deimos could not disagree with the crones, for it seemed Ares had no will to return. Which meant the Mantle of War would remain with Deimos. It also held sinister connotations for the recovery of Aphrodite, who was so well aligned with the dying Ares.

Swearing under his breath, Deimos turned away from the bier.

It was time for him to visit Anteros with the news that Hera wanted Harmonia. Deimos had no intention of bringing the child back to Olympus, however, his brother deserved fair warning of such connivance.

From the corner of his eye, Deimos caught movement. With the flick of a black robe, its owner stepped toward Ares and into the light. The visitor was Thanatos, better known as Bitter Death.

"Is he to die, then?" Resignation was heavy in Deimos' voice.

Thanatos shrugged. "Ares fights me."

"He would. It is his nature."

"A nature that will someday weaken." Thanatos circled the bier, watching Ares with an intensity that bordered on covetous hunger. "When it does, I will be waiting for him. For now, he lingers in my brother's realm."

"Sleep."

"Yes, Hypnos holds tightly to him."

"Does Hypnos claim Ares or does Ares choose to stay?"

"That question is not mine to answer. Yet when he does enter my realm, he will never leave."

"Sometimes I believe he refuses to awaken in order to punish me."

"Punish? Next to Hades, War holds the greatest power between Mortal and Immortal Realms. That seems not a cruelty to me."

Thanatos ran his fingertips along Ares' bare arm to his naked chest, tracing down to the ever-draining wound. He was careful not to get any of the blood on his skin for fear there was still poison in the gash. With a frown, he wiped his hand on the linen coverlet.

"The art of War belongs to Ares. I merely hold the reins until he recovers." Deimos wanted to strike Thanatos and his unbearable arrogance but resisted. Instead, he remained stern-faced and unrelenting. "He will return."

"I beg to differ. Ares recedes. I see the Mantel of War firmly upon your shoulders."

Deimos heard deep envy in Thanatos' voice. "So, Cousin, you would take your father's throne, if the opportunity afforded itself?"

Thanatos grimaced and did not reply. Instead he focused on the inert body before him. "To carry Ares to the Shadowland would be ultimate proof of my control. Imagine, an immortal who is not immune to my power."

Thanatos' breath quickened and his tongue flicked over his lips in a disturbingly salacious manner. "The consequences would be far-spread. No one could truly escape my touch."

Deimos eyed his cousin with a skeptical gaze, wondering to what degree Thanatos was willing to go for this kind of leverage. One would speculate he was after no more than the souls of the departed, and to deliver them to Persephone for healing.

It would seem that Thanatos had a much more sinister agenda.

From the mortal viewpoint, Bitter Death was a frightening, unknown and unseen creature from the spirit realm, a skeletal horror creeping up on an unsuspecting body with scythe raised to harvest its soul. Thanatos encouraged such fearful images. He delighted in them.

Truth be known, Thanatos was far from that reflection. So far from such musings that one would not realize Bitter Death was at one's side if not for the hair that rose on the back of one's neck.

Beneath the ominous black cloak worn with deliberate glee about Thanatos' shoulders, stood a tall youth in a purple tunic. Forever young and pretty, with wide innocent eyes the color of wet sand, cheeks sprinkled with freckles and dull red hair, Thanatos was hardly the portrait of a ghoul ready to steal away life.

Were he to remove his cloak and walk amongst the mortals, he would be admired for his beauty, yet Thanatos did not appreciate the incongruity. The obvious was lost on him, for he lacked any sense of wit or humor. Those who claimed Bitter Death played tricks had not truly met the son of Hades.

Thanatos was substantial, not gaunt or hollow-eyed from the rigors of the Shadowland. He was quite vigorous, in a softer, more rounded manner than Deimos himself.

Softer of body, but still imminently capable.

Accomplished enough to capture an immortal? Deimos shuddered at the very idea. If Thanatos could take Ares, then it was true, no one was safe, not even Zeus himself.

The immortals could scarce allow that to happen.

Could they?

Deimos cast a glance at his cousin and noted the calculating smile that graced Thanatos' face. There was no doubt Thanatos intended to do his best to bring Ares to the Shadowland. If Thanatos succeeded, both Mortal and Immortal realms would shift with irrevocable and frightening consequences.

"Does Hades agree with this deed?"

Thanatos sniffed. "Why would my father oppose? He would

have the ultimate authority over all living creatures if I brought him a prize such as Ares."

"If you brought Ares to the Shadowland, it would reinstate Chaos. Everyone is aware Hades detests anarchy. He appreciates order. And Persephone, even more so."

At Thanatos' pouting frown, Deimos mocked, "Queen of the Shadowland, Healer of Souls, Bringer of Spring and New Life. Hmm, what would your mother say of this desire to take down an immortal?"

Thanatos voice was frosty. "Step-mother."

"Ahh," Deimos nodded. He was beginning to understand. "Persephone moves so frequently between the worlds that she does not know of the battle that rages. I must wonder if the Queen is ignorant of this mission, is the King also uninformed?"

"Do not make light of my quest." Thanatos ground his teeth. "I do my father's bidding, as always, just as you obey your father."

"Have you not paid attention, Cousin? I no longer follow my father. I have become my father." Deimos could not keep the edge of resentment from his voice.

"You do not appreciate the gift you have been given. Would my father pass the crown to the Shadowland to me, I would readily accept it."

"Then you know nothing of what Hades does."

"Your ego shows, Deimos. I serve my father's realm every second of my existence. I know the balance he holds between the worlds."

"And you think you could do as well?"

Thanatos sneered. "More so than you. I am, at the least, a willing subject. You, on the other hand, reject your true calling."

"Be careful or the question you will be pressed to answer is *can Death die?*"

"You dare threaten me?" Thanatos grabbed the front of Deimos' tunic. "I will drag both you and your father to the

Shadowland for all eternity."

"Touch me not, Thanatos, or I will do worse by you than a simple killing." Deimos raised a hand and bid Amason to come. A mere blink later and the menacing sword vibrated in his grip. The lust for blood beat heavy in Deimos' heart - a true gift of War.

Thanatos blanched and moved not a twitch at the hot fury in Deimos' gaze. It was whispered that the deadly Amason had the ability to dispatch immortals to their demise.

"Brother. Cousin. I beg of you to cease this nonsensical argument." Hypnos, he of Dreamless Sleep and Thanatos' twin, arrived beside them, hands upheld in a request for peace. "This is not the time or place to quarrel."

As fiery as Bitter Death appeared, Dreamless Sleep looked ambiguous. He, too, was pretty in a forgettable way, his thick hair white, and his lips bloodless in his pale face.

After a tense moment of silence, Deimos nodded. He withdrew his blade but not before he nicked Thanatos with the razor edge, drawing a single drop of blood. Thanatos let out a shriek and released Deimos to clap his hand to the cut.

Deimos turned away with a slight smile as he released Amason back to her resting place at Athos. "Bitter Death is not so heroic after all, is he?"

"You will regret this, I swear it upon Hades' realm." With a snap of his black cloak, Thanatos disappeared.

At the spot where Bitter Death had stood, the Moerae could be seen frozen into a cluster of alarm, their lips moving in silent prayer.

"Do not let the ramblings of my brother frighten you." Hypnos spoke with soothing grace to the old women. "He is merely discouraged that Ares resists him, no doubt because of your fine ministrations. Rest, Grandmothers, take a well-deserved rest and forget you gazed upon Death this day."

Still murmuring, Hypnos waved his fingers toward the staring women, and then, with a slowness born of the need to slumber, they lowered to their chairs as sleep enveloped them.

"Ahh, so simple." Hypnos faced Deimos. "But such is my lot in life."

"Is it that easy to hold War in the grip of Dreamless Sleep? You wield more power than you let on, Cousin."

"Because you are who you are, I will tell you a little secret." Hypnos beckoned Deimos closer.

"Because I wear the Mantel of War, or because you take pride in thwarting your brother?"

"Hmmm." Hypnos glanced at Ares, a pensive expression etched onto his features. "Perhaps both. Though Thanatos and I are twins, we are at odds with our individual concerns for the living.

"He seeks no more than to satisfy our father with the souls of the mortal ilk. I, on the other hand, offer peace without death. The blessed oblivion of dreamless sleep, whereby all can escape the dangers of existence for a short time. The sacrifice is in hours, not lives."

"And Ares, who could never find rest now slumbers in your realm unconcerned with the consequences?" Deimos' tone held a serious threat.

"Cousin, Cousin. You should relax more yourself. You would not be so quick to judgment." Hypnos smoothed his clothing, a gray tunic similar to Thanatos' but without the black cloak.

Deimos could not decide which of the brothers annoyed him more, each with their own self-involved diatribes. Both were unbearable. He stilled the urge to soundly thrash Hypnos and turned a threatening gaze upon the young man.

"I must go. Keep my father safe. Return him when you tire of this game."

"And there you go again, opining when you do not have all the facts." Leaning closer, Hypnos whispered, "I told you, I have a secret to share if you would be polite enough to listen."

Biting back a curse, Deimos shook his head. "What is this secret? I do not have the luxury of time that you seem to have."

With a clucking sound, Hypnos waved his hand across

Ares' body. "Such bitterness. You were not like this as a boy. I liked you much better then."

"Do not ask what has happened. You know full well my position. Get on with this secret, or I swear, out of spite, I shall cut your throat."

"Very well. I will tell you with one condition." Hypnos winked at Deimos. "You inform no one. Thanatos, Hera, Aphrodite, Anteros or anyone else."

"Fine. Yes. Get on with it."

Hypnos raised his hands chest high, palms turned upward in a gesture of defeat, though he implied it was no fault of his. "I do not hold Ares in the Realm of Sleep."

"He stays there because he wills it. That comes as no surprise," Deimos growled. "He would do such to torture my mother, if not all of us."

"You do not understand me, Cousin," Hypnos corrected. "I do not hold him. He does not reside in my Realm."

"He is not there? Where is he?"

"That I do not know. He has utterly disappeared."

"How is that possible? He must be somewhere." Deimos stared with hard eyes at Hypnos, sensing a lie. He would not stand for it.

"He is Ares the Destroyer. No one has ever been able to hold him prisoner for more than a fleeting moment." Hypnos flipped his fingers in the air.

"His body, yes, is like a bull that cannot be held, but his spirit, too, escapes?" Deimos looked askance at his cousin.

"Yes. It seems he did not find my domain to his liking and has taken himself to a realm he prefers."

"Where is that, pray tell?"

Hypnos shrugged, his lips lifting in an infuriating smile.

"This is madness." Deimos stared at his father's body. "How could his spirit disappear? Where would it go?"

"Again, I do not know the answer."

"Well, then, who does?"

"I cannot guess for we of the Shadowland have never lost our charges. It is beyond my ability to comprehend."

"What of Hades? What does he say?"

"You would have to ask my father that question."

"Hades is a recluse who speaks to no one."

"Agreed, Cousin. You see my dilemma. I cannot gain audience with my father and I certainly cannot advise Thanatos of the situation."

"Then we must sound the alarm, call in help to find him." Deimos strode to the heavy door but before he could pull it open, Hypnos was at his side.

"To advise the world that Ares is truly missing will only cause more destruction. You must wait for him to reappear when he is ready, or find him yourself." Hypnos' pale gray eyes sparkled with delight.

"Of one thing I am certain, Ares will never concede either to Thanatos or to Libertina, even though she would bring Sweet Death. He will not fall into either my brother or my sister's clutches. This I know as sure as I am standing here."

"You advise we do nothing, Cousin? On the sound reasoning that you win the battle and your siblings do not?"

"Think hard, Deimos. Do you want to return the Mantle of War to your father? Ares is without mercy, allowing the human tides to rage wherever and whenever they choose. By his very nature, he is unconcerned with bravery or righteousness. He remains contemptuous of triumph as long as there is bloodshed to be had.

"In the short time you have born the Mantel of War, things have changed. Or are you so wrapped up in your own woes you fail to pay note to this?"

Deimos' hand flexed, ready to call Amason once again. "You have no dealings in my Realm, Cousin. You would be wise to keep clear of me and mine."

"Ahh, the misery of such power," Hypnos mocked. "It appears that it is your destiny."

"You ridicule me, but what of you, Hypnos? What is your

destiny?"

Hypnos stroked his clean-shaven cleft chin and tapped one finger against the side of his nose. "I have no desire for places and things, no longing for love, or hate, such as it is for you." He glanced at Ares' body. "Or my brother, as it seems."

With a soft exhale, Hypnos moved his hand to a brooch at the front of his tunic. "Just hear me, Cousin. Whether you approve or not, I have seen both your daydreams and nightmares and you are most certainly not your father.

"You wear his Mantel, but it does not lie the same way on your shoulders. Take note of this, for you are certain to change the shape of War if you pay attention. Do not follow his footsteps. Create your own path."

"Begone with your lunacy," Deimos snapped, "War is what it is, and I have no choice but to be as my father was."

"You are wrong about that. I have seen the changes." Hypnos shrugged. "Be that as it may, it is your choice."

Hypnos took his leave as Deimos continued staring at the bier holding his father's nearly lifeless body. How much truth had his cousin told? If Ares was not in Sleep's Realm, where was he?

SEVEN

Dark. So dark. No sound, no light. No sensation, no sentiment. No thought, no memory. No breath, no heartbeat. Floating in darkness, there was naught save the tiniest flicker of awareness that there was nothing.

Nothing.

Ares drifted in and out until a tiny spark took hold and grew into dim understanding. He fought to retain that one moment of clarity, that one speck of alertness that might give him the momentum to pull out of the depths of incomprehension.

Yet with each flash of insight came more darkness. He could do no more than helplessly waft in the endless quiet. With each attempt to awaken, he grew tired, receding back into oblivion until the next flare caught his distorted attention.

How long between those moments of lucidity? There was no time, no measurement of distance. He had no means to sense the length or breadth of his prison. It was all he could do to hold onto those flickers of awareness, and with each reoccurrence, widen the door a bit more before he fell back into the black hole of senselessness.

He could not be certain when the fabric of mindfulness began to knit a larger pattern, one to which he could cling for a longer stretch. He could not identify when he became aware of his body or when he gained the ability to open his eyes. It just happened.

Darkness swaddled him like a blanket within his cocoon. Ares could hear the faint creaks and groans of timber and stone settling onto a foundation. He could hear the soft trickle of water deep within the walls and smell the aroma of burned incense and lamp oil.

These sensations also came and went. He could not hold any one of them long enough to question what it was or why it was there, other than to wonder if it was all a dream. After long periods of acquiescence, he would struggle back to the question. The only question he had.

Where was he? Not his fortress on Athos.

Or Olympus, or Cos.

It was not anywhere he had ever been.

Or had he?

Some niggling illusive reminder of the past made him believe perhaps he had, indeed, been in this state before.

But what was it?

Exhausted by the uncertainty, Ares fell once again into a sleep as sound as the dead.

When next he awoke - and how long he slept, hours, days, months, even years, he could not tell - it was with physical feeling restored to his limbs. He felt the frame beneath him, iron and wood supporting a firm pallet that cradled his body. A woolen blanket tucked around his naked torso, covering him down to his feet.

He was conscious that every part of his skin burned, his left side seared with red hot pain, his extremities lie heavy with fatigue and his fingers and toes tingled with numbness. In spite of it all, Ares sucked the cool moist air into his body with gratitude. He could not force himself to move a thread's width even by sheer willpower. His body lay like a tree with roots buried far into the earth.

Staring straight up, he saw nothing but blackness. Not a flicker of light. He could hear the trickling of water somewhere far away but could not identify the source. There was a certain degree of relief that he had not imagined the sound, that it was real, that he was alive.

With each breath, he began to sort out the smells lingering in the air around him. Lamp oil. Incense. Damp wool.

Good.

He had not dreamed those either.

There was something else riding in the air: the delicate scent of returning spring. Newly budded flowers, greening grass, warm dirt laced with burnt ash. Lilies. Fields of lilies.

As if all that grew now burned to dust once the cold winds of winter set in, this fragrance lingered in the far distance. Ares could not pull it close enough to identify the aroma. Trying to remember, trying to place the essence fatigued him and he once again slipped into a stupor.

The muted sound of humming brought Ares back to himself. Disoriented, he tried to speak but found he could not. He could only lie unmoving, mindful of his useless body that ached with each breath.

There was a faint glimmer of light and the acrid smoke of a lamp. He could better see the details of his prison, or at least, what was directly above him. Hewn rock, uneven in the flickering light, shot with streaks of sparkling dust. A cave? What else would have such distinctive markings?

The aroma that tickled his senses was again present and he fought to remember the familiar odor. With huge effort, Ares managed a slight turn of his head and a croaking gurgle came from his lips. There was an immediate response, a rustling of cloth and a sharp intake of breath, the scrape of a chair leg against the floor. A feminine shadow was cast against the ceiling. The shadow danced and wavered as it moved.

Ares heard the ping of a key placed into a lock and the grate of metal on metal as it turned. His mind registered danger, for he surely was imprisoned, and yet he could not summon the strength to sit up, let alone prepare for battle.

Words would not emerge from his mouth, only guttural grunts conveying no discernible meaning. He was trapped and yet felt no fear. He felt nothing save curiosity as the figure approached his resting place. The fragrance grew stronger as the light grew brighter. Whoever she was, she carried a lantern with her.

Burning oil overlay the scent of spring growth. He closed his eyes, ever willing himself to remember.

The humiliation.

Ares struggled against his bonds: grunting and sweating, attempting to free himself. The ropes binding his hands behind his back stretched to his feet, and then tied together so he could not gain leverage. A filthy cloth gagged his mouth and his eyes were blinded by another rag. Fear wove with pain to fuel his fight. He could feel the rough walls of his prison against his naked body as he squirmed round and round, trying to loosen the oiled cord.

He was sealed inside a huge bronze urn, one of two that decorated the entrance to Poseidon's palace. He and the other boys had often played games of hide and seek or tag among the marble pillars and statues, running from the wide steps all the way down to the shore and back, laughing wildly.

Ares had trusted his playmates, the twins, the Aloadae.

The dishonor.

What a fool he was, believing that he, Ares, could have friends. At thirteen, filled with a bloodlust and fury that he could not understand, Ares was a child on the verge of embracing his power as War. No one wanted him, not even his mother, and especially not his father. Sad, lonely, in desperate need of allies, he believed Otus and Ephialtes, those monstrous and cruel children of Poseidon.

They took him under their care, and assured him they were worthy companions to the emerging God of War. The twins who were his playmates - the only ones to befriend him when all others turned away.

Otus and Ephialtes tricked him. They hated him. They betrayed him.

The agony.

Tears soaked the blindfold and ran down his cheeks. Ares choked on the grief that threatened to tear his gut apart. He could not cease crying as a new feeling emerged, a feeling not yet birthed but growing within him: panic. The ugliness gripped him in its vengeful vice and sent him into uncontrollable loathing. He swore that should he ever be freed, he would kill them, the Aloadae. He had believed and confided in them.

He would kill both of them - a slow tortuous death that would show them how strong he truly was. They captured him only because he was caught unaware, stupidly unaware. Now he was locked within this ignoble prison, unfit for one such as him.

What would he prefer - something glorious? A volcano or in the heart of a mountain, but this? He set up a howl muffled by the gag, a cry no one heard.

 Would he ever be released from his prison? He had been curled up inside the bronze urn for a very long time and no one came looking for him. No one.

Not his mother.

Not his father.

Not a single one of his siblings.

No one cared if he was missing.

Did they even notice he was gone?

Ares fell into an uneasy sleep, dreaming of his prison only to awaken and know that it was not a dream at all, but a reality.

How long? How long had he been locked away, filthy, starving, a frightened child who needed someone to rescue him?

And no one came.

He swore he would never shed another tear, never show weakness ever again as the rage built. It built and built, red hot wrath swathed in a murderous brutal desire to destroy everyone and everything around him.

Revenge. Mutilate. Slaughter.

Destroy them all without discernment. Kill or be killed. The rage surged through his body, filling every fiber of his blood, his lungs, his heart with such hatred he thought he would burst.

And then he did.

He erupted from his prison, shattering the urn into metal slivers that glistened in the sun like bronze colored ribbon. The ropes that bound him split apart, shredding into nothingness. With a roar that thundered throughout the land, echoing between the water and the sky, a roar that struck terror into the hearts of all inhabitants of Olympus. Ares was free. The trusting child was dead.

Ares the Destroyer was born.

With an involuntary shudder, Ares came awake, eyes wide open and staring into the darkness. Where was he? Not in the urn.

No, not there.

That was eons ago. The Aloadae twins were long dead. He had most cruelly killed them.

Where was he? Lying on a narrow bed, the smell of hot oil and incense hovering in the air, water dripping deep within the walls. Ares raised his throbbing head from his bed and tried to focus on the light next to him.

As the lamp was placed on a small stand, the female leaned over to gaze at him.

Aphrodite. His Beloved, his mate, his heart of hearts.

No, it was not Aphrodite. Her scent was the delicate and shy moonflower that appeared only at night. This was the aroma of warm earth and spring growth. The perfume of lilies.

"Persephone." As Ares forced the single word from his throat, he went into a wheezing fit that hurt from head to toe.

"Yes, Ares, it is I."

"What? Why?" he gasped as another choking cough threatened to rip asunder his ribcage. A brilliant point of pain was focused on his left side, an agony he could scarce contain.

"Please do not concern yourself with those questions at present. You must rest and gather your strength to heal. I will explain soon enough."

Ares fought to move, lifting one hand to grasp at her. "Where am I?"

"With me. You are safe but damaged. You must rest."

Persephone touched cool fingertips to his forehead. Moments later, Ares drifted back into sleep, a protest still on his lips. Her smile was thoughtful as she watched her captive dropped into a deep slumber.

"You know not the favor I have granted you, Ares the Destroyer. What will you do to repay me?"

After tucking the blanket around his body, Persephone took up the lantern and went out, locking the cell door after herself.

"Perhaps a better question: what will I ask of you?"

*****

Ares stirred, limbs jerking, mouth dry. Where was he? Why was it so dark? What was that sound? Water dripping? Remnants of lamp oil and the lingering scent of lilies.

Memory flooded in of conversations with Persephone, many, over long periods of time.

How long?

Groaning, Ares forced himself to sit up, though his arms and legs were leaden and his head throbbed with harsh pain. With great effort, he rose to his feet. Pausing there until he caught his balance and the bursts of color stopped whirling in front of his eyes, Ares took a few steps. The darkness was so consuming that he could not see any detail of the room, he could only feel his way around the area with excruciating slowness.

Rough walls, iron bars, narrow bed, a small stand next to it and a single chair. Nothing else. He shouted out, hoping he would get an answer but there was none. His voice echoed in the larger chamber outside his cell but he could not see into its depths.

Ares circled his quarters numerous times, feeling his way up and down the walls, along the floor, under the bed, between the bars, looking for a way out. He had no strength to bend the bars apart, no force to break through.

There was no way out.

Once again, Ares was trapped yet, oddly enough, this time, he felt nothing. Not fear, anger, or even annoyance.

He was calm and quiet. He was resigned.

EIGHT

The moment Deimos set his feet upon Cos, like smoke, the memories from his very distant childhood rose up. A warm salted breeze played with his hair as the scent from the pastel blooms winding about the pillars took him back to a time when life was simple. A time when he and his twin brother, Anteros, ran naked upon the sandy beaches. A time when Deimos was as comfortable in the water as he was on land. A time when they swam with the dolphins or chased the myriad of seabirds along the shoreline. A time when they held no responsibilities.

Time that was long past.

His was a different world now, obscure and violent. The aching beauty of sunny, green and flowering Cos did not belong to him. Aphrodite's palace was formed of billowing white fabrics and open air save for the sleeping quarters deep within the structure. Deimos was now accustomed to windows that looked out upon cruel rocks, dreary and dank walls and closed doors.

Always closed doors.

This openness was uncomfortable.

The heat did not help him adjust as Deimos was dressed for

Athos: thigh-length leather tunic, long-sleeved undergarment, leggings and boots. Already, he was sweating.

"Ares grows weaker." Deimos spoke in a low voice, aware that Aphrodite was not far from where he met with his brother, Anteros.

"Is that what you have come to tell me?" Anteros embraced his twin. "There was no need. I can see it in our mother's face that Ares shifts further and further from our Realm."

"There is no change though the healers do everything they can." Deimos hesitated. Should he speak of Thanatos' threats or Hypnos' tale? Was there any truth to it or was it mere fabrication to cause more grief?

As Deimos looked into the reflecting gaze of his twin and saw the heavy load already carried as Aphrodite faded, he decided to keep this piece to himself. At least until he could better understand what may, or may not, have happened to Ares' spirit.

"Libertina, she of Sweet Death, has left Ares' side. She has given up on an easy transition for him." Deimos turned away so that Anteros would not see the lie.

"Libertina has never cared for Ares."

"And to this moment, our father will have none of her gentle embrace to carry him off to the Shadowland."

"Then there is no hope he will awaken?"

"I am doubtful, Brother, for I fear now that Libertina has abandoned Ares, Thanatos, will step in."

"Thanatos, he of Bitter Death. Yes, well, that would be the more appropriate passing for Ares, would it not?"

"I suppose that is true, and yet he clings to life, allowing neither Sweet nor Bitter Death to release him from his bodily prison."

"Stubbornness." Anteros laughed without mirth and the sound echoed against the vaulted ceiling.

"Ares' most predominate characteristic. True to himself, he does nothing on command. Death cannot take him, Brother, I see that now. Ares must allow himself to pass." Anteros began to pace with an air of restlessness that was unusual to Love's Response.

"And he does not allow it. I can only assume he is not agreeable to joining Hades in his Kingdom of Shadows." Deimos shrugged within the heavy leathers. "For now. Thanatos will make it his unswerving duty to wear him down."

"Perhaps that is for the best." Anteros paused to stare out at the ocean before them. Aphrodite's main residence sat close to the sandy shores of Cos where her cherished sea could sing her to sleep. "Perhaps the world is a better place for Ares having left it. Perhaps the face of War has been irrevocably changed and there is no need for Ares to return."

"I do not want the burden of War upon my shoulders for the rest of eternity. He must return."

"Are you certain? I advise you to search your soul before answering in so final a tone. Though you suffer under the Mantel of War, you have put your mark upon it. Do you truly wish to give that up?"

A sharp retort sprang to Deimos' tongue but would not pass through his lips. He swore he did not want the Mantle, swore he would find a way to restore Ares, the way it should be and had always been since Chronos gave way to Zeus.

But there was a tiny spark of resistance building within him. A remote part of himself that whispered seductive words of power yet to come.

Deimos shrugged, unwilling to voice thoughts of embracing the Mantle of War. It seemed wrong, somehow, to dismiss Ares as lost when he still breathed. It seemed even more dangerous to assume Ares would not return and take his power back. Woe to any who had not shown loyalty to the fallen god when he finally awakened.

"And what of you, Brother? What of your place in Love's Realm? Although the Mantle of Love has not completely descended upon you, you bear all the grief and duties of her role."

"I am caught between the worlds, Deimos, and I find it a most difficult place to be. If there is no change in Ares, then there is no hope. Aphrodite suffers with the poisons of guilt and remorse, just as Ares lies poisoned by Cedalion's blade." Anteros continued his walk back and forth across the inlaid turquoise tiles of the open air chamber.

"She sinks further away from us every day. If Ares dies, I fear Aphrodite shall also. Then what are we to do?"

Deimos stared at Anteros, noting the difference in posture and tightness of features. Though he had allowed the golden abundance of his hair to return to its former flowing beauty, after Ares had shorn his locks out of spite, Anteros appeared different.

Although he was clad in the usual white tunic with blue edging, his skin glowing warmly in the sunset, Love's Response was not the same. Anteros was forever changed by the same circumstances that changed Deimos.

"I will have no choice but to keep the Mantle of War. And you, I fear, will have little choice as well."

Anteros grimaced. "The responsibility of Love's Realm weighs heavily upon my shoulders. The balance of power has not fully shifted but each day, there is more pressure. I do all that I can but I do not know if I do right by Love."

"What is right and what is wrong? I am not the one to ask, for I do not know myself."

"It is agony. I do not know how long I can continue in this manner. I was not prepared for such burdens. My role has been in support of Love, not to become Love."

With a snort, Deimos retorted, "And it is your belief that I was ready for this? How many times have I told you that I, too, was a follower, not a leader? I did Ares bidding without question, never suspecting that such a thing as this could happen. No one did. Everyone lives in fear that it could happen again, and that is the only reason Hephaestos has been banished. They do not want him to create another weapon that could slay an immortal."

"You do not believe Ares will rise from the miserable place where he has been cast to demand his realm back?"

Deimos shook his head. "It does not appear so."

"Then Aphrodite is lost as well." Tears rose in Anteros' eyes and he turned away to stare out at the distant horizon.

They stood in silence, listening to the ocean's wail, as if the water grieved with them. Just as Aphrodite rose from the sea, it awaited her return.

Before sadness overwhelmed the brothers, a child's shrill shout echoed upward and a tall laughing boy chased after several smaller children. They ran along the beach, darting in and out of the breaking waves until the boy caught one of the giggling children up in his arms and ran back into the shadows of Aphrodite's palace.

"Eros."

"Yes. It has been very difficult for him. Worse for Harmonia, for she has scarce known a mother since her birth."

"Ahh." Deimos shifted from one foot to the other. "Speaking of Harmonia."

"I am quite concerned for Eros, for he senses his power and longs for it to descend, though he is too young to assume Erotic Love. Could he force his trial as Phobos did?"

"At twelve? It is possible, I suppose, but in regards to Harmonia...."

"It seems as Phobos becomes more regimented, Eros becomes less constrained. I have been unable to rein in his natural enthusiasm."

Anteros began to pace again, biting his thumbnail. "On the other hand, though Eros runs a bit wild, what boy does not? We made our share of mischief when we were children, did we not, Brother?"

Deimos thought back on his beginnings as a pawn of War. He was allowed no such freedom once he was taken to Athos. A few short years exploring the shores of Cos with Anteros were followed by the terrors of his father's realm.

He was younger than Eros when snatched by the ravenous jaws of War, no longer allowed the comfort of companions other than the hateful hounds that slunk the halls of Athos.

"My time for play was short. Once Ares claimed me, there

was only discipline." Deimos glanced about the tranquil quarters, a peace so utterly foreign to him.

"Eros should not be allowed to do as he pleases. The behavior you describe will not serve him well when he assumes his power. And in particular, it is not good for Harmonia to be without the nurturance of her mother."

"It is truth you speak." Anteros continued as if Deimos had not spoken. "But I am at a loss as to how to put a stop to his disobedience. I am consumed with the worries of Love. Thaleia will not leave Aphrodite's side, Aglaia disappears for no good reason and Euphrosyne has become a hindrance."

A tide of red began at Anteros' neck and moved up to his face, staining his fair skin. Deimos hid a smile at his brother's discomfort, for the moment his missive forgotten.

"Euphrosyne stalks my every step." Anteros spoke with a lowered voice, his gaze moving from side to side as if the girl would leap at him even now.

"What does she want?"

The color deepened on Anteros' cheeks. "She wants to be by my side."

Deimos raised his chin in question.

"As my consort." Anteros turned away, his hair sliding past his shoulder to hide his face from his brother's sharp eyes.

"Your consort? How bad could that be, Brother? She is a beautiful woman."

"Yes, yes, she is but I am not comfortable with her. If she were part of Ares' court, would you take her to your bed?" Anteros finished with unaccustomed awkwardness.

"Ahh." Deimos understood. "She belongs to Aphrodite and you fear retribution should you take her."

"Something such as that." Anteros gathered his mane between both hands and lifted it above his sweating neck before releasing it in a shimmering cascade. "It would be best if I did not indulge in that particular way."

"Then advise her of your disinterest."

"I would, but I somewhat promised."

"Promised?"

"Swore, rather."

At the burst of laughter from Deimos, Anteros jerked around to face him. "I do not see the humor in this, though obviously you do. It was necessary to know the true conditions of Aphrodite's stay at Hephaestos' palace and none would tell me save Euphrosyne. At a price, of course."

"So our little Euphrosyne has become wise to the ways of the world."

"Too wise. She attempts to hold me to my vow even though we are not free from our crisis."

"It might be of benefit to accept her offer."

"No, it would not. Do not encourage her."

"It is not Euphrosyne I urge."

"Nor I," added Anteros. "I am in no mood to indulge her."

"If you have made a vow, there is little you can do."

"I did not say when I would honor that vow."

"It appears the time has come." Deimos was relieved to have a moment of humor, even at the expense of his twin. "How long would you make the poor woman wait?"

"I expected her to find other companionship, yet she determinedly does not."

"Then serve her and be done, if that is all there is to it."

Anteros pressed a palm against his forehead and squeezed his eyes shut as if in pain. "That is not all. I do not wish to insult or hurt her, yet I find I am not attracted to her womanly ways. I am fraught with…."

Before Anteros could finish his thought, Zelos, she of the Jealous Heart, appeared between them, anger sparking from every fiber of her being.

"Aphrodite would have settled this long ago." Zelos stood with her fists balled at her sides while she raged at Anteros. "Unlike you, she would not let Ares keep my talisman. She would have forced him to return it to me."

Naked, wild red hair tumbling down her back, brilliant green eyes flashing, Zelos gave Anteros a violent shove.

"I want my talisman back this instance."

Anteros reacted with a slap to Zelos' face. With a gasp, Zelos took a step backward.

"You struck me!" Her features twisted into an ugly mask. "How dare you? Aphrodite will punish you."

"I will do worse if you do not control yourself." Anteros gestured at Deimos. "We have a visitor, and I will not tolerate this absurd behavior."

Deimos raised one eyebrow and gave Anteros a long appraising look. Gentle Love's Response had changed after his time with War. As Deimos' attention shifted to Zelos, the pulsing waves of hostility emanating from her naked body enveloped him. His breath caught as he stared at her.

Jealousy wore nothing to hide the lean lines, the small tight breasts or angled hipbones that drew into a triangular patch of neat red hair between her legs. Deimos could not help the surge of lust that gripped his heart, nor the impulse to stroke the smooth skin stretched between her shoulder blades as she turned toward Anteros.

"Ahh, Zelos, you tempt me." Deimos spoke softly.

Zelos whirled upon Deimos, smacking his hand aside. "*You!* You have my talisman. Give it back."

"I do not know what you speak of."

"My beautiful talisman, the chain that connects me to the Mortal Realm, is somewhere in Athos. I demand its return."

Deimos had a brief flash of Ares rolling golden links between his fingers before they disappeared into his pocket. The memory of instant distrust edged with aggression that rose up at the sight of the chain brought an end to his covetous thoughts of Jealousy.

Allowing his own power to eddy to the surface, Deimos pushed back the second wave of insolence from Zelos.

"I know not where it is. Further, I suspect there was a good reason he took it from you. Only Ares can give it back, and since he lies in a stupor between life and death, it is unlikely."

"A hateful reason with no cause other than his cruel nature." Voice lowering into a wheedle, Zelos continued her argument. "I did not merit such punishment. Ares denies me what is mine out of spite."

Anteros and Deimos exchanged a glance that spoke volumes. Knowing both Ares and Zelos, who could be certain of the truth behind their exchange?

"Things are not as they once were. Do you see, Deimos? There is not a moment without interruption. Though my time spent with Ares was brutal, at least it was blessedly silent."

"Agreed." A smile touched Deimos' lips. He was not accustomed to the disorder that held Cos within its grip.

"Zelos, you belabor a point that is beyond either of us to fix." Anteros cast a dark look at the young woman. "It would be best if you left us."

"I think you do not have the ability to force the return of my talisman." Zelos curled her upper lip in contempt.

"It is true, I do not have the same power as my mother, but even if Aphrodite, or I for that matter, were able to demand the chain from Ares, he is in no position to grant the request. Go attend to your duties. Deimos and I have unfinished business."

"Do not dismiss me as if I were nothing." Zelos stomped one bare foot. "I serve Love as well."

"Yes, you do, in which case, you are mine to command." Anteros' gaze hardened. "Now leave us before I find some way to make your distress worse than it is."

"You have changed, Anteros. There was a time when you would have responded to my needs. You would not have allowed this to continue."

"As I have stated, things are not what they once were." Anteros' tone remained flinty, though his gaze held sympathy. "I know this has caused you great misery, Zelos, but there is naught I can do about it."

"What about you, Deimos?" Zelos turned green liquid eyes upon him; eyes that had drowned many a poor soul with irrational jealousy.

Deimos felt the immediate surge to throttle Anteros, resisting only out of sheer will.

"Zelos, do not be foolish and play games with War." Anteros touched Zelos on the arm. He was immune to the rise of jealousy that he saw in Deimos.

"Yes, desist, before I do something I should not."

There was a frightening hunger within the depths of Deimos' gaze. Zelos shivered at the intensity, knowing she brought carnal desire to War. She licked her lips and offered a wicked and sensuous smile to entice Deimos further.

"What can I do for you, God of War, so that you will restore my talisman?"

Without realizing, Deimos reached for her as if in a trance. Anteros pushed him back, and gave Zelos a stern look.

"Zelos, you are out of order."

"Oh, I see, you hope to quiet me. Deimos must have power over you." Zelos' eyes narrowed. "Are you afraid of him? Since he has taken on the mantel of War, his strength is greater than yours, for you only do Aphrodite's bidding. You are her minion, her slave, unlike Deimos, who has become War."

Anteros could not help the upward quirk of his lips at Zelos' attempt to make him jealous. At the same moment, his shoulders tensed for there was truth to her words. With a deep breath, Anteros forced himself to relax.

There was always truth to Jealousy. Truth gave Zelos her power - she called the emotion forward and used her chain to bind those who fell under her spell.

"Stop, Zelos, you cannot hook me into your game. I am not Aphrodite, but I am your master while she is ill. You will not attempt to play your tricks on me or you will suffer punishment."

Zelos blinked once. The expression on her face was enough to tell Anteros she did not expect such a response.

"Make Deimos give me my talisman!" Zelos went back to anger.

"Do you have it, Brother?" Anteros turned to Deimos, noting the dazed expression and glassy-eyed stare. With a snap of his fingers, Anteros brought his twin back to the moment. "Do you have Zelos' talisman?"

"No." The answer was slow as Deimos inhaled and gave a quick shake of his head. "No, I do not have it."

"Zelos, you are ill-behaved and create much mischief in both Realms. I would hesitate to give it back to you, if it were me, but there it is: he does not have your chain."

"I do not believe him," Zelos spat. "He does not like me and now he lies."

"Deimos cares not for you one way or the other and he does not know where your chain might be found."

"Lies, lies, lies!" Zelos jumped up and down with both feet, flailing her arms as if to attack them both. "Deimos gave it to you and you have hidden it from me."

Watching her breasts bounce was little more than a fleeting moment of entertainment for Anteros. Deimos, however, was entranced and gave devout attention to the lithe body of Jealousy.

"What Ares did with it before he was struck down, neither of us can say."

"I cannot continue this way - I am losing my essence," Zelos sobbed. "I have little effect and cannot hold anyone under my spell for more than a few moments. I shall fade away."

Throwing herself onto a well-cushioned couch, she began to wail. "What have I done to deserve this? I am loyal to my mistress. I always do as she bids. Why would you steal the very breath away from me? Why, Anteros? Why?"

Anteros gazed skyward with a sigh. "I wish I held a modicum of sympathy for you, Zelos, but it would seem the Realms are better off your talisman is not returned to you. It is despicable to shackle unfortunate souls to your poisonous deeds."

"It is who I am. Aphrodite understands my role - she is

aware there must be darkness as well as light. And now, both mortal and immortals will see right through me. I am nothing. I am invisible without my chain."

"Though you are lovely to look at, I am certain there is some truth to what you say."

"Then will you?" Zelos raised one tear-stained eye to Anteros. "Will you retrieve my chain?"

"I cannot, Zelos, nor can Deimos. You will have to wait until the day Ares awakens." With a thoughtful head-to-toe glance, Anteros continued. "However, I believe you would command more attention if you were better attired."

"What do you mean?"

"Instead of a naked presence, perhaps a bit of clothing would not hurt."

"I do not understand. Do you find me offensive?"

"I find you very offensive, but it has nothing to do with your unclothed appearance."

"And that is why you can never fully rule Love's Realm. You are locked within your own conformity. You see nothing beyond your role as Love's Response." Zelos gave Anteros an ugly look and then smiled at Deimos. "Do you object to the way I appear?"

She lay on her side in a most alluring pose, one arm thrown over her head and her hips pushed forward.

With a sharp exhale, Deimos started toward her, unmindful lust surging through his body. Anteros stepped between them, breaking the contact. "Brother, what is it you came to tell me?"

With a wrenching twist, Deimos turned away from both and stared at the sun-speckled waves of the sea. "Our grandmother intends to use Harmonia as leverage."

"What do you mean?" A gnawing concern began in Anteros' belly, one he did not want to entertain. "Surely, Hera would not attempt to overthrow Aphrodite's rule during this most trying time?"

"Exactly that." A muscle in Deimos' jaw twitched. "Hera requested I bring Harmonia back to Olympus. She believes the child would be better off under her care. In exchange, we would be given full respect at Council. Our voices would be heard."

"And you agreed?" Anger sparked in Anteros' sea-blue eyes as if lightening gathered on the horizon.

"Yes." Deimos shifted and caught sight of Zelos once again. She wiggled her hips and blew a kiss his way. A shudder ran down Deimos' body and without thought, he took a step toward her only to have Anteros stop him with a hand upon his chest.

"Brother, I warn you, I am not the same as I once was when Phobos was taken. I will fight you."

"And you would lose." Dark eyes met light as Deimos grasped his twin's wrist with hard fingers. "But it will not come to such an end.

"That our grandmother professes to know what is best when she keeps Aphrodite from Ares is disgraceful. Now she wants their child as well. I will not be party to such humiliation. Anteros, heed my warning: be watchful another does not come for her."

Though Deimos spoke serious words, his gaze kept moving to the lounge where Zelos lay. His breath grew shorter as the heat spread throughout his body.

"Deimos."

The sharpness of Anteros' tone brought Deimos' focus back to their conversation though it was a struggle to release his attention from Zelos.

"Deimos, I am fair warned and I thank you, but I feel it is now time for you to leave." Anteros cast a fierce glance at the laughing Zelos. "Before Zelos wins this skirmish."

With a quick shake of his dark curls, Deimos agreed, "Perhaps you are right. I will speak with you later."

Anteros contemplated the spot now vacated by Deimos, certain that worse trouble was headed their collective way.

"I would not have thought Deimos could be so easily rattled." Zelos rose to her feet and preened as if looking into a mirror. "Even without my talisman. How interesting."

"Very. Now go, Zelos, you wear me out."

With mocking laughter, Zelos took her leave.

NINE

Inni glanced over her shoulder, taking care she was not followed. She managed to slip from under Ajah's watchful eye as quick as a slippery fish from a child's grasp when the younger priestess was called to tend to one of the townsmen. His frantic wife appeared in the medicine hut doorway screaming for help. She was covered in blood and sobbing that her husband was dead.

Chopping wood, the dolt chopped his leg instead.

Giggling at the image, Inni sang, "Chopped himself, chopped himself, chopped himself, how silly of him, silly, silly man."

When Ajah ran to assist, Inni did not follow. Instead, she went the other way, out the rear exit and into the gardens. She pretended she was to gather eggs from the fowl who pecked at the far end. As soon as she was away from the king's guard - Razi, the only one she liked - she tossed the basket on the ground and hurriedly made her way upwards, though Jahmed had forbidden it.

Inni could hear Jahmed's strong voice cautioning all of the women to stay away from the hidden cave's entrance for fear it would be discovered and sealed.

We must not lead anyone else to our sacred ground. We must only go under cover of darkness.

"But I must go to the cave." Inni talked to herself as she climbed. "No, I should not. I will go to the top instead. Ajah goes to the plateau every morning and I want to see what she does there. I will not go to the caves, Jahmed."

She was resolute in her determination to avoid the cavern even though she heard the voice of Gaea on their last ritual. Even though Jahmed claimed she imagined the voices.

"I did not imagine the voice of our goddess. She asked me to help Niala Aaminah. How can I refuse?" Inni paused and shook her head from side to side, her thoughts suddenly foggy. Why did she need to help Niala? What was wrong with her? Niala was the strongest among them, why did she need help?

We must not lead anyone else to our sacred ground. We must only go under cover of darkness.

Again, Jahmed's voice sliced through the confusion.

"No, I will not go to the caves. Why would I? It is daylight. I am going to the plateau. We have gone to the plateau before, yet I do not recall why. It was important, what we did, this I know. If I visit the top, perhaps I will remember."

With a glance over her shoulder, Inni was certain Razi could not observe her progress up the mount. She continued her arduous climb, much slower than her first eager steps.

"Hmm. Razi will not see me, no, because he has eyes only for Ajah. Hmm. Ajah and Razi. Hmm."

Inni paused as she reached a split in the trail, pressing fingertips to an indention at her temple as a sudden flare of pain struck behind her eyes. Jahmed told her the blinding bouts of pain would go away as time went on but lately the headaches were worse. Inni crouched, waiting for the onset of nausea to pass. She would not throw up her breakfast. She would not. The sickness would pass in a few minutes.

It always did.

If she could only recall how she came to have the slight hollow where a scar had formed. There were so many things she could not remember, things that lurked on the outskirts of her memory, just out of reach.

Some days she cried with frustration, trying to bring back the lost events that left blank black holes in her existence. Names and faces that were vaguely familiar yet illusive. The way everyone spoke to her, as if she were a child simply because she could not recollect how she was injured.

She did not understand why Jahmed was afraid to leave her alone. Ever since she was well enough to walk beyond the little yard surrounding their house in the woods, Jahmed insisted Inni go everywhere with her. Jahmed was frightened of something yet Inni could not fathom what it was.

To the right, the path went across the face of the ridge to the sealed cave entrance and continued on, sloping down to the lakeshore. She chose the left path, the one that would take her straight to the top of the ridge.

She wished she had brought a staff to lean on as the incline steepened, and when she heard an odd whistle, she did not know if it was her labored gasping or something else.

Taking a moment to catch her breath, she stood silent and listened to the sounds around her: rustling leaves in the breeze, birds chirping, the skittering of small stones from her last footstep.

Then she heard it again, a faint humming above her. Inni hesitated, trying to trace the source. It was bird-like, yet breathy, as if someone attempted to imitate the songs of those feathered creatures perched in the scrub trees but could not quite hit the correct tone.

Now the call came further from the left and had changed. Now it sounded like a faint whispering of her name.

"Innnnniiiii."

The hair rose on her neck and her skin prickled. "Hello?"

There was no response but Inni straightened, certain of what she heard. Forgetting her promise, Inni stepped off the worn path onto an overgrown trail that led toward the backside of the plateau.

Jahmed would be very angry to know that Inni was going to the caves. Once again, Inni heard Jahmed's voice warn her to stay away from the sacred cave.

"I promise, Love, I will take care. No one will see me. No one will know our secret, but Gaea is calling to me from the caves. "

Inni hesitated, uncertain if her mind was playing tricks. The headache rebounded, pulsing with double the vengeance. Pressing her palms to her temples, she sat on a large boulder.

"Am I mad? Am I hearing things that do not exist?" Squinting, she tried to remember what she wanted to do. "I was going to the top. Or was it to the caves? No. I am not supposed to go to the caves. I should go back before I cannot move my limbs enough to climb down."

"Innnnniiiii."

Startled, Inni dropped her hands. The voice was insistent though no louder than before. She rose and stumbled forward, eager yet frightened, the pain forgotten.

"Hello? Gaea?"

The voice was the same as the night of their ritual - the whispering of Gaea. She remembered. She remembered Gaea speaking to them. Relief flooded through her - she was not mad - she was receiving a message from the Great Mother.

Slowly, Inni picked her way through weeds and rocks, the trail very narrow and steep, and at times, seemed to disappear. Her steps faltered when she reached the far side of the plateau. She held back the desire to run away.

"Gaea, what is it you want of me?"

As soon as she spoke the words, an image of Niala Aaminah blossomed in her mind. Her compassionate smile and oddly colored amber eyes filled with kindness, the thick auburn hair that was always a bit messy with curling strands escaping the severe braid, the way she stood tall with her chin lifted yet humble in her graceful movements.

"Niala." Inni reached out one hand as if she could touch the fallen priestess.

Niala was dead. That was what Jahmed told her. Dead, entombed within the mount. In the main cavern that was Gaea's sacred ground, sealed shut for eternity. They would never look upon her face again.

Inni did not remember Niala's death or anything that followed. She only knew what she had heard in the cave during their last ritual.

She remembered Gaea calling to her, asking for her help. Gaea said Niala was not dead, that she lived.

"What do you want from me, Great Mother?"

"Innnnniiiii."

A light wind played at her back, urging her forward. At that moment, Inni knew Gaea wanted her to look for Niala. Gaea wanted Niala found. Gaea wanted Inni to help Niala return to her people. Suddenly brave, Inni nodded.

"Yes, Gaea, I will help. Niala is lost in the cavern tunnels, and she needs me."

Inni recalled another misplaced conversation in the recesses of her disoriented mind. Ajah had assured her that she would help her find Niala. Ajah did not tell the truth. Ever since that evening, Ajah avoided speaking of Niala Aaminah.

"As if I would forget." Inni shrugged away the point that she did, indeed, forget, until now. "They treat me like a child. They all believe I am mad. That I do not know what I heard, but I do."

Gathering her strength, Inni continued until she could see the dark treetops of the forest surrounding the west side of the plateau. The forest ran northwest, thick and foreboding except for the glimmer of water that was the Maendre.

The Maendre River emerged from the wooded edge on the west border and flowed through the valley to meet with the Bayuk River. Together, they formed a great lake before splitting once again as the Maendre continued on its twisting eastern path and the Bayuk curved away to the south in a shining ribbon.

Panting, Inni wiped away a bead of sweat and stared at a cave opening partially disguised by vines. "Hello? Niala, are you in there?"

There was no response other than the flutter of wings as a startled bird took flight. Stepping with care, Inni drew closer to the entrance. The flowering greenery was deliberate in its placement, for a supporting web of ropes held it in place and allowed the vines to grow like a cloth thrown over the entrance.

Inni pushed aside the tangle of leaves and let the morning sun shed light within the cave. She felt the moist sweet breath of Earth wash over her and a shiver of anticipation left her impatient to enter the depths of the cavern. She stepped inside, leaving the vines to one side, leaving her better able to see in the gloom.

As her eyes adjusted, she could make out the ring of stones and smell the leftover ash of wood mixed with bitterroot. Following the rough stone of the small chamber, Inni reached the back wall only to find her hand on an empty space. A cool brush of air told her she stared off into the depths of a tunnel that led somewhere deeper into the mount.

She hesitated, the urge to take the path into the heart of the cavern strong.

"Innnnniiiii."

The murmur seemed to emanate from the tunnel. Shivering, skin crawling, Inni backed away, her heart hammering inside her chest like the beat of a ritual drum. What had not frightened her with the warmth of the sun shining on her now sent fear sliding along her spine.

How could she be certain it was Gaea? What it if was someone else? Someone who tricked her. Someone who wanted to hurt her?

Turning, she started toward the entrance only to step on a rock and fall to her knees. She cried out and heard her voice echo within the chamber. Crawling to the wall, she leaned into the rough rock, panting. The scent was of dark soil and water that had never seen daylight. Above her head the ceiling of the tunnel was a swirl of glinting light from the reflected sun. The dancing shadows emphasized the small jagged edges of the rock.

They appeared as teeth.

Teeth that could rip and tear flesh without notice.

Panic clawed at her belly as flashes of a distorted ugly face careened through her mind followed by punches and kicks and violation that tore her to pieces.

"Please do not hurt me." Crouching, with her face buried against her knees, her whimpers were muffled. "I am sorry I entered the sacred cavern without permission. I swear I will not…I will not…tell anyone." Further speech was choked off by a throat that refused to breathe.

"Innnnniiiii."

The voice whispered directly into her ear. Scrabbling at the stone walls, she ripped her fingernails and drew blood while trying to stand. With a gasp, she fell again. Fear and pain left her sobbing with her face in the dirt and no strength to get up.

"Innnnniiiii."

An invisible hand touched her. Inni shrieked and covered her head with her arms. All reason left her.

"I am sorry. I am sorry. Please do not hurt me."

Sobbing, Inni lay on the damp earth, terrified to move. How long she lay in the chilly cavern, she did not know. There were no more whispers, only the echoing sounds of her own weeping.

Dirty, cold and hungry, Inni finally staggered to her feet, unaware of how much time had passed. She made her way down the trail until she reached the gardens and then she collapsed.

Razi saw her and raced to her side. His face registered surprise at Inni's filthy appearance.

"Priestess, what has happened to you? Did someone hurt you?" Razi's stance was battle-ready. One hand rested upon the pommel of his sword, the other fist ready to strike. "If someone hurt you."

"No, I fell. I went for a walk and I fell. That is all."

"Let me help you." Razi relaxed but his gaze reflected doubt. He brought Inni to her feet, one arm around her thin waist.

"I am fine." Though Inni protested, she was grateful for Razi's strength as she leaned into his chest. Her ankle pained her and the best she could do was limp forward.

As the two entered the medicinal hut, Jahmed choked.

Features sharp with fear, Jahmed laid the pestle on the table and gaped at the soiled clothing and tear-streaked face of her beloved. She sniffed at the moist soil, the clinging scent of the cave.

"Who did this?"

Jahmed felt faint at the thought that Inni had once again been attacked. There would be no bringing her back from another rape. She glared at Razi until he released Inni and backed away.

"I found her at the rear of the gardens." Razi lowered his gaze to the floor. "She said she fell."

"I did. That is all, I stumbled on my walk." Inni pointed toward the rear gardens and the ridge that shaded their little piece of the valley.

"Where did you go? You were supposed to be with Ajah." The knot in Jahmed's stomach clamped tighter as she cast a sideways glance at Razi. "Never mind, it does not matter."

"Razi helped me." Inni avoided Jahmed's frightened gaze, knowing Jahmed knew the truth of Inni's whereabouts. Jahmed did not want Inni to say she had been in the cave, Inni could see that but it did not seem wrong for the guard to know.

After all, he liked Ajah.

"Razi would not...."

Pulling Inni into a hard hug, Jahmed kissed her cheek. "Hush. Let me see to your scrapes and bruises. Razi, thank you, you may go now."

"Of course, Priestess." With a quick bob, Razi left the women but not before he threw an assessing glance their way.

"We must never talk about these things in front of the king's men."

"Razi is different, the way Zan is different. They would not tell."

"We do not know that, my Love. You are too trusting, especially now." Jahmed paused. It seemed to all of them that during her illness, Inni had lost the ugly memories of the invasion. Jahmed preferred Inni's innocence to the horrifying truth, but she could not allow Inni to tell of their secrets.

"Too many still believe their ways are better than ours."

"What does that mean?" Inni jabbed at Jahmed's ribs, wanting her to let go. Closeness made Inni feel twitchy and upset. It was something she could not control even though she knew it hurt her mate. She simply could not help the rebellion that caused her to push away when she was held in any manner.

Jahmed released her as relief brought lightheadedness. She sat on a stool next to the table and stared at Inni's disarray. "You are certain you were not harmed?"

Poking at a drying stalk of leaves before bending to sniff at it, Inni brushed the question aside. "These are ready to grind."

"Then grind them." Pushing a bowl and pestle towards her, Jahmed continued to watch for signs of the illness that laid claim to Inni.

"What do mean about their ways? Who are they?"

Sighing, Jahmed began to mix salve for insect bites. "I mean those that follow Hattusilis." She pretended to spit on the floor after saying his name. "He has learned nothing in all this time. We saved his life and we continue to minister to his followers, and yet, they have not learned to honor our goddess."

"Not learned, or not told?" Inni kept her eyes downcast as she twisted the pestle so that the rounded sides crushed the leaves, releasing a pungent scent.

"Told what?" Jahmed paused to push back a long braid that had worked free from the many that were tied with a cloth at the nape of her neck. "They do not listen to anything that is said."

"Razi listens."

"Yes, he does and a bit too much, if you ask me. Inni, what is this really about? Why did you go up to the cave?"

"Niala."

"Niala is dead."

"I know you have told me this, but I did not see her. I do not believe it." Inni dropped the smooth wooden pestle.

"You were very ill at the time."

"The invasion. The fire. I remember more than you think."

"How much more?" Jahmed watched for signs of the terror that had stolen the old Inni away but saw only the naive blue eyes of one who did not know the full truth.

"But you do not remember Niala died, or how she died."

"That is just it, Jahmed, Niala Aaminah is *not* dead!"

"Oh, my Love, she is gone. I swear it. I saw her die. I washed and dressed her body, wrapped her in a shroud. I was there when we…." Jahmed paused to swallow hard, fighting grief that was still raw. "When we gave her body back to Gaea."

"And yet, Gaea has told me Niala Aaminah is alive and waiting for us to find her."

"Stop." Jahmed fixed a sad gaze on Inni. "You are imagining such things."

"Imagining what things?"

Ajah entered the hut with a distracted glance between the two women. Both Jahmed and Inni's heads jerked up to stare at Ajah. Her hair was pulled loose from its braid and her apron was soiled with patches of dried blood and what appeared to be vomit.

"Niala. She is…." Inni flushed as Jahmed gripped one shoulder.

"Niala is what?"

"Alive. And you promised you would help me look for her." Jahmed's hand slid off as Inni ducked away from her.

"And you promised to stay by my side as Jahmed requested." With a tired accusing gaze, Ajah plopped her supply basket on the table. "I needed help stitching Meir's leg and do you know he nearly bled to death without someone to assist?"

"His wife was there." Inni shuffled her feet, staring down at her toes as if she had never seen them before.

"Sian was so distraught, she puked as she tried to do your job."

Heaving a sigh, Inni took the basket from the table and began to put away the unused items. She placed the bloody cloths into a pail of soapy water next to the doorway.

"Have you nothing to say for yourself?"

Inni hunched her shoulders and did not reply.

"Inni is tired, and no doubt hungry - she went to the cave by herself this morning and just returned." Jahmed met Ajah's gaze over Inni's bowed head. "Let us forget this foolishness for now and see to our work."

"It is not foolish," Inni protested. "Niala is alive. I swear it. Ajah promised to help me look for her. She promised."

Jahmed shook her head and held up a palm to Ajah before the younger woman could respond. "Come, Inni, you need to wash and eat and then lie down for a rest."

Grasping the protesting Inni by the elbow, Jahmed pushed her toward the dining area. "Ajah, you may need to do the same thing. You look exhausted."

Ajah watched them leave, instantly sorry for snapping at Inni. She promised Inni she would 'help' and then did not. She regretted that she let days pass, being too busy with the needs of the temple.

She intended to guide Inni into the woods to create a small cairn in honor of Niala, hoping to do so would put to rest the ghosts that plagued Inni's mind.

"That is all she needs, to grieve. To say good-bye. She was not able to mourn with us so she has not accepted that Niala is gone. It is like a dream to her. Not real. I understand why she is in such denial, and yet it distresses Jahmed so much."

Removing her apron, Ajah pushed it down into the bucket to soak along with the clothes. "I do not know what is the right thing to do."

Before she could ponder more on the subject, Tulane and Deniz entered the medicinal hut together. Both had been attending to those who could not walk to the temple, the elderly, the crippled and the very sick.

In exchange for their help, the village folk gave whatever they had to give: food, herbs, cloth, any number of things were offered up and now needed to be stored.

Letting her troubled thoughts go, Ajah joined the two girls in the work of sorting the basket and putting away the donated goods.

TEN

Crossing the blue and green tiled floor of Aphrodite's quarters, Anteros leaned against the white rail of the terrace and stared at the waves crashing against the shore in an unusual display of elemental force. He could smell the brine as it was whipped into a froth, spewing foam onto the wet sand. The beach was deserted, no children or animals played while under the watchful eyes of their caretakers.

Not even the seabirds were about as all creatures large and small took refuge from the storm brewing on the horizon. Dark clouds gathered like heavy smoke and distant rumbling could be heard across the water. As he watched, a streak of lightening stretched from sky to sea, disappearing as quickly as it appeared.

The weather reflected his own disturbed thoughts. Aphrodite continued to weaken yet the Mantel of Love would not completely abandon her. He could feel it hovered somewhere between him and Aphrodite, leaving them both vulnerable. It was as if the Mantle was a sentient being that was confused as to who held the true power.

"There must be something I can do." The words were torn away as the wind increased and the white drapes behind him whipped about in a frantic dance to free themselves from their rods.

One corner of the curtain caught his eye as he turned to go inside. With an irritated snarl, Anteros yanked the ceiling to floor shutters closed and then held one palm over the abused area.

If the Mantle did not settle on him, unbelievable chaos would ensue. The Realm of Love was unstable and those minions of Aphrodite who could run amuck were already taking advantage.

Minions such as Zelos, who made threats. Minions such as Nemesis, Love's Revenge, who trolled the Mortal Realm with glee, causing immeasurable damage.

Where was Nemesis' softer side, Forgiveness? Was there no forgiveness left? Anteros, too, felt a hardening of his heart to those who caused his mother more grief.

And then there was his wayward brother, Eros. The youth continually taunted the other children and caused major upheaval within their little community. Anteros was deeply concerned that Eros, Erotic Love, would leap into his rites of passage trial without support.

"I am uneasy about Eros' behavior. He seems to seek out mischief at every turn. I pray the boy is too young to discover sexual pleasure, the act of which might very well capitulate him into whatever ordeal awaits him." Anteros spoke to Thaleia, who paused her soothing hum as she ministered to Aphrodite.

"You may hope all you want, but there are troubling signs that Eros hovers on the edge of his birthright, even at the tender age of twelve."

"Yes, you are right, and his birth date is not so far off. At thirteen, it is more than possible Eros will engage in carnal activities." Anteros ran fingers through his long hair and exhaled loudly.

Thaleia nodded in agreement. "Thirteen could bring about a serious shift. When you were thirteen, you came fully into your power."

Anteros nodded absently. "Yes, I did, though with Mother there to assist, as well as all three of you Graces, I managed without any damage. However, Deimos was much younger and Phobos was a mere ten years of age when he discovered his role as Panic." Anteros left the ocean view and retreated to a narrow table that held bowls of grapes, peaches and a flask of wine.

"It is my duty to help Eros through the ordeal and yet, I am so thoroughly pulled into holding Love's Realm in balance that I have not the time to monitor him."

He opened the wine and poured dark red liquid into a delicate goblet, splashing drops onto the table surface. He ignored the beauty of the intricately inlaid pattern of sea turtles beneath the bottle, scarce noticing the spilled wine as it stained the wood.

"And I cannot appear weak-willed, Thaleia. Even though I do not have Aphrodite's full power, I must uphold the stability of both worlds. How am I to maintain dominion when all beings fight me, immortal and human?" Anteros drank deeply of the full glass, draining half of it.

Thaleia frowned at Anteros for not offering her a goblet of the rich wine. Truly, he was distracted for it was not in his nature to be rude. She considered her response to him before speaking it aloud.

"Perhaps if you yourself experienced true love, you would find the influence you lack."

Anteros faced Thaleia with an insulted expression on his handsome face. "How can you say such a thing? I experience love each moment of each day and it has brought me naught but pain."

"You manage love, my Dearest, but you do not feel it. You are detached from the depths of your own emotions."

"Detached? When I lie awake each night, consumed with the madness of such sentiments gone amuck? Of course I feel it. I feel it in my bones, in my blood, in my every breath. I am bred to feel Love and live my life around the reply to such confusion."

"Indeed," Thaleia smiled. "You are Love's Response and it is your obligation to hold that awareness for every creature, for without an answer to the mating call, there would be nothing. No one. You have been consumed with such things since accepting your role."

"And yet?"

"And yet, you do not experience the pleasures of Love, only the pain and rejection. Here, on Cos, finding the balance should be an easy task." Thaleia lifted her palms as if to display light and dark and how they held even ground in the Realm of Love.

"What you speak of appears easy, but it is not that simple. It is made more difficult with Aphrodite drifting away from us. I have neither the power nor the influence to make changes, let alone have authority over my own desires."

Thaleia came to stand next to him, touching one finger to the back of Anteros' hand. "You serve your mother well, but you have no passion for another, as she does for Ares. I urge you to find sincere love, for it is the only way you will find the authority that is lacking."

"It is not that simple, dear Thaleia. Would that I could find such a sustaining passion but heartfelt affection eludes me." He took another gulp of his wine and frowned. It did not taste as sweet as he remembered.

"There is one who loves me, and yet I do not feel the same. It would be unfair of me to take advantage, would it not? Physical lovemaking is not the same as two tender hearts that join, is that not true?"

As if by deliberate invocation, Euphrosyne dashed into the chamber, her hands fluttering, her lovely face tear-stained and fretting.

"Eros is tormenting the other children again and he will not listen. All he does is throw things at me when I caution him against displaying meanness. I wish we could send him off to Ares' fortress for a bit of training. It would certainly do him some good."

"Euphrosyne." Her name, spoken with sternness, brought the youngest Grace to a halt.

"Yes, Thaleia?" Folding her hands with a meekness that belied the belligerence in her eyes, Euphrosyne paused, then added quickly, "Anteros, why do you not take Eros in hand? He is devoid of all respect."

"A question of substance." Anteros swallowed the last dregs of his goblet and felt the wine go to his head. "But I have no answer."

"Euphrosyne, you overstep your limits. Anteros does all that he can under the circumstances." Thaleia set her gaze upon the listless countenance of Aphrodite, who took no notice of the quarrel.

"Yes, Thaleia. I am sorry, but what are we to do with him?"

"*We* do nothing." Anteros took the girl's hands into his own, noticing the softness of her skin. "*I* will make this right. Do you trust me?"

Anteros met Euphrosyne's blue gaze and looked sincerely into her eyes. There he found the adoration he knew resided within the girl. He searched his soul for a flicker of attraction and found there a tiny seed that held potential. Could mere physical desire blossom into the kind of love deemed necessary? If it could, would he allow it?

Was Thaleia right? Without true love, without a mate, that he, Anteros, could not possibly know the depths it would take to command the Realm of Love? He was not unschooled in the art of pleasure but it had not been the motivating force behind his nature.

Not like his father, Ares, who was driven into the arms of lust to quiet the noise of War, and not like Deimos, who appeared to have embraced the same pattern. Until this moment, Anteros had viewed all such behavior with disgust. Now, he wondered if there could be sacred purpose behind carnal indulgence.

Could the balance of power be had with sexual

extravagance?

Euphrosyne trembled at Anteros' touch and the yearning in her gaze was unmistakable. All thoughts of Eros' misbehavior fled. Her expression reflected naked desire.

Anteros closed his eyes and saw her exposed and willing, the virgin ready to surrender her treasure. In that moment, its own powerful need and long-held hunger consumed Anteros. In the farthest reaches of his mind, he knew something about this was wrong, but he had promised her, had he not?

"Come, Euphrosyne, we will talk further of this in private."

Breathless, Euphrosyne let Anteros lead her from the chamber. Already she imagined his exploring hands and mouth, and feel the sensual strength of his body. She could not wait for the moment when she would give herself to him.

Sighing, she clung to his arm as they made their way along the corridor. She envisioned their union as supreme, beyond the mere physical - their union would be spiritual, a binding of their souls forever, just as that which bound Aphrodite and Ares.

Euphrosyne frowned as the image of Aphrodite languishing, nearly gone from this world because of that love for Ares, came into her thoughts. She shook her head, refusing to have this moment destroyed.

"What is it, Euphrosyne?" Anteros paused to look down at her. "You seem unsure."

"No, not at all." Euphrosyne's quick intake of breath was not from fear but from desire at the turquoise gaze and handsome face of her love. "Kiss me, Anteros. Kiss me, please."

She reached for him and as his lips touched hers, Euphrosyne's knees buckled just a bit, enough that Anteros had to catch her. He grabbed her up in a crushing hold, one hand pulling her skirt to her waist, fingers caressing her bare skin.

It shall happen. Now. Here. Finally.

Frantic lust leapt into Euphrosyne's heart. It mattered not that her first time be in a golden chamber filled with the scent of roses and soft candlelight. No, she wanted him, now, hard and fast. She was ready.

Anteros pressed against her, his manhood ready to relieve her of her virginity. So excited she could scarce stand it, Euphrosyne moaned and parted her legs so that he could enter into that long deprived womanhood.

He was there, eager for the first thrust when a shrill voice cut through their fervor.

"Anteros! Anteros, where are you? Oh, please, we need you, something terrible is happening."

It was Solan, one of the nursemaids, shrieking his name. Her voice echoed in the vast hallway linking Aphrodite's private quarters with the rest of the palace. He knew the caretakers and children had taken refuge from the coming storm in an enormous gallery constructed over an ocean inlet. The express purpose of the area had been to protect Aphrodite when she had need of her cherished sea during inclement weather.

It had evolved into a playground. The children delighted in swimming beneath the walls spanning the inlet to the outer shores and back within to eat their refreshments while the storm lashed the isle.

"There will be death if you do not come with haste," Solan squawked. "Anteros, where are you?"

Anteros drew away from Euphrosyne, in spite of her grasping fingers that tried to hold him. Her legs dropped and her feet touched the floor as her gown slithered across her aching flesh.

"Eros," Anteros gasped. "The children."

And he was gone from Euphrosyne's side. She slid to the floor into a sobbing bitter huddle, once again denied his promise of pleasure and love.

Anteros appeared inside the gallery and demanded, "What is it? Are the children hurt? Has Eros done something?"

Her hand extended toward a noisy disturbance, Solan cried, "No, they are fine. It is the water nymphs - they caught someone and threaten to tear him limb from limb."

As Anteros followed her shaking finger, he saw the waters of the covered inlet roiling with bodies and a red stain flowing towards the white sands lining the pool.

"Why do they do this?"

"Each has claimed this man for her own and none will relinquish him. Each would rather see him die than part with him. Please, stop them. The children must not witness such a horrible thing."

Indeed, as the screaming nymphs fought over the unfortunate male, the cove was lined by the children of the island. Eros first among them, shouting encouragement, his face flushed with excitement.

"Stop," Anteros commanded.

None listened. With Eros as their leader, the children of Cos continued screeching, clapping and throwing rocks at the water maidens.

Furious, Anteros strode to Eros, snatched him up by the back of his neck and tossed him against the furthest wall. Stunned, Eros lay pale and unmoving, eyes closed against the pain.

The other children, wide-eyed and silent, scattered as fast as their feet would carry them, disappearing through the doorway into the depths of the palace. The nymphs dragged their find beneath the wall and continued their fight over their treasure in the pelting rain. Long streaks of lightening reached to charge the water yet they ignored the danger, wanting only to claim rights to the battered unconscious man.

Anteros followed them to the outer cove and raised his fist in fury. As he beckoned the surf that was his birthright, a huge wave swelled upward and rolled toward shore. The quarreling nymphs paid no heed until the upsurge broke over their heads, flinging them right and left like so much driftwood.

A fine mist of red water blew back upon Anteros and stained his white tunic. In that moment, blood to blood, he felt the call of his father, and was ready to do corporal harm to any who defied him. It was a dizzying explosion of power and it made his head reel with the notion of pain caused by his own hand. It was a foreign feeling and yet exhilarating: to punish with pain.

With a gasp, Anteros stopped in mid-stride and shook his head. This was not who he was. He did not bring about anguish to innocents, however rebellious they were.

"My father's influence is wicked and I shall defy him in this time of anger." Anteros spoke only to himself, for no other was listening. And then he paused again for he knew it was not Ares' influence that brought this sudden rage.

It was Love.

It was the darkest side of Love; it sought revenge against those wrongs of the heart. In a flash, he knew it was not the nymphs for whom he wished retribution. It was his grandmother, Hera.

What was happening to him? Vengeance did not represent power to him, yet now, he lusted for blood.

"Further, is not Nemesis a minion of the Goddess of Love?" Anteros stared at the still-churning waters of the cove. "She is. Revenge belongs to Love."

It was the Mantle of Love moving ever closer to his shoulders. As the Mantle shifted, the power weighed heavier and each of Aphrodite's' underlings sought out Anteros for guidance.

Nemesis, she who represented revenge, had yet to call upon Anteros. She was a being of great independence. She came only when Aphrodite bid her presence on Cos. Locked in mourning, Aphrodite neglected to control her minions and Nemesis was on the loose to wreak whatever havoc she felt was her due.

"Perhaps it is time Revenge is called home." Rather pleased with his own thoughts, Anteros turned away from the chaos.

The nymphs converged upon him all at once.

"He is mine," came one reedy voice.

"No, he is mine," came another.

"I found him," burbled one more.

"I rescued him from Pegae nymphs where he was sure to drown," came another voice that sounded much like the waves. "He is mine."

"You left him, so he is mine."

"I slept!"

"He was alone. He is mine."

"Enough!" Anteros shouted, raising his arms as if to strike them down. Even the rain ceased in that moment, pulling back into the scuttling clouds.

The nymphs drew away in fear. Never had they seen the son of Aphrodite behave in such a manner. Silence fell for one moment before they burst into their babbling song once more, each trying to outdo the other.

"Help me." A hand reached from the shoreline waves as a new voice spoke. "Help me."

A weak yet thoroughly masculine voice called above the high-pitched tones of the nymphs.

Anteros stared as a naked young man rose out of the surf and lurched forward. A most beautiful man with a well-kept body decorated in a plentitude of tattoos and curling brown hair that fell across wide shoulders. Though he sported dark welts, claw marks, and many wounds oozing blood, he was a vision of strength and vitality.

The young man staggered a few steps and then collapsed on the sand. Before the nymphs could leap upon him and drag him back into the water, Anteros commanded them to desist.

"Who is this?" Anteros spoke to Clio, the eldest sister of the Nereid Nymph Clan of Cos.

Clio sniffed. "A human."

"Perhaps, but what is his name?"

"He belongs to me." Clio swung her sea-blue hair and glared at Anteros. "How dare you interfere? Aphrodite would not allow it."

"I am the law of Cos now and you will answer me. What is his name?"

Hesitating, Clio searched the churning angry gaze of Anteros.

"Hylas, son of Dryops, King of Oeta."

"Where did he come from?"

"He was first taken by the Pegae Clan and then I stole him from them." Clio was proud of this accomplishment. "It may well start a war between us though I do not care. Hylas is not like all the rest, and I want him."

"Hylas." Anteros repeated the name several times as he gazed upon the body of the young man. In that moment, Anteros' heart filled with a warmth such as he had never felt before. He knew there and then it was his destiny to save poor Hylas from the clutches of the Nerieds.

And perhaps, save himself from a loveless existence.

Plucking Hylas from the white sands of Cos, Anteros carried him back to the palace as the nymphs' screams of frustration followed the entire way.

Rude sounds intruded. Sounds that did not belong in the silence beneath the sea. Her dream receded though Aphrodite fought to hold onto the sensuous feeling of water flowing across her naked body.

Lifting her head, her hair a tangle of snarls, she stared at Thaleia with weary eyes. "What means this?"

Thaleia came away from the open veranda, rushing to Aphrodite's side. "What, Princess?"

"That noise, the uproar, what was it about?"

Taking Aphrodite's pale hand between her own, Thaleia pressed her warmth into the cool flesh. She was uncertain as to what commotion Aphrodite referred to, for all was quiet now. The storm had passed and all the children were fed, bathed and tucked in for the night. Euphrosyne cared for little Harmonia in her own chamber, and Anteros had made himself absent after advising her of the fracas along the inlet.

Yet it was the first time in these many months that Aphrodite had been aware of anything outside her grief and Thaleia did not want to discourage the interest. The story of how the nymphs fought over a human was rather amusing, therefore she thought to relate it as a means to peak Aphrodite's curiosity.

"My Princess, it was the Nereids. They found a treasure and fought over it. A human male that was quite the worse for wear after the nymphs nearly tore him limb from limb. They can be ferocious, those Nerieds, when they have their hearts set on a worthy prize." Thaleia patted Aphrodite's hand.

"But Anteros put a stop to their nonsense and all has grown quiet."

"I see." Withdrawing her fingers, Aphrodite touched their slender tips to her forehead. "I was lost in a dream. A beautiful place. No room for discordance and arguments."

"I am surprised you heard it as they were on the other side of the isle beneath the gallery." Thaleia picked up a brush. "Shall I comb out your hair?"

"I wish it was a dream. Everything." With effort, Aphrodite sat up and moved her feet to the floor.

"Yes, Princess, I, too, wish we were in happier times."

Her mistress waved the brush away. "My head aches and I do not think I could bear the pulling."

"Of course." Thaleia replaced the brush on the table. "Would you like food or drink? A piece of fruit?"

"No. No, nothing."

"Then perhaps we could visit the bathing pool?"

Aphrodite sighed and finally nodded.

Thaleia had only to think it and they were upon the hillside, standing within the pavilion. The rising moon appeared to sit upon the waves as it cast a silvery sheen across the dark water. The two women were white wraiths moving amongst the draperies that hung in quiet relief against the tall pillars. There was not even a hint of a breeze to billow, or even ripple, the silk fabric.

Night birds and insects made soft sounds in the trees and grass as the surf pounded the beach in the background. The air was warm and tasted of lemons and mint and the hint of rain.

Thaleia lifted one hand and the pool began to waft with the

fragrance of the flower petals floating upon the surface. The many candles that surrounded the rim of the spa burst into flame as the evening became like a cloak around their shoulders.

Unclasping Aphrodite's gown, Thaleia waited for it to slide to the floor before helping her mistress into the bathing pool. Then, she, too, disrobed and slipped into the water.

Aphrodite sighed and sank lower into the steaming water. Her chin touched the surface as the slight eddying rocked her back and forth in a blissful caress that only an oceanic princess could understand.

Thaleia filled a pitcher and tipped Aphrodite's head back to pour water over her head. Lifting a vial of soap made from the essence of moonflowers, she drizzled the shampoo onto Aphrodite's wet hair and then combed her fingers through the heavy strands.

As the suds came to life in a foamy white lather, wet curls clung to Thaleia's wrists and arms, as if mindfully seeking the comfort of another's flesh.

Instead of waiting for the pitcher to rinse her locks, Aphrodite submerged her whole being and floated beneath the surface until she could hold her breath no longer. When she emerged, she smiled. A wan smile. A sad smile.

But nonetheless, a smile.

The first Thaleia had seen since Ares fell.

Aphrodite came to Thaleia and laid in her arms, staring up at the dancing figures in the ceiling.

"I have spent many an hour in this pool with Ares." Aphrodite's voice was filled with bittersweet memories. Her body tensed, as if she awaited his touch. After a moment of silence, and a single tremor, she continued. "I know Deimos was here today. Did he have news?"

"I am sorry, Princess, there is no good news. Lord Ares continues to lie between the worlds. How I wish it was otherwise."

"I do not want to live without him."

"Lord Ares is strong-willed. Surely he will recover."

"I pray you are right." Aphrodite sighed again.

It seemed to Thaleia that Aphrodite was forever sighing over all things lost to her. Running one hand along the pale arm of her mistress, Thaleia laced fingers with her and kissed the top of her head.

"I am certain. There is no force powerful enough to keep Lord Ares from your side."

"It should be I locked within that poisonous sleep, for it is my fault this happened."

"What is done is done, Princess. We must now go forward. You have Harmonia to think of."

"I can scarce look at her, though she is a beautiful child. It is too painful to remember how she came to be. Poor Hephaestus did not deserve such dreadful behavior on my part."

With an absent gesture, Aphrodite trailed her fingers across her left breast. "What has become of him?"

"Ahh, Princess, may we speak of other things?"

"No. What has the Council done?"

Thaleia hesitated. "Hephaestus has been banned from ever again setting foot in Olympus and all immortals have been forbidden to attend to him.

"Although he remains on Lemnos, the fires of his forge have been extinguished. He is barred from working with the bounty of the Earth. No metals whatsoever."

Tears ran from Aphrodite's eyes and joined with the water beneath her as her heart swelled with more grief. "And what of Cedalion? Though I find his actions repugnant and know not if I can ever forgive him, he behaved out of loyalty to his master. I understand Cedalion's love for Hephaestus."

"Alas, Princess, Cedalion is chained deep within the dungeons of Olympus. He will never see light again. And should Ares...." Thaleia clamped her lips together, reluctant to continue.

"Should Ares?"

"Ahh, I deplore speaking such an awful thing aloud."

"You must, for I need to know all that I have wrought."

Giving Aphrodite a slight push to lean against the side of the pool, Thaleia braced herself against the tile as well. "Should Lord Ares succumb to his wounds, Cedalion will be put to death. The Council preferred to carry out this sentence months ago."

"How can he be destroyed? Cedalion is an immortal."

Thaleia looked away from the tortured gaze of her mistress. "By employing the very blade Hephaestus created, Princess. But since Amason resides in Deimos' hands, it is up to him to carry out the sentence, yet he has refused to abide the Council's wishes."

"Deimos will not slay the dwarf?"

"Not as of this time. Should Ares pass into the Shadowland, I do not know what action Deimos will take."

"Ares will not leave me." Aphrodite's voice was tight. "He cannot. If I could just see him, I am certain he would awaken."

"Perhaps Anteros will find a way. We must keep up our hopes, Princess."

"Yes. Yes, you are right."

"I do not think the Council is a match for your clever sons, Princess. Between Anteros and Deimos, they will fix this, I swear it." Thaleia smiled with encouragement. "Now let us have a bit of sweets, yes?"

Engulfed in the warmth of the water, feeling for the moment as if all would end well, Aphrodite agreed. Thaleia called for Aglaia to bring a tray. Instead, Euphrosyne appeared, bearing fruit, pastry and wine on a silver plate.

Thaleia frowned at her youngest sister. "Where is Aglaia?"

"I do not know." Euphrosyne glanced over her shoulder, as if she expected her sister to appear. "She has taken leave once more without a word."

"Aglaia said nothing? That is unlike her."

"Agreed, and yet, these days, it is her way."

"Why have I not noticed this?"

Euphrosyne inclined her head toward Aphrodite. "You have been disengaged. There is much you have not noticed."

"Explain yourself."

With a one shoulder shrug, Euphrosyne took a step backward. "We stand upon the cliffs of great change, Thaleia. Everything we know hangs in the balance. May I be excused?"

"Perhaps." Thaleia saw the unusual jumpiness with her sister's twitching hands and feet ready to run from the room. "Sister, what ails you? What is it that you cannot explain to me? At least you must try."

"It is too much for me to bear and I am ashamed." Euphrosyne stared at the marble flooring while she twisted her fingers together as if to break them off one by one.

"Come, Sister, it cannot be that bad, can it?" Out of the corner of her eye, Thaleia watched as Aphrodite drained a glass of wine.

"Anteros, alas, he does not love me." The youngest Grace pressed the fingers on one hand to her breast. "He dallies with another and I cannot bear it."

"Anteros has taken a lover? Why would that disturb you? It is not the first time and will not be the last. I do not understand all this madness," Thaleia inhaled deeply. "Wait, sister. Where is Harmonia? I thought you were to care for her this evening."

"She is with Lyda. It was time for the babe to feed and then she fell asleep. I will go to her in a bit. I felt the need to be alone. Being ever so distraught over Anteros and his conduct, I could not bear to be in company with others."

"Why are you upset over Anteros? I do not understand."

"Because I love...."

"Harmonia?" Aphrodite rose to her knees and crossed her hands at the wrists and laid her palms over her breasts. Water streamed along her bared arms as wet hair clung to her shimmering skin.

Aphrodite's delicate features were twisted in confusion. "If Harmonia needs sustenance, am I not the one to provide it?"

Euphrosyne ceased complaining and stared at her mistress. Thaleia glanced first at Aphrodite and then at her sister. They were both speechless, for every attempt to suckle newborn Harmonia at her mother's breast had failed and a wet nurse was of necessity engaged.

"Where is my child? I should care for her."

"Ahh, Princess, the little one is with Lyda and we shall bring her to you when we are finished with our bath."

"But she is hungry and she needs her mother. My little Harmonia, my beautiful girl, I have waited so long for you."

Aphrodite's crooning dissolved into a faint hum as she splashed about in the water, catching the rose petals and then dropping them back into the ripples.

The giggles that accompanied the play were disturbing. Something was unmoored about Aphrodite's behavior. Thaleia gestured to Euphrosyne to disrobe and join them even as she kept her gaze riveted on her mistress.

"I will be of little assistance." Euphrosyne protested though she did as her sister asked. "Anteros has deceived me and I am upset."

"Anteros is not for you." Thaleia did not intend to sound harsh but her concern for Aphrodite overrode Euphrosyne's distress.

"What do you mean, he is not for me? What would prevent Anteros from loving me?"

"We will talk later." Thaleia pointed at Aphrodite. "We must sort this out. Where is Aglaia?"

"I do not know." Euphrosyne sulked in one corner of the pool. "She disappears often and I do not know where she goes."

With a frown, Thaleia drummed her fingers on the side of the pool. "Her absence must stop as of now." Sitting straight, Thaleia shouted, "Aglaia. Come."

There was no arguing with Thaleia's command. Aglaia appeared beside the marble steps with an expression of rebellion upon her pretty face. The eldest Grace was not accustomed to her sister's authority. She did not care for it at all.

"Yes, Sister?"

Aglaia's tone was cool. Thaleia tilted her head at the unusual tenor of one who was meant to be an uplifting influence. "You have been neglecting your work."

"That is none of your concern."

"Our mistress has need of you."

At this, Aglaia's long-lashed gaze flicked to Aphrodite's countenance but her expression did not change. "Why, then, has Aphrodite not called to me herself?"

Thaleia's lips thinned at the disregard in her sister's voice.

"If you had been in attendance as you should have been, you would know how severely stricken she is."

"She is not the only one who carries grief like a cloak about her shoulders."

"Aglaia!" Euphrosyne's astonishment was reflected in her rounded lips.

"Please, do not argue." Aphrodite lifted one limp hand from the fragrant water and sank back into the pool as if her request for Harmonia had never happened.

"Dear ones, please do not argue on my behalf. It is I who have been neglectful. May we have peace, if only for a short time?"

Downcast, Aglaia nodded but did not make a move to join them in the bath.

"Aglaia, please forgive me." Aphrodite spoke with sweet sincerity, her voice trembling with the effort.

Both Thaleia and Euphrosyne stared at their mistress and then at their sister. Something unspoken passed between Aphrodite and Aglaia, something that caused the very air around them to crackle as if lightening had struck nearby.

"Of course, Princess." Aglaia's voice seemed to stick in her throat. She cast off her clothing and slid into the pool. "Of course, but how did you know?"

"How could I not? I am Eternal Love." Aphrodite held Aglaia with the tenderest of embraces. "You have helped to soothe my own heart."

"Truly?"

"Truly."

"Know what? What does she know? Truly, truly what?" Thaleia and Euphrosyne spoke at once in confusion.

No response was delivered from the two women who clung to each other and wept with the sorrow of a thousand years.

ELEVEN

"Mursilis is so happy to see you." Pallin smiled at Inni as she shifted the chubby little boy to the other hip.

The babe reached for Inni, drool wetting his chin as a row of tiny teeth showed through his grin. He babbled with excitement, most words indistinguishable save for 'Inni'.

"You see, he knows my name." Inni smiled in response and took the child from his mother. "He speaks to me. He tells me many secrets." She kissed his round cheek. "Just like Gaea speaks to me. She tells me secrets, too."

"She does?" Pallin wiped her son's face with a cloth and chucked him under the chin. "What does she say?"

Breathing in the sweet scent of the boy's dark curls, Inni winked at Pallin. "You may wonder why she speaks to me but it is because I am the only one who will listen."

"Do not encourage her." Jahmed entered the hut and gave Mursilis a welcoming pat on the back. With an admonishing shake of her head toward Pallin, she laid freshly dried and folded linens in a basket.

"The spirits do not speak, Gaea does not speak, we do not speak, no one speaks since *they* came." She threw a sidelong glance at the wide-eyed Mursilis before turning back to her work. There was something about the child that bothered her but she would not ask Pallin about it.

"Why? What harm is it to hear her tale?"

"Why, indeed?" Jahmed's tone sharpened. "Pallin, you are far removed from the workings of our temple. It would be best if you did not question my requests."

Pallin's back stiffened. "I try to carry my share of the work but it is getting more difficult." She cast a glance toward Inni and frowned. "Inni, would you take Mursilis to play?"

"Of course. And I am hungry. Are you hungry little one? Let us find something to eat."

The two went off to search for a treat, the babe gurgling and Inni giggling as he grabbed at her hair.

A moment later, Jahmed heaved a sigh and turned with a wry smile. "I am sorry, Pallin, I am overtired. I worry so about Inni." Jahmed leaned against the work table. "I do not wish to burden the younger girls with my concerns but of late, she wanders about at all hours and speaks nonsense. I fear she will get into trouble."

"It is troubling and I do not blame you for being upset. Have no concern as far as myself, and yet there is something I need to discuss with you. I fear it will only add to...."

"Pallin!" Tulane burst through the curtains that led to the sleeping quarters and ran to her. She threw her arms around her, rocking Pallin back on her heels with enthusiasm. "We have missed you so much."

"I have missed you also." Hugging the girl, Pallin breathed in the soft scent of the floral soap used by the women and closed her eyes. If it was within her power to turn back time, she would be here with them, and Hattusilis would have gone on to whatever reward he was to have.

She would be free to raise her son the way she wanted,

within the walls of the sanctuary, not amongst the dirty warriors that camped out in the field near her home. Pallin feared that as the boy grew older, Hattusilis would force him into warrior training. He would be wrong to do this for Pallin had only to look into her babe's eyes to see the tenderness within him. Mursilis was not meant to be soldier.

In spite of his true father. Deimos did not know of his son's existence and Pallin did not want him to find out.

"Pallin, you are so quiet, and thin, too." Tulane kissed her on the cheek. "Are you unwell?"

"I am fine, Dearest. Jahmed has just chastised me for being absent these past weeks."

"Jahmed is cranky because she was up all night. Did you know that Suni had her babe early this morning?"

"Suni. Did she wed one of Hattusilis' men?" Pallin ran her finger through a pile of fresh flower petals in a bowl, stirring them around and around.

"Yes, she did, and now she has given him a fine son. Jahmed let me assist." Tulane beamed with pride.

"It is good she had a boy," Jahmed frowned. "A girl might be set aside to die."

"What? Why would you say that?" Pallin froze under the harsh claim. "What do you mean by such awful words?"

But she understood, though she was loathe to admit it. Her husband referred to all women in a disdaining tone as 'the females', implying no worth. Always, Pallin showed her disapproval, but Hattusilis would pat her arm and say, 'you are the only woman in my life, what does it matter what I call the others?'

Of late, Hattusilis was showing signs of a much deeper disturbance. She closed her eyes for a moment, wishing to block out the most recent fit of anger he flew into without provocation. One moment he was the attentive husband, gentle and caring, the man with whom she had fallen in love. The next moment, he was raging about the lack of respect due him and the punishment that would be inflicted for the insult.

Pallin was on the edge of being truly afraid of her husband, and yet she did not want to speak of it to her sisters. Instead, she responded with a smile. "These men come from a different world but they are here now and it is up to us to teach them our ways."

"Of course." Tulane returned Pallin's smile but her eyes held an uneasy glint. She retreated to the table to help Ajah put away the supplies, leaving Pallin and Jahmed in an uncomfortable silence.

"Am I to understand that *he* will not allow you to come here any longer?" Jahmed laid the pestle down and began to brush the crushed contents into a small glazed jar with a lid.

"It is not because of Hattusilis that I have not been present. I have not felt well." Pallin flushed. "I am with child again. I have had sickness, and that is why I have not been here."

Tulane laughed and ran to hug Pallin once more. "Wait until Inni hears there will be another babe to care for. She will be overjoyed."

Ajah lifted her gaze from her work and exchanged a glance with Jahmed, who refused to look up, keeping her bowed head over her work. Without making eye contact, Jahmed spoke in a low tone.

"Does this mean you will no longer come to the temple?"

"No." Brushing a few crumbs that fell from the pestle to the table, Pallin reached across to drop them into the bowl. "I will do my duty as always, but there is something I need to speak about with you."

Pallin glanced at the two younger women, her blush deepening. Ajah touched Tulane's hand and jerked her head toward the next room.

"No. Ajah, Tulane, please stay. This concerns all of us. What is it, Pallin? Does your king refuse to let you be part of our mission?"

"No, but he does not approve that I bring Mursilis to the temple."

Astonished, Jahmed paused with the jar midway to a shelf. "Why ever not?"

"Mursi grows so fast - he is crawling at six months, already pulling up to my knee. It will not be long before he walks. And now, he is saying words."

"Why would any of that matter?"

"Because of what he said." Heaving a sigh, Pallin continued. "Mursilis speaks Inni's name over and over. That alone irritates Hattusilis, and then, when his father took him from me, he began screaming." Pallin paused at the knowing look Jahmed cast her way.

"While Hattusilis held him, Mursilis did not cry for me, he cried for Inni." Sinking to a low bench, Pallin pulled her long black braid over her shoulder and began to pluck at the end. "You may well guess that Hattusilis was very unhappy about it. I fear he will forbid me to bring Mursilis here."

"It will kill Inni to lose Mursilis. You cannot allow that to happen." Jahmed slapped her hand on the table. Her gaze was filled with distress.

"I am so very sorry. I will do what I can to prevent it but Hattu grows more and more strange as the days pass." Pallin's gaze was downcast. It seemed all she did was mourn for that which had been in their lives but was now gone.

Pallin stared at her clasped fingers. "I will not leave my son with one of the horrible women that came with the legions. I will not do it. If it comes to that, I will no longer be in attendance to the temple."

"Hattusilis seeks to control everything." Jahmed's voice rose. "They have taken over every aspect of Najahmara, save for our work, and then only because we serve their needs. Soon, they will no longer want us and then what? Will they kill us? Banish us? Sell us into slavery?"

The image of the day Inni arrived at Najahmara as a beaten, sex-ravaged slave was forever seared into Jahmed's mind. It was only through Niala's intervention that Inni was taken from the coarse men and brought into the temple fold. It was only because Niala frightened them so much that the slave traders abandoned the women they sought to sell and fled Najahmara for good.

Niala had seen the real Inni beneath the filthy child who cowered at every touch, whimpered at any attention given her, ultimately turning inward and vacant-eyed in resignation of more pain. That Inni, the frightened child, did not speak. That Inni would soil herself rather than be noticed. That Inni would rather die than live through more torture.

Inni had survived so much, Jahmed feared taking Mursilis away from her would reverse the progress she had made since the soldiers attacked. It scared her to think Inni would sink further into the darkness, into the lunacy of this belief that Niala was still alive.

Jahmed's shoulders sagged. Without further comment, she began placing her medicines into a basket in preparation to attend to the ill of Najahmara.

"Jahmed, you have been up all night, I will care for those who are suffering." Ajah reached for the basket.

"I am not tired."

"Jahmed," Pallin began.

"I do not want to hear anymore. You should rest, for another child so soon is not good."

"It has been long enough."

"Mursilis is not yet a year old, it is too soon."

"If I birth a girl then Inni could care for the new babe and she will forget all about Mursi."

"Listen to yourself, exchanging one child for another as if they are the same. Inni would be destroyed if the boy is not allowed to see her."

"Would she truly mind so much?" Pallin lifted her chin, a rare sense of rebellion icing her words. "It is you, Jahmed, who makes more of this than should be. You are not being fair."

"Is it fair to take Mursilis from Inni? It would kill her. But it seems you do not care, and that, Sister, is not fair." Jahmed tossed her braids, snatched up her basket and swept out of the hut.

One tip of Ajah's head and Tulane rushed to follow Jahmed outside.

"What can I do, Ajah?" Pallin sagged, cradling her already protruding belly. "I cannot stand against Hattusilis. He is different these days."

"What do you mean by that?" Ajah laid a bowl of eggs to one side and took Pallin's hand between her own. "Has he not always been different?"

"From us, yes, but in spite of Hattu's beliefs, he cared about our people and did not want his men to destroy what was left. He wanted harmony between us."

"He no longer does?"

"He does not speak of it these days. His interest lies in building an exchange port, one that will accommodate the ships that travel across the oceans."

"What will that mean for Najahmara?" Ajah's gaze darted above Pallin's head to the hanging bundles of dried herbs and to the rows of jars and bowls.

"I do not know, but please, do not tell Jahmed of this. It will only make the division worse. She detests Hattusilis as it is."

"She will learn of it at some point."

"Yes, but let us convince her that all will be well and this too, shall pass."

"I hope that is true." Ajah returned to the table and began tucking the supplies onto the shelves.

Her thoughts had moved to the next task, preparing bread dough. Once upon a time, there was enough women to cover all the duties of a prospering temple. Now there was only a handful to do the work.

"What can I do to help?" Pallin stood, swaying just a bit as a wave of dizziness overtook her. The moment passed with quickness but not before Ajah took note.

"When was the last time you ate?"

Pallin gave her an apologetic smile. "I am certain it was this morning after I rose."

"And not since then? Mercy, let me get you a cup of hot tea and some bread and cheese. We cannot have the new one taking all your strength."

Grateful, Pallin returned to her seat on the bench. "It will be alright, Ajah. I promise, we will all be fine, even with the changes."

"I am certain that is true, Zahava." Although Ajah nodded and smiled in agreement, she did not believe everything would be fine.

In her dreams, the Sagittariidae returned to claim his rightful place and Ajah knew if she did not accept her role as priestess this time, disaster would strike them once more.

Mursilis grinned at Inni showing eight teeth, four on top, four on the bottom, all bathed in slobber. He grabbed at her nose and leaned in as if to bite her. Instead, he left an open-mouthed kiss upon her cheek.

Laughing, Inni pressed her lips to his shining face in return. "My sweet boy, I am so happy to see you. What shall we explore today? We may find some Wildroot if we go deep enough into the woods."

"But it is not time for Wildroot." Inni answered herself, her face scrunched into a thoughtful expression. "Wildroot is found after the spring rains."

Inni hugged Mursilis and ruffled the soft tendrils of his hair. "Ahh, what will we find, then?"

Tilting her head to one side, Inni peered in the direction of the timber that lay on the northwest edge of the village.

"The days grow shorter and cooler. It will soon be time to harvest Redberry. Yes, yes! Shall we search for Redberry?"

Inni spoke to Mursilis as if he responded with words. Though he could yet not speak, his babbling meant the same thing to her.

"Eat them? Is that what you said? Silly boy," Inni chided.

"Of course we will eat our fill and then bring back the rest. What do we do with those?"

The babe chewed on his fingers as they left the temple. "That is right, we will make dye from the skins and jam from the berries themselves. But I think today we will go to the cave."

"Cave?" Inni kissed the chuckling babe. "What cave? You may ask."

Smiling to herself, she whispered into the dark silky curls lying against Mursilis' ear. "It is a secret place and we must be careful. We cannot go the back way through the gardens, someone will see us. We must go along the edge of the woods to reach a different path to get to the plateau."

Inni set Mursilis on the woven reed rug and continued her monologue while she gathered candles, a blanket, a few choice bits of food to feed the babe and a flask of water.

"It goes up the back side of the ridge and is very steep, but no one will see us. It is a long walk and yet, I think we are up to it today. However, little Mursi, you must swear by your blood that you will not tell anyone about it."

When all they needed for an afternoon adventure was placed in a basket, Inni scooped Mursilis up and they set off through the village. Inni nodded and spoke to those she passed though she did her best to keep to herself. She did not have time to chat and, what's more, the ravages of fire were still apparent and she did not like seeing the damage.

It made her sad. She hugged Mursilis. "You will not be like Hattusilis when you grow up, will you? You will be so much more, kind and loving. And I know I can trust you. I trust you with my secrets, Mursi. Now, you must be patient for this path is not well trod and is dangerous. I do not want either of us to fall into the ravine."

"I know you wonder about the ravine." Inni skidded to a standstill as one foot went over the edge of a steep downslide. Below them was scrub growth so tangled in vines it appeared to be a green net. She let out a hiss and clutched at the child.

"You see? We almost fell. You must always listen to what I tell you."

Backing away, Inni took better care to watch her footing as she moved up the mount with her precious charge.

"Now, let us go have a look at the cave."

They crept forward a bit at a time until Inni found the wall of vines and pulled them back so they could enter. The cave was dark and a damp breeze flowed like water over the babe's flushed face. He sniffed the air and then shivered at the chill.

"This is our sacred cave." She sat the babe on a blanket and struck flint against a rock until a spark jumped. A circle of stones had already been laid, and within that ring a small fire began to burn, illuminating the interior of the cavern.

"Do not be afraid, Mursi. This is the home of the Great Mother, Gaea. She loves all of us.

"That is why I brought you here, so you can learn our ways, so you will understand. When you grow up, you will be different. But it must be a secret. You must tell no one what you learn here within the sacred cave. Do you promise?"

Inni smiled at the babe and brought out a tidbit she swiped from the kitchen.

"Here, my little love, enjoy. Now let us begin your lessons."

The ring of wavering light cast by the fire was welcome, pushing back the darkness to the edges as Inni told stories of how Gaea, the great Earth goddess, would bless their rituals with her spiritual presence.

"If we listen closely, we may well hear the voice of the Great Mother. You may find this hard to believe, like so many others, but I have heard Gaea speak right here in this sacred place. She talks to me. She does, Mursi, she really does.

"But remember, I have never called Gaea into myself. Niala Aaminah was the only one who truly could. None of us have been so wholly able to give ourselves up as she did. She sacrificed all connection to give Gaea room."

Inni's eyes glowed in the firelight as she spoke of her Zahava, her teacher. "Gaea lived within her in ways that not one of us understood. And yes, there was fear. Always the concern that Gaea might not choose to retreat.

"What would happen then?" With a shrug, Inni chuckled. "I do not know, my little friend, for Niala was always strong enough to keep her boundaries. But since she has been gone, we have not had such a ritual."

Inni leaned over to pick up Mursilis. "Are you asking where she went? Why is she not here to help us now?"

"Well." Inni dropped her voice to a whisper. "They say she is dead, but it is not true. Gaea told me Niala Aaminah is still alive. Gaea told me Niala needs my help but I do not know how to help her."

Inni cast a glance behind her, into the shadows of the cave. "But I feel Niala strongest here.

"She is not a ghost, of that I am certain. A spirit, perhaps." Inni tilted her head to one side in thought. "Yet, I know she lives. I wish I could better understand what Gaea desires. "

Inni sighed. "How about another story?"

Mursilis was growing heavy in her arms as he settled into a nap. Satisfied, Inni lay down with the babe cuddled into her arms and began to describe the time of her first arrival in Najahmara. "I was a slave, forced to do only as I was told or be punished. It was not until Niala Aaminah saw me that...."

When next Inni awoke, it was dark. Their fire had died back and no hint of sunlight filtered through the vines. She snatched up Mursilis and rushed outside to see torch-lights up and down the streets of Najahmara. Even from a distance, the lights held a certain frenzied movement. Perhaps it was the way they were lifted up and around, down and over. As if searching for something.

Or someone.

Inni groaned. "I fear we are both to be reprimanded for over-staying our visit."

The babe began to whimper. Hungry, no doubt.

"Hush, little one. Do not worry, no one will be angry for long once we are back amongst them safe and sound."

Smiling with encouragement but with a sinking heart, Inni put out the last vestiges of the fire and started down the path with the full moon as their only light.

Inni expected, and received, Jahmed's ire once they returned to the priestess quarters. She ducked her head, burying her face in Mursilis' chubby neck.

"We must take the boy home right now. If Hattusilis finds him here, we will all be punished."

"Perhaps he should stay the night. We can take him home in the morning. He is hungry and I must feed him."

"No, Inni." Jahmed took the babe from Inni's protesting arms. "He must go home. You only add fuel to his father's hatred of us. We will be fortunate if we are not cast out of our home as it is. Our temple, or what is left of it, will be destroyed. Is that what you want?"

"Of course not." Inni avoided Jahmed's angry gaze. "I want peace, for everyone."

"And that is what we attempt to keep, but you continue to stir trouble, every day it is something new."

"Please do not be upset. I would never hurt him. I love Mursilis."

"We all love the boy." Jahmed kissed the babe on the cheek and was rewarded with a toothy grin. Every time she saw the boy, she was astonished at how fast he grew. Given that Mursilis' true father was Deimos and not Hattusilis, there should be no surprise in the way the child developed.

"Think of Pallin, then, if nothing else. She weeps endlessly for her son. For you. Everyone thinks you have been injured in the woods, maybe dead. Why would you do this?"

"It was not on purpose. We fell asleep."

"Where? Where were you? I know you were not in the forest, for we combed every bit of it."

"We were in the caves and lost track of time. I just wanted

to show Mursi where we honor the Great Mother, and then we fell asleep. When I awoke, I saw the commotion and came straight down."

"In the caves?" Jahmed's lips thinned with further disapproval and a tinge of fear. "You must never go there again. Do you not recall how you fell on the slope and nearly killed yourself? And further, we do not want the soldiers to find our sacred ground."

"No one saw us, I made certain."

"How many times have you taken the boy there?"

"Just this once."

Inni smiled at Mursilis and rubbed one dimpled fist. When she met Jahmed's gaze, she put on an expression of contriteness.

"I am sorry, my Love. I should not have taken him there. I will not do it again. But, can Mursilis stay here tonight? Just tonight."

"By all that is sacred, Inni, do you hear yourself? Why would you inflict this pain on Pallin until dawn?"

"They will all be calm by morning."

"No, they will not. I would not put it past Hattusilis to burn this sanctuary to the ground as a punishment. You do not understand what you have done."

"Then send them a message and tell them he is here."

"Oh, to have such a simple view of the world." Jahmed put one palm to her forehead and rubbed as if she could force the ache from her head. "Mursilis must be returned to his parents tonight, and I pray that they will forgive you."

"I do not want to take him back."

"He is *their* son, Inni."

"I do not care. I do not like Hattusilis."

"He does the best he can do," Jahmed snapped.

Inni's brows rose in surprise. "*You* defend him? After your suspicions that he beat her?"

"Sshhtt." Jahmed glanced behind her, at the knot of anxious girls watching their exchange.

In a quiet voice, Jahmed went on. "I do not approve of Pallin's choices but at heart, she is a priestess. Her intent is to bring harmony to both sides. Though I fear for her, I trust she loves her children and would let no harm come to them."

"But she lets *him* do as he pleases. She will let *him* take Mursilis away."

"Nonsense. Mursilis is no more than a babe and a babe belongs with his mother. Even Hattusilis must respect that." Jahmed straightened her shoulders. "I am taking him home."

Tears trickled down Inni's cheeks. In her heart, she knew that Hattusilis would forbid her to see Mursilis again. Hugging him, she kissed his cheek and bid him be a good boy.

Wrapping a shawl around both herself and the babe, Jahmed started for the door, dread deep in her heart.

Nothing good could come of this. Nothing good at all.

Ajah could no longer contain herself. She had seen too much and understood Jahmed's fear was based on something very real. The build-up of an unseen enemy was disturbing; she could not let Jahmed go without an escort.

"Jahmed, wait." Ajah stepped forward, one hand outstretched. "Do not go alone. I fear there is much more below the surface, much we cannot see."

"What? What do you speak of, Ajah? Am I so old that I do not even know what goes on beneath my very nose?" Jahmed held Mursilis closer as she pulled the scarf around her braids, unwinding it, hoping the pain in her head would be relieved. "I no longer can contain all that happens within these walls."

"No, Zahava, you take good care of us. It is just that I feel things. I see things, sometimes in dreams, sometimes it is an impression. I do not know how to explain. Sometimes it is a vision that unfolds before me." Shame flushed her dusky cheeks. "I should have told you before, but I was afraid."

"Told me what, Sister? Told me what?" Jahmed frowned over the babe's head. "What do you know?"

With a full body shudder, Jahmed raised one hand. "Never mind. We must get this child home before something worse happens. You will tell me all about this later."

"Yes, Zahava." Ajah bowed her head and followed along behind Jahmed as they made their way along the shore.

Those with torches out searching for Mursilis and Inni were far away from the lake and their path was safe for the moment, at least until they reached the guard near Hattusilis' cottage.

As they approached the area, the smell of briny water gave Jahmed a slight pause, as did the moonlight shining across the dark water. In the distance, the two women could hear the encampment of soldiers in the meadow past where the Maendre and Bayuk went their separate ways.

"They destroy the beauty of our valley." Jahmed spit upon the ground. "I curse the day we were invaded."

Ajah could only nod in agreement. There were no words to express her sorrow.

The return of Mursilis to his parents was every bit as tedious as Jahmed anticipated. Zan and Connal stood at attention as they entered the hut turned into a king's dwelling. In spite of her worries, Jahmed could not help but notice the additions to the residence, expanding it far more than any simple shepherd would consider.

Neither man would meet the eyes of the priestesses, nor even those of Hattusilis and Pallin. They merely held the space as best as possible while the exchange took place. Other soldiers hovered nearby as if the women were common thieves and were to be clapped in irons before the evening was done.

It was disrespectful.

Jahmed kept Ajah behind her, fearing they would be struck dead where they stood with no opportunity to explain the circumstances.

While Pallin wept with joy and held her babe to her heart with all her strength, whispering 'thank Gaea, thank Gaea,' Hattusilis cursed at them in his own tongue. His face was red with rage as he beat his cane upon the floor to emphasize his rant.

Zan edged forward, his gaze locked onto his king as if he feared the same thing. Connal, too, stepped closer.

Jahmed knew Hattusilis was near crazed that his son had

disappeared and yet all Jahmed could hear in her mind was *'It is your own fault - you should never have come to Najahmara.'*

She had no real sympathy for her sister priestess either. It was the first time Jahmed allowed herself to think the word traitor when she looked at Pallin. Yet she did not express these thoughts, instead, murmured an apology.

"I offer our deepest regrets for this unfortunate incident. It was an oversight in time."

"Yes, it was just that...." Ajah closed her mouth, recoiling from the murderous expression on Hattusilis' face.

"I do not accept your defense." Hattusilis' brown eyes were filled with something undefined moving behind the harsh cold gaze. He gripped his cane until his knuckles lightened, lifting it up as one would a weapon. "Mursilis will never be allowed back into your presence."

"That is uncalled for." Jahmed tensed, her glare betraying her unadulterated hatred for the man. "No harm was meant to the child."

"It is true, my husband. They all adore Mursilis and care for him as if he was there child. Please reconsider."

"I will have no more of this foolishness. I have allowed you freedom long enough." Hattusilis turned his ugliness to Pallin. "You are forbidden to return to the work of these misbegotten shrews."

"Do not speak to my sisters in such a foul way!" Pallin stood at rigid attention, clutching Mursilis to her breast. "You cannot prevent my life's work, Hattu."

"I can. I am."

Hattusilis turned away from Pallin and stared at Jahmed. A sudden desire to strike her rose with a vicious burst and Hattusilis had to clench both fists around the cane to thwart the urge. It was not like him to want to harm women and children, but he found that he wanted to beat them all half to death. He despised their manipulative controlling ways.

Swallowing hard, he fought the light-headedness but

stumbled as his feet turned leaden.

"My King." Zan moved to Hattusilis' side, an expression of concern pinching his eyebrows together. With one hand beneath Hattusilis' elbow, Zan attempted to steady him, though Hattusilis jerked free and near fell with the exertion.

Connal appeared at Hattusilis' other side and between the two soldiers, seated their king on a low couch. Hattusilis leaned back, eyes closed, fingers relaxed, allowing the cane to slide to the floor.

Hattusilis could not account for these bouts of wrath that came with more frequency. He was frightened by the aftermath and had needed to rest for three days after the last round of violence.

Weak and dizzy, unsure of his steps, he had lied and said he was ill with a burning gut. He struggled with the feelings on a daily basis, and here it was again, threatening to overtake him. He did his best to quiet the inner beast and repeated in a lower tone. "I forbid you to go to the temple again."

"There is no reason for this. You will sleep, feel better, and reconsider these harsh words."

Pallin flicked her fingers at Jahmed and Ajah. It was a signal for them to go. Jahmed and Ajah retreated even though Jahmed was afraid to leave Pallin and the babe with Hattusilis. Though he had calmed, there was madness reflected in his eyes.

Connal caught Jahmed's gaze and nodded his assurance that he would not leave Hattusilis and Pallin alone. With a prayer that she would not live to regret their departure, Jahmed returned his nod and the two priestesses made good their escape.

"I will never allow my son to be in the presence of that white witch ever again."

"You now speak of Inni, whose injuries have caused her to be different. How can you be so cruel?"

Hattusilis gritted his teeth against more of a torrent. "I do not like her, she rambles on with foolish notions. I do not want my son exposed to such nonsense."

"Inni is confused." Seeing a change in her husband's posture, one that was less aggressive and much more like the old Hattusilis,

Pallin continued. "It was you who brought this illness upon her."

Pallin had discovered that when she could pluck the guilt from within her husband, he was much more pliable. She was convinced the aggressive behavior that reared its ugly head from time to time was due to his injuries.

When he was himself, she felt deep affection for him, and when he was himself, he was kind and caring to all. She saw the man with whom she had fallen in love. This other creature was a stranger and she did not like that Hattusilis.

Momentarily, he appeared to revert to his former self.

"It is not my fault." Hattusilis felt the stamina drain away as if stolen from his very essence. He was suddenly exhausted.

"Had I been here, I would have prevented Telio from the revenge taken upon Najahmara. In truth, he did only what he deemed necessary."

"He attacked us under the guise of finding you but he wanted power. I believe he would have killed you had he discovered your whereabouts."

"Never. Telio was my blood, he wanted to rescue me."

"That is not what I was told." Pallin rocked Mursilis as he began to fuss. "By Zan."

"My liege, it is true. Telio wanted power and used your disappearance as an excuse to invade. He would not listen to reason. I have told you this many times."

Hattusilis shook his head, irritation rising as the exhaustion faded. His skin began to prickle and he dug his fingers into his thighs, allowing his cane to fall to the floor.

He no longer knew Zan. The changes that occurred during their short time in Najahmara were astounding. Hattusilis could scarce believe Zan was once a brilliant warrior.

"I would not have caused such death and destruction. It would have been less painful."

"*Less painful*? To have our lives stolen from us, to have our homes wrecked and our peace shattered, that is what you call *'less painful'?* You and your army brought ruin upon us and now you forbid me to serve my own people?"

"You do not understand the strategy of war." The itching spread and became unbearable, as if his skin attempted to slough off his body. He could sit no longer. Standing, he lifted his chin up, straight and proud. "You are a simple woman who does not know what is best for yourself or our child. You will not return to the temple. I have spoken as your husband and your king. You will abide by my degree."

"I will not stand for your demands, Hattu." Reckless anger consumed Pallin. Again, Hattusilis shifted from humble to arrogance. She could not, would not, live in such absence of affection or concern.

"There is naught you can do, Wife."

"If you demand I give up my duties, I will forsake you as my husband." Pallin ignored Zan's gasp and kept her gaze fixed to Hattusilis. "I will, I swear it."

"You cannot. By law."

"Your law, not ours. Do not push me, Hattu. I will not be held captive. I have done everything you asked but this I cannot and will not do."

"You would return to the very ones who attempt to pull us apart?"

"I will."

"No, you will not." The burning sensation ceased and Hattusilis felt the stamina flow into his body, a vigor unknown to him in months. With the exhilaration came a surge of scorn. "You have no power. You can do nothing save rail at me and I will no longer listen."

"If you refuse to let me work at the temple, I will leave you. We do not force anyone to remain in a union that causes pain. I will return to the priestess quarters. I will no longer be your wife."

"You are my wife unto death."

"Only in your world, Hattu, not in mine. It is my right to separate from your side if I no longer...." Pallin pressed her lips to her babe's soft hair to hold back the words that would wound the most.

"If you no longer owe me loyalty?"

"If I no longer love you." The words spilled out in spite of her best efforts.

Hattusilis stared at her, stunned, eyes blinking, nostrils flared, fists knotting until his knuckles bulged. "Is that it, then?"

He spoke softly now, but his fury was scarce contained. "You have decided you no longer love me and do not wish to be my wife, although you bear my children? You want to return to your humble beginnings, live in that burned out hovel they refuse to give up, serve others when they should be serving you? That is what you want?"

Though frightened at the red-eyed rage reflected in Hattusilis' gaze, Pallin refused to lower her gaze. "No, it is not what I want. I want my husband restored to the man I wed. If that is not to be, then I will…."

"Say it, Wife. Speak it aloud so that all our ears can hear this traitorous declaration."

Connal shifted from foot to foot, uncomfortable with the argument. Zan pleaded in silence for Pallin to speak with care, to say nothing she would regret, yet knowing all the same that she would, for Hattusilis had pushed her too far.

"Yes, Hattu, I want to return my sisters. I no longer wish to be your wife."

There was a long silence. Neither spoke but the air was filled with such rage it seemed as though a blanket of fog wrapped about them in a stranglehold.

"You no longer want to be my queen?"

Hattusilis' eyes were constricted and mean, his face twisted into something Pallin had never before seen in her husband. Her fright grew stronger and her belly lurched as the babe kicked.

"Zan, bring me my son. Connal, take her away. She wishes to be banished from my home? So be it."

"No." Pallin shielded the boy with her own body as the Zan

approached. "Do not touch him."

"Please, my Queen, do not make things worse."

"He is mad. Please, Zan, do not do this."

"It is best if I am the one," Zan whispered. "Please, let it be me and not one of them."

More soldiers came running into the chamber at their king's command. Terror swept over Pallin as she saw the ugly eagerness in the men's eyes. They were not sympathetic to the Najahmaran way. The majority resisted, causing trouble for those who chose to be part of Gaea's rituals.

Pallin had seen these men and their bestiality first hand. She had used her power as queen to stop their behavior. Why had she not seen that Hattusilis had increasingly surrounded himself with these cruel types, what he called his 'loyal troops'?

As Pallin thought back to the arguments she and Hattusilis had raised their voices over, she knew these men had been close by, listening, waiting for this very moment. Sobbing, she released her now-squalling babe into Zan's arms.

"Forgive me." Zan's brown eyes held torment and grief as he cradled Mursilis in his arms. "He will be well-cared for."

"Take her away," Hattusilis screamed, spittle dripping from his lower lip. "She is no longer my wife. Lock her in her quarters."

"Hattu, no, please, what are you saying?"

"You will not defy me, woman. You will not turn away from me and go to those shrews who wish to kill me. Lock her away."

"No, Hattu, please, I beg you, please do not do this. Do not separate me from Mursilis. He is my son, he needs me."

"It is too late. I have long wondered about your loyalty, and now you have said it with your own lips."

Shrieking, Pallin reached for her child as Connal held her about the waist and fought to pull her from the king's presence.

Connal spoke in a low voice next to her ear. "Do not struggle. All will be well, I swear it. For now, come with me and you will not be injured."

Pallin moaned and sagged in Connal's grip. What else could she do?

Lying in bed, unable to sleep, Hattusilis was filled with regret and sadness at being so alone. It was the first time since Mursilis was born that Pallin was not beside him, and even then, he sat vigil with her until the babe had entered the world.

It was the first time he was completely alone, with no one in the room save himself, not even a servant. He sent everyone away in a continued fit of rage, a rage so deep that Hattusilis did not know where it came from. The hatred just bubbled up like a wellspring, spewing all the bitterness and resentment hidden beneath the surface.

"It was all unnecessary," Hattusilis moaned. "What has come over me that I treat my love with such disrespect?"

Yes, yes, life had been difficult for him since he had lain in the cave with an urn the size of a horse lying atop him, crushing one leg and badly damaging the other. Yes, he knew the people of Najahmara held him responsible for all the death and destruction even though it was Telio, his nephew, whose hand had nearly destroyed the village.

Hattusilis held himself responsible. He was a good king, a caring man, one who wanted to build Najahmara, not annihilate it. The town was, after all, the place of his dreams. Not paved with gold, as he was told, but no less valuable.

Hattusilis felt he was on the verge of insanity, no longer in control of his actions. More and more, he had become mean and petty, harping like an old woman, complaining and condemning everything.

He was truly not himself and he did not know why. The happiness he felt when he moved his family away from the burned out temple evaporated. His interest in building a ship harbor waned and the joy of his son turned to disappointment and frustration that Mursi so adored the white witch.

What was happening to him?

His head ached with a fierceness that rivaled those of his

lower extremities. And on this night, the light from the bedside lamp hurt his eyes more than usual. He could scarce stand the brightness of the burning flame and yet he was afraid to snuff it out. The darkness would be far worse than the light, for what lurked in the corners was terrifying.

Pallin kept the ghosts away. Her sweet nature calmed the spirits that hung about Hattusilis and they left him alone when she was nearby. He could not tell her this without appearing weak-willed and timid. He could not tell her that was the reason he demanded she spend most of her time with him and not with the women on whom she doted.

And now, by his own hand, he had lost her forever. She would never forgive him for this, never. With tears leaking from under his eyelids, Hattusilis wondered why he did not die from his injuries. He should have. He should not have survived such wounds. Yet here he was, still in agony, still scarce able to walk, appearing an invalid to his men. No strength, no ability. Why did they even follow his orders?

Pallin would not forgive him for this.

She will forgive, it is her nature.

Hattusilis started up, eyes bulging as the sibilant whisper curled around him, taunting him. It was the voice of his nightmares. The voice that came often in his dreams. It was the voice from the caves and it would not leave him alone.

"No, she will never forgive this. I have gone too far. You have made me go too far."

She wounded you.

"Yes, it hurts when she fights against me, but to banish her. That is wrong. I must make it up to her somehow."

Hattusilis grew frantic. Once again, his skin crawled as if a thousand tiny insects sought to burrow into his body. His limbs began to twitch and jerk about.

She does not love you.

"She did not mean it." Hattusilis clawed at his arms as the itch grew deeper and coldness enveloped him.

She abandons you.

"You lie. She did not want to leave me. She is justifiably angry with me."

She betrays you. They betray you. They betray me.

The whisper became more intense, closer, close to Hattusilis as if this invisible being sat in bed with him.

I watch. I listen. I see. They want you gone. They will do anything to be rid of you. They keep you from their temple. They hide from you.

"Stop! Leave me alone. Have you not done enough? Is it not enough that I have banished my love? Leave me alone."

They did it, not I. The women of the temple turned your mate against you. They turned my mate against me.

"I do not know what you speak of. I do not know you. Why do you badger me, what do you want?" Hattusilis threw the blanket off and slid his feet to the floor. Panic took hold and he shook with abject terror. The voice had never been so insistent, so demanding.

Hattusilis must go to Pallin and beg her forgiveness. He must give her son back. He must not be this cruel.

Let me in, Hattusilis, and I will fix this for you.

"Let you in where?" Wailing, Hattusilis made a lunge for his cane, his heart pounding. Even though he was cold, sweat stood on his forehead and ran down his face. "Leave me alone!"

I will make it right, if you let me in. Let me in. Let me in.

The cane was knocked from his grip as if by an invisible hand. Stumbling, Hattusilis flailed to recover his balance but instead, his foot met the cane and rolled forward. He crashed to floor and struck his head against the wooden washstand. The wound throbbed with such pain that Hattu's eyes blurred and his tongue swelled, becoming dry and foreign in his mouth.

The pounding in his head grew to enormous proportions. He could not cry out as his body spasmed and nausea overtook him. The last he recalled, he was vomiting where he lay, his face resting in a puddle of his own foulness.

TWELVE

This time, when Ares opened his eyes, it was to a warm pool of lamplight. Not overly glaring but brighter than he remembered. Laced in with the smells of his prison was the familiar scent of Spring: newly turned soil, early budding blooms, fresh air, and above all, hope.

As he stirred, he felt stronger, more like himself than a walking corpse. Though his left side still ached, it was bearable, as if it healed, yet he had not found a wound upon the site.

With a deep breath he sat up, fully awake and ready to fight for his freedom. He had spent long days building his vigor, waiting for the moment when Persephone would return.

He looked toward the outer chamber, squinting for better focus. There burned a single candle casting no shadows upon the wall. Turning toward the brighter light, he was startled to see Persephone sitting in the chair next to his bed with an oil lamp on the little side table.

"You are restored, I see." Persephone smiled with a compassionate curve of her lips. "I am glad."

"You hold me prisoner and yet you are glad to see my revival?"

"Ahh, Ares, always the romantic. Your spirit is healing because of my ministrations." She gave a slight satisfied nod. "I have kept you safe while you are recovering."

"*This* is how you protect me?" Disbelief colored his words. "Attempts to contain me have led others to lethal disappointment."

"I had little time to prepare when your spirit received its grievous wound." She gave a tiny shrug of one pale shoulder. "Do you recall how you came to be here?"

A faint memory surfaced, one that had been sliding around the corners, just out of reach. He saw glimpses, one of his beloved Aphrodite as they lay together in a bed shrouded with gold, and then another of a sharp pain, a dulling of his senses, distant screaming - and then nothing. He could grasp no more regardless how hard he tried.

"You were poisoned by Cedalion, a dagger in your side. Had the blade touched your heart, you would not be here." Persephone waved one small hand toward the iron bars at the far end of his cage. "You would be in a different sphere of my care."

"Then I am not dead?"

"Not entirely. Your body still breathes, lying in state and at her command, in Hera's temple."

"That would explain my shaven face and shorn locks." Ares ran a hand across his clean chin. "My mother disliked the unruly wayward appearance I felt was in keeping with my role as War. I should have known she would have it her way the moment I was incapable of disagreement."

"She feels it reflects a more honorable you."

"There is no honor in my Realm." Ares shifted his feet to the floor. "As for Cedalion, I will rend his limbs from his body with my bare hands for this crime."

"Ahh, Ares." Another tender sigh from Persephone. "In my Realm one must accept responsibility for his or her life in order to heal. You blame the hapless Cedalion."

"It was he who attempted to end my life."

"It was he who did the bidding of Hephaestos. How can you blame one who remains true to his master, down to the ruin of his own life?"

"He has been put to death, then, for this traitorous act?"

"No, though the Council sought his execution. Deimos refused to carry out the sentence. He wields the only blade that can bring death to an immortal." Persephone tilted her head and her blond curls fell forward across her exposed neck. "Yet he will not abide their order."

"Why would Deimos refuse?" Cold anger colored Ares' voice as he stood up. The blanket dropped from his hips and he stood naked before Persephone. "He dishonors me."

"Deimos does not explain himself though I believe he is more his father's son than you would see. It appears he does not like the Council telling him what he must or must not do."

At that, Ares calmed. This observation rang true for he, too, took umbrage at following the dictates of the Council.

"Do not fret, Lord Ares, for a far worse fate has befallen Cedalion: he has been separated from the one he loves most, Hephaestos.

"Cedalion's act was not one of a traitor. He was bidden by his master. Must not your minions follow your every command or be punished by your hand? And are their actions not considered heinous to others?"

Ares blinked once before the red tide of hatred enveloped him. Aphrodite's betrayal surged forward. She went to Hephaestos; she abandoned him for the lame Forge god.

Betrayal? No, she had been coerced, stolen from Ares by Hephaestos, his sworn enemy. He would not tolerate it. He would destroy the Forge God.

"Hephaestos. He caused this grievous act. It is he who must pay. I will use his most prized work against him when I am released from this prison. My blade, Amason, will separate his head from his shoulders and we will be done with this horror."

Ares paced back and forth across the small space with no thought given to his unclothed state.

"It is understandable. Your rage is fueled by Jealousy."

"Zelos, that bitch. She brought this on."

A memory surfaced of Zelos teasing him while he watched the fortress on the Isle of Lemnos and waited for the moment when he could retrieve Aphrodite from Hephaestos. Another recollection forced itself into his thoughts. A dim reminder of brutal sex on a mountaintop with Zelos bawling as she reaped what she had sown.

Ares rubbed his face with both hands, memories washing over him with a vengeance. He groaned with the weight of it all.

With great patience, Persephone watched Ares stride back and forth, his long legs making short work of the distance within his prison. Two steps, turn, two steps back, repeat endlessly. She smiled at his agitation.

"Your temperament drives you to battle, yet not all answer the call of War. Zelos does what is in her nature. Who can blame her for that? Is it not up to us to resist her charms?"

Head pounding, Ares buried his fingers in his short curls and ripped at his hair to drown out the babble of voices shrieking in his mind. Most disturbing was Aphrodite's screams as the fine gold net fell upon them as they lay satiated after making love. He then recalled the sting of the dagger entering through his ribs, the blood spurting and the quickness of the poison which stole his life.

Through fogged eyes, the last thing he saw: the smirking self-satisfied Hephaestos standing at the foot of the bed. The last thing he heard: Aphrodite's inconsolable weeping.

"Aphrodite, my Beloved. What has become of her?"

"Her heart breaks and she recedes. And though she begs Libertina to take her, Sweet Death will not approach."

Rage shook him. "I will kill Hephaestos, I swear it."

"Look further, Endless War, for you place erroneous

blame."

Confused and tormented, Ares dug fingers into his eyes as if to blind himself to the truth. Pinpoints of light danced as he inflicted more pain upon himself. "It was Hephaestos."

"Was it? Did not the Forge god act with fealty toward his wife? What would you do had you found your true love lying with another?"

"I did." Ares slammed one fist against the stone wall of his prison, bruising his flesh. "Aphrodite is *mine*, not his."

"Ahh, once again, Ares, awaken and see the veracity. Did not Aphrodite annul your union and go to him with a clear heart? And did Hephaestos not accept with honor? Were they not wed by their own agreement?"

"She was coerced. She would never do this to me."

"Aphrodite left your marriage bed for that of Hephaestos by her own free will."

"I cannot accept that as truth."

"Ares, consider the facts."

From the depths of Ares' mind came a blurry commotion, the heated arguments, and Aphrodite's shrewish demands for another child. Her threats to forsake him.

"*She*," Ares hissed. "*She* did this."

"Aphrodite was driven." Persephone shifted in her chair, rearranging her skirts. "All of us are driven when the call to bring a child into being is placed upon us. Harmonia was destined to be born. Aphrodite was left no choice."

"Harmonia?" Ares collapsed onto the narrow bed, holding his head in his hands. "Who is Harmonia?"

"Aphrodite's daughter."

"My daughter?" Ares lifted his face and gazed with an edge of panic at the unshakeable woman seated before him.

Again, a delicate shrug moved flawless shoulders. "Her parentage remains a mystery for Harmonia truly is a perfect portrait of her mother. She exhibits no sign of her paternity."

"I must be her father. It must be me." Anguish filled Ares' voice before he froze, his fingers waving in the air.

"Wait. A single child? We have always had twins. A pair to share, one for her Realm and one for mine. Oh, by blood and bone and all that is mine." He released a great moan. "The babe is not my daughter."

Tears began to run down his cheeks.

"What is this?" Scrubbing at his eyes with the heel of his hand, Ares stared at the wetness on his palm. "Am I mad? This is not who I am. I do not mourn for that which cannot be changed. Wicked one, you seek to trick me." But the tears continued to streak his face no matter how much he raged at Persephone or shook the bars that held him prisoner.

Throughout it all, Persephone remained at peace as she watched his outburst. When Ares fell silent, she spoke with quiet conviction.

"One cannot say for certain to whom Harmonia belongs."

"I have done this." Ares' voice filled with plaintive disbelief. "With my own obstinance I have done this. It is *my* fault." Exhausted, Ares lay down on the thin mattress. "My fault. It is all my fault."

The tears continued to run from his eyes and he had not the strength nor the ability to stop them.

Persephone nodded. "You have done well, Ares. And now you may begin the task of true healing."

Ares sank into yet another deep sleep from which he could not rouse himself. His body refused to obey and his mind relinquished all thought of revolt. He felt Persephone's light touch upon his forehead and all else save restoring sleep swam away.

From that moment on, each time Persephone visited, Ares felt the balm of her existence. He finally came to understand why she was Queen of Souls. She had only to stroke his forehead and his agitation calmed, his sorrow dissipated and his pain eased. Even the throbbing in his side ceased and he could take in deep breaths once again without the sting.

Wellness coursed through his body.

The will to heal, to fight, to live became his single focus. No longer did a shadow hang over him. Grief did not tempt him to linger within its darkest clutches.

Once again, Ares believed in his own fortitude and ability. He could think of his unjust deeds toward Aphrodite without rancor. He was without desire to retaliate against Hephaestos. Persephone's touch healed even that wound and now he had no care for what became of Hephaestus or the dwarf Cedalion.

He wanted only to return to his beloved so that she, too, could heal. He was satisfied. He was whole again.

All that had been stolen was restored.

It was time he reclaimed his mantle.

Persephone knew the moment she entered the cavern Ares was recovered. His aura was clean and strong, shifting in color as it should when he spoke. At his arrival in her domain, his aura had been gray and lifeless. Over the months he spent in her care, his aura had lightened and now, appeared fully regenerated.

She smiled upon seeing the cleared aura, but was keenly aware that with Ares restored, he could not be trusted. He was, after all, Endless War. Whether Deimos held the Mantle or not, Ares would always be War. She took care not to approach within touching distance. And she was right. The first words from his mouth on sight of her was a demand.

"Release me." Ares shook the bars as if to tear them apart. "Return me to my body."

"I would if I could." Persephone's expression was solemn. "That is not the way a soul is regenerated."

"You have said yourself that I am not truly dead, but in a state of limbo somewhere between the worlds."

"That is true, my friend, but it should not be. I could not help myself when I saw your spirit wandering, lost and confused, I intervened. Had I not, you would certainly be in Hades' Realm of the Dead. Thanatos seeks to claim your soul for his father, even now."

Persephone wrinkled her nose at the mention of her husband's son. She knew Thanatos' keen interest in Ares was not to impress Hades - it was to gain more power for his personal use. This was one reason she had snatched Ares' from beneath the cold fingers of Bitter Death. She would not have Thanatos extorting power and using it to claim any part of her realm.

"Thanatos." Ares flicked his fingers in a gesture of dismissal. "He is no match for me."

"Perhaps in your former state. In this, the Spirit Realm, he would prevail."

"Return me to my body and I will show you who is the stronger."

"I cannot." Persephone avoided his gaze, and instead, stared at the uneven stone floor.

"I do not understand." Ares' voice was fast rising as fury took hold. "Restore me or you will regret this action."

"Ahh, Ares," Persephone responded with sadness. "I had hoped your time spent with me would help you find a gentler side in your demands. Perhaps even one that would allow you to see another's perspective."

"I see that you hold me here for no apparent reason."

"You do not hear me. You were in great peril. I saved you from eternal anguish. Thanatos would not have been so generous as to help you resolve your conflicts and heal your wounds."

Persephone finally met Ares' angry eyes. For one brief moment, her knees weakened. Within that darkest gaze laid more than a desire to leave the Shadowland. Within those black eyes was a conflagration of lust that would consume anything that came close, including herself. She took a single step backwards.

"Thanatos would have you drink the waters of the River Lethe so that you would never remember who you are. Yours was not to enter into the Elysian Field of Dreams to heal nor ascend to the Isle of the Blessed to be reborn. Yours was to remain in the Kingdom of Shadows' Field of Punishment."

"And you, dear Persephone, did not feel I deserved such a reward?"

Ares' mocking tone send a twinge of regret up her spine. She had saved him from a punishment that he had, perhaps, earned. And yet, it was not in her nature to set judgment upon a soul. It was her nature to heal, to give an errant spirit another opportunity to go forth toward an uplifted life.

Such dire verdicts she left up to her husband, Hades, for he was quite aloof regarding his decisions. Detached, with no emotional connection to his subjects.

Persephone frowned. He was also detached from his wife. At times, she accused him of having no heart and no love for her. When she would complain, Hades sought her grace and begged her forgiveness. He expounded on how much he adored her. Did he not make her Queen of the Shadowland? Did he not give her a free hand with the souls that came unto his realm? How could he be more devoted to her than that?

She would once again be mollified, and look past his inability to satisfy her need of connection. After all, Hades bore many burdens, some so difficult that it was impossible for any to understand.

"Why would you save a soul such as mine?" Ares leaned into the iron rails of his prison and spoke in a low voice, so low that Persephone could scarce hear him. "Am I not the epitome of wickedness? Of brutality and bloodshed?"

"That is what they say, and yet I believe every soul deserves a second chance."

"Have you not seen those I have dispatched into the arms of your adored husband?"

"I have witnessed their pain, yes."

"And yet, you still believe that I am not beyond redemption?"

Fear migrated throughout Persephone's body and yet, she could not resist moving closer. She was entranced by War's power, however diluted it was. His heady sandalwood scent was like a beacon, drawing her in though she knew it was dangerous.

"I believe even you should have the opportunity to review your misdeeds."

"And then what?"

"Change. Become a better version of yourself."

"Never." Ares reached through the bars and yanked Persephone against them. "It is not my nature."

Persephone gasped as Ares closed his mouth over hers in a fierce kiss. Heart pounding, she melted against the bars and let him. When he released her, he gave a slight push causing her to stumble before catching her balance.

"But I thank you for trying. No other has ever cared enough to give my salvation any thought." Amusement colored Ares' words.

Persephone leaned against the cool wall without comment. She was unable to catch her breath and instant regret leapt into her heart. Was a simple kiss that she did not fend off considered a betrayal of her husband?

"We are still left with the question of how I am to leave this lovely prison and return to my own body." Ares stepped back from the gate and sat upon the narrow bed. "It would be best to release me. If I stay here, you will succumb to me. They all do."

Persephone turned her head away, hating his arrogance and yet afraid that he spoke the truth. Her body hummed with desire though she fought against it.

"There must be a way. Think, Persephone, or next time, this prison will not prevent me from having you."

"I will not allow it." Persephone smacked her small hand down upon the table top. "I will not allow you to touch me again."

"You will." Ares laughed and the sound echoed into the larger chamber, chasing after her defiant thump. "You need me. You want me."

Persephone shivered as the terrifying truth of his words made her belly clench. It had been too long since Hades had held her with passion, too long since she had been kissed with heated longing and the overall hint of force made her breath catch in her throat.

Curling fingers over the front of her bodice, as if that would keep Ares at bay, Persephone retreated to the safety of her chair. It did seem it would be prudent to release Ares as soon as possible and yet he could not go into the arena of the truly dead. He was neither dead nor alive but caught between.

Cradling her chin in one palm, Persephone half-listened to Ares' sexual taunting. At long last, she lifted her head and spoke.

"Here is the quandary: I wish very much for you to go but those souls that return to the mortal realm with me are reborn into infants. They are the healed and renewed spirits of those who have lived before, who have worked through the suffering of their mortal lives and are ready to incarnate once again.

"Every other month, when I travel through the portal as Spring into varying parts of the Mortal Realm, the souls who are regenerated pass with me. There they await the appropriate time of imminent birth to join with the physical body of a newborn child. If you would accept this and be born into a mortal babe, I will help you. Otherwise, I have no way to return you to any realm other than this one."

"I want *my* body, not that of some fragile brat that may or may not survive the mortal existence." Ares bared his teeth in a growl. "How could you steal my soul and have no way to return me?"

"I have explained the alternative which would have been much worse than this."

"There must be a way to liberate me. There has to be."

"I do not know how. I have done what it is I do and that is heal the wounds of your spirit. It has never been done with an immortal." Persephone exhaled to calm herself. "I am at a loss as to what to do now. I confess I did not think that far into the future. I sought only to save you."

Sadness filled her heart as she viewed Ares. She did not blame him for his rage. He was well and truly trapped. All she wanted was to help him. For this, had she doomed him to stay in this small cell, to fall into the wicked hands of her step-son, Thanatos? Or worse, return to life as a mortal babe?

Persephone was positive none of it was acceptable to War.

THIRTEEN

Zelos skirted the corridors of Athos, her back pressed against the rough walls. The fortress was deathly silent, the air undisturbed by the breath of any being. The difference between Ares' rule and Deimos' tenet was startling. In Ares' presence there had been brawling drunken warriors, the smell of death and decay and a sense of hopeless ruination. Now there was only the musty scent of disuse.

She began her search of Athos in the altar chamber. She could not contain her laughter at the dusty yet pristine altar that had not seen a sacrifice since Ares was laid low. She heard of the woe brought to Anteros for disturbing Ares' rostrum and could only imagine Ares' fury at its sight.

Why had Deimos left it? Why had he not established dominion over what was now his? To have such power, to have all of War's creatures at his call, including those mortals who would bring aggression into the world.

Zelos shrugged her slender shoulders.

To own all this.

She always enjoyed causing jealousy amongst the warriors

gathered to pay tribute to their god. Because of her, there had been many fights, and on occasion, she bedded the victor. She, of course, preferred Ares himself, until he raped her on the mount of Lemnos and stole her chain.

After that, she was terrified of him. She felt no sympathy when Ares was struck down. He deserved such punishment for his barbaric ways. That day on Lemnos, she meant only to stir his resentment. She wanted to see if he would drag Aphrodite from the arms of Hephaestos. Instead, Ares turned on Zelos with painful brutality.

She shuddered at the memory as she made her way deeper into the fortress. Where had Ares hidden her talisman? It was here, she could feel it, albeit, faintly. She called to the amulet and felt the answering pulse of energy as she moved up a staircase and into yet another gray corridor.

She imagined the chain slithering toward her, the links crawling along the floor with the movement of a golden serpent. She felt the longing reply and yet the talisman did not come to her.

That could only mean the chain was imprisoned in such a way that it could not break free. Even near death, Ares would not let go of his power over her.

"Curse you, War, and all your demons. I hope you rest in Hades' arms soon."

"What an unkind thing to say, particularly since I am now War."

With a shriek, Zelos whirled, red hair flying about like shooting flames. Deimos stood behind her, his countenance grim, his clothing bloodstained and tattered. She could hear Amason singing in triumph, and though sheathed, the unearthly trill brought a chill to the back of her neck.

"Deimos. I was looking for you." Zelos managed a weak smile as she leaned against the wall. Her legs shook at his sudden appearance, but more profoundly, she was struck by his beauty.

Deimos was always handsome in a boyish way, much like Anteros, yet both were a mere shadow of their father's countenance. She had not truly looked upon Deimos, preferring to toy with him as she did Anteros. Tease, torment, but not take with any seriousness.

Until now.

Warmth spread in her belly as she recognized the man Deimos had become. His features were more defined, rugged, a dark beard outlining his chin. His eyes were wary and carried the distant struggle of the Mortal Realm.

Maturity brought a crease between his brows and a certain dangerous set to his shoulders she had never noticed. At Cos she was too absorbed in her frustration to pay attention to the changes in Deimos.

Zelos' gaze moved to stare at his hands, filthy from battle, scratched and bleeding, yet emanating strength.

How many men had those hands killed?

How many legs had they parted for pleasure?

Zelos licked her lips and brought her gaze back up to meet his. Erotic interest flickered in the black depths yet he made no move toward her.

"What do you want?" Deimos' tone was curt.

You, she wanted to cry out. Instead she drew in a steadying breath. "I search for my talisman."

"I told you I do not have it."

"And you may not."

"I *may* not? You say I lie?"

"No, no, never that." Color rushed into her cheeks. "But I feel its presence. It is here, somewhere. When I call, it answers. Though it has not yet come to me."

She lowered her gaze to see that her nipples stood stiff with anticipation. Inwardly, she scolded herself but could not stop the dampness that was beneath her arms and between her legs. Deimos was all that Ares had been, and more. Deimos wore an aura of emotion that Ares did not allow to surface.

Passion smoldered just below the surface. Enough that she could drown in his arms. It was his mother's blood, Aphrodite, Eternal Love, that called to Zelos. She belonged to Love and could scarce fight the response to the silent summoning of ardor.

It was clear that Deimos was unaware he sent such a strong message. Zelos fought the urge to leap upon his strong body and have her way with him. Instead, she gulped air and spoke in a low voice.

"If I may have your permission," taking another deep breath, she continued, "to search. I will not bother you, I swear it."

"You have already come into my home without my consent. Is my brother aware of this treachery?"

"Anteros does not know I am here. I am sorry if I offended you." Zelos cast her gaze to the floor. "Truly, I would be glad to make it up to you."

"I see." Deimos' gaze moved to the rapid rise and fall of her breasts. "And what would that be?"

"Anything you desire." Zelos brought her green eyes, bright with lust, to meet his. "Anything."

"It means that much to have your talisman returned to you?"

"Yes, I am lost without it."

Deimos nodded once. "I would feel the same without Amason."

"Anteros thinks the world would be better off if my chain was not returned to me." Zelos could have bitten off her tongue for uttering those words. What if Deimos agreed and would not let her search?

"And so it would, Zelos." Deimos reached up as if to touch her face. "But the world would also be better off if War were not in it."

His hand dropped back to his side. "But we are like puppets and the Mortal Realm controls us. It is by their twisted needs that we even exist, and by their own desires we deliver such evil into their lives."

Deimos stood silent for a moment, staring off into a cobwebbed corner of the corridor. When he spoke, it was with a touch of kindness. "Go. Find your talisman."

He brushed past her into the room whose door she was ready to open. With a delicious shiver, Zelos realized she was about to enter Deimos' private quarters. Oh, if he only was delayed further for a small amount of time, she would have be privy to his bedchamber.

What then? Had he found me there, would he have resisted taking me to his bed?

She thought not. Yet he did not invite her in. The door was not quite closed and through the crack she could hear Deimos moving about the room. He did not completely shut her out. Did that mean he wanted her to follow?

Dare she take such liberty? And what if she did not please him, would he curtail her search for her talisman?

No, better she did not risk losing the opportunity. With great reluctance, Zelos crept down the corridor - in part, hoping Deimos would forget she was there, and in part, hoping he would follow her.

Zelos found she did not have to enter most chambers. Standing outside each room, she could feel the absence of her chain. Why waste precious time with curiosity when she was drawn toward the uppermost floor?

She could think of several reasons to know what was beyond all those doors but there was not enough time to indulge. She needed to find her chain and leave as soon as possible. A sense of doom pervaded the fortress now that Deimos had returned.

Making haste would be prudent.

Zelos scurried up a staircase and emerged in yet another corridor, before another chamber.

She knew where she was - outside Ares' private quarters. She had been there more than once and should have known that if the chain was not in the altar room, it would be here.

The sensation of her talisman grew stronger. The thread that bound them felt like a taut vine strummed by the wind. The sway made her delirious with joy and she danced with eagerness as she pulled open the heavy doors.

She moved inside the dark quarters and allowed the doors to swing shut. The room was a void, with no sound, as if all life had been sucked away with Ares' spirit. And yet, the tiniest of tiny hums reached her ears.

Ahh, there it was! She could hear her talisman now. Within the walls of this chamber. The sweet, seductive call to immerse oneself in the life of another, to control every breath, to be all there is for the loved one.

To protect, to shield, to keep that one away from any other.

With an index finger lifted, Zelos brought life to the dusty oil lamps. Light flickered, casting weak shadows across the walls. The scent of a chamber fallen into disuse made her nose wrinkle and she wondered why Deimos had not taken such fine quarters for himself.

It appeared all was left exactly the way it was the day Ares fell to Hephaestos' poison. The chair before the cavernous hearth still bore the indentation of Ares' body and the stool held scuff marks from his boots. A woolen cape lay draped across another chair as if casually tossed aside by its owner. A garment that did not belong to Aphrodite, for she would never wear anything so drab.

Did it belong to the female who drove Aphrodite to the madness of forsaking Ares?

Zelos touched the soft cloak out of curiosity, smoothing a wrinkled corner of the cloth. The image of a woman sprang into her mind. A woman whose great sadness brought an unaccustomed sniffle to Zelos; a woman whose essence bespoke of stoic courage and a refusal to accept the inevitable.

Zelos snatched her hand back. She did not want to know more of this woman, or to care what had become of her. Zelos was here to find her talisman and nothing more. She turned back to her search, opening the large wardrobe against one wall.

Inside she found clothing, plain gowns, slippers, stockings, more cloaks but no chain. Frustrated, Zelos turned toward the bedchamber. Where did Ares hide it? The chain was here. She could hear it, feel it, but not see it.

Where was it hidden?

"Come to me, my Pet," Zelos commanded. "Do not make me wait any longer."

The responding cry was like a stab to her heart. Her beloved talisman could not move - it was indeed imprisoned. Zelos followed the whimper until she stood before the hearth. The arch was so high, Zelos could duck inside if she wished. Instead, she stood with hands on her hips, staring into the dark depths.

"Are you inside?" Zelos bent to peer at the scorched bricks. The cry came again. It was higher, above the grate.

Zelos dragged the stool over and climbed up, grasping the mantle for support. As she touched the marble, a current ran through her fingers and into her arms.

Her talisman.

Excited, Zelos reached out to feel along the uneven edges of the surface. Nothing. Her hand came away filthy from dust.

Leaning her forehead against the cool stone, Zelos sobbed, "I know you are here, Dear One, show me where you are."

A faint glow drew her gaze upward. Just above the ledge there was a horizontal line of light imbedded in the wood. Zelos held out her hand and a lamp flew from the wall to the mantel. With the illumination, she could now see the top half of the links of her precious chain.

Ares had sunk his trophy into the wall beneath the place where Amason stood guard.

Or where Amason once was. Ares' talisman holding her talisman captive while he watched from his chair by the fire. Zelos imagined him smiling in hateful triumph.

Zelos clawed at the timber in an attempt to free the chain. She suffered broken nails, bleeding fingers, splinters in her skin, but to no avail. With a twist of her wrist, she pulled a knife from the air and dug at the wall until one link was open and she could insert the tip through it.

She pushed and pried. Pulled with all her strength but could not release the chain from its prison. Screaming with fury, Zelos threw the knife across the room and beat on the mantle with her fists.

Panting, crying, she knew she would never be able to reclaim the chain unless someone helped her.

Deimos.

He could give it back to her.

Leaping from the stool, Zelos took herself down levels until she was standing in Deimos' quarters.

She was spoiling for a fight and damn the consequences.

"Deimos! Deimos, I bid you come here." Zelos turned in circles, checking each gloomy corner as if he would hide from her. Fury turned her vision red. To be so close to her chain and have it denied was unbearable.

Shrieking, Zelos demanded Deimos to appear before her, "From whatever flea-ridden place you have gone, return here for I need your help."

Still nothing. Zelos made another sweep of the room and only then did she see the drapery-disguised doorway on a far wall. Throwing caution aside, she stormed into the chamber, still screeching. Once inside, she came to a stunned silence.

The interior was not the four walls and ceiling she expected. It was, instead, a waterfall. Boulders climbed uphill as if there was truly an embankment behind them and at the mount, water rushed through the opening as if propelled by an invisible river. Sheets of water channeled down to collect in a basin lined with moss-covered rocks.

Beyond the rock, where walls should be - and maybe were but Zelos could not see them - was the hint of forest. The scent of trees, decaying leaves, and damp air flowed past, stirring her hair with a cool breeze.

Deimos stood naked beneath the falling water, his back to

the doorway. His black hair clung between his shoulders in ringlets, drawing her eyes downward to the swell of buttock and strong thighs, to the graceful curve of calves and ankles.

Zelos forgot her anger.

The broad expanse of his back gleamed as water sluiced from his shoulders. Zelos swooned at the sight. She wanted nothing more than to lick the drops of water from his skin, to kiss along the line of his backbone to his hip and around to his manhood.

She sighed, unable to hold back the desire. Stepping into the pool and under the spray of warm water, Zelos slid her arms around his waist. He did not protest.

Even though Deimos did not turn to face her, she knew he wanted her there. She could feel it in the way he tensed at her touch. She slid one hand down to grip the straining line of hardness along his belly and rubbed her breasts upon his back.

Grinding her hips into his buttocks, she was already teetering on the edge of release. As she moved against him, she stroked his manhood, her thumb circling the tip until Deimos groaned with pleasure.

Zelos slipped around to his front and fell on her knees, taking his member in her mouth. She ran her tongue along the exposed head as the foreskin pulled back, biting, sucking and kissing until she felt the hot splash of his juice on her lips.

She licked at it and sucked more for his hardness did not decrease. She held him with one hand while the other stroked between his legs, tickling the spot that would send him reeling once more over into the chasm of bliss.

Before she could bring him again, Deimos yanked her to her feet, his hands strong on her thighs. Lifting her up until she could hook her legs behind his back, he thrust into her bringing a pleasure so exquisite, Zelos screamed out. He filled her completely, his body molding to hers until she thought she would split in half and be overjoyed to die.

Deimos shoved her against the rocks, heaving into her as if he fought in battle, as if he slashed at his enemies with Amason. No weapon could draw her soul from her as much as this body that speared her to the stone behind her.

Zelos shrieked as she came, clawing at Deimos, her body bucking in response to his own release. The heat sprayed inside her this time and she felt it spread through her belly, her womb, and she could not help but think, what if she were to carry his child?

Ahh, Deimos was not finished and they went again and again until they were exhausted, bleeding from the rocks, cross-eyed from satisfaction and collapsed into the pool of water in each other's arms.

"Zelos?" Deimos' voice was hoarse.

Panting, she kissed his lips first before answering his unspoken question. "My talisman. I need your help to get it."

"And this is my payment?" Deimos smiled. "I think you could have simply asked."

"Where would the pleasure have been in that?" Zelos sank deeper into the pool, luxuriating in the heat of the water. "My chain is embedded in the wood above the fireplace mantel in Ares' quarters. I cannot release it myself."

"And you wish for me to get it for you?"

"Yes. Please."

Deimos ran his fingertips along the smooth line of Zelos' upper arm. "If I could, I would."

Zelos sat straight up. "What do you mean, *if I could*?"

"That which Ares has taken away can only be given back by Ares. I have no power to undo that which has been done."

"I do not believe you."

"It is true. There are many deeds that I would retrace if I could, but it is not allowed. We can only go forward."

"How, then? How will I regain my chain?"

"As long as Ares lies between the worlds, so shall your talisman."

"Then Ares must awaken."

"It is not within my power to bring him back."

"You do not want him to return."

"Ares is on his own path. There is nothing I can do to alter that."

"If Ares stirs, the mantle of War will leave you and find its true master. You will be left with nothing."

"I would be left at peace, no longer an unwilling servant."

"You lie." Zelos looked into Deimos' black eyes and saw there the truth. In some ways, it filled her with sadness and yet, she understood what it was to be the minion. The one who was always ordered about, nothing more than a servant.

"You have changed, Deimos, you have embraced the power of bloodshed, pain and fear."

"I see it not as change but of maturity. I am, after all, Terror."

"Reluctant terror, more like. You were drawn to such things but fought the mindless crusade of torment."

"A mindless crusade of torment, yes, that well describes Ares but I have fully learned my lesson: to think too long upon the cruelty of the mortal world is to sink into madness."

"You deem Ares mad?"

"Does not the entire realm? Have not both worlds breathed easier knowing that he is lost between them?"

"Having assumed the role that drove him to this dark place, I can only believe you, too, have lost your sensibilities." Zelos stood up, droplets cascading along her lean torso to return to the water lapping at her thighs. "I beg of you to consider the ill effect the mantle of War has upon you. Do not become Ares."

"I am not, and never will be, my father." Deimos reached for a drying cloth.

"Of course," Zelos answered, a sly glint to her eyes. "Be something that he is not. Force him to awaken and take back this ugliness so that you may claim your own power. Your destiny, not his."

"Zelos, do not attempt to play your paltry tricks upon me. Should Ares survive, the mantle will return to him, but he must find his own way back. I cannot help him."

"You mean you will not help him."

"None of us may help him." Deimos clenched his teeth so the truth would not slip between his teeth. How could anyone help when no one knew where Ares was?

"You would just let him lie there in peace while you have none? You would let his every need be cared for while you listen to the petty aggressions of every living thing?"

"Above all the creatures that are deployed between Love and War, I would think you, Zelos, would understand me best."

"I do. And the truth is, you are afraid of Ares, of what he will do. Afraid he will take your power from you if he returns."

"And you are a foolish girl who comes too close to War for comfort." Deimos threw the cloth aside and took her in his arms once more.

His kisses sent her spiraling out of control and into delirious abandon. She bit his lip and their laughter echoed amongst the rocky waterfall.

"What is going on here?" A lyrical voice laced with disapproval intruded upon their pleasure.

Both Deimos and Zelos snapped their heads to the side to see an open-mouthed and dismayed Iris staring at their nakedness.

"Deimos." One hand came up to cover her lips as Iris' eyes rounded with insult.

"Iris." Deimos' sudden release sent Zelos tumbling into the water with a great splash. He snatched the cloth from the side of the pool and covered himself. "Why are you here?"

Iris could not speak for a moment as the swirls of color upon her skin brightened into a blueish hue. She could not move her gaze from the knowing grin that bedecked Zelos' face. It was as if Zelos could see right through Iris, into her heart. As if Jealousy could pinpoint the love Iris felt for Deimos and then turn it into something ugly.

With ragged breath, Iris kept her dignity and forced calm to return. She would not allow herself to succumb to the rising sense of betrayal that would tear itself from her belly as she gazed upon the naked and aroused Deimos.

He had no shame, no shame at all. The scent of sex lingered in the air and Zelos, though she remained crouched in the pool of water, kept that maddening and devious expression upon her face. Her nostrils flared with the hunger of a rabid animal on the trail of prey, and she, Iris, was the hunted one.

No. No, she would not become the target of one as base as Zelos, who would rather cause trouble than create harmony. No. Iris refused, her body stiff with rebellion, driving away the insidious resentment that would overtake her natural elation.

"I am here to deliver a message from Hera." Iris lifted her chin and kept her voice steady. "Why have you not delivered Harmonia? The Queen has been expecting her grandchild and has been patient up to this point. Where is Harmonia?"

"Iris." Deimos stepped from the basin and reached for Iris. In turn, she stepped further from his grasp. His hand lingered for a moment in the air between them as if to beseech her forgiveness. "Can we speak in private?"

"You have heard Hera's message. Am I to return with a response?" Iris could not keep the hurt from her voice and hated that Zelos snickered at the tone.

"Zelos, leave us now."

"Oh, so once you have had me, you would dismiss me as if I were no more than a servant?" Zelos rose and stretched arms overhead. Her breasts swelled and her hips moved with a delicious invitation to visit her woman's cave again. "Because the prudent Iris is here?"

"Zelos, be careful, or Hera will hear of your behavior. She would not approve your alliance with her grandson."

"Hera would prefer you as a mate to Deimos?" Zelos threw her head back and shrieked with mirth. "I am the perfect consort for Terror, not you."

"I said no such thing." Iris' complexion was fully stained blue. "I am here to deliver a message. That is all."

"Ahh, but you were hopeful for more, were you not?" Jumping

to the edge of the pool, Zelos tiptoed to Deimos' side, a finger to her lips.

"Was that a secret? Oh, my, forgive me." Zelos ran a hand along his naked back, leaning in to kiss his shoulder blade. "But here I am and I do not believe there is anything left for you."

"Stop." Deimos shoved Zelos away. "Do not torment Iris."

"Why not? She wants you nearly as much as I." A cunning gleam lit the emerald eyes. "Or perhaps she has already lain in your arms and knows the delights you bring."

Seeing the stark truth written across Iris' lovely face, Zelos hooted with unadulterated amusement. "Are you so protected within the confines of Olympus that you believe Deimos would be faithful to you? So dreadfully naïve. Oh, and Iris, I have been told that Deimos has a son by a mortal woman. It is not just with me that he dallies - he spreads his seed across both realms, just like his father."

Before Deimos could seize Zelos, she disappeared. She left behind loud mocking laughter that was a reminder of her other side: Truth.

"Iris."

"She is right." Folding her hands against her breast, Iris withheld the tears that threatened to spill from her eyes. "I did think perhaps we were destined to become mates. Yet I realize it is not to be. You are too much like Ares, and I am not at all like Aphrodite."

"I am not like Ares." Deimos' dark brows knitted together. "I do not have a child. I would not allow that to happen. Zelos seeks to enrage you to suit her own purpose."

Iris cast her gaze to the stone floor, humiliated by her disappointment. She should have known better than to believe, after one wanton moment, that Deimos would swear allegiance to her. Since the Mantle of War descended onto him, he was changed.

"There is no more that needs said other than your response to Hera. Where is Harmonia?"

At Iris' sharp tone, the jagged edge of War rose to the surface. Deimos tightened his lips and his gaze hardened into a cold indifferent stare. His ways were his own. He did not answer to either Iris or Zelos. Or Hera, for that matter.

"Harmonia remains on Cos, where she belongs."

Deimos paced back and forth across the bedchamber, restlessness driving his steps. He kicked at the rug depicting ocean waves lying in the center, resenting the intrusion of his mother's realm into his world. The small carpet was the only piece of Cos he brought with him to Athos, the only reminder he would allow in his chamber.

Love.

Both Zelos and Iris were in love with him. Even he could see that, and though he took pleasure with both, he did not return their affections. He loved only one woman in all the eons he had been in existence, and she was dead.

Grief became a sudden jabbing wound. Deimos grimaced as he relived Niala's death and his part in it. The fierce coupling that brought on the birth of her child and the gush of blood that ended Niala's life.

Staring at his hands, Deimos could once again see the blood running between his fingers as he held the infant, still attached to her mother by the birth cord. He heard Niala whisper, *Take care of her.*

He had not honored his promise. When, in past months, had he inquired about the child? Caught up in the Mantle of War, Deimos had not given the infant another thought.

Hot shame sent a flush throughout his body. The heat crawled up his neck, suffused his face and brought tears to his eyes. Fingers cupped, he could feel the tiny girl squirming against his palms and hear her thin wail, as if she knew her mother had passed beyond their reach.

Dropping his hands to his sides, Deimos closed his eyes and pushed the images aside. Niala's death was in the past and there was naught he could do to change the outcome.

He turned to Zelos' declaration of a child, half human, half divine, a child she claimed was fathered by Deimos. He knew of no such babe.

"It is not possible." Deimos paused in the center of the round rug, his voice bouncing upon the rafters as another memory flooded into his mind.

The harvest ritual, the cavern, his heart connection with the earth goddess, the overwhelming realization that he, Deimos, was not just Terror, but also Survival. A naked and eager young woman who sought her own truth in the waters of the lake.

Pallin.

Had he impregnated Pallin without realizing it? He was not in control on that wild and sensuous night. The earth goddess, Gaea, took charge of them both and neither he nor Pallin refused. They made love with abandon, without thought, embracing the physical pleasure and the spiritual heights they reached. He returned to Pallin's bed after the invasion, when each of their defenses were down to seek comfort from each other.

At either time she could have conceived a child. For Deimos realized, no, he had not maintained control. He had allowed himself to be immersed in the simple delight of physical contact.

To know the truth, Deimos would have to visit Pallin, to view this child, to see if there was a spark of divinity within the human form. To do that, he would have to return to Najahmara, to the source of his deepest sorrow.

There he would relive the guilt of Niala's death.

FOURTEEN

As soon as the evening meal of soup, cheese and bread was ended and the clean-up complete, Inni slipped out of the temple and began the trek along the lakeshore. She wanted to see little Mursilis.

Jahmed told her Pallin did not feel well and could not come to the temple. If Pallin could not visit then Mursilis could not visit. Jahmed refused to speak further of it in spite of Inni's pleas to go to the so-called palace where they lived.

Inni was not stupid. She knew it had something to do with the night she fell asleep in the cave with the little boy. She also knew if she could apologize to Pallin and Hattusilis all would be well. She was certain of this, so certain she was going there now to say how sorry she was and that it would never happen again.

She missed little Mursi so very much, she had to try. He was such a good-natured child and a fun playmate. He made her laugh.

"It is very important to laugh," Inni told a wandering dog. The dog ignored her and continued on his path.

"And he seems much older than six months," Inni continued to no one in particular. "If you saw the way he gurgled, as if trying to speak already, and he grabs at my face, but touches me with a gentleness uncommon to a child of that age.

"I have a great deal to teach him, to show him, to let him experience, things he will not learn locked inside. He has to be out amongst the plants and dirt and water and air to understand how to make potions and salves. He will make a fine healer someday."

Inni ducked her head, averting her eyes until a strange man passed by. She could feel his eyes upon her, searching through her clothes to see what kind of woman she was. Shuddering, Inni drew her cloak tightly about her and prayed there would be no others along the shoreline.

Her thoughts quickly returned to Mursilis. She wanted to show him the sky this evening for there would be many shooting stars to watch. The past few nights had heralded the arrival of a brilliant storm of lights making the heavens particularly entertaining. Mursi would love it.

Inni knew Mursilis was not an ordinary babe. She knew this because he talked with her about many things the others did not understand. Pallin claimed the babbling of her son was no more than nonsense, but Inni knew better. She heard words of great wisdom from the lips of that clever child as his brown-eyed gaze searched Inni's rapt blue stare.

She had cared for the little boy since he was born. She held him, rocked him, and fed him bits of sweet treats even though Pallin frowned on this practice. She was concerned it would make the babe too fat.

"It will not," Inni muttered. "He has the sense to eat only when he is hungry. Mursi has more sense than everyone put together. Especially his father. Especially Hattusilis."

Frowning, Inni kicked at a stone in her path. "Who is not really his father, now is he? I know the secret. You cannot hide the truth from me for I see it in his little face. He does not belong to that horrible man who claims he is our king. No, Mursi is not his, this I know. Pallin lies. They all lie."

Inni paused to watch a few water birds waddle along the

shore in front of her. The birds hoped for a handout and Inni did not disappoint them. She scattered breadcrumbs and as the birds fought over the crusts, Inni talked to them.

"Pallin and little Mursi have not been to the temple in a week's time. Whatever this illness, I must see to it. Jahmed said I should not go visit them, but I must. I must be certain they are well. It is right that I go to see them, is it not?"

The responding fuss of the birds sounded like an agreement to Inni and she laughed aloud. "Even the fowl understand it is necessary to go for a visit."

Inni continued rambling to herself as she approached the perimeter of the king's residence.

"What Jahmed does not know will not hurt her," Inni giggled.

"Halt." A narrow-eyed guard stepped in front of Inni, staff raised to bar the way.

Inni ducked her head in confusion. She did not like this man. He was not Razi. Razi always smiled at her. This one's voice was filled with suspicion.

"You cannot enter the king's domain. Turn back."

Inni fought the panic that climbed from her belly up her ribcage and tried to choke her. "Where is Razi?"

The soldier pursed his lips but did not lower the staff. "Razi stands guard at the temple. If you wish to see him, return the way you came. You are forbidden to continue on this path."

From behind the fall of her hair, Inni caught her breath and cast an inquisitive glance at the soldier. There was more than distrust in his tone, there was a hint of fear. Did he reflect her fright or did he have his own?

More sure of herself, Inni smiled. She meant it to be a coy gesture, one that would encourage the man to let her through. Instead, he glanced past her shoulder toward the village and back to her, searching for a sign of ill intent.

"What do you want?" he barked

"I am here to get Mursi." Inni responded with her head down. Did this man not realize that she spent much time with the king's son, who was also the son of Pallin?

"Prince Mursilis? I doubt that. Now be gone."

"But we are to go up and watch the stars on the plateau. Tonight will be an exciting night as the gods will throw lightening at each other as they play. Mursi must go with me."

"The Prince is a babe in arms, he would have no interest in watching the sky." The mean-eyed guard looked Inni up and down as if she was a troll.

"But he always wants to go with me."

"Leave, you foolish woman, before I beat you senseless."

Inni stared at the ground. How could she tell this man that to sit atop the world was to be embraced by Gaea herself? She raised her chin ready to shout at him but then knew he would not understand. That much she could see in the beady gaze directed at her with such suspicion.

She felt a flare of daring and whispered, "Do not anger Gaea."

"What do you mean?" He slid a glance toward the plateau rim.

"Nothing." Inni answered with a slow grin. "And everything."

"You are mad. Go away." The soldier curled his lip.

"But I must see Mursilis." Inni pointed one skinny arm toward the cottage.

"Go away."

"But I," Inni hesitated. Words sometimes failed her and the one she searched for swam somewhere in the murky depths of her memories. "I am with Jahmed."

"I do not know a Jahmed. Go away."

"Pallin is my friend."

"The Queen has not told me to expect a visitor. Be gone."

"But I am…priestess." There, the word emerged, and Inni straightened her shoulders. "Priestess to Gaea. Do not defy our goddess. Let me through."

"Your goddess does not frighten me. I recognize no other

than my king and my god."

"Your dreadful god." Inni pursed her lips. "He destroys all that he touches." A memory tried to surface, one of blood and pain, filled with smoke and screams. Inni shook her head; she did not want to remember. "Someday, you will see the strength of Gaea and you will be ashamed."

Grunting in disgust, the soldier grabbed Inni by the hair and shouted at her, "Go away, stinking whore. You are not allowed here."

Inni shrieked in terror. All feeling in her legs was lost and she collapsed to the ground as the guard held tight to the long blonde strands.

"Let her go." Ajah rushed along the remaining few feet of the path. Thank Gaea that while she was preparing to visit a pregnant woman of the village she saw Inni leave through the front entrance of the temple and followed her as quickly as she could. It was not fast enough, it seemed, for Inni was already in trouble with Hattusilis' guard - the very thing they all sought to prevent. Ajah shouted again.

"Let her go!"

Before the man could reply, Ajah was upon him and swung her heavy staff at his head. It struck him on the temple, opening a wound. Releasing Inni, the guard fell back with a grunt, one hand slapped over the dripping blood on his face.

"Foul thing, never touch me again." Spitting on the fallen guard, Inni crawled to meet Ajah.

"You whores will pay for this," the guard howled as he climbed to unsteady feet. Already he was heading back to the king's home to summon other men.

"Hurry, Inni." Heart pounding, Ajah dragged her to her feet and urged her along the shoreline in the opposite direction.

No one else was about and with any luck, they had not been seen. Or heard. All the noise and yet not one soldier came running to check. Strange but fortunate. One glance back saw the single guard pausing to press a cloth to his bleeding head. With a relieved sigh, Ajah pressed forward.

The two women did not slow their pace until they were within sight of the village edge. At least there, if she screamed, help would come running. Ajah stopped to catch her breath. It was only then she realized the depth of her actions. Clapping one hand over her mouth, she groaned. A choking cough rattled her chest and gasped with a pain that was not in her body but in her spirit.

"Oh, mercy, what have I done?" Ajah leaned on her staff, too weak to move. She had struck one of the king's men. Woe to her now. The last one who defied Hattusilis was whipped within an inch of his life.

A warning, the townsfolk were told. Let this be a warning.

Inni leaned forward and whispered, "Do not worry, you did not kill him." Inni's smile was heard more than seen as twilight descended. "It was not Razi. I do not understand why it was not Razi. He always helps me."

"Razi stands guard at our temple, he is no longer at the lake path. Jahmed said never go to the cottage where Hattusilis lives. Never. None of us."

"I did not think it would be so troublesome. Pallin does not mind if I care for her babe, why should he?"

"Because he is a tyrant and cares not what Pallin wants or needs." Still worried at her confrontation with the guard, Ajah felt something much deeper: the unaccustomed fury that rose up in her and made her act with violence.

With a heavy heart, Ajah trudged along the remaining route, mindful of the slower woman. Yet Inni was not as frail as she appeared. Even though her blonde hair had grown paler in the aftermath of the invasion of Najahmara, and her legs were bent after the broken bones, Inni moved with grace.

Until a stick snapped beneath her foot. Inni paused with one hand clutching at Ajah as the memory she fought to keep away swept over her. The sudden recollection brought a dizzy spell and a renewed sense of panic. Inni pressed her hands over her ears and began to scream as she relived the brutal details of the invasion that destroyed their lives.

With a growl, the soldier leaped forward, seized Seire and with one quick chop, slit her throat. The old one did not even know what happened, for her film-covered eyes never saw him. She died swiftly at his feet, her blood soaking into the woven rug.

The women set up a shrill howl as one save for Inni. With eyes narrowed into slits, all the rage she suppressed during her years as a priestess fell away. All the abuse she suffered at the slave trader's hands resurfaced and brought with it a frenzied desire to make the soldier suffer.

She lunged for him, clawing and shrieking like a banshee, determined he should die for his travesties. The foreigner struggled with her as the other men fought to subdue the women, beating them back into a corner with fists and dagger hilts. Here and there a blade flashed forth and one fell, and then another, while the grief and horror rose to a higher level.

Inni fought with Seire's attacker, ripping open great gashes with each swipe of her nails. Rivulets of blood and sweat ran into his eyes as he throttled her, shaking her like a beast. Still she kicked and punched at him until he heaved her to one side. She felt her thin nightshift tear from her body as she went face first into the pool of Seire's blood, retching and naked.

Ah, Seire, loyal one, loved one, was all Inni had time to think before the soldier kicked her in the ribs with his rough boot again and again, until she felt her flesh give way and her bones break beneath his foot. She moaned in agony though she did not want the man to know how she suffered. Before the pain had time to recede, he fell upon her from behind and viciously impaled her with his sex.

Inni collapsed in a swoon and would not get up. She wrapped her arms about her knees, releasing pitiful moans that left Ajah frantic. Thankfully, they were not far from their quarters. Tulane heard their cries and fetched Jahmed.

"Ajah, what has happened?" Jahmed could only close her eyes and pray when she heard where Inni had been. "I told you to stay away - why did you not listen to me?"

Once again, she failed to protect her beloved. She noticed Inni was not with the rest of the women immediately after their meal and yet did not look for her. There were too many things calling for her attention to leave the temple.

Inni paid no attention to Jahmed's agitation as she raked at her hair, trying to erase the feel of the guard's fingers. "I wanted to take Mursi up to watch the shooting stars. I know he is very small, but tonight there will be many and I know he would love to see them. I suppose it will have to wait for another time."

Biting her lips, Jahmed nodded. Inni did not understand the danger. She did not understand Hattusilis would just as soon see them all dead as let Inni touch Mursilis.

She did not know that Hattusilis forbid Pallin to bring the babe to the temple. This alone wracked Jahmed with resentment. Why did it need to be this way? Merely because Hattusilis feared them?

She should have told Inni the truth. But how could she? How could she destroy the one thing that kept Inni focused on life rather than cycling down into the darkest of dark places?

What's more, to think her beloved Inni could be further harmed by Hattusilis or his men was insufferable. Jahmed knew she would have to prevent Inni from ever attempting such an outing again.

How, she could not fathom. She could not watch Inni every minute, and yet there must be a way. There must.

Jahmed wiped Inni's face with the edge of her skirt. "Let us get indoors before this madness causes further harm."

The two women half-carried Inni the rest of the way, sending Tulane ahead to make tea. Once settled onto a cot with a hot drink between her fingers, Inni began to cry.

"I am sorry, my Love. These old frightful thoughts, they come upon me without warning."

"Be still, Inni. Please rest and let me finish my work."

"You are angry with me." Inni fussed with the bowl, turning it around and around as she stared down into the amber liquid.

"No, not angry. I am worried you could be hurt. You must never go there again. Will you promise me this?"

"But I just wanted to take Mursilis up to see the stars. I would not hurt him, or lose him. Why can I not see him? When will Pallin bring Mursilis to see me? I miss him. Mursilis loves me. I love Mursilis. I must see him soon or he will cry."

"The babe cannot come here anymore."

"Why? Where is Pallin? She will bring Mursilis to us."

"His *father* will not allow it." The words left a bitter taste in Jahmed's mouth

"Silly." Her tear ceased as Inni began a soft sing-song rhyme. "Silly, silly, silly. Mursi loves me. I love Mursi. Silly, silly, silly."

"Inni, stop, there is nothing we can do to change this. You must accept the way things are now."

"I love Mursilis."

"Yes, I know you love the boy, we all love him." Jahmed smoothed the scarf tied around her many dark braids in a habit she repeated countless times a day. Much of that time, she considered cutting all of them off. She was tired of her hair, tired of everything.

"You must listen to me. Do not go out at night. Do not go near the king's residence. I fear for your safety."

Inni tapped on the side of the small bowl. "I have upset you, Dearest, but I did not mean to. I just wanted to see the babe."

"Truly, Inni, it is dangerous to think you can approach Hattusilis. He is different these days."

"What do you mean by different? Are we not all changed?" Inni shifted and cast her gaze back into the swirling tea. She did not finish her thoughts but withdrew into a huddled ghost of the woman she once was.

Turning away so Inni could not see the worried frown etched upon her face, Jahmed retreated to the medicine room. There were far too many illnesses these days, the healers could scarce keep up.

And besides, work chased away the grief and guilt and allowed her to do something to help.

Ajah watched Jahmed flee the room and felt sad for both women. Life was being squeezed out of them right before their eyes and naught could be done. With a heavy heart, Ajah trailed Jahmed into the healing area.

"There is more, Zahava. I am so sorry but I…" Ajah pursed her lips and blew out an uneasy breath.

"There is more?" Throwing down the rag she used to wipe the tabletop, Jahmed faced Ajah with hands on her hips.

Shamefaced, Ajah bit her lips before replying in a low voice. "The guard had Inni by the hair and I feared he was going to hurt her, so I hit him in the head with my staff. I know it was wrong but I did not know what else to do."

"Mercy!" Jahmed collapsed onto a stool, one palm pressed to her forehead. "Did you kill him?"

"No, Zahava. He was bleeding but standing when we ran."

"He will raise an alarm. Their king will send soldiers for us." Her shoulders slumped in resignation.

"For me. The rest of you did nothing. They will come for me." Kneeling, Ajah took Jahmed's hands in hers.

"They do not know the difference between us. We will all be punished, perhaps put to death. Oh, Gaea, deliver us from this evil." She pulled free from Ajah's grasp and closed her eyes.

As Jahmed leaned against the wall, her dark complexion turned ash-like, Ajah was wracked with guilt. "What can we do? Should I leave? Should I hide? Zahava, I am so sorry."

"Give me a moment. Let me think, child." Holding up one palm, Jahmed met Ajah's gaze and saw the newest heartache etched upon the young woman's face.

"We have had enough grief." With a quick inhale, Jahmed squared her shoulders and lifted her chin. "They can all be damned. They will take none of us away. I will die first. Come, Ajah, help me up."

*****

After the many trails of light ceased arcing across the dark sky, Inni pulled the blanket to her chin and sighed with pleasure. How wonderful to sleep beneath the stars! She was quite pleased that Jahmed bade Ajah take her to the top of the mount to see the celestial event. There even seemed to be a bit of relief in Jahmed's weary expression when she told them to go and enjoy.

And something else, a tension of some kind that lingered at the corners of her eyes as she helped pack bedrolls and a small amount of food and water before the trek up. Jahmed told them to spend the night up on the plateau so they would miss none of the shooting stars.

Inni sighed. She did not mean to be a burden. It made her sad to know she caused Jahmed more angst than already laid upon her back. There was so much work and not enough women to take care of it. There were few girls sent to train with the priestesses and fewer volunteers from the men to help, though she did not understand why.

"And I am not much help, am I? No, I am not. I am sorry, Jahmed. Sorry to be such a burden."

Lifting one thin shoulder, Inni pushed away the trials, wishing only to embrace the beauty of the heavens.

"Ajah, I especially liked the stars when they looked like rain, all falling at once. Ajah?"

There was no immediate answer. The younger woman was right beside Inni only moments ago. Where could she have gone?

"Ajah?"

Inni's concern deepened when there was no response. She could not hear even the hint of Ajah's held breath, as if the younger woman was playing with her. Hide and Seek. Perhaps it was a game.

Inni clapped her hands and called once more to the girl. "Ajah, I do not wish to play tonight. Where are you?"

Pushing the blankets off, Inni rose to her feet and stared into the shadows. The night was still save for the chirping of insects and the rustling of a breeze through brush. A sudden movement to her left tore a sharp gasp from her throat and she jerked backwards, just managing to catch her balance before falling over a boulder.

Concern turned to fright. What if Ajah had wandered away in the dark and fallen over the side of the ridge? What if she lay on the side of the mount with broken bones, unable to climb back up?

Inni's head bobbed from left to right, her gaze going from one end of the plateau to the other. What should she do? Get help to search? She could not climb down the backside of the ridge herself. Even if she found her and Ajah was hurt, she would not be able to lift her.

But if she brought men to search the hillside and possibly the honeycomb of caves, the priestess' secret place would be exposed and they would never be able to return. Hattusilis would have this entrance closed off just like the other side of the mount.

Jahmed would never forgive her.

What if Ajah went into the cave? What if the same voice that called Inni also called to Ajah? What if she were lost deep within the caverns?

"What should I do?" The cold sweat of fear dampened beneath her arms and along her spine. "What to do? What to do?"

She crouched and began to rock back and forth. Her mind clouded as terror took her back to blood and flames, hoarse shouts, screams, and her own ruin. Whimpering, she buried her face in her skirt, her arms wrapped around her knees.

"It is over, it is over," she moaned, "it is done, it is done, do not plague me this way."

But the carnage washed over her in all its horrifying detail as if she lived it again. The murder of Seire, the rape of the girls, the attack on Inni, the crunch of bones breaking and the acrid scent of the serpent as Kulika was summoned.

"Why, why?" Inni sobbed. "We did nothing to you."

She shrieked as a hand settled on her shoulder.

"Inni?"

Ajah's voice was scarce more than a whisper but her touch brought Inni back to the present. Shaking, Inni put her arms around the younger woman and clung to her, ear pressed to Ajah's chest. The sound of her heart beating brought Inni back to a place of calm.

"Are you ill? What is wrong?"

"I…it…." Inni sat back on her heels and looked into the solemn eyes staring down at her. The darkness played tricks on Ajah's face, and for a moment, Inni saw not the priestess Ajah was becoming, but someone much older.

Inni shook her head, blinking away the thought. She hugged Ajah again. "I was frightened I had lost you forever."

"Hush. I am not lost, nor will I be." Ajah lightened her tone. "Now we must be very careful climbing down the mount in the dark, but I dare not light a torch. We do not want to be seen."

"Where were you? I looked all about and I did not see you."

"I am sorry, Inni." Ajah glanced away. "I thought I heard something, over there, behind the broken stone markers. I went to see if we were followed."

"Were we followed?" Inni caught her breath.

"No. No, there was nothing."

"I thought you might have gone into the caverns. You could be lying within the tunnel and I would not be able to find you."

"Why would I go into the cave at this time of night? Why would I leave you here by yourself?"

"We are to find Niala and help her. I thought perhaps you had gone looking for her."

Ajah replied with gentleness. "Niala is dead. I saw her body placed in Gaea's sacred chamber within the mount. You were too ill to attend the ceremony, but I was there. She is gone."

"Mayhap her body was placed in a tomb, but Gaea tells me Niala is not truly dead. Her spirit lives." Inni grasped Ajah's hands.

Ajah's chest tightened and though she did not want to acknowledge the sensation, it was a response to some bit of spoken truth. She, too, had heard the whispers. They rode on the winds, rustled in the grasses, hissed in the rains, and even warmed her face when the sun was out. Their undertones were loudest in the dark.

It was the murmur of voices that took Ajah behind the stones. She was certain they were followed and feared it was soldiers coming to capture them. With her hand resting on the hilt of a dagger at her waist, Ajah went to see.

As Inni stared with rapt attention at the sky, Ajah crept to the stones, one hand resting on the hilt of a dagger tucked into a belt at her waist. If it was, indeed, Hattusilis' men, she was prepared to defend them to the death.

No one was there. Not a soul about, thank Gaea. It was merely the night wind swirling about the broken monuments. Yet she swore it sounded like a voice calling out to her.

"Inni, I, too, have heard something but I believed it to be the voice of my spirit guide. He is pressing to become part of me. He wants to share his power yet I am afraid." Ajah swallowed hard. "I am afraid to go through with the rites of passage and have his image put upon my body."

Inni gazed off toward the horizon. "We have all stood in that place of fear, Ajah. The ceremony is difficult. I recall mine very well. It was both awful and exhilarating, though I cannot properly describe it."

"You recall that far back?"

With a laugh, Inni touched Ajah's arm. For once, her sensibilities felt like her own, as if she was returned to her former state. She felt strong and at ease, truly a priestess of Gaea and not some fumbling lost and wounded child.

"I do and I do not regret one moment of dedicating my life to Gaea. We are always led to our own destinies. It is whether we accept or decline that is important."

"That is very wise, Inni."

"I am not always a fool." Inni smiled. "We have the choice to do as they request or turn away. What do you want, Ajah?"

"I do not know but I also feel the answer is within the

sacred cavern. I have felt this for some time now."

"Then let us walk through the tunnels tonight and see what needs to be seen. Let us hear the voices, let them guide us and we shall put this to rest, one way or the other."

Ajah paled at the thought and yet she knew she had to decide if she could accept the spirit guide. If not, she would never become a full priestess. She would never be able to lead her people.

"Yes, Inni. Let us find an answer, one way or another."

With great care, they moved along the steep path from the plateau to the hidden entrance of the cave. Once inside, Ajah lit a torch. The two women looked at each other and nodded before slipping into the tunnel that led to Gaea's sacred hall and Niala's final resting place.

Trembling, Inni stepped into the ritual chamber. The earlier clarity - that bright moment of seeing both their paths lit before them - waned and fear-driven weakness settled into her bones.

Echoes of long-gone chants, of drums and whispered words from Gaea spun through her head. The throne made from natural rock formation sat waiting for Gaea to grace it once again. A small sob tore from Inni as she looked past the throne to a shrouded bier.

A figure was outlined by a thin cloth, draped in such a way that could be either male or female. It lay silent, without rise or fall of its chest, but Inni did not smell death. Instead, there was the faint scent of lemongrass and cinnamon, of myrrh and frankincense. No rotting flesh. Instead it was the clean scent of the herbs used to wash and prepare a body for burial.

Inni's heart thumped as she moved toward the bier, pulling Ajah along with her. As Inni reached for a corner of the shroud, Ajah broke from her grip.

"I do not want to look under the cloth." Ajah wagged her head from side to side in vehement disagreement as the torch threw shadows upon the rough walls. "I do not want to see what these past months have done to Niala Aaminah. And, I have been told it is bad fortune to look upon the face of Death."

"Who has said such a thing?" Inni fingered the edge of the dusty shroud. "Someone who forces his belief upon us? Razi, perhaps?"

"There is no force." Ajah lowered her chin with a sharp exhale. "Razi is not like the others. He is kind and gentle."

"Razi comes from a land where the dead are burned, not buried. Our custom is to return the dead to the earth, to Gaea. To do otherwise is to insult to the goddess."

Ajah agreed. It was a constant struggle and many tears were shed over burning funeral pyres. Ajah had seen women gather the ashes with care and knew it was to bury what was left. Something had to return to Gaea, some little piece of the dead, or the sacred circle was broken forever and one could not return in another life.

"It is a sacrilege that Niala was not buried. Here she lies, between the worlds, neither here nor there. How could you have done that to her?"

"Consider it an honor, Inni. Only Niala could be put to rest within Gaea's chamber. Only Niala could have been preserved and handed to Gaea above ground, as a jewel of the heavens who gave herself to Earth. It was the right thing to do. It was all we could do. Please try to understand that."

"But her spirit has been captured. She was not released to the Great Mother, which is why Gaea speaks to me." Wringing her hands, Inni stared at the dusty bier. "Niala must be released from this prison."

With shaking fingers, Inni lifted the edge of the shroud. Her breath caught and would not release. Her chest ached with grief at the silent tender face of Niala Aaminah.

There was an ashen cast to Niala's skin instead of the sunny warmth that Inni remembered. The skin stretched tightly against the bone, hollowing her eyes and cheeks. Her lips were thinned in repose, and yet, Niala was whole, untouched by the decay of death.

Tears rained down as Inni touched Niala's hair with

shaking fingers. She bent and placed a kiss upon the cool forehead. Her tears left a damp trail behind.

"Ahh, Niala, I thought never to gaze upon you again. I thought you were lost forever yet I knew you were not dead. Hidden so you could not be harmed, but not dead. Not at all. But why do you lie here now when we most need you?"

The only response was a dry rattling sound that slithered around the corners of the cavern and raised the hair on Inni's neck.

"Zahava, you must awaken, we need you." Inni stroked Niala's cheek. "Open your eyes, wake up and see me here with you. I have come to help you."

The rustling sound repeated, much like the wind through the dried grasses in the winter. No words. Still Inni understood it was Niala Aaminah speaking to her, trying to tell her something.

A tremor ran down Inni's back as she thought she saw a slight rise and fall of Niala's chest. The faintest of breaths, like a cloud wisp floating in the sky, scarce moving and yet in a different place with every blink.

"Ajah, what should we do? We cannot leave her here." Restless, Inni began to stroke Niala's thick braid. It was no longer tight and smooth the way Niala liked it.

Without thought, Inni untied the scrap of leather that held the braid together. The sections of hair came loose and spread across the wooden bier, hanging down and nearly touching the floor.

Inni combed out the strands with her fingers, each stroke with love. The scent of honeysuckle rose from the rough curls as the warmth in Inni's hands warmed Niala's hair. It was traditional to wash the deceased with water infused with the flowering vine.

Honeysuckle was endless - it never died back, it continued to live on. It represented the grace of the Great Mother and eternal life within her bosom.

Inni brought a handful of Niala's hair to her nose and inhaled. If Niala were truly dead, there would be no lingering smell of flowers. There would be a putrid decayed scent that would make her gag.

"Niala, I know you can hear me. Please open your eyes. Be here with us now."

The more Inni begged, the more frantic she became. With a whimpered moan, she stepped away from the bier. "She cannot be dead. It is not possible. Gaea said she lived. Niala cannot be dead."

Inni reached for Ajah but her hand did not encounter the younger woman. Her fingers met air. With a strangled shriek, Inni whirled about. "Ajah?"

Ajah sat on the stone formation, her shoulders against the smooth back, her arms placed along the side bolsters. Her eyes were closed, her head tilted as if she heard the drums. Her lips were parted as if to whisper the invocation to Gaea.

The words Niala Aaminah always said before the harvest ritual could now begin. These were the words that would bring the spirit of Gaea into Niala's body so that the great mother could bless the people of Najahmara, the same words that would start the milk flowing from her breasts as shared bounty of the earth.

Stumbling forward, Inni fell to her knees in front of Ajah. "Great Mother, do you wish to speak to me?"

At first, there was no sound. Ajah's lips moved but nothing escaped, not even a whisper. Inni rose to her feet and bent near to Ajah, to better hear the words of the Great Mother.

Stop him.

A faint murmur, scarce loud enough to reach Inni's ears.

"Stop who?"

There was no response. Inni puzzled over this, then decided Gaea spoke of Hattusilis and the madness that gripped him. Accepting this as the meaning, Inni leaned closer.

"How?"

Another long pause.

Invoke me.

Inni's gaze slid to the silent figure lying on the bier.

"How? We no longer have Niala to hold your grace."

This one.

With a huge gasp as if she had held her breath, Ajah jerked and opened her eyes. "Inni, why do you stand so close to me? And why am I sitting here? I should not be here, I should not be here at all. Let us go, now. Now."

Cold, shaking and utterly frightened, Ajah slid from the throne and grabbed Inni's elbow. "We must go. Now."

"Of course." Inni gave her arm over to Ajah's persistent tugging and with one confused backward glance, left the sacred cavern.

Humming to herself, Inni allowed Ajah to lead the way to the temple gardens. She forgot they were to sleep upon the plateau, yet it did not matter. Niala could not be dead and appear the way she did. Inni smiled, she was right. She knew it all along. Niala was alive.

All seemed quiet at the temple, to Ajah's relief. The guard at the rear was not Razi but someone different, one who snored peacefully in his chair next to the entrance. For this, Ajah was grateful, for Razi asked too many questions. On this night, she had no answers.

As they tiptoed into the recesses of the temple, all seemed calm. Nothing was out of place or appeared as if violence was done. They crept along the corridor, and in passing, she saw Jahmed curled up on a pallet in one corner of the medicinal area.

No harm had come to her, thank Gaea. With a soft cluck, Ajah led Inni to her quarters. Inni would sleep with her tonight and on the morn, she prayed all was truly well.

Perhaps they had dodged a disaster after all.

FIFTEEN

Phobos glanced behind him with an uneasy twitch of his skinny shoulders and hurried to catch up with Eris. The forest was dark, without a speck of sunlight allowed to shine through the heavy canopy of branches. Eris would not call any source of light to them other than a tiny glowing ball he held in his palm.

"What was that?" Phobos hissed. "It sounded like a giant crashing through the undergrowth of this forsaken place."

Eris shrugged and kept a careful pace as he watched for signs of his mother and sister having passed through the woods. Tracking skills were taught to him as a child growing up in the very same forest that now swallowed his kin.

"There may be some horrible beast waiting to devour us," Phobos continued, his voice rising. His dark curls were damp with sweat and sticking to his face and neck while the insects buzzed about his head in a noisy celebration of their next meal.

"Do you not hear that?" Phobos demanded. He paused to listen, grabbing at Eris' arm. "What is that?"

"It is nothing." Eris whirled about and gave Phobos a shove, causing him to stumble back a few steps.

A low branch stabbed the boy in the back. Phobos shrieked and thrashed at his invisible attacker.

"Phobos, calm yourself. Your panic will draw every creature in this forest to our sides. If they smell your fear, they will call to their packs and we will be surrounded. I command you to stop your wailing."

"What creatures? Ogres? Trolls? Monsters? What lives in this wilderness that will kill us?" Phobos' breath came in great huffs. With every creak and rustle, he turned in circles watching the gloom at the edges of their small lamp with wide eyes.

"And I am hungry and thirsty as well. If we do not die at the hands of some terrible beast, we will surely starve to death."

"Stop moaning. We are of the immortal race and will not die in these woodlands."

"They can still capture us, hurt us, torture us, and keep us from ever going home."

"There is nothing here that is a match for us, Brother. You have braved the bloodiest of battles and yet are afraid of a few shadows and creepy crawlies?" Eris scoffed. "Remember who you are, and the loins from whom you sprang."

"In battle I can see what I am fighting." Phobos shivered. "Here, I cannot. Anything could attack us, pounce on us, tear our eyes out, and we would be helpless. We would not see it coming. We could be blinded for eternity!"

"Be quiet, Phobos. Allow yourself to surrender to the living forest. Let the trees speak. Listen to them. They will help us."

"Even after the demon-spawns burned the Sacred Grove?"

"Even then. I am a child of this woodland - I may have the red blush of War in my bones but I carry the green blood of my Sylph ancestors in my veins. The ancient ones will help us if you would but silence yourself."

"What *is* that racket that follows our every footstep?"

Eris took in a deep breath, lifting his nose to better catch the scent. He closed his eyes and savored the earthy smell of the forest floor, the layers upon layers of plants and wood returning to dirt.

The aroma of damp shade, of cool water and thick growth washed over the Sylph, bathing him in wistfulness for a simple life he no longer claimed.

As a child playing within the depths of this very timber, his mother taught him to fear nothing for all things draw their energy from the same source. If honored, all things are amiable, according to the Sylph creed.

Chuckling, Eris gave a quick shake to his head. War taught him the opposite. To survive in the forest, one learned to identify every creature that lived within the deep woods by the trail of odor it exuded.

What followed them was not a beast. It was the Kobaloi. He had no doubt the extra noise was meant to trick them into following the sound and therefore wind up trapped.

Eris held up his hand in a gesture to pause the non-stop, anxious chatter of his brother.

"What is it?" Phobos whispered.

"Rather, *who* is it?" Eris whispered in return. "The Kobaloi follow us."

"What...what are they?"

"They are a tribe of dark elves that inhabit the deepest part of the forest. It would be best if we could avoid them."

"What do they want?"

"No doubt they would like to roast us on a spit and eat our flesh."

"They are cannibals?" Panic rose like fog on warm ground seeking cooler air. "We must leave, now!"

"Brother, there is nowhere for us to go."

"Please take us out of here and back to Athos." Phobos danced about his brother in a terrified shuffle.

"I will not leave until I have found my mother and our sister."

"What if these dark elves have captured, killed, and feasted on them already? What good would it do for us to follow them to this fate?"

"They cannot kill us."

"Argh, that is worse," moaned Phobos. "We would be roasted alive!"

"If the Kobaloi wish a fight, then we will provide one. I have only to think of a battle and the Hordes of War will descend to assist us."

"Oh…oh…yes…that…is…right." Phobos' breath came in gasps as he leaned over, palms resting on his knees. As he stared at the ground, eyes watering, nose running, he noticed the clatter around them had ceased. He felt Eris grip his shoulder in warning. Slowly straightening, Phobos sucked in a deep breath.

They were surrounded by small savage elves with sharp teeth and sharper spears. Their skin was clay-red and heavily tattooed in swirling indigo designs. All eyes, big, round, black eyes that filled the socket leaving no room for white or any other color, they stared with malevolence.

Phobos put one hand on the dagger at his side. "Can you call the Hordes now?"

Eris and Phobos sat back to back on the bare ground, hands and feet bound with a thin rope looped about both their necks. They made little to no movement. They had been in this position for long hours without food or water or rest. The Kobaloi had taken them prisoner, which was far better than being murdered. Nevertheless, Phobos was frightened out of his mind.

When they rode with War, they were protected. Here, they were plain and simple victims of circumstance, though why Eris allowed them to be captured without a struggle was beyond Phobos.

As night fell and the single guard nodded off, Phobos whispered, "Eris, I am sorry for your mother and for our sister, but please take us out of this muddle."

When Eris did not readily answer, Phobos slammed his head back against his brother's, eliciting a grunt of surprise.

"I do not see how this is helping anyone. Why do you leave us like this when you could easily release us so that we may fight, or take us back to Athos? Or at the least, call Deimos or the Hordes, as you promised. I cannot bear much more of this."

"They mean us no harm. Now be quiet."

"I will *not* be quiet," hissed Phobos. "They are going to kill us."

"They cannot kill us, we are immortal."

"What if they found a way?"

"The only way is Amason and Amason is at Athos."

"Perhaps there are other ways. Look at what happened to our father from the poison concocted by Hephaestus. These *things* are savage - we cannot know what they might do to us. Please take us out of here. I am begging you."

Although Phobos could not see Eris shake his head, he felt the movement. "Do not cry like a baby, Phobos. You are part of War. We face all battle conditions with courage."

"I hate you." Phobos spat on the ground. "You are arrogant and selfish."

"Besides," continued Eris, "We must wait with patience as they hold my mother somewhere within the Kobaloi confines. She, too, is a prisoner."

"Patience? That is...." Phobos fell silent for a moment. "Wait. She is here? How do you know?"

"I was raised in these woodlands and I, of course, speak their language. Or at least enough of it to understand what they are saying."

"And you did not try to reason with them?"

"I do not want them to know I understand. Unlike the older immortals who can adjust to all cadences of the Mortal Realm, we are thought to be ignorant of these private conversations. It is to our advantage."

"You are certain your mother is here? What of our sister?"

"I have heard my mother's name repeatedly but not Alcippe's." Eris shook his head again. "We must be still and wait. We have no other choice."

"But I am hungry and thirsty."

"You must break yourself of this indulgent habit of food and water. Your body does not need sustenance."

"But I like it. And I know you also indulge, so do not tell me I am too much a child because I am not."

"Keep your voice down. Do not draw attention to us."

Too late. Moments later, rough hands yanked them to their feet and drove them forward with spears cutting into their sides. The young men shuffled with an awkward two-step since they were still bound together. Neither could see where they were going and could do no more than follow orders. They were brought within a cave of fragrant tree boughs lit by a single torch and unceremoniously shoved to the ground.

Phobos lay face down in the dirt as Eris rolled atop him to have a view of the shelter. Therein his gaze fell upon a startling sight.

"Mother?"

"What?" Phobos' voice was muffled by the ground. Coughing out bits of debris, Phobos rolled over, forcing Eris into the dust. "Your mother is here? Where? Where is Alcippe? Is our sister here?"

"I do not know, you fool-monger." Eris shoved his brother, jabbing with his elbows. "Stop moving, I cannot see who is here."

"But I want to see, too." Phobos struggled, digging his heels into the loose soil.

"Stop," Eris kicked at his brother, "before I break all your bones."

"You can try." Phobos' words came out muffled as his face was once again buried in the earth.

The boys were jerked upward by the ropes that bound them. Standing on their feet, they could both see Kobaloi tribesmen surrounded them with spears pointed and ready to disembowel the two if they made any movement. The wave of scowling men parted to create a path for one with a large headdress made of bones and feathers. He approached with a double-edged blade gripped in one fist.

Aglauros could be seen huddled beyond the circle of fierce sentries with her own guards ringing her. A half-moon of Kobaloi women lined a fire pit with leaping flames. Their ominous silhouettes loomed large on the stone walls, appearing as ghouls who watched and waited for bloodshed.

Both young men shuddered.

"Call the Hordes," Phobos screeched.

Aglauros lifted one finger to her lips before lowering her head, her gaze averted.

"Ni'madra," Eris whispered, his eyes hardening at the sight of his mother, bruised and battered, her clothing torn. There was no doubt she was abused.

Dirty, sweating and frightened, Eris and Phobos fell silent. Bravado gone, worry now in its place. They could not be dispatched to the Shadowland but Aglauros could.

The Kobaloi shaman stood before them, feet apart, blade glistening in the light of the fire. He tapped its tip against one palm while he studied the two filthy boys. He spoke over his shoulder, clearly addressing Aglauros.

"What did he say?" Phobos jiggled up and down with apprehension. "What is he saying?"

"He is asking my mother if we are truly her sons." Eris tilted his head to better hear. He could not understand every word but enough to get the sense of their conversation.

"He says we don't appear to be great warriors. Just little boys who cannot fight the beasts that attacked my mother and stole," Eris choked. "The beasts who stole our sister and the Kobaloi children."

"Are they the same ones that burned the Sacred Grove?"

"Be still, I cannot hear them."

"But are they the flying monsters your grandmother spoke of?"

"I do not know. Be quiet." Eris bristled. "They want us to find the children and bring them back, but they do not think we are fierce enough to fight these fiends."

"The flying monsters. They want to send us after the flying monsters?" Phobos choked, panic rising once again in his blood.

"We are without Deimos and the Hordes of War - we do not even have the hounds. How could we possibly fight these awful things? Eris, we cannot do this."

"Oh, yes. Yes, we can." Just as it was in Phobos' nature for panic to rise under strain, the thought of mayhem rose up in Eris. To cause strife, to create chaos and confusion, to set one against another - that was Eris' nature. He grew excited by the prospect of displaying it to its fullest power.

"I will do anything for my mother and sister." Eris spoke through gritted teeth as the shaman turned back to them with his wicked blade extended. "Anything."

"She is my sister, too. I am not a coward. If you go, I go."

"Then it is settled. We do as they ask. We go after the flying monsters."

"We do not even know what they look like or where they went. How will we find them?"

"I am certain they will advise us."

As Eris' last words were whispered, the shaman cut the ropes binding them together. The boys stumbled, fell, and were again lifted, this time with less roughness.

The shaman crooked his fingers at the boys.

"He wants us to come with him," Eris murmured. When his gaze met that of Aglauros, his heart leapt at her weary smile. He was going to save her. He swore it on his heart. He and Phobos would save them all.

They were taken to a small creek to bathe, and after, given sustenance. Even Eris was grateful for the attention. Although his portion was much smaller than the amount Phobos wolfed down, he indulged in a bit of the dough-wrapped meat and flask of clean water,

Phobos stuffed his mouth full amid the coos of the Kobaloi women who brought food. The women patted Phobos on the head, shoulders and back, stroked his cheeks and one woman even leaned in to sniff his curly black hair.

"Yes, of course, you are quite pretty, are you not?" Eris waved a hand at his brother. "But do not get used to this consideration. We are being prepared for war with their finest feast."

Phobos' reply was stifled by the warm pie crammed in his mouth.

"And we do not know the source of that meat. It may be one of their enemies. I told you they are cannibals."

Phobos opened his mouth and let the food drop out onto the ground. "What? Ugh. I think I shall be sick."

"Eris, you are cruel to tell the young one such a thing." Aglauros came to sit beside Eris, her high-pitched voice music to his pointed ears. "The meat is from their hunt, some woodland animal not quick enough to escape."

Grunting in disgust, Phobos made a face at Eris and continued eating his way through a basket of pies.

"It is because he is still a child that they are attracted to him."

"I am *not* a child."

"To them, you are." Aglauros smiled at Phobos.

"Ni'madra, I am so happy to see you but what are these things that have stolen our sister? Tell me what has happened."

"My brave son." Aglauros hugged Eris with both arms, rocking him as if he were a small babe. "It was because of the Kobaloi I survived the attack that took your sister."

Aglauros closed her eyes and swallowed hard, nearly unable to continue. Tears slid from the corners of her eyes as she went on. "I took Alcippe and ran into the forest to draw the creatures away from the Sacred Grove. Once we were under the shelter of the trees, I could no longer see what they did. I could only smell the smoke. We could not return therefore we went forward, away from our village."

"Ni'madra, we first went to our homeland and there I saw Pehun. The beasts abandoned their quest once they saw you flee and the fire was extinguished when it began to rain. It appears they only wanted Alcippe. No doubt because she is the daughter of...."

"Shhh, my Son. Do not speak of her parentage, it will only make matters worse." Aglauros held up a cautionary finger.

"Where did these beasts come from?"

"I do not know. I ran after they attacked the Sacred Grove, ran until I was exhausted and could carry your sister no further. I found a small clearing in the woods to rest for the night. I heard nothing, saw nothing until they were upon us." Shuddering, Aglauros rubbed her arms and held herself in a tight huddle.

"The fire had dwindled, but I still saw them. There were two creatures with great horns wielding awful blades astride giant horses. They shouted at me in a language I did not know.

"I am certain their intention was to kill me and steal Alcippe from my arms save for a small band of Kobaloi hunters resting nearby. They heard the commotion and attacked the creatures with a vengeance. These brave souls shot arrows and spears, forcing their retreat."

"The Kobaloi saved you and for that I am grateful. I owe them a great debt. Are you certain these beasts are the same that attacked the Grove?"

Nodding, Aglauros sniffed and wiped her nose on her sleeve. "It was dark when our home was raided, but I saw them by the leaping flames of the many burning trees. Giant snorting horses that flew through the air as if riding on land, horned creatures astride with great spears. I knew in my heart the monsters wanted Alcippe."

"It would appear you are right."

"Your sister and I were cared for by the Kobaloi tribe." Aglauros touched her bruised and scratched face. "Save for them, I would be dead. As it is, Alcippe was later taken.

"One early morning there came an unearthly wailing, a warning of sorts. Before, the attacks came out of the darkness. This time it was daylight when an entire batch of these dreadful things spilled out of the air and raided the Kobaloi encampment.

"This time, there was an addition - great four-legged, shaggy beasts with blood-red ears and eyes that snarled with great gaping maws. Their drool burned when it touched my skin while they tore at me. These beasts distracted the Kobaloi warriors, it took every adult, women included, to fight them. This allowed the horned ones on horses to do their wicked deed.

"All of the children were snatched away." Aglauros released a gagging sob. "I can only guess they did so because they did not know which child was Alcippe."

"Alcippe was born of immortal parents. They cannot kill her."

"I do not know what these things intend, but I fear they will slay every Kobaloi child until they discover her."

And there she stopped as the full intent of her words soaked into the boys. Phobos laid the last meat pie down and stared at Eris, who returned his grave expression.

"Alcippe does not look like the Kobaloi - why would that be necessary?"

"Then perhaps not for that reason. Perhaps out of spite since the Kobaloi wounded some of their own. I do not know." Aglauros moaned into her hands. "I do not want the blood of these children upon my head. I already bear the burden of my own folk dying."

"Ni'madra, I am sorry to bring this pain upon your head. I swear, we will find her. We will find all of them and bring them home." Eris felt his own power surge forth. "If I must, I will call Deimos. He has assumed the Mantle of War and can destroy these things with scarce effort."

Phobos' eyes glittered as his countenance also shifted to one answering the call of War. "We will avenge the Kobaloi and find our sister. She will return with us."

Eris put a hand upon his mother's shoulder. "These creatures did not have appear from thin air. Where did they come from?"

Aglauros inhaled a faltering breath. "It is hard for me to say. They shot out of an opening that appeared amongst the boughs of trees. It looked like a giant hole shimmering with every kind of light and color, like a round rainbow."

"A rainbow? Quite odd."

"I have not seen such a thing before. It was as if the beasts slid out of this glistening tunnel and into the camp."

"I know of only one who connects to rainbows. One who might know what this means."

Eris and Phobos exchanged a glance.

"Iris."

Iris of the Rainbows stood before Eris with a most perplexed expression on her pretty face. With hands on her hips, she surveyed the forest clearing, taking careful note of the small dark beings with pointed teeth and even more pointed spears standing in silence around them.

She saw a woman with pale green skin and hair several shades darker standing to one side of the area. The woman was known to Iris as Aglauros, mother of Eris. Curious that she was present, Iris also noticed Phobos, his gaze cast down upon the ground, one bare toe digging into the lichen and dirt.

"Eris, may I ask what this is about?"

"Of course. I will explain." Eris brought forth his best placating smile. "I am grateful you accepted my call."

Iris shifted from one dainty foot to the other and smoothed the front of her short white tunic. "You sounded a bit distraught. I thought perhaps you summoned me because Deimos has need of me." She glanced over her shoulder, hoping he was close by.

"Ahh, no." Eris blinked. "Deimos is not here."

"I can see that. Why, then, did you call me? A message for my mistress, perhaps?"

"Ahh, no." Eris jerked on shoulder as Phobos jabbed him in the ribs.

"Ask her."

"Be quiet." Eris jabbed Phobos in return.

"Just ask her." Phobos pushed Eris.

Eris shoved hard and the younger boy stumbled. "I will. Now stop."

"Boys, I have no time for your games. What do you want?"

"Iris, have you ever seen a round rainbow?" Eris waved his arm in a circle and pointed at the tops of the trees. "A very large round rainbow? In the sky? Sort of wavering, with all sorts of colors? Have you ever seen anything such as that?"

The iridescent tone of Iris' complexion darkened with hues of blue. Biting her lip, she followed the line of Eris' hand to stare up at the thick canopy of branches.

"You cannot see the heavens from this vantage."

"No, but if you could, would it be possible to see a round rainbow?"

"From here, I would say not."

"Not just from here." Impatience edged Eris' tone. "From anywhere?"

Aglauros stepped forward and dipped her head in acknowledgement of Iris' station. She spoke in her high-pitched reedy voice. "What I saw appeared as if in the boughs of the trees, very much like a flat bubble of soap."

"Have you heard of such a thing, Rainbow goddess?" Eris rushed to cut off Aglauros' words for he did not want to frightened the amiable young woman, who already stood with her nose wrinkled, wearing a distressed frown.

After a moment of hesitation, Iris spoke. "Rainbows come in many shapes, for they are a reflection of the Sun's fire caught in water."

"A rainbow could not, then, appear at night?"

Iris shrugged. "If there was water in the air and a fire on the ground, a rainbow could form. Unlikely and unusual, but I suppose it could happen."

"There was no rain. Our fires were burned to embers and yet this rainbow-like thing appeared. Out of it leaped horrible creatures with red ears and red eyes." Aglauros came forward and refused to cease her description even though Eris grabbed her arm.

"Upon their backs rode warriors with cold eyes reflecting

the dark rainbows. They held wicked blades aloft and we feared for our lives. As they passed through," Aglauros shuddered, "I heard wailing like I have never heard before. They came from amongst the trees, straight from the rainbow above our heads. Honored one, do you know of these spectral beings?"

Pressing the back of her hand to her forehead, Iris closed her eyes. Her worst nightmare had just been described. She could not part her lips enough to utter a single phrase, so shaken was she by their account.

"May I sit?"

Eris assisted Iris to the fire and found a smooth log for her to rest upon. He sat at her feet, staring with rapt attention at the young woman. The back of his neck and shoulders tingled and his hands grew restless. He felt a battle was in the offing and was glad for it.

Phobos crouched nearby as Aglauros and the Kobaloi gathered to listen. Though the Kobaloi did not understand the language in which Iris spoke, they were aware of the importance of her words. Aglauros translated for them as best as she could.

"I scarce know how to begin this story, for it is not what you will expect from me." Iris twisted her fingers together, staring at her multi-hued skin. She remained quiet for a few moments, gathering her thoughts, before she continued in a soft voice.

"I was not born to an Immortal of the Olympic Realm - I hail from the Fey Realm There is only one other who knows the truth of my existence, and that is Hera, my mistress.

"My given name is Branwen. My mother is Pennarddun, a queen of the Sidhe folk. I am of the Blue Water Tribe." Iris straightened with a touch of pride and an inhale of those things now lost to her.

A moment later, she exhaled in a defeated slump and continued her story. "My brother - whose name I refuse to speak - bade me enter into a marriage with Matholwch. In my brother's eyes, this was the perfect match, for Matholwch is also a king of the Sidhe folk and our union would create a strong liaison between the two dominions.

"Although I protested mightily, my mother did nothing to

prevent the wedding. In fact, I believe she was relieved to see me upon this journey for reasons I do not wish to go into. Upon the first night of this marriage," the word dripped venom unheard before in the gentle voice of Iris, "my husband ravaged me."

Eris' pointed ears twitched as he leaned forward but he did not interrupt. Phobos, too, listened with rapt attention.

"Broken and bloodied, I ran from his castle until I found a pond on his land. I draw strength from water and therefore, I hoped to find the courage to destroy Matholwch, and any affected dominion be damned.

"I should add that though the Tuath De are not eternal, they are very long-lived. Thousands of years can pass before one is struck down, yet they can, indeed, die. I, however, am the daughter of Llyr, a god of the great Northern Ocean, a true immortal, and will not suffer the hand of Death."

Iris sighed and stared into the flames in the center of their little circle. "I sat the rest of the night by the pond praying for the strength to seek revenge upon my husband. When the sun rose, the rays struck the surface of the pond and it began to flicker with an inner light.

"Entranced, I waded into the midst of the light. The water moved as if alive and colors of the rainbow appeared, vivid hues I had never before seen seethed around me as if they were serpents coiling about my very body. My skin began to take on these tones until I vibrated with the same energy. I felt as though I would faint from the beauty of this creation.

"As I peered down at the flickering ripples gathered upon the surface, I saw images begin to form. One of a young man like none I had ever witnessed. I was mesmerized by his beauty and grace. He was dark, unlike my very pale people."

Iris paused to offer an apologetic shrug to the colorful folk before her. "It was clear he was a warrior built lean and hard, used to difficult labors."

"Deimos," Phobos whispered.

"It was indeed Deimos." Iris nodded, her lips curved in a smile. "I fell madly in love with him that instant though I knew not who he was nor in what world he existed, for it was certain he did not hail from my homeland. But I did realize I was looking at a portal that led from one realm to another. These portals are opened with regular basis in the Fey provinces. It is how the Sidhe, among others, travel back and forth to the Mortal world.

"In that moment, I knew I would never return to my brutal husband, even to punish him. I wanted the handsome youth reflected in the water, the one who now held my heart whether he realized it or not. I did not care what would become of my tribe's alliance with Matholwch, nor if they slaughtered each other over resources.

"I dove into the portal without regrets, caring not about the consequences. When I surfaced, expecting what, I cannot tell you, I was alive and healed, and no longer in the Fey Realm or under control of the Tuath De. I was on the Mortal Plane, yet unlike any human, for as you can see, my skin retained the rainbow hues of the pond.

"I wandered a bit but mortals were frightened of me. I sought the man I loved, yet I had no idea where to search. Tired, hungry and frightened, I lay down to sleep in a forest not unlike this one. When I awoke, I beheld another astonishing site, a ravishing warrior woman stared down at me, just as I had stared at Deimos. Unknowingly, I had caught the attention of Artemis, who was hunting in the same woods.

"She saw my confusion and knew I did not belong in the Mortal Realm. Out of kindness, and perhaps a bit of lustful interest," Iris arched an eyebrow and gave a tinkling laugh, "Artemis took me to Olympus, to her mother. There, under Hera's tutelage, I learned about the Immortal Realm. I became Hera's loyal messenger. It was also there, at Olympus, where I first met Deimos in the flesh."

Iris sighed. "That was a very long time ago and the end to that story has not yet been written. As to what you saw, I believe it is a portal into the realm of the Tuath De. Perhaps the same portal I passed through to arrive here."

Eris blew out with a heavy breath and shook his head. "You have kept this secret well, Iris. And no one suspected your true origins?"

With a slight tilt of her chin and a small shrug, she indicated without words that there may have been suspicions but no one questioned too closely because of Hera's protection.

"Do you know what those terrible beasts were that took my sister?"

"I believe it was Arawn and the Wild Hunt."

"The Wild Hunt? Arawn? Tuath De? The Fey Realm?" Eris bit his thumbnail. "I have never heard of such folk."

"But they have heard of you. Or rather of Ares. Ares ignores all boundaries and rides into their battles whenever he feels the pull. You, Eris, have gone with him into these conflicts."

"I do not recall such a place."

"When bloodlust is upon you, do you take note of where you are?"

Eris blushed a deep shade of green and ducked his head. "Perhaps not. It is like a madness, consuming all of Ares' minions. We follow his command and that is all. Where we are or whom we fight is inconsequential. All that matters is bloodshed."

"My Son." Aglauros clicked her tongue against the roof of her mouth in a Sylph reproof.

"Ni'madra, I am sorry but I have no control over this."

Iris continued her story. "The Wild Hunt is the stalking of poor souls who cannot escape, no matter where they hide. The beasts you saw are the Cyn Annwyn, hounds of Arawn, Master of Death in the Fey Realm.

"Though the Tuath De cannot invade an Immortal Plane, they can ride into the Mortal Realm anytime they wish, though this is not their usual haunt. I am surprised they partook in this region."

"They will rue the day they came here," Eris growled.

Iris unlocked her fingers long enough to motion toward the ancient forest. "I am deeply puzzled as to why they would choose to ride here. Who were they hunting, if they were indeed led by Arawn?"

"I know why. And who." Aglauros rose to her feet, anger written upon her face.

"Ni'madra, please." Eris, too, rose to his feet, blocking his mother's advance toward Iris.

"Do not quiet me, Eris. These folk, the Tuath De, have caused terrible loss amongst the Sylph and now the Kobaloi. We have done nothing to deserve such violence. But there is one who has: Ares. Once again, death and destruction lie at his feet."

"What do you speak of?" Iris stood up as well.

"The child they sought, Alcippe, the child they took, the child they were willing to burn our Sacred Grove for and kill many of my people - this child is a daughter of Ares the Destroyer."

"The Tuath De took a child of Ares?" Iris staggered a step backward, bumping her heels against the log, causing her to sit with abruptness. "I have heard the Tuath De celebrate Ares' demise, for they would stop at nothing to revenge their people slaughtered by Amason."

"But Ares is not yet gone into the Shadowland, and Amason still draws blood through Deimos." Phobos spoke up with sudden concern as he edged closer on his knees. "And now they have Alcippe, Ares' daughter, our sister. What do they intend to do with her?"

"I cannot imagine," Iris breathed. "But their desire to punish Ares knows no limits."

"Alcippe is a babe in arms, an innocent child, along with the Kobaloi children. Do they intend to hunt these little ones?"

An anguished gasp arose from the Kobaloi as Aglauros explained to them the words of Iris.

"That cannot be. No one is that cruel." Eris cringed, for he knew he did not speak the truth.

All eyes turned to Iris, waiting for her reassurance.

"Children are not prey. They are cherished, just as they are in all realms. Arawn does not hunt children. If they are to be taken, it is by Gentle Death."

"But they hate Ares." Aglauros' lips were peeled back from her pointed teeth and her eyes blazed with the fierceness born of protecting her young. Though she had not birthed the babe, Alcippe, she was still mother to her. "We must do something. Fight them. We must find the children before harm comes to them."

"We cannot fight Arawn. The Wild Hunt always wins. When Death stalks, Death wins." Iris clutched at the edge of her tunic. "I do not know how to call the portal. It just appeared in my moment of need."

"I think you do." Gaze harsh, Eris pressed Iris. He was no longer the playful youth - he was the right hand of War.

"I do not."

"You created a portal in a simple pond of water. You can do it again."

"I have no idea how it happened. It may well have been the goddess Danu or my father, Llyr who made it possible for me to escape."

"Whether you manifested the portal or you did not, you will at least try." Eris gripped Iris' slim wrist in his own battle-hardened fingers.

Iris resisted, straining to get away from him. "You do not understand - I cannot return there. I will not go back there." Pulling at her arm with her opposite hand, Iris' face grew blue with exertion. "That beast."

"Your husband." Eris let go so quickly Iris slid into the mud at the edge of the river.

"And if not Matholwch, then my brother Bran would seize and punish me for disobeying his command. He is worse than the hounds. If I could set the Wild Hunt upon them both, I would."

"And why could we not?" Eris stroked his chin, his gaze rolling up in thought.

"That is not how the Wild Hunt engages." Lifting her muddy palms in disgust, Iris wrinkled her nose. "The moment I return to my own realm, they will know. There would be no time for Arawn to seize upon either, even if he would."

With a sly glance toward the disheveled girl, Eris went to the edge of flowing water. It was quite beautiful, reflecting the green cradle above them as it coursed along the corridor cut out of the ancient woods.

"Then let us call Deimos. I am certain he would be happy to sort this out with your husband and your brother."

"No." Iris swayed to her knees and attempted to stand up in the slick muck. "No, do not tell Deimos of this story. It is in my past and has nothing to do with my life here."

"But you hunger for Deimos - should he not know you are already wed?"

"I do not believe it counts here." Iris pressed her lips together and crossed her arms over her chest, leaving muddy prints upon her once-glistening tunic.

"I believe it does. Wed is wed."

"Please, do not summon Deimos. I beg of you." One step toward Eris sent Iris toppling backwards onto the slippery bank. Her efforts only worked her further along the slope until she splashed into the water.

"There, you see, you agree whether you know it or not. Iris, there comes a point when you must face your demons and fight for your life. This is not merely about your existence, but that of my sister. We must also concern ourselves with the missing Kobaloi children. We have no choice but to go after them."

"You intend to go through the portal - if I can create it - with me?" Iris' blue eyes widened. "I thought you would send me to my fate alone."

"Ha." Eris' lips turned up in a wicked grin. "And miss taking our revenge upon Arawn? I think not."

"I fear he will destroy you."

Eris shrugged in spite of Aglauros' whimper behind him.

"He does not know who I am or whence I came. I hold the element of surprise, and I too, am immortal. He can do no more than wound me. Just get me there, Iris of the Rainbows. Just get me through the portal and I will take care of the rest."

Phobos came to stand next to Eris, though his knees knocked together in unbridled panic and his voice squeaked when he spoke. "I stand with my brother. Take us there before we summon War."

Pinching the bridge of her nose with mud-caked fingers, Iris thought long and hard of this decision. Had it been a full-grown offspring of Ares, perhaps it would be different but Arawn had stolen a babe. And other children. All of whom must be terrified, for she did not speak of the slavery that awaited them and the cruel life of the non-Sidhe in the Fey courts.

Without further protest, Iris waded into a pool of water created by a fork in the small river. The water was cold and she shivered as the icy stream sluiced around her waist.

"I cannot even be certain this will work."

"It will work, Iris. Have faith."

At this, the Kobaloi shaman raised his rattle and began to chant to the heavens. All the Kobaloi chanted with him, an unintelligible noise to Iris. She covered her ears and frowned at Eris.

"Concentrate," Eris commanded. "Think of the Fey Realm as you would when you want to move from one place to the other here. Picture it in your mind. Remember what it was like, how it felt, how it smelled. Remember, Iris. Create it."

Iris closed her eyes and let her hands float upon the surface of the moving water. She felt the way it ruffled through her fingers in a gentle eddy that brought calm within her. Though her nature was Water, she also embraced Air, for a rainbow is both elements.

She thought of the iridescent layers of color held within the beauty of a water bridge formed in the sky by sun and rain and how each felt different.

Red vibrated deep within her body, at her root, between her legs. Iris felt fear laced with exhilaration, survival versus surrender. Her breath came in gasps as the power began to build. The surge moved to her belly and the color changed to orange.

Vivid scenes of raw sexuality rose up and Iris once again was locked into a desperate embrace with Deimos. Just as the force was close to sending her into an orgasmic state, the color changed to yellow.

The glow surrounded her torso, throbbing with her own will, that piece that defined who she was, and better, who she would never be again. The source of her shame and at the same time, the source of her strength. From this place she gained command of her destiny. No longer was she afraid to face those from her homeland.

Iris' head tipped back and a loud 'Ahh.' issued from her throat as the color changed to green and her heart expanded. She was consumed by compassion and she cared not what drove those who wished her harm, only that she could hold them with deepest love.

Green shifted to blue and her throat opened wider. The 'Ahh' became a victorious shriek. The sound echoed in the tops of the trees and sent a flock of birds winging away in alarm. Her fierce noise was born of freedom.

Blue gave way to violet as her mind snapped into the awareness that she was everything and everything was she. All that was necessary was to follow her instincts, go where she sensed the thread, grab hold and flow through to a different realm.

Violet turned to white. A pure white light, transcending her physical body, surpassing the simple existence on any plane of being. Iris connected to all realms as a spider is connected to her web. She could see the facets of each domain and those who inhabited them. The people, too, were connected, in ways that were indescribable.

Iris felt them become legion, merging together until there was only one. The one they all sprang from before they fought and separated into their private empires. In and out, the web was created. She could see the map against the stars. She could choose where she would go.

Her body went liquid, flowing like the stream, and she slipped away from the Mortal Realm to return to the Fey.

Eris saw Iris melt away and become a rainbow portal on the surface of the pool.

"This is it, Brother. We go to rescue our sister."

Phobos gave one quick nod before the two young men dove into the multihued water and disappeared from sight.

Aglauros began to wail. Both children were now lost to her. Would she ever see them again?

SIXTEEN

Deimos allowed the swarming warriors to flow around him as if he was invisible. He observed both sides as they waged war one upon the other slashing, hacking, tearing at limbs and torsos, heads and necks, all with the brutal intention of annihilation. Each tribe wished for total destruction of the opposition. It was clear there would be no prisoners, no protectors left for the weak when the strongest prevailed.

In the southern hemisphere, in the jungle where this battled raged, women were left at camps, along with the children, the infirm and the old. Deimos could read the savage expressions and knew that whomever won - and it mattered not which - there would be no survivors amongst the losing tribe. Everyone, from eldest to youngest, would be slaughtered.

And why?

Deimos looked upon the curled lips and rage-filled eyes and saw no difference between the two sides. Why did they fight? Was it rich soil? Clean water? Mineral deposits? Appearances? Betrayal? Murder?

What was worth this bloodshed?

Even though Amason hummed within her scabbard pressed against his spine and demanded to be unleashed, her razor sharp edge lusting for the taste of flesh, Deimos resisted. Even though every vicious and cruel act sent a siren call to the Mantle of War, Deimos refused to engage. He stood in the center of the violence and closed his eyes, listening to the sounds.

Above the clash, he heard the baying of his hounds and the shrieks of his minions, those who would bring further destruction down upon the heads of these warring nations. The descending Erinnyes, the Keres, and worse, Enyo, who would strip more than her share of souls from the face of the earth. There was no hope for peace.

It was curious. Neither Eris nor Phobos was within the crusade. Deimos noticed yet took little time to consider where they might be or why they did not respond to his command. Instead, his patience frayed.

He no longer wished to be at the mercy of the Mantle.

There was no honor to this battle, no purpose other than death.

"Cowards," he hissed. "Not of dying, but of living. Cowards, all of them."

If it was death they wanted, Deimos would give them to Thanatos. With a mere whisper of his thought, Death appeared next to Deimos.

"It is not like you to invite me to partake, Cousin." The youth smirked as he flipped aside the tip of a spear from a warrior who did not see his presence.

"Most of the time, I am bid wait until after the carnage and then I must fight that despicable one for souls to deliver to the Shadowland."

Thanatos jerked his head toward the spectral Enyo. Shuddering, Thanatos gathered his cloak and held it as if a piece of cloth could protect him from the ravening nightmare come to life. "Even I cannot abide the site of that hag."

"Prepare yourself for you shall have your fill, Cousin."

With that, Deimos lifted both hands and slammed his palms toward the ground. Every single man dropped with the motion. One gasp and their eyeballs rolled back into their sockets. Tongues protruded from open mouths and their faces mottled as if strangled.

Thanatos gaped at the sight but did not speak, for now his work began. His posture shifted with the weight of the dead climbing onto his shoulders and clinging to his limbs. He was surrounded by the clamoring souls of the departed as they tore at him in a frenzy to avoid Enyo. Their cries of fear rang in his ears. There was no calming them as they poured themselves upon him in a torrent of terror.

It mattered not to Deimos if Thanatos was mute, for he did not care. He left the massacre to those who reveled in it. Deimos left the battleground and took himself to Najahmara. He was not a coward. He would face the grief and loss that was left in his wake.

He would see if there was truth to Zelos' declaration.

The moment his feet touched the barren soil of the plateau he forgot his mission, for he felt her. Deimos sensed the pull of energy was from Gaea, magnifying his sadness. Her primal energy supported and sustained but could not shield her people from danger, thus Gaea's entreaty to Deimos to protect them.

And he had failed her. Even though she forgave him, he did not forgive himself. He would carry the wound for eternity.

"Great Mother, I come in peace."

The ground shimmied in response yet the air was void of any wind lending itself to Gaea's voice. As the plateau settled back to its barren existence, it was clear the Earth divinity had nothing further to offer him.

The former Deimos would have begged forgiveness again and again, never satisfied, never accepting absolution. The Deimos that walked upon Gaea now pushed the sensation away.

He could not change that which had already occurred - not even Divinity could alter the past. He was left with his memories. Gaze drifting to the single white pillar at the far end of the ridge, Deimos was drawn to stand before the monolith. Niala's name was inscribed upon its face and with great care, he traced the letters with his fingertips.

Behind the marker, within the shadow of her grave, was where she had left her earthly presence. Tears stung his eyes before he could shove his emotions out of reach.

"Niala, my devotion holds true. I cannot, regardless how hard I try, I cannot love another. They are empty vessels without steerage yet I cannot become their captain. Though I have made the attempt, it is an impossible task."

Again he felt the pull of energy from the soles of his feet. It was a vibration this time, less intense than the first. He knelt and touched the soil, picked up a handful of dry hard dirt, crumbled the clot and let it sift through his fingers. The ground was undisturbed. There had been no burial here.

"If not here, then where?"

The words were scarce out of his mouth when he felt a tug at his elbow. Was it Gaea directing him?

Deimos rose and returned to the center of the plateau, at the spot he entered Najahmara. The pull was stronger now that he stood near the ring of stones built to contain fire.

Where was it coming from?

He walked a tight circle, eyes cast to the ground. He felt the pulsation strongest to the right of the largest rock. The energy pulled him like magnet, down, down, deeper and deeper.

Inside the mount.

Within a second, Deimos descended into Gaea's cavern, the inner sanctuary where the harvest ritual was held. To the same place he once fed upon the milk of the goddess herself. Where Gaea first blessed him. Where he was reminded of the duality of his nature. Yes, he was Terror. He was also Survival.

With a quick gesture, the old torches revived with light. Deimos' gaze fell upon the shroud-covered body of his beloved Niala Aaminah. As he approached, he could not cease the tremor emanating from his core. He reached to uncover her face, but his hand trembled so that he withdrew.

Did he want to see the ravages of death etched upon her beautiful face? Did he carry the courage to view the horror he brought to her? Grief was a raw wound that would not heal but seeped forever to the depths of his soul.

It mattered not whether he wanted look upon her.

He knew he must.

Inhaling the dusty stale air of the cavern, Deimos steeled himself and folded back the shroud. His startled gasp echoed off the stone walls of the cave. With one flip of his wrist, he flung the linen cloth the rest of the way off and threw it to the floor.

Though her complexion was ashen, Niala Aaminah was untouched by time. There was no decay or decimation, only perfection. With gentle fingers, he stroked her cheek. Instead of mummified remains, his touch met pliant flesh. Hope rising, he sought the pulsing blood in her neck but felt none. He moved his palm to her chest, praying for the rise and fall of one who lived.

He found nothing. There was no breath in her body, no beating heart. She seemed well and truly dead, and yet her condition could not possibly be of a mortal deceased these many months. Without thought, Deimos kissed her cold lips, begging for a response.

There was none. Not a flicker of an eyelash or a twitch of her fingers. Deimos contemplated her state. Niala was somewhere between life and death, just as Ares. While Ares could not be helped, Deimos wondered if he could restore Niala to her former state.

Was it possible?

And if he did, what of her spirit, the spark that had been ripped from her at the moment of her physical demise? Would it return, or would he animate a soulless vessel that would be vacant of any prospect, much less love?

It did not matter. He would risk anything to bring her back.

With tenderness, he grasped her jaw and parted her lips. Taking a deep breath, Deimos blew into her mouth. Niala's chest rose and fell but did not rise again. He drew in another breath that held the scent of roses, the same used to bath her before interment.

Deimos blew into her parted lips again. Her chest expanded but failed to maintain. He called upon every entity, every being that could assist. He implored Gaea to return life to her daughter. He poured his desire into each breath that he blew again and again into Niala Aaminah's body.

Three times three he exhaled into her mouth. Upon the ninth attempt, Niala continued to breathe on her own. Warmth began to seep into her limbs and the ash tone left her skin. Her eyelashes fluttered though she did not open her eyes.

Deimos grew weak at the knees as his heart leaped with joy and gratitude. Laced within the elation was wild fear. Was she truly restored or was her body merely reanimated? He could not be certain. And yet he felt her energy surge forth as her heart beat.

"Niala? Do you hear me? Ahh, my Love, can you hear me? Come back. Please, come back to me."

Deimos gathered Niala into his arms, his fervent pleas whispered into her ears. She was light as a feather as if her bones were hollow. Her head lolled against his chest without further trace of her existence save for the slightest movement of her chest.

"My Love. My only Love, return to me."

Without further consideration, Deimos took Niala away from her tomb. Not to Athos, the site of her imprisonment, the place she hated, but to Cos, the dwelling of light, love and healing.

*****

"Zan, what brings you to the temple?" Jahmed plucked a bunch of freshly cut mint, the last of the season, and began to tie the stems into bundles. The herbs would be hung up to dry and later used for a medicinal tea to relieve bellyaches.

It was all that was left of the harvest, and though she had sent the others off for their noon meal, Jahmed wanted to finish. She was not hungry, and thus, found it better to work than play with her food and make small talk as others ate.

She glanced up at Zan and smiled. In truth, she did not mind Zan's company. Even though Zan appeared as a rough warrior who would sooner gut a man as look at him, she suspected inwardly he was much gentler. She could see kindness in his heart and a distinct interest in the daily work of the sanctuary.

It was not unusual for Zan to visit the temple under the guise of collecting medicines for the soldiers who camped in the meadow. Many of those men were suspicious of the priestesses and resisted seeing the healers themselves. The women did their best to give appropriate powders without knowing with any certainty what ailed the men. The women, too, were wary and would not go out to the encampment.

When Zan did not reply but stood at stiff attention in the doorway, his big hands tightened into fists, a pained expression on his weathered face, Jahmed laid her work aside.

Her first thought was in fear for Ajah and Inni, fear that Hattusilis demanded their arrest for striking a soldier. Though days had passed with no such action and all the women went about their work in the temple with no mention of reprisal, here was Zan ready to deliver bad news.

"Zan, what is wrong? Does Hattusilis seek to punish Ajah for striking a guard? Mercy, what are we to do? And Inni, he cannot take her from me. He simply cannot."

"No, that incident has been forgotten, thank the gods. In truth, it is far worse than that."

"What could be worse?"

A sick feeling settled in Jahmed's gut. The last she saw of Pallin was upon the return of the babe, Mursilis, to his mother's arms. That night, Hattusilis had ranted like a madman about her work in the temple, leaving Jahmed to worry that all was well with Pallin.

Two weeks had passed since then but given the fear for Inni and Ajah, Jahmed did not question nor interfere. It was Pallin's decision and since she did not request assistance, Jahmed left them alone.

"Does Pallin suffer an issue with her pregnancy? Is it little Mursilis? Does she have need of me?"

"No." Zan looked at Jahmed with a strange light in his eyes, as if it just dawned on him that Pallin was indeed with child again. "Neither is ill or dead but it is a grave situation. King Hattusilis has placed Queen Pallin under house arrest, locking her in her quarters. He allows no one to see her, save for serving her food and water. I fear he has abused her." Zan stared down at his big hands, unable to meet Jahmed's horrified gaze.

At her distressed huff, Zan took a single step into the room. "There is more. He plans to send Pallin and Mursilis away."

"Away? But where? Where would he send them? And why? Why would he do such a thing? Why would he imprison her?"

"My king has embraced the lunacy that has plagued him for many months after his injury. It seems he has finally lost all sense of sanity.

"King Hattusilis bade me escort Pallin and Mursilis to the Steppelands. I refused, believing it was a momentary spell he would move past, just as he has all the other times."

Zan's shoulders slumped from the perfect warrior's attention. "But he has not recovered. He continues his rant with the intention to send them away at the dark moon. Even now, he readies the supplies for the journey and selects the men who will accompany Pallin and the babe on their journey."

An expectant woman and a small babe sent out of Najahmara into the harsh wilderness to make a journey so perilous that grown men died? Jahmed's head was reeling. She scarce knew what to think.

"The man is without reason." Jahmed's voice shook and she found she could no longer stand. She sank onto a wooden bench.

"We cannot allow this."

"No, we cannot."

"You would defy your king?" Bitterness tinted Jahmed's words but a spark of hope leapt into her heart.

Zan bowed his head. "Hattusilis no longer speaks as a strong leader. Something has happened to him, something I cannot describe, nor comprehend, only that it is."

The way he spoke, the way he shrank within, the way the bulky man showed more fear than with his earlier announcement caused Jahmed to pause, afraid to ask what this new terror was.

When Zan lifted his head, the whites of his eyes showed. "Hattusilis has changed. It is more than the madness that curses him. His body has altered as well." With a quivering breath, Zan went on.

"When I returned this morning in the hopes he had calmed, it was not so. No, not at all. Hattu greeted me as if I was a stranger. I thought perhaps he drank too much last night and did not feel well.

"I thought he teased me, let me think he did not forgive my refusal to go. Then he rose from his chair and walked across the room. Walked, not limped. Walked without use of his cane. Walked tall and strong, not bent and weak."

Jahmed was speechless. It was not possible for Hattusilis to ever again move without help. His legs were crushed, one foot nearly severed in the accident in the caves.

"How could this be?"

"I do not know, Priestess. I hoped you could tell me."

There was no immediate reply, for Jahmed did not have an answer, or at least, none she cared to share. She was long disturbed by Pallin's talk of ghosts and nightmares that routinely visited Hattusilis. Some descriptions did not sound like lost spirits or mere night terrors - even if Hattusilis warranted a haunting - but these things Pallin spoke of were suggestive of another being.

The Blue Serpent, Kulika.

The Sky god was last invoked during the Summer rites at Gaea's insistence. Those indifferent heartless beings who wanted only to lie in each other's arms. Their selfish actions brought about Niala's death.

Jahmed clamped her lips together at the memories as overwhelming grief enveloped her. Had either Gaea or Kulika been concerned for Niala? For any of them? It did not seem so, for both fled the moment Niala birthed the babe and bled to death. The deities left broken bodies and broken hearts behind.

Jahmed questioned why Gaea allowed the suffering of so many to take place, why so many died and so many others were injured beyond repair in both body and mind.

Like Inni - gone without trace. All intelligence and humor, grace and wit, disappeared in the same fire that burned much of the town. Jahmed could not, with any conscience, summon Gaea back amongst them.

And Gaea understood. She quietly took her penance and receded into the depths of Earth to wait until her children were ready to call upon her once more. Gaea grieved along with them, knowing she had gone too far, and allowed Kulika to do the same.

In her deepest heart, Jahmed knew she must forgive Gaea and made inroads during these past months to move beyond the betrayal. As for Kulika, she would never absolve him for his travesty. She believed he returned to the Sky Realm in disgrace, just as Gaea retreated to the bosom of the Earth.

Instead, did Kulika run rampant through Najahmara? Did he discover the weakest link in Hattusilis, seeking to use the broken body of a king to do his bidding?

It had happened once before during the Spring rites. With all that had transpired since, Jahmed had forgotten the moment when Hattusilis rose from his chair and tried to strangle her at the lakeshore as she carried out the wishes of the Great Mother. At that moment, Hattusilis held the strength of the Blue Serpent. Was it any surprise that he did so once again?

Jahmed was filled with shame, for she should have seen it. She should have known the serpent would refuse to leave. She should have known he would take advantage of the ensuing chaos after Niala's death to hide amongst the mortals.

She met Zan's gaze. "There is much more to this. I fear it is more complicated than even you believe. I fear your king's behavior has been guided by another, yet it is a long story and one we do not have time for now. What are we to do about Pallin and the babe? We cannot allow them to be sent away."

With reluctance, Zan nodded. His first allegiance should be to Hattusilis, but his connection to the kind folk of Najahmara had grown to an enormous proportion. He felt a kinship with them. He could not let the Queen and her child suffer needlessly.

"I agree, Priestess. I have a plan, however dangerous. I wish to enlist your help."

"Anything."

Zan nodded and spoke in a low voice after first looking right and left to ensure they were alone. "I advised Hattusilis I reconsidered and agreed to take the Queen and little Prince to the Steppelands. Of course, I will not, but it placated Hattusilis long enough to map an escape for Pallin and Mursilis. But first, we must find a place to hide them."

"How will you do it? What of the other guards? Oh, please, do not get Pallin and her child killed." Jahmed could not help the rising panic. Which was worse? Banishment or death?

She saw the haunted look in Zan's brown eyes. She saw that to defy his king would mean his death. She saw absolute courage and a willingness to sacrifice his own life to save Pallin and her son. She found she trusted Zan and was astounded at her own sadness at his probable loss.

"At night there is a single guard on duty within the king's quarters. On the eve before they are to leave, it will be Connal, my brother." A glint of satisfaction reflected in Zan's eyes. "Outside, there are two, but I am still second in command of the legion and no one will question my decision to relocate the queen. However, we must have somewhere for them to go. Somewhere no one will look."

With a sharp exhale, Jahmed rose from the bench. "I know

where we shall take them. Bring Pallin and Mursilis to the gardens behind the temple, and do not concern yourself with the guards, neither here nor there."

At this she offered a grim smile and moved to her work table to concoct a sleeping potion. After grinding a few leaves together, she poured a powder into a square of leather.

"Put this in their drink and no one will be the wiser. When they wake up, there will be confusion."

Zan grimaced. "At last I understand why some of the men have no memory of their time watching over the temple."

With a brief salute Zan turned to leave.

Jahmed hesitated but felt in her heart the bond of trust between the grizzled warrior and the priestesses. If she could not rely on Zan, then there was no one who would take up their greater cause, to send Kulika back to the Sky Realm.

"Zan, a moment more of your time, if you will."

"Yes, Priestess."

"I believe your king has been possessed by Kulika, the Sky God, who is mate to our great Earth Mother. We must find a way to force him out."

"Possessed?" Zan blew out a great breath through pursed lips. "I have heard of such things but never witnessed it. Are you certain it is not some deeper illness afflicting Hattusilis? A sickness of the head?"

"From all you describe, no. I believe it is Kulika. There are many things I cannot explain about our rites but the last time he was called, he was not released properly." Jahmed stared at a spot on the wall beyond Zan's head. "It was the night Niala died, the night Pallin gave birth to Mursilis. We were in a great distress and did not notice. I believe he has been here ever since, no doubt looking for sway over a body. Your king."

Zan lowered himself to a bench, a dazed expression upon his bearded face. "It is far more wicked a situation than I believed." He repeated Jahmed's own words back to her. "What are we to do?"

"I need time to think." Jahmed placed one hand on the warrior's thick shoulder. "Will you help us?"

Their eyes met and Zan gave a short nod. "Yes, Priestess. This madness must stop. Just tell me what you need."

"We are at war again." Jahmed spoke in a low voice, afraid they would be overheard even within the confines of their quarters.

Ajah and Tulane sat to the front while Inni was at one side next to Deniz.

It was Pallin that Jahmed spoke of first.

"Our sister and her son are locked away at the mercy of one who should not be here. His intention is to send them away."

Inni made a low keening sound and rocked back and forth at the mention of the boy. Jahmed cast a worried glance at her but Inni would not meet Jahmed's gaze. She averted her eyes, wiping away tears, her lips moving in a constant whispered monologue.

"However, Zan and I have a plan to rescue them tonight. It will take some effort, but we can and will make them safe."

"Why has this happened?" Ajah's eyebrows knit together in a frown. "Does it relate to Mursilis?" Her gaze slid to Inni's distraught expression and then to her fingers laced together in her lap.

Jahmed cast a warning glance at Ajah and gave a quick shake of her head. Inni could not be blamed for this folly.

"He who calls himself king has been taken over by a creature not of this world. Kulika, the Blue Serpent that is Gaea's consort, has inserted himself into the body of this man."

Ajah appeared ill and grasped Tulane's shoulder in support. "I knew something was wrong when last we saw him."

"He has been hovering nearby all this time, slithering about, looking for a way in. I blame myself." Jahmed paused to swallow the bile rising in her throat. She went on in a hoarse voice. "Had I not pushed the Great Mother aside, had I not let my anger and bitterness consume me, had I paid more attention to the changes in the town, let alone to Hattusilis, it would not be so."

Jahmed released a shaking breath, unable to go on. She sank to the bench behind her as the weight of her guilt pushed and pulled and made her weak in the legs.

"Kulika lied to Gaea. He apologized for abandoning his place as her protector, but he was not sorry. He rebelled against her power and only pretended to do as she bid. As soon as Gaea left Niala's body, as soon as he released Deimos, Kulika escaped our notice." Jahmed closed her eyes against the memory.

"Yes, Zahava, I remember." Ajah rose to her feet, her own guilt weighing heavily upon her shoulders. "It happened when our beloved Niala fell into the pangs of childbirth and the babe emerged too quickly for any of us to help her."

"For *me* to help her." Jahmed pounded on the bench with her fist. "And I could not. There was too much blood, too much damage. Oh, mercy, even now I can scarce stand to think of it."

Ajah went to sit beside her and placed an arm across her shoulders. To see Jahmed in such a state amplified her fear. "Zahava, you cannot blame yourself for what happened. Niala would not allow it."

"Niala told me I was to take care of everyone, to continue in her place. I rejected this because of pride. I did not accept that Niala would leave us even though she had a vision. I refused to contemplate such a thing."

"You have taken care of us." Ajah clung to Jahmed. "Without you, without your healing, many more would have perished."

"Ahh, yes, the medicines," Jahmed ranted. "That is all I know: herbs and pastes, powders and teas. I can care for a fever, or dress wounds, cure coughs and deliver babies. Healer, yes, that is my calling, but that is all I am. I did not bother to notice the spirit haunting our village."

"You tried, Zahava." Tulane patted Jahmed's back. "You did all that you could do."

"But I blocked Gaea from returning to us. I was so angry

with her that she fell into Kulika's arms at the first sign of his regret. She did not punish him for all the death and destruction at his hands. She let him get away with murder, and then rewarded him with pleasure. How could she?"

"She does not think as we do." Ajah squeezed her eyes shut for she knew she could have prevented this had she allowed herself to go through the initiation. When she continued, her voice was steady. "This lesson I learned well at Niala's knee. Gaea is not like us, she does not view things as we do, therefore she does not answer to the same rules we have set for ourselves."

"If I had forgiven her, called her to us, she would have known Kulika did not return to his realm. She would have forced him back to the Sky, as she should have forced him the first time."

"We did not know."

"I should have sensed this." Jahmed shook off Ajah's arms and rose to her feet, pacing back and forth in agitation. "If I had listened to Pallin and her complaints instead of judging her. If I had befriended Hattusilis instead of ignoring him, I would have seen the changes. If I had just let Gaea come through me."

Her voice dropped. "But I was afraid. The only time I attempted it, I could not hold her power and it did not turn out well. Even then, Gaea and Kulika fought with each other." She paused to shake her head at the memory of the Summer Solstice when the immortals had once again taken charge and then fled after creating trouble.

"The only one who ever could amongst us was Niala. And always, afterward, she was exhausted and sick for days. Finally, she was abandoned, left to die, by our own goddess. I was afraid."

"Zahava, do not be troubled by this. We all have been afraid."

"Stop calling me that. I am not worthy."

"Zah...Jahmed," Ajah grasped Jahmed's hands, "please, I feel your pain and hold my own hurting heart, yet we cannot lose sight of what we must do. First, we must save Pallin and little Mursilis. Then we will banish Kulika. Somehow, someway, we will do it."

"You are right, Sister." Jahmed inhaled and gathered her wits together. She was ashamed of her lack of control in front of the young ones. "I am sorry for my outburst."

"It was necessary." Ajah raised a finger and pointed at Jahmed. "You are always the one we come to for answers, always the one who must bear the burdens, and yet you must forgive yourself, for you did what you did to protect us."

Jahmed nodded even though she did not agree. There were many things she did to safeguard her people. There was just as many things she did not do. No matter, there was no excuse for not sensing Kulika's manifestation.

"The past is the past." The ever practical Tulane put her hands on her hips. "Let us move forward."

Jahmed had to smile, even if it was just a small curve of her lips. If she did not know better, she would think Tulane was the new incarnation of Seire, the elder priestess murdered by the evilest of all men that dark night of fire and death.

"Tonight we hide our sister and her son. In two weeks, on the full moon, we call Gaea, for she is the only one who can banish Kulika. I am old and useless. I will be her vessel even if it causes my death."

"Old? Useless? What nonsense," Tulane scoffed. "You are our leader. Without you, we would flap in the wind. We cannot risk you."

"I must, Tulane. There is no other."

"But there is." Ajah straightened her shoulders and lifted her chin. "I will do it. I am young and strong, and I have heard the ritual calling. I have seen Niala and you host the Great Mother. I can do it."

"You have not been initiated. Without a spirit guide to keep you tethered to this world, you might never return." Jahmed's eyes flicked toward Inni and back again. "I will not allow it."

Ajah's jaw tightened. "I have been chosen by the Sagittariidae, the Snake Eater. Who better to battle Kulika? We must perform the sacred rites and beat his image into my skin as a symbol of my strength."

"We have no one who can hold the image of your spirit

totem, or place it upon your skin, not since Seire and her apprentice died. We cannot hold the sacred rites without them. No. It is impossible."

"Yes, Jahmed. I was ready long before the fire. Niala told me herself that I was to take flight with the Corvidae's kin. I feared then she meant her own death was near and did not want to do it.

"So, you see, you are not the only one who turned away from duty. But I am no longer afraid. I embrace Air and Sky, just as Niala did, and I must be the one to bring Gaea here, to enable her to send Kulika back into the heavens."

"There is no one to perform the ceremony." Jahmed leaned against the table, fingers flat against the surface, head bowed. "And even if we had a Spirit Walker, it would not matter. Niala was different and that was why she could host the Great Mother."

"I believe the Corvidae allowed Niala the strength to hold a goddess within her body. And there is someone who can walk between the worlds. Someone that…"

Jahmed cut Ajah's declaration off with a wave of her hand. "And did the Corvidae write her name upon the white stone on the ridge? The stones that stood watch over the graves of the women who discovered this valley?"

"Yes, the Corvidae was her magic." Stubbornness flared Ajah's nose and tightened her lips. "And the white stone is just a symbol of her leadership, a monument to her, just as the stones were monuments to the other women who were once leaders."

"Ahh, you are young and foolish." Jahmed met Ajah's scowl. "Those women were the founders of this town. Niala was with them when they first came to this valley. "Do you know how many years ago that was? And yet, she appeared not a day older."

"That is just a story told. I do not believe they all lived at the same time, but were in succession as priestesses of Najahmara."

"A story?" Jahmed's voice rose. "Niala herself told me of her journey here. She was not human, though I do not know what she truly was."

"Who is foolish now?"

Jahmed shook her head. "You are naive. There was more to Niala than mere flesh and blood. That is why she could allow Gaea into her body."

"You held Gaea in your body during the Summer rites."

"Not well. I came near death myself that night."

"Once I am initiated and the Sagittariidae is etched into my flesh, I will be able to hold Gaea within me."

Jahmed's features softened as she gazed upon the earnest face of the younger woman. "Dear Sister, everyone initiated into our priestess tribe has a spirit guide that visits us in the form of an animal. Each guide fulfills a role much larger than that of ritual, and each has its own attributes, but it does not mean we are strong enough to hold an immortal energy such as Earth."

"I disagree. It can be done, and I will do it, I swear." Ajah's jaw set. "There is nothing else for us to do."

"She lives."

Ajah jerked as Inni clutched at her arm.

"Niala lives. Ajah saw for herself. She saw Niala - she lay as if asleep and not a rotted corpse. Ajah saw her."

"Inni, be still." Ajah tried to pry Inni's grip loose. "Do not speak of this."

"Niala lives."

Jahmed shook her head, irritated by the incessant intonation. Though she loved Inni with all her heart, it was clear that her illness progressed. Until now, Jahmed had been able to keep Inni's ramblings limited to their private conversations, but now Ajah was also involved?

"Inni, stop this." Jahmed's tone was harsher than she intended. "Niala is dead."

Inni pointed upwards to the caves as she sang the same words over and over. "She lives. She lives. Niala lives."

"Stop, please!" Angst filled Jahmed's eyes. "I can stand no more of this lunacy."

A crafty look passed over Inni's features as she paused for a moment, then redirected her gaze toward Ajah, resuming her recitation. "Ask Ajah, ask her, ask her, ask her."

Ajah looked from Jahmed's stricken expression to Inni's insistent demand. Her heart welled up with compassion for Inni, and also with a fierce need to protect Jahmed. Yet there was no other choice, she had to confess.

"It is true, Jahmed. I saw Niala Aaminah. She does not appear as a corpse after these many months. She looked the same as the day we placed her within the sacred cavern."

SEVENTEEN

"Why would you keep this from me?" Jahmed grew dizzy as her heart thumped against her ribs.

"I was uncertain as to what I saw that night. I feared it was an illusion. "

"You did not, you could not have seen Niala alive."

"I do not know if she truly lives, only that she has not decayed."

"Did she breathe?"

"I saw no sign of it though she looked as if she could at any moment."

"Again, I ask, why would you not speak of this to me?"

"I feared the concern over whether I would be imprisoned or punished after striking the guard was causing me to imagine things that were not real." With palms pressed to her breast, Ajah bowed her head in shame. "I should have told you, Zahava. Please forgive me."

Jahmed waved away the apology. "Niala was never what she seemed. Still, I cannot believe this. I wrapped her body and helped carry her to the cavern. I must see this for myself."

With a grunt, Inni came to her feet, needing only a little assistance from the younger women. "I will show you and you will finally believe me."

Jahmed bade Tulane to return the girls to their work while she visited the caverns. Because it was daylight, the three women took the long way around through the wooded area and made the difficult climb up the backside of the plateau. The entire time, Inni continued her monologue though no one listened. Ajah and Jahmed walked in silence, each lost in contemplation.

With great trepidation, Jahmed allowed Inni to lead them through the connecting corridors. Some were mere grottos or narrow indentations in the walls. Others were sizeable and still held the large containers where winter supplies were once stored. These wares were no longer brought into the cool depths of the mount but concealed in underground cavities.

When they neared the chamber where Niala's body was laid to rest, Jahmed felt stifling panic rise within her. There was no smell of decaying flesh to greet them, only dust and moldering cloth and the damp rock walls and ancient dirt creasing the floor.

And something else. The smoky scent of torches.

The flickering light cast eerie fingers into the antechamber.

"Did you leave the torches lit when you were last here?"

"No, we did not light them, we used a lantern." Ajah felt her skin prickle and she rubbed her arms to erase the chill. "It has been many days since we were here."

"Aaiee! Niala is gone!"

The sound of the lantern crashing to the ground and Inni's shriek sent the two women rushing into the main chamber.

In her eagerness to see Niala once again, Inni had wandered away their discussion and entered the burial chamber alone. With the still burning torches in their holders, they could see the cast off shroud and vacant bier.

"Mercy, how can this be?" Jahmed pointed a trembling finger at the stone. She felt near to fainting.

"It is because she is not dead, just as I have said many times but no one listens. Our Niala Aaminah lives."

Ajah slipped her fingers along the cold slab in disbelief. "Where could she be?"

All three women turned to stare at the corners of the chamber, both fearing and hoping to see a figure crouched in the shadows.

There was no one.

"Gaea, Mother of All, please tell me what has happened here. Who has stolen our dear sister's body?"

Just as Jahmed prayed, so did Ajah and Inni.

There was no immediate response. Then, like eddying pools of water swirling about their ankles, energy began to rise around them. The awareness swept up their legs, stirring skirts, and circling torsos with a vibrating presence. The force fanned Ajah's hair away from her face, touched her cheeks and crept along her arms in a tingling sensation that made her jerk her hand away from the stone altar.

Ajah's head dropped forward chin to her chest and her shoulders slumped down. Eyes closed, she began to hum. It was a haunting melody, one that was sung during rituals before the invasion, one that called the great goddess Gaea into their midst.

The hum grew louder and Ajah raised her chin, a smile flitting across her lips. Brown eyes opened but it was no longer the young one who looked out at Jahmed. The change was subtle but clear - Ajah receded and another waited to speak.

Jahmed's mouth dropped open at the sight of Ajah holding the spirit of Gaea. Inni clutched at Jahmed's arm.

"Gaea? Dear Mother Goddess, where is our beloved Niala? Who has taken her? Please, tell us."

The Rebel has risen.

Although Ajah's voice carried the words, the intonation had changed and the words slowed as if chosen with care. Or as if someone had forgotten how to speak with lips and a tongue.

Rebellion lives.

"Who? Who do you speak of? Kulika?" Jahmed could scarce force out the question. She felt her heart might hammer right out of her chest and could hear little else than the surging noise in her ears.

My daughter. Rebellion has risen.

Jahmed stared first at the blank expression on Ajah's face and then turned to stare at the empty bier. She was breathless but calmer. The din in her ears subsided. "Do you mean Niala?"

Ajah's chin dropped in a nearly imperceptible nod.

"She is not dead? She is safe? But where? Where is she? Who took her?"

He is misguided.

"Who is misguided? Who took Niala Aaminah?"

There was no immediate response. The humming resumed as if Gaea was contemplating her next words.

Forgive him.

Please, Gaea, tell us, where is Niala?"

There was a long silence during which Ajah swayed as if nudged by a gentle breeze. Jahmed feared a human touch would send her into a spasm. To hold the essence of Gaea without a totem could bring instant death in the event that Gaea were to release Ajah too quickly. Inni paid no attention. She knelt on the floor, her fingers running over and over the shroud as if she would find Niala hidden somewhere within it.

When Ajah's lips parted again only one word emerged.

"Deimos."

Ajah sucked in a wheezing breath and collapsed into Jahmed's arms as the energy receded. With wobbling legs and a tight chest, Jahmed lifted the semi-conscious Ajah and shouted at Inni to help. Between them, they half-carried, half-dragged the younger woman along the steep path to the temple.

Sinking to a footstool, Jahmed closed her eyes. The enormity of all that had transpired in the past few hours was overwhelming. Ajah remembered nothing and was gripped with a weakness that sent her to rest. Inni sat babbling to herself in the corner, unable to comprehend that Niala's body was missing. And now, as the shadows crept across Najahmara signaling sunset, she was reminded the time was drawing near to Pallin's rescue. A few more days, at best. Jahmed knew she must rally her strength to prepare the provisions that would allow Pallin and Mursilis to hide in the caves, however temporary.

In the caves.

Jahmed blanched. Her shoulders slumped as the weight of the day laid upon her. Deimos had stolen Niala's body. Gaea claimed her to be a rebel rising, but Jahmed had no concept of what that meant to the Earth Mother, or what it was supposed to mean to them.

Gaea had spoken through Ajah. It was now clear that Ajah could hold the immortal energy during a ritual to release Kulika back to his own realm.

"But not without a tether. We must perform the ritual to tie her to her Spirit Guide, otherwise we could lose her altogether." Jahmed spoke to herself. "We cannot risk it without the bond to the Sagittariidae. Is it possible there is one among us who can walk between the worlds and tie the cords?"

She jerked as Tulane touched her shoulder. "Zahava, what has happened? Is there something I can do?"

"Ahh, Child, here is the long and short of it." Jahmed described the events, taking comfort in Tulane's presence. She was young in age but mature in her outlook - she would become a superb priestess, one fit to lead when the time came.

"I sit here wondering if Ajah can hold the spirit of Gaea long enough to finally rid Najahmara of Kulika's deceitful presence. Would that in and of itself relieve the foolish plan to send Pallin and the boy away? Once Kulika is sent back to his own realm will Hattusilis cease his madness?"

"If Kulika has taken possession of Hattusilis, it would seem banishing him would change everything."

"He is a god drunk on power." Jahmed rubbed her temples

to ease the headache that would not go away. "Gaea will want to protect him. I say banish him, and may he never be allowed to return."

"Pallin and Mursilis can only hide in the caves for a short time. They cannot stay there forever."

Tulane spoke aloud the very essence of Jahmed's worry.

"No, they cannot. We must correct this situation and send Kulika back to his own realm, no matter what the outcome. It is possible that in Hattusilis' feeble condition, he might not even survive the withdrawal of Kulika's energy."

In a grave voice, Tulane again spoke the truth. "Would it be for the best if Hattusilis did not survive? For then, Pallin would have no fears as it is clear Zan would assume command of the soldiers."

"You have sharp eyes and ears for one of your age." Jahmed smiled for the first time in what seemed like months.

"We must go through with the ritual to unite Ajah with the Sagittariidae for if she has not been initiated, she cannot be the one to hold Earth's energy for a prolonged time. It would kill her."

"Yes, Zahava." Tulane nodded, her hands folded in front of her. "Please allow me to bring you sustenance. I fear you are ready to collapse."

"Tea would be nice." Jahmed smiled again as the girl retreated to the cooking quarters.

After mere moments of Gaea possessing her in the cavern, Ajah was exhausted, vomiting and unable to eat. She had no protection, no tether, and no way to release the energy. She was, in essence, poisoned from the contact. Gaea had no concept of such carnal stress - to her it was a simple act of energy exchange. She did not understand the priestess' need to have dominion over her own body.

Startled, Jahmed rose to her feet.

"Is that the real reason Gaea continues this use of Ajah without her permission? She spoke of the rebel rising. Is she, herself, the rebel? I thought she meant Kulika, for he disobeys her command and stays on this earthly plane. But now, I am not certain.

"If Gaea can force her being into Ajah, she could stay as long as she wishes. If she does not need permission perhaps she would never leave. Earth and Sky united in physical form. And what then? Are we doomed to be pawns in the games of Divinity?"

Jahmed paced to the doorway of the medicinal hut and peered out through the curtain. The moon was growing smaller and soon it would be very dark, casting only a few shadows. A new moon was to their benefit. Pallin and Mursilis could be moved with more ease and without their every step highlighted.

"Please forgive me, my Dearest Pallin, for all my judgment," Jahmed whispered. "We will save you, I swear it on my life."

"I agree, we must remove Kulika's hold over Hattusilis and banish him back to the Sky Realm." Ajah stood at the doorway that joined with the sleeping quarters.

"Why are you up? You should be resting." Jahmed released the curtain and let it slide across the entry.

"I find you here speaking only to yourself."

"Tulane was here only moments ago, I swear."

"Even so, it would appear you, too, should rest. The strain has taken a toll on your strength."

"I will not lie." Jahmed rubbed her forehead in response to the headache still in residence. "I am tired."

"Inni is inconsolable."

"If Deimos has taken Niala's body, there is nothing to be done. Perhaps it is for the best. If she does, indeed, live then he may be able to help her where we cannot. And if she is truly dead," Jahmed looked away from Ajah. "Then he will honor her in the manner of his kind. Either way, it is out of our hands. We have other things demanding our attention."

"And that is what I want to talk about." Ajah came to Jahmed and took her hands in her own, gripping with the intensity of youth. "I know you fear that I cannot hold Gaea's energy, but I have done so twice and lived to tell the tale. I can do this. I must do this. It is our only way."

"Ajah, there is a plot much deeper than we can see." Jahmed gripped the younger woman's fingers. "Gaea should not inhabit you without an invitation, without ties to the Spirit Realm. What if Kulika is calling her to him? What if she intends to keep your body for herself?"

"Gaea would not do such a thing!"

"We worship her and yet we do not truly understand her greater plan. It is all a mystery that we mere mortals fall prey to. My trust of these divine beings has vanished into thin air for they appear to take advantage of our weakened state."

"She is the Earth Mother. She loves us and cares for us. She would not betray us." Releasing Jahmed's hands, Ajah sat down on the longest bench.

"She already has. Especially you, Ajah. I fear deeply for your life. You have held Gaea's presence for short moments - to do what we must do is a thousand times more draining. You are not initiated. It could kill you without a Spirit Guide. And we cannot even be certain Gaea will assist us."

"If that is the sacrifice I must make, then so be it." Ajah's jaw set with stubbornness. "Come, Jahmed, we must be strong. I am our last hope. If Kulika cannot be forced back to the Sky Realm, we are lost."

"You have not yet received the rites of the Sagittariidae. It cannot be done without the Spirit Bird to assist."

"Then we must hold the initiation rites as soon as possible. We cannot wait any longer." Ajah trembled at the thought of the ritual where the image of the Sagittariidae would be etched onto her back. Still very frightened of it, she was determined to go through with ceremony.

"Niala Aaminah herself told me that I was ready before the invasion. Before all the tragedy that has befallen our people. Now we are faced with further grief if we do not dispel Kulika. No one else can do this but me. Jahmed, you are too important. If we fail, you must be here to lead our people.

"I was a coward the first time this power was offered to me, and here I am, no better than before. Because of me, our people died. I cannot let that happen again."

"A coward?" Jahmed sat beside the younger woman and lifted her chin. "What is this about cowardice? This is the bravest thing you could ever do. You would sacrifice yourself for the good of your people."

"If I had let the Sagittariidae's spirit to enter me at the first rites of passage, I could have prevented...." With hollow eyes, Ajah stared at a vision of the violated and scarred walls that lay beyond the doorway into the depths of the sanctuary.

Jahmed's gaze followed. "I will not allow you to blame yourself. The temple survived, as did we. Things transpire within this world without our knowledge. We have no control over the life and death that is around us."

"Does the ritual hurt as much as it appears?" Ajah's gaze was fixed on a row of jars set upon a shelf.

"It does, and yet it is a good pain. It has been so very long since the spirit wrote upon my flesh, but I recall the joy with which I accepted my gift."

"Not so long ago, Zahava."

Jahmed touched her own dark face with a rueful smile. "I am much older than I appear. My people do not show our age until one day...poof...we dry up and turn to dust. So yes, long ago."

"Ahh, you jest with me at a time when I cannot laugh."

"A bit, perhaps, but I do not lie to you. Having the spirits join with you is without description."

Inhaling deeply, Ajah smelled the familiar herb and spices of the medicines and the underlying scent of charred wood that would not leave in spite of all the scrubbing. In her head, she could hear the screams of panic and mayhem when the soldiers invaded, and the terror of her people.

With straightened shoulders, Ajah nodded. "I am ready now. Please, Jahmed, you must let me do this."

"Even if I agreed - and I am not saying that I do - we no

longer have a healer who can commune with the spirits and receive the image to connect you to your guide. Seire and her apprentice are both gone. No one else has the ability."

"There is someone."

"Who? Who among us can journey into the spirit realm? None that I know of."

"You will not approve, Zahava, but there is a man - a very gentle man - who came here on a ship from far away. He fell ill and sought out my assistance. He has described his visions of Najahmara and how he came to this land to find us."

Jahmed frowned. "I do not know who this is."

"He will help us."

"How can we trust a simple traveler? It is too dangerous."

"I feel a great bond with this man. Please let me bring him here so that you, too, can know he is trustworthy."

Jahmed placed her hand at her throat, as if the gesture would keep the sharp words of suspicion from spilling out. Had Gaea sent this man to them to help? Closing her eyes, she went within her own heart and decided there was no other choice.

EIGHTEEN

Ares awoke to muffled sobbing. Lying on the narrow cot with only a dim shaft of light from the oil lantern casting shadows, he took a moment to listen before sitting up. Persephone was seated at the small table in the outer chamber, but not in her usual quiet repose.

Instead, her face was buried in her hands, elbows on the table top, shoulders sloped in despair. Little spurts of crying alternated with distraught muttering and gestures toward the indistinct passage behind her, as if she spoke to someone who could not be seen.

This was all very out of purpose with the Queen of the Souls. Perhaps Persephone of the New Spring held doubts - maybe even shed tears over the many spirits needing her services - but this crazed ranting was contrary to her demeanor. It was unlike any behavior Ares had witnessed in his extended visit to the Shadowland.

It was a trace worrisome.

Persephone promised to find a way for him to return to the

land of the living. Whether she swore it out of concern for her own fidelity or because she was tired of his company or because of guilt over his imprisonment, Ares knew not. Nor did he care her reasoning.

He wanted his freedom at whatever cost, but this grief-stricken wailing was difficult hear. With a grunt, Ares rose and went to the bars separating him from the outer chamber.

"Persephone, what troubles you?" He intended his tone to be compassionate. What emerged was a bored quality even he recognized. Trying again, Ares spoke with deliberate tenor. "What has happened to make you weep in such a manner?"

Startled, Persephone fell silent though her breathing continued on in a ragged wheeze. When she spoke, it was with a cracked voice and scarce concealed emotion.

"You are awake."

"I am. Throughout my existence, rest has been elusive and yet here I find myself asleep more than alert."

"Even now, you are healing. Although your spirit is parted from your corporal body, you are attached at your core since it survives. Through this connection, you are restoring your body as well as your soul."

Persephone recited this response without inflection. It was the same answer she had given him numerous times, one Ares well knew. Oddly, he was being polite, which gave Persephone a flicker of amusement.

Imagine War courteous - would anyone believe it? She hardly did herself. Pushing back tear-dampened curls, Persephone dried her face on her sleeve. Ares was only patient because he desired his release.

And she had found a way to liberate him.

Persephone could not regret that Ares would be away from her domain - even though it would not be hers for long. As that thought wiggled back into her awareness, the tears began again.

"What ails you, Persephone? This is unlike your gentle countenance."

"I must return to the Mortal Realm in three days."

"That does not seem a reason for tears." But rather than pursue the whys of this fit, he allowed the spark of excitement to launch within him. Did this mean that he, too, would be able to return? "And I?"

Persephone lifted one hand in weary acquiescence. "Yes, you also will depart, though you may not welcome the terms."

Ares frowned. Agreement might be dangerous. He could find himself emerging as anything. Yet, he could not languish in the Shadowland any longer or he would go mad.

"I accept any tenure that brings freedom."

"As you wish, War god. In three days, you will go with me through the portal between the living and the dead, at which time, Libertina will assist in the rest of your journey."

"Sweet Death will assist *me*?" A tingle at the back of Ares' neck suggested that there was, indeed, a trick at hand.

Libertina detested him. Upon the very sight of Ares, her elegant nose would wrinkle as if she smelled something dreadful and then turn her face away, refusing to give him any kind of homage.

"She has agreed to grant me a favor."

"I can scarce believe she would help me."

"She would not, save for my request." As the lamplight caught in Persephone's eyes, there reflected a wary glint.

"And in return?" Ares gripped the bars and leaned forward, better to hear each word.

"In return, I require a favor from you."

Ares paused, brow creased. He did not care for Persephone's tone and yet he had already agreed to the terms.

"Do you wish to tell me of this favor or are you content to spring it upon me at a later time?"

Persephone's laugh was laced with bitterness. "Well said. *Spring* it upon you. It is in my role as New Spring - Regeneration - that I will need this assistance."

"And what is this good deed I will owe you?"

A pained wail erupted from Persephone's throat. She could not hold it back.

"I fear Hades will not claim me when it is time."

The well-known scent of panic rose from her body and trailed like smoke to the bars of Ares' prison. He had smelled the acrid aroma at every battlefield when the defeated ones realized there was no hope.

"What do you speak of? I do not understand."

Everyone knew the story of Hades and Persephone, the legendary theft of virginal New Spring called Kore, from beneath the proverbial nose of her mother, Demeter. All knew of Demeter's rage and the demand to return her daughter to the Mortal Realm so that Spring could thaw the vicious winter which had fallen upon the Earth.

Except it was not true. Hades did not steal his bride. Persephone went willingly - she was wildly in love. She knew her fate was more than bringing warmth to the Great Mother. She was destined to become a healer of souls, to assist in the continued cycling of human life.

During the struggle between Demeter and Hades over the innocent girl called Kore, Persephone stepped into her own power. She swallowed 6 pomegranate seeds while in the Shadowland. This simple act ensured she could remain with Hades six months out of the year. The other six months, she would visit the Mortal Realm to bring warmth to Earth.

No one said she had to do it all at once. Clever Persephone chose her own destiny by splitting her time in a different fashion: one month with her husband, one month with her mother, and so on, thereby fulfilling all of her duties.

Ares smiled. Persephone was no one's fool. And yet, here she was, weeping like a child denied a toy.

"Each time I leave Hades must reclaim my love. He must renew his vow to me or I cannot return to the Shadowland. If he does not appear to me, if he does not profess his love, I cannot come home." She waved her hand in a vague gesture toward the outer walls of his prison. "But now, my husband has rejected me. He has taken another to his bed and I fear that he intends to make her his new Queen. I fear he will not fulfill our marital contract and I will not be able to return. Ever."

Astonished, Ares' mouth opened and then closed without comment. Of all the pairings in all the Immortal Realms, Hades and Persephone were thought to be the most loyal to each other. For a millennium there had been not even a whisper of infidelity between them.

Except one. There had been one hint of Hades straying from his beloved. Unproven save for Ares' own notions when he looked upon the face of Niala Aaminah. He knew she was an immortal being even though she denied it. Why would a child of the gods be cloaked in such a fashion?

To avoid discovery.

And why that?

Indiscretion.

Children were not born to immortal parents with random ease as are humans. The children of gods were created with intention, distilled through the needs of the Mortal Realm.

Niala Aaminah held a greater purpose than a mere priestess of Najahmara. Her parents had gone undetected for centuries but Ares knew when he looked upon her face for the first time that she was something more. He recognized familiarity in her features.

Not when they first met, when she was a budding girl, but later, after she had grown into a woman. Then he began to see the possibilities of her parentage.

Hades was the first to cross his mind.

"Who is this you fear will displace you?" Ares asked more out of curiosity than concern. Could this new infatuation of Hades be Niala's mother?

Persephone's chin quivered as she attempted to speak the name of her husband's lover. Thrice she tried before the name was whispered aloud.

"Leuce."

"Daughter of Oceanus? Humph." Ares frowned. "Leuce is unexpected."

Raising a tear-stained face, Persephone's voice rose with outrage. "Is there another?"

Tapping his fist against the bars, Ares turned away from her without a response. It was not his place to make his suspicions known.

That thought made him chuckle. In the past, it would not have mattered, his place or not. He would have taunted her with the idea regardless of the truth. Had time in the Shadowland softened him?

"Is there? Is there another? Ares, you must tell me what you know."

"And why would I do that?" Ares turned a cool stare upon Persephone.

"I saved you, healed you." Persephone gave a sharp shake of her curls and straightened her shoulders. "I have found a way to free you. Do you not feel I am owed the truth?"

"I do not know for certain. My thoughts are mere suspicions."

"Just speak what you know, or suspect, please." Pulling her hair across her shoulder, Persephone began to twist it into a knot. She stared at the lantern flame, unable to look at Ares as he told her the story of Niala Aaminah.

"And this woman, she is of the immortal race?"

"Yes, though she denies it."

"Who...is...her...mother?" Persephone ground out the words.

"This I do not know, nor could even guess."

"You could. You did!" Persephone rose quickly and the chair fell over with a clatter. "You know who it is."

"There have been, shall we say, a few hints that have come to my attention."

"If you will not tell me, then instruct me as to how to find this Niala Aaminah so that I may see for myself any resemblance to my husband."

Ares lips quirked upward into a quick smile before

straightening into a firm line. His black eyes went flat. "If you want more details, it shall not be until I am restored to my own body."

"Your cruelty has returned, I see." Persephone came to the bars and twined her fingers around the metal.

"*My* cruelty?" With a throaty laugh, Ares waved at the small cell. "What do you call this?"

"I have told you, it was for your safety. Of this I swear."

"You could not release me into the outer chamber, even for a moment?" Ares put both hands over Persephone's delicate fingers and gripped until she flinched. "You do not trust me?"

"I do not. With good reason." Her gaze dropped to his hold on her.

Ares released her and stepped back, hands held palm up.

"Forgive me, I forget where I am. Could we return to this favor I will owe you upon my release?"

"Hades has taken Leuce to his bed. He will not see me, even for a moment."

"That does not sound like my uncle. His honor is well known."

"Something has changed and he has turned away from me." Once again twisting her dark red locks into a plait, Persephone contemplated the wall as if she could read the truth within the flickering shadows cast by the lamp. "Are you positive this woman is a daughter of Hades?"

"No one knows for certain."

"But you know she is an immortal?"

"In over three hundred mortal years, Niala scarce appeared different. A human would have been long dead."

"There is no question that she is one of us?"

"No question.

"Does she look like him?"

Ares called up Niala's image, brown hair burnished auburn, wild with curls, gold eyes that glowed from within, generous mouth, skin the color of fallen leaves darkened by the approach of the winter season.

"She carries the mark of Hades upon her face."

Persephone leaned her forehead against the bars. "Does she carry her mother's presence?" Head lifting, Persephone stared at Ares. "Do you see another immortal etched upon her face? Do you know who her mother could be?"

Ares leaned close to Persephone, their faces touching, save for the bars between them. "Open the door and I will tell you."

"No, you seek to trick me."

"Trick you into what? I cannot go anywhere without your help, now can I?"

"You know who this woman's mother is, you truly do know?"

"Again, I cannot say for certain. I can only tell you what I believe." Ares cocked one eyebrow up in an amused expression. "Let us speak without a prison between us."

"Tell me."

He stood back and waved at the cell. "Your choice."

"You are a horrible creature." Persephone stomped one foot. "No wonder you are hated so across the realms."

"Indeed."

Arms folded, Ares waited in silence while Persephone ranted about his ingratitude. At the end, when the tears of frustration dried up, a trembling Persephone unlocked the door and stepped inside.

"There, we have no bars between us."

"Do not," Ares stepped closer to her, "lock me inside again."

Persephone's breath caught but she would not move away in fear. She was the Queen of Souls. Ares could not hurt her.

"Tell me who bore my husband a child."

With a tight smile, Ares nodded. "Artemis."

"Artemis?" Persephone closed her eyes against the pain in her heart. "No. Never. Artemis is well known for her chastity. She would not do this. She has slain her own followers for far less, for the mere thought of lying with a man. You are wrong."

Persephone searched Ares' bottomless gaze for duplicity but saw only truth.

"I could be wrong, but it is unlikely. Niala bears a great resemblance to Artemis, not only in body but in determination."

"Hades made love with Artemis? And a child sprang from this union? It cannot be." Persephone sank down onto the cot. "How could I not know of this?"

"Our chaste huntress is no longer a virgin, which is reason enough to keep Niala's existence a secret." Ares sat beside her, his wicked laughter tickling her ears.

"I have longed for a child, and is it not irony that I - Regeneration, she who brings the seed of life and hope into the mortal world - have not conceived? Why is that?"

Ares shrugged. "This very puzzle bests me beyond comprehension: why does every female place so much importance on birthing a child?"

"You speak now of Aphrodite."

"It was her fatuous desires that brought me to this existence. Had she waited...."

"Waited for what? For you? We should not be at the mercy of male fertilization. I bring my own seed to the Mortal Realm."

"But there is more that makes those seeds spring to life. You need...." Ares ran his palm along Persephone's arm. He spoke the last word with his lips against her neck. "...heat."

Persephone shivered but did not draw away. It was with a reckless and bruised heart born of anger and betrayal that Persephone turned to Ares and kissed him.

Surprised, Ares paused to look into her eyes. Though he intended seduction, he did not expect the Queen of Souls to fall into his arms. It was more of a game, to see her flee his presence, leaving the cell door open for his escape.

That she kissed him - at first in gentle exploration, and then with a shuddering passion contained far too long - was more than he could resist.

He fell upon her with ravening lust, and Persephone pressed back with aching desire. Ares ripped her garments and threw them to the floor. His body, already naked, needed no more encouragement. Persephone opened to him and he took her.

There were no tender moments, no sweet words, no delicate touches. Their act was violent. There was no thought. Animal instinct swept them away. They strained against each other as if they could merge and become one. As if they could erase the pain.

They came to a shuddering crescendo and lay gasping in each other's arms. Persephone clung to Ares, her face buried against his smooth chest. Ares did not push her away. Instead, he drew the blanket over them and held her close.

"I am not sorry." Persephone's voice was muffled.

"Nor I."

There was a moment when Ares wanted to laugh at the absurdity, he with Persephone, but thought better of it. They lay in quiet contemplation, each reluctant to break the silence. In the end, it was he who first spoke.

"What is this favor you would have of me?"

With a soft exhale, Persephone shifted into a more comfortable position. "Did you know that when I return to the Earthly Realm as Regeneration, as New Spring, I will remember none of this?"

Ares made a sound deep in his throat.

"No? I am not surprised. I do not believe anyone knows this great truth, save for myself, Hades and my mother, Demeter." Persephone ran her fingers along Ares' chest. "And Zeus."

"Each time I move through the portal as Queen of the Shadowland, Healer of Souls, Purveyor of Life and Rebirth - each time - I lose all memory of my reign here. I become just like those I usher from spirit to the physical plane. Newborn with no memory of what was before. A clean slate to start over as each soul is given the opportunity to grow into infinite possibilities."

Persephone turned her gaze to Ares, her blue eyes wide with fear. "Do you understand what I am saying?"

Ares met and held her gaze, amazed at the swelling empathy within his heart. "You are saying that if Hades does not come to you and offer himself each time, every time, if he refuses to find you and you do not fall in love with him, then all of this…." Ares pointed a realm he had never seen save for his prison. "...is gone. You will no longer reign as the Queen of Souls."

"I will forever be New Spring."

"How could that be?"

"My mother." Persephone's tone grew bitter. "It is the agreement Demeter forced upon Zeus. Each time, she has the opportunity, the possibility and the rash hope I will forget Hades and stay with her. Each time she does her best to thwart Hades and stop him from claiming me as his wife. Each time he has circumvented her and found me. Because he loves me. Or has until now."

"And now he loves another. You are uncertain he will come for you."

Persephone hid her face, unable to speak.

"And what can I do to help with this? It appears to me that I have no power in this matter."

"You are Ares, god of War. Everyone fears you, even Zeus himself. You wield Amason, the only weapon that can end the life of an immortal soul. You can compel them to change the agreement, give me my memories, my knowledge of the Shadowland. If Hades does not come for me, I can find my own way home."

"Is that what you want?"

"What I want is for my husband to love me the way he always has."

"What if I cannot influence Zeus and Demeter to alter their agreement?"

"Then you must force Hades to come for me. Coerce him." Persephone spit the last words out between gritted teeth. "Or kill him."

"That is the favor I will owe for my release?" Amusement and something more chilling colored his words.

Persephone hesitated for a mere moment. "Yes. That is my request."

"You are certain?"

"Absolutely."

Ares took only a second to consider his reply.

"So be it."

Persephone knew she should be afraid for Hades. She may have signaled his end, but she could not find it in her heart to care.

She could not forgive him.

*****

The sailor flailed in the churning sea, struggling to breathe with naught but salt water swallowed through nose and mouth. The agony as his body convulsed, vomited and silently screamed for help when there was none to be had. Clawing hands reached for anything to keep his body above the surface but found nothing.

Waves crashed over his head and pushed him down into the depths. Though the sailor fought hard, he was weakened and sunk further with each surge.

He was drowning.

Live by the sea; die by the sea. It was the way of the water born. The sailor spent his life on board ship. He saw distant lands, monsters in the deep, strange folk and many a storm, but this last swallowed them whole and spit them out in pieces.

Everyone was dead, gone when the deadly wall of water converged upon the ship and smashed it to bits. He was alive only because he was lashed to the steerage, but then the wheel broke apart under the thundering rage of the sea and he joined his fellow shipmates.

With one last gasp, the sailor gave up and let the sea claim her son. He sank below the surface, relinquishing his body to the only mother he had ever known.

Libertina watched and waited. She could not take a body from a soul without acquiescence, without that soul first choosing to abandon his physical temple. As she searched the mortal realm for just such a body, many were presented but all were rejected as unsuitable to house War.

No, Ares needed strength, agility, endurance and youth to hold his energy. So Libertina waited, watched and denied each one until now. This one caught her attention because, although battered and bruised by the ship debris, this one was unharmed. No mortal wounds, no broken bones, no disease. This man was well built, young, sturdy and with a pleasing face.

This one was acceptable.

Libertina waited until the sailor knew his last breath was upon him, waited until he let go, separating soul from body. She saw his spirit rise up, recognized the confusion stamped upon his energetic presence as he stared down at the corpse floating just beneath the waves.

She waited as the spirit hesitated, considering whether to return to his mortal remains and try again to survive this ordeal. Saw the flitting thought that he had endured through many other torments and lived to tell the tale. Saw the grief cross his spirit's awareness.

With one hand outstretched to greet the soul that was in need of escort to the Shadowland, Libertina bid Ares to prepare.

"Come, War. I have found a mortal body for you to reside within until such time that I can put you into your own body."

"Remember, Sweet Death," Ares replied, "I do not want to lose my identity. I must know who I am when I open those mortal eyes. It is imperative I retain the knowledge of Ares the Destroyer and not become some human flotsam for the rest of this weak life."

"Do you threaten me? For if you do, I shall return you to Persephone's prison where you may stay for all eternity."

"I must recall everything. Do you agree to this?"

"I cannot say. What you request is beyond my power. Perhaps you will know and perhaps you will not. Do you wish to take this chance, for time is running out for this mortal to breathe once again?"

Libertina pointed to the floating body being tossed about in the angry ocean and then turned away, her arm around the ethereal form of the newly released sailor.

Ares cast a sidelong glance at the white-robed purveyor of death. Her pale countenance did not reflect any dismay at his demands, she merely responded as if they conversed about the weather. He weighed his choices: one, to return to the Shadowland where he, at the least, had form. Two, remain in the ethereal dimension that was neither here nor there, to drift with endless longing. Three, accept the sailor's body and pray that all memory would travel into the Mortal Realm with him.

A quick nod was all that was necessary.

It was now up to Ares to survive or not. Libertina did as she promised and what became of him was none of her concern. She disappeared with the sailor's soul within her comforting embrace.

Momentarily, there was no sensation in the body. It was, after all, dead. It was beyond feeling pain, surrendering to the organic nature of the Mortal Realm.

Ares summoned his power and pushed into the body, through every muscle and tissue until the lungs exhaled mightily and water spewed out. He leaped above the surface of the sea, flailing both arms and legs, back arched, face to the heavens, gasping for air.

When he came down, it was within reach of a broken piece of the mast. He clung to the wood while growing accustomed to the human body and thought how close the sailor had been to a reprieve, had he just forced himself to swim a few more strokes.

The first wave of pain hit upon the second deep breath. The stressed lungs protested the expansion and the heart heaved, frantically pounding to beat with a steady rhythm, to push blood and air throughout the fragile system. Ares took it well, forcing breath after breath until the body stopped jerking and the torture receded.

He rested on the thick length of wood, drifting, unsure of his next move. This body had no power other than physical strength, and that now drained. He could not move from place to place by sheer will. He could not exist without food and unsalted water.

He did not even know where he was.

But he knew who he was.

His laughter was weak and self-mocking: for the first time in his existence, he found himself at the mercy of the gods.

"Hear me, Poseidon. I am your humble servant, a minion of the sea," Ares croaked through a throat raw from saltwater. He marveled at how much it hurt to even speak let alone swallow. "Help me. I beg you."

The last five words were the most difficult Ares had ever spoken. War asking for help. How rich. Would Poseidon take pity on the poor sailor whose body Ares inhabited? Or was Poseidon just as fickle with his followers as Ares himself had been with the warriors who came to his temple?

Time would tell. Meanwhile, Ares felt his consciousness ebbing even as he fought to maintain control. Though his energy was of that of the immortal race, his body was not. He fell into a stupor, unaware of the waves attempting to dislodge him from his makeshift raft.

One turn of the sun and moon and Ares heard shouts and bells, felt hands upon his sunburned skin. He was beyond pain as hard fingers dug into his arms, dragging him over rough wood. Delivered by Poseidon or the Fates, he did not know. He felt another unfamiliar sense: gratitude.

The sensation lasted for mere seconds before he blacked out and his body was hoisted upward.

Light. So light. Shadows flickered against his closed eyes, eyes that would not open. A flood of thoughts, memories of choking on water, of drowning. Then came the awareness of clear air filling his lungs and his heart beating in a solid thump against his ribs.

There was sound all around: the jumble of voices, creaking wood, metallic clangs and the screech of birds overhead.

Sounds.

The sounds of life.

Ares drifted in and out, aware when a covering was laid over his shivering body and again when clean water was dribbled into his mouth. He was indebted as the liquid ran down his parched throat. Tears slid from the corners of his crusted eyes.

He was alive.

Ares attempted to awaken, to look out upon the Mortal World he once again inhabited, but he could not even twitch his appendages. He could not lift his head. He could not force his eyes to open even after someone wiped his face with a wet rag.

There was movement beneath his body, a rhythmic shifting back and forth.

The deck of a boat?

He was cast into the body of a drowning man lost on the waves of an endless ocean. What other manner would come to his rescue than a sailing vessel?

A ship had saved him.

He was on his way home.

*****

Aphrodite jerked as a searing flame coursed through her body. She felt on fire, as if charring from the inside out. The flames seemed to lick through bone and blood and skin causing her watery nature to bubble and burst from the heat.

Her eyes flew open as a strangled shriek emitted from her lips. With a wild gaze, she stared at the serene cherubic faces that peered back at her from the gilded vault ceiling and thought she was possessed by demons.

Her mad gaze turned to the open air between the pillars framing the cobalt sea. The white draperies fluttered in the gentle breeze, bringing the scent of briny water and the cooling spray of salt-laden mist into the chamber to caress her face.

Beyond, she could hear the cry of gulls as they chased after each other in an attempt to steal a tidbit. She could hear the tide sucking at the sands and pounding against the boulders that lined a great deal of the shore. In the distance, there were children laughing and adult female voices calling out in chastisement.

All of it seemed foreign.

Aphrodite did not know where she was. She did not recognize these smells or sounds, nor did she feel the comfort of her favorite lounge or the soft swathe of the gown upon her body. The unfamiliar sensations rubbed against the grain of her very being as the fire consumed her. She could do naught but gasp and moan and roll about on the cushions of a chaise, while tearing at her clothing until she fell naked to the tiled floor.

She tried to rise and found herself too weak to get up and her throat too dry to call for help. Her voice was no more than a hoarse croak. She could only lie upon the cool surface where she had fallen as tears leaked from her eyes.

Burning up, inflamed, incautious with growing histrionics, Aphrodite felt the call of her beloved. He was out there and needed her. His soul beckoned to her, his spirit yearned for her, yet she could not go to him. She could not help him. All she could do was weep with a helplessness that went bone-deep.

Thaleia discovered her thrashing mistress upon the floor moments after and with a scream of alarm, rushed to her side.

"My Princess, my Princess - what is it?"

"Ares!" Aphrodite clutched at Thaleia's hands. "Ares drowns in the living waters of my mother's womb. He sends his fire to guide me to him. He needs me. He needs me!"

"I do not understand, Princess."

"Drowning, drowning." Once again, Aphrodite broke down in shrieks as the inner flame of her beloved's struggle consumed her body and soul.

Thaleia knelt beside her mistress and wrapped her arms around the writhing woman. Thaleia knew not what was happening, nor did she know what to do to alleviate Aphrodite's pain except to hold her so that she would not injure herself.

Thaleia's shouts for help brought no immediate response. Now crying herself, Thaleia rocked her sobbing mistress back and forth as she smoothed Aphrodite's disheveled hair away from her sweating face.

Covering Aphrodite's cheeks and forehead with kisses, Thaleia murmured, "All will be well, I promise. Breathe, Princess, just breathe."

The wailing grew louder as Aphrodite fought to free herself from Thaleia. "I must find him, I must find him."

"We will. I promise, we will."

Thaleia shouted again for help, to Aglaia and Euphrosyne, to Anteros and Eros, to the nymphs and dryads, to the all those who served in Love's Realm. Not one soul came to assist until Zelos stumbled in, appearing confused and beleaguered.

"Beloved, I would come to you if I could," moaned Aphrodite. "But I do not know where you are."

"What in tides is happening here?" Zelos demanded. "What is wrong with her? Why did you call me? I am not good with histrionics."

"No, you merely create them. I know the mischief you do since our mistress fell ill. Now bring your sorry self over here and help me."

Wide-eyed, Zelos inched forward. "What do we do? It appears as if lunacy grips her and her mind flown off."

Thaleia twisted with frantic haste, looking for some way to calm Aphrodite without harming her. The fluttering white drapes caught her attention, as did the sparkle of blue water from the spa upon the veranda.

"The pool. We will take her to the pool and hope the water can soothe her."

Together, Thaleia and Zelos carried the struggling Aphrodite to the spa overlooking the sea. Aglaia climbed in and supported Aphrodite's weight as they lowered her writhing body into the warm water. Aphrodite sank to her chin and a sigh escaped her lips. She stopped fighting.

"What is wrong with her?" Zelos withdrew her arms and put her hands on her hips. "I have never seen our mistress in such a state before."

Thaleia shook her head. "I found her this way, in terror, as if the

Hordes of War were upon her. I know not what has happened."

"Where is Anteros? He should be here, tending to his mother."

With narrowed gaze, Thaleia replied, "I, too, would like to know where Anteros is, as well as my sisters, for none of them have answered my call save for you."

"I did not willingly do so," admitted Zelos. "I was compelled."

Thaleia frowned. "It is not within my power to compel you or any of Love's minions to assist me."

"Then why was I without sway? I had no choice but to appear."

"The mysteries grow and I am frightened. There is mischief afoot, to be sure." Thaleia shifted to a more comfortable position, still cushioning her mistress so that she did not sink below the surface.

"Yes, but what has brought this on?"

"I have said already that I do not know."

Thaleia paused and stared at Aphrodite. Love's turquoise eyes were open but no longer stared with blankness. Instead, ignited within that oceanic gaze was a murderous rage fuelled by jealous vengeance. Coiled tension launched Aphrodite up through the water to her feet as a loud ululation vibrated from her throat.

Before either could speak, Nemesis - Love's Revenge - appeared in a tumbling fall across the walkway. She sat sprawled before them with a bewildered expression.

Zelos and Thaleia looked at each other, at Aphrodite and then at Nemesis.

"Oh dear," Thaleia whispered. "This is bad. Very, very bad."

On the heels of Nemesis came the twins, Odyne and Oizus, Love's Pain and Misery. The two young women fell to their knees with confusion etched upon their identical faces. Before any could stand, Zelus, Love's Rivalry, appeared. She took a fighting stance with an imperious glare at her companions.

"Why have we been called here?" Zelus addressed Zelos. She refused to look at Thaleia. "This is no mortal battle for love."

"No, Sister, it is not. There is something amiss with our Princess."

Splashing and sliding, Aphrodite struggled to throw off Thaleia's hands. With one final push, Thaleia fell back into the pool as Aphrodite rose out of the water, naked and glorious. Droplets cascaded down her flawless body. Her long hair clung to her curves as if embracing her flesh with loving hands. The air around her crackled with static, sending Thaleia into utter panic.

Eternal Love focused on the ocean's horizon with fierce intention. In one swift move, Aphrodite yanked Nemesis to her feet. The twins, Odyne and Oizus, rose as one to stand with her. Zelus joined them as they all stared toward the sea.

Aphrodite cast one chilling glance backward at Zelos and Thaleia before releasing another blood-curdling howl. She then disappeared, taking her minions with her.

"We must stop them," Zelos screeched, as an alarmed knowing passed over her features. "Where is Anteros?"

Speechless, Thaleia lifted her shoulders and shook her head. Anteros had been lax in his duties since discovering the young man washed upon the shoreline of Cos.

"Find him." Zelos froze in place as her eyes widened and a froth appeared on her parted lips. Her shoulders rolled back and her breasts lifted, as did her chin. Her gaze lengthened and her head tilted as she listened to something Thaleia could not hear.

Zelos' body quivered with anticipation. With great effort, she whispered, "Do something, please." before she was gone from Thaleia's sight. She left a small whirlpool trying to fill the vacated spot.

Thaleia sat in the bath, her gown floating serenely about her legs as if there was no concerns. She could not right off comprehend as she stared at the movement of the water until it stilled. It was then she closed her eyes and allowed the moment to relive within her mind.

What she saw was Aphrodite being consumed by the ignominious side of Love: Revenge, Jealousy, Rivalry, Misery, Pain - Nemesis, Zelos, Zelus, Oizus, Odyne and the horde of other minions that laid waste to the human heart. Each Realm held the balance between light and dark. Each Realm was responsible for this balance as it reflected in the mortal world.

Aphrodite always kept tight rein over the entities that brought such distress to her beloved mortals born of water, demanding that the difficulties be tempered by their softer sides. In the past, she was able to hold dominion over them. Now it appeared the dark side of Love was in deep rebellion and on the loose with Aphrodite in the lead.

As the depth of the situation sank in, Thaleia climbed out of the pool and went in search of Anteros. Her sopping gown left a wet trail as it slid along the marble floor as she marched through the interior of Aphrodite's palace.

The spacious beautifully-appointed chambers were a reflection of Thaleia's mistress right down to the palette of seaside colors. Always, Thaleia felt calm and centered when she wandered through the sunny warmth of these quarters. She was duly grateful when she was alone to enjoy the serenity.

On this day, however, she fumed and fussed that there was not a soul about. And why would there be anyone lingering indoors when the call of the sand and surf was strong within any of those who resided upon the isle of Cos? Of course, they would all be scattered about the island either in play or work, and no help to Thaleia.

"My sisters should be within calling distance," fretted Thaleia. "Where have they gone and why do they not hear me when I have need of them? And Anteros, shameful that he is not in closer unity with his own mother. Shame, shame, shame."

Thaleia continued talking to herself as she searched for Anteros. She intended to admonish him for his lack of attention. He was the only one who could find Aphrodite and stop the lunacy that had taken hold of her.

"Madness. This is all complete madness. Where will it lead? Oh dear, oh dear, oh dear."

Anteros heard none of the outburst. Although he felt the surge of power from Aphrodite, he ignored her call. He had never before pushed aside his responsibility to his mother's realm, never turned away from his duty. And yet, in that moment, it felt good to rebel.

Extraordinarily good.

He worked tirelessly to maintain order within the mortal scheme of devotion, to keep those darker instincts that inhabited Love's Realm from doing too much harm. It was a thankless job. There was never enough given and too much taken, to the point of exhaustion.

Because of all that, Thaleia's words - that he had not ever known real love - reverberated in his head like a canyon call echoed into the skies. She spoke the truth. Since Anteros was a child, since his first awareness, his entire existence was wrapped around Aphrodite's needs. Her struggle to stay afloat with all the emotion that constantly swirled around her was the one consistent element in his life. For Eons, Anteros was the only one responding to the balance of Love in the Mortal World.

This time, however, Love's Response was already engaged in answering the call of unmitigated infatuation. Perhaps even 'real love'. The young man, Hylas, captured all of Anteros' attention. As Hylas lay recovering from his wounds, Anteros could not take admiring eyes from the beauty of this youth. To discover his father was Poseidon further added to the titillation, for Hylas was only half mortal. The other half belonged to Anteros.

From the perfect symmetry of Hylas' features, the wispy locks of dark hair that stuck to sweaty skin, the shapely arms and legs and the torso that rippled with the demands of hard labor, to the perfect curve of buttock and well-developed manhood, Anteros could not tear himself from the sight of the naked young man sleeping in Anteros' own bed.

The few times Hylas awakened was merely long enough to be fed a simple broth and bathed. Then he fell back into an exhausted slumber, covered by a light linen sheet that hid nothing from Anteros' gaze.

Anteros sat by the bedside for several days watching the miracle of this lovely youth. He was amazed at the breathlessness he felt while gazing upon Hylas, and surprised by his own racing heart. Anteros could hear the pounding in his ears and feel the response of his phallus pressing against his leg.

He wanted this young man. He wanted to possess him in every way possible. Was that true love? To kiss and lick and suck, making love for hours until they were both spent? Until they fell into a dreamless sleep entwined in each other's arms?

Was that love?

Or was that lust?

Either way, Anteros could no longer restrain himself. He slipped out of his tunic and crawled into bed with Hylas, lying tight against his back. Anteros stroked the sunburned skin along Hylas' hip and kissed the back of his neck.

Hylas moaned and turned to face Anteros, his lips offered in sacrifice to Love's Response. Their limbs tangled and bodies strained against each other as passion ignited and they were lost within each other.

Anteros did not hear Thaleia's call, nor sense his mother's distress. He was consumed by the heat, oblivious to all other distractions.

NINETEEN

"My sister calls to me." Euphrosyne blotted sweat from her forehead and turned to Deimos. "And I can do no more for this one."

She glanced back at Niala, bathed, clothed in a simple gown, her hair combed into a burnished halo about her head and shoulders, lying in repose in one of the many spare beds in Aphrodite's palace.

"I cannot say that she will awaken, for her spark is very faint."

"She will. She did. She opened her eyes for a moment and looked at me."

Deimos brushed past Euphrosyne without a bit of gratitude for her service - a point she did not miss. Hands on her hips, Euphrosyne blew out a breath of air in response to the rudeness. She could see how enamored Deimos was of this woman, and indeed, Niala Aaminah was beautiful in an earthy lush sort of way.

Not at all like her mistress, Aphrodite, delicate and fragile, swimming in the emotional tides of her watery nature.

With head cocked to one side, Euphrosyne studied Niala. Now that there was some color restored to her face, she appeared to be in a natural sleep. Still, there was no movement other than the rhythmic rise and fall of her chest.

"Deimos, Thaleia demands my attention." Euphrosyne twitched as if jabbed by a sharp stick. "If you have need of something, please call Lyda."

"Go if you must." Deimos sat on the edge of the bedstand and caressed Niala's cheek. "But say nothing of this to anyone, including Anteros."

"He is Master here. I...must...tell...him." Euphrosyne jerked as if her hair was hardily yanked. Yelping, she lunged forward and crashed into a chaise.

"This must remain our secret." Deimos cast a single dark look at her antics before his gaze returned to Niala. "What are you doing?"

"I do not know." Euphrosyne huffed, out of breath from the effort to regain control of herself. "Something is very wrong." With that, she disappeared from sight.

Just as Euphrosyne took her rather hurried leave, Deimos felt a rush of undiluted jealousy followed by the desire to kill those who locked Niala in the cave. His hands balled into fists as he leapt to his feet. He turned in a circle, eyes red from rage, wishing to rend limbs from torsos, to throw fresh meat to his hounds, to cause pain and misery, to destroy everyone who would cross his path and get in his way.

Moments later there came a crushing jolt of adoration for the silent woman in front of him. He fell to his knees next to Niala's bedside as an upsurge of bittersweet love, unrequited love, abandoned, wandering and lost love brought tears streaming down his cheeks.

Deimos struggled to contain his passion. It tore at him in the most wicked way, worse than the battering of War's desires. He understood bloodlust. He did not understand emotive lust. As he looked upon Niala's beauty, he wanted nothing more than to tear her clothes away and possess her. His fingers moved with restless arousal, ready to do his bidding should he let go of his control.

No.

He would not ravage the woman he rescued. He would not let go and let Love have an immoral victory.

No.

But he was drawn closer, ever closer, until his mouth touched hers. He exhaled the warmth of his breath and inhaled the scent of mint, now a mere touch of it remained upon her lips. Closing his eyes, he rubbed his cheek against hers, his nose to her nose, his forehead to her forehead.

He could not help himself. He lay down next to her and pulled Niala into his arms. He held her close to his heart. Nothing more. Nothing sexual, though he ached for her.

When her head tipped to the side and her cherished lips were once again next to his, he covered her mouth with his own and kissed her, releasing, finally, all the grief around her death.

Through his tears, he whispered, "I love you."

He knew then why Aphrodite and Ares always returned to each other, no matter what. They had no choice - they embodied half of the same heart.

As Deimos kissed Niala for a second time, he felt her stir against him. A small tremor, a slight tensing and release. He thought he lost her once again as she then went still. He drew back to look at her beloved face, and gasped for he saw that her eyes were open and she returned his gaze.

Though he wanted to speak, though he thought so many times what he would say to Niala Aaminah should he get the chance, Deimos was spellbound. His throat locked and he could scarce draw a breath, let alone pour out his troubled guilty spirit or repeat his profession of love.

All he could do was stare into her amber eyes and pray that it was, indeed, Niala Aaminah who stared back. He searched behind the distant nearly blank expression hoping to see some spark of the woman he loved.

Tiny flecks of black floated in the depths of her tawny eyes, moving about, hinting of secrets that made Deimos uneasy. He brought one hand up, first to smooth the curling auburn hair away from her face and then to cup her cheek with his palm.

"Niala." It was a question more than a declaration.

She blinked once, slowly as if to clear away the debris lodged in her mind by her long sleep.

"Is it you, Niala? Have I truly called you back?"

She touched the tip of her tongue to moisten her lips and swallowed twice before trying to speak. A cough interfered with the first attempt but on the second Niala spoke.

"Where is my daughter?"

*****

Iris, Eris and Phobos emerged in the center of a large lake with all three shooting upward in a spray of iridescent water only to fall back and go beneath the waves. Phobos shot up again with a hoot of joy and slapped his hands against the surface before settling into a float upon his back.

Water was his natural element, his birthright and his childhood all wrapped into one wet parcel. With a satisfied grin, Phobos savored the sensation of being supported by the lake's loving arms.

Iris tread the surf as she scanned the horizon, hoping to get her bearings. She was not certain where they were even though she pictured a specific spot for them to emerge from the portal. Many things could have, and most likely did change in the many hundreds of years she was absent.

Eris screamed as he was hurtled out of the watery threshold, and howled in terror as he plunged back into the cold waves. He came up spitting, snorting and coughing as he floundered and splashed looking for something solid to grab.

The nearest thing to him was Iris. He latched onto her and pulled her under. With a swift kick, Iris brought them both to the top.

"Cold," Eris's teeth chattered as he clung to Iris. "Freezing cold! Where are we?"

"Sshhtt. We are in Llyn y Fan Fawr, a lake in my homeland." Holding him with one arm and using the other to keep them above the surface, Iris stared at the snow-covered slopes beyond the shoreline. "Do not awaken those who live within these waters."

"Who…what lives in the lake?" Phobos came upright, his brown eyes wide with sudden concern.

"Many creatures. Some dangerous. Some not. It is best if we do not call attention to ourselves. Let us make our way to the shore. Our destiny is between those hills.

With strong strokes, in spite of Eris' clinging to her shoulders, Iris, with Phobos close behind, reached the rocky shore within minutes. As they climbed out, shivering and grateful for what little warmth the weak sun gave them, Phobos frowned at his brother.

"You do not know how to swim?"

"No, and why would I? War does not take place in the sea and my homeland is the Sacred Forest. Did you see large bodies of water there? No, you did not."

"That is sad, Brother. To swim is to be free. I do not know how you can exist without the great oceans." Phobos wiped his face with one hand and glanced at the whitecaps dotting the dark lake. A thin layer of ice ran along the boulders that received constant splattering from the waves. "This water is quite cold. I prefer a balmier swim."

"I prefer none save a heated bath, thank you very much."

"Sshhtt. The both of you. This land has many eyes and ears, most of which are hidden from your sight."

"Where are we?" Eris turned in a circle, noting the direction the sun stood in the sky, which side the lake was on as opposed to the wintry hills. He also noticed they stood in snow-covered gravel.

"We are in the Fey Realm. It overlays the Mortal World in a most deceiving manner. Unlike your people who choose to inhabit one or the other domain, the Fey stand with one foot in each. We are on temporal soil and this lake, Llyn y Fan Fawr, serves both Mortal and Fey, yet the human eye cannot see us or our dwellings unless we lift the veil and reveal ourselves."

"Like a curtain?" Phobos twisted the edge of his loincloth between his hands and watched the stream run down his legs.

"Like a curtain," Iris agreed. "Our castles and manors might well sit next door to human lodgings but they would not know it. Unlike Athos or Cos, or any number of immortal habitats, which are quite solidly seen and visited by anyone passing by. *You* may make yourself invisible, but the Fey can make all of it disappear."

Iris spoke with a bit of pride and flipped her soggy hair away from her face. With this gesture, both boys stared at her.

"You are blue." They spoke in unison, mouths agape.

"Pale, like the sky, but blue," said Eris. "No more rainbow hue."

"Every bit of you is blue," Phobos added. "That I can see."

Holding one hand in front of her, Iris turned palm up and then over as her gaze followed her arm and then down to her legs and feet. Then she began to laugh in a soft tinkling trill.

"So I am. Well, my friends, you see my true identity: Branwyn of the Blue Water Tribe."

Iris chuckled again and then brought a more serious expression to her pretty face. "We must make our way through there." She pointed at a gap between the hills. "My mother's barrow is just beyond Bwlch Giedd."

"Are you certain that is where we should go? It did not sounds as if your mother was inclined to assist you before. What would stop her from taking you prisoner now?"

Eris studied the hills and saw no more than a rude shack here and there with trickles of smoke rising from the roofs. Many sheep dotting the land, though they were difficult to distinguish as their coats were nearly the same color as the dirty snow.

"Two things." Iris held up two fingers. "One. I am no longer the innocent girl married off against her will. I am Iris of the Rainbows, messenger to Hera, Queen of the Immortals." She folded her forefinger down, leaving a rude gesture for the boys to smile at.

"Second. I have War at my back. I have you." With a sly glance toward the pass between the hills, she added. "I cannot wait for our meeting with Queen Pennarddun and her court. And as for Arawn, he will pay dearly for what he has done."

With a tilt of her head, Iris clothed them all in warm garments and boots appropriate for the winter months. Next the boys knew, the three travelers stood before a wooden fence entwined with blood-red roses boldly blooming against the snowy backdrop.

"We have arrived at my mother's residence," announced Iris with a one-handed wave.

Beyond the gates lay a burial ground.

TWENTY

Kulika fidgeted with the bedcovers, annoyed with even the lightest blanket. The human body he inhabited, that of King Hattusilis, needed rest, yet Kulika resented the intrusion of physical necessities that plagued the mortal.

Sleep, eat, drink, groom - even clothing was an irritation. Kulika much preferred the body of an immortal, one that did not need anything, an indestructible dwelling that he could do with as he pleased.

Alas, such a fine residence was not available. He must make do with the feeble one he was in. Even with a body as infirm as Hattusilis, there were many pleasures to be had.

The taste of food on his tongue, in his mouth, the feeling of fullness as he ate and the fermented liquids he was plied with during meals were delicious. The scent of exotic flavors and spices filled his head with delight, this he could not deny. He could not forgo the inclinations even though he wished to be free of the need.

Licking his lips, Kulika thought of another indulgence he enjoyed, that of sexual gratification. Heretofore, his only opportunity was when his mate, Gaea, called him into form. She demanded his presence when *she* was filled with desire, when *she* wanted carnal bliss.

The choice was never his, until now.

Rising, he dressed in blood-splattered trousers and tunic, a result of a beating he gave a servant the day before. That, too, was delightful - to give vent to his rage without recrimination. He was not at all certain the man survived. Not that it mattered, there were so many more to replace the dolt.

Kulika shrugged and turned his thoughts back to Pallin.

He used the female form of the queen to satisfy his hungers, even when she cried for him to stop. Her begging empowered his lust. He spent hours with her, excited by her milk-filled breasts and rounded belly, fecund with another child. Kulika kept at the queen until she was sobbing, trembling and exhausted from his efforts. Only then would he leave her chambers and seek out sustenance for the body he wore.

The more he envisioned Pallin spread beneath him, the harder his phallus became until he could contain himself no longer. He made his way to her chamber for one last encounter before he sent her away at dawn. He regretted the decision to dispatch the queen to King Hattusilis' homeland but he had no choice - she interfered too much with his plans.

Pallin's threat to leave him and return to the temple was beyond acceptance. Hattusilis went into a frothing fit over it - which allowed Kulika to possess him - yet the serpent had to agree: the female was unnecessary and a nuisance. Killing her seemed overdone. Banishment was the next best thing.

The short corridor was oddly quiet with no one in attendance at the female's doorway. His command was to have a guard posted day and night - why was there no sentry?

Kulika could feel anger building and had to admit, this sentiment was also pleasurable. He could let the emotion take control of the body and do whatever he pleased. He often used the cane, once necessary to support Hattusilis' weight, as a weapon. He could freely beat anyone he wanted with no argument, for he was the ruler of this land.

Someone would die for the revolt against his orders.

Flinging open the door, Kulika strode into the room only to discover it was devoid of all humans. A single lamp cast shadows upon the walls, revealing the rumpled bed was abandoned. The pallet in one corner where the boy slept was empty. Pallin did not sit in either chair. She did not stand at the window gazing out as she often did. She and the child were gone.

A manic frenzy overtook Kulika. Howling at the top of his lungs, he swung the cane and struck the lamp, knocking it over. Flames immediately began to lick along the wooden platform bed and caught the linens afire.

He hurled swaddling and lotions and empty dishes to the floor. He pulled drapery from the window casing and threw it upon the now-spreading flames. He watched the room burn, just as Pallin would burn when he found her.

Hattusilis' frenzied howls brought the first guards running, with Zan on their heels. From there, the alarm was set in motion. The greater contingent that patrolled the streets and meadow came flooding onto the grounds. These men had been stagnant for many months, unused to the sluggish life to which they were relegated while their king recovered from his wounds.

Now, at last, it seemed there was something to fight for.

"Fire," Zan shouted to the soldiers. "Set up a brigade to bring water from the lake. The king's residence is on fire."

"Where is she," Kulika raged. "Where is my wife? How did she escape? Who allowed it?"

"My King, calm yourself." Zan yanked Hattusilis by the elbow. "You must come with me before you injure yourself. How did this fire begin?"

Guiding the king away from the inferno and out into the cool night air, Zan noticed the strength with which Hattusilis resisted. Entirely odd, considering the king was enfeebled by pain from the earlier wounds.

"She has taken flight. I want her found. Now." Spittle dripped from the corners of Hattusilis' lips as he continued to rant. "Her punishment will have no bounds, I swear it."

"What do you rave about? Queen Pallin has left on her journey to the Steppelands, at your command."

"Dawn. She is supposed to leave at dawn." Kulika struck Zan in the face with his cane. "Do you see sunrise? No. She was not to leave until then."

Zan rubbed the welt on his cheek, his thoughts whirling with an explanation. "My Liege, I felt it was best for the caravan to get a head start. I sent the legion on its way a few hours ago with Connal in the lead. A storm is in the offing and we did not want the queen to get caught up in it.

"I will overtake them very quickly as the caravan moves much slower than a man on horseback. My King, there were a few things I had need to do before setting out on a journey I might not return from. My wife…"

"Your wife? You have never wed."

"But I have." Zan kept his gaze locked upon that of his king and old friend. Or what used to be the man he respected, the man he would sacrifice his life to save. "You have been too ill to speak of it."

With narrowed hate-filled eyes, Kulika stared at Zan. He sensed the truth. There was no caravan, no journey. No wife. It was a lie.

"I burned it all, just as I will burn you for this treason. Now, where is the female?" Hattusilis raged, face flushed, eyes bulging from their sockets as veins throbbed in his neck.

"My King, please regain control, you will harm yourself if you overexert." Zan prowled in front of Hattusilis, moving back and forth, first with concern, second to avoid the slashing cane.

"Where is she? What have you done with my mate?" Hattusilis' pupils carried the shifting shadows of a sky filled with thunder clouds. The scent of madness rose off his body, sweat and drool mixed with the metallic odor of blood.

Zan could see the frightening change in his king and feared

the worst, that the corruption was now permanent. No matter what the priestess Jahmed said, he could not comprehend how they were to drive the demon from Hattusilis.

"Hattusilis, you speak madness. We are your loyal servants." Zan attempted to soothe him with a calm voice and a hand on his shoulder.

Kulika shook him off and moved away from the big man. He flailed his arms as he wildly shook his head, still screaming at the top of his voice. "It is the female with the many braids - it is she who has done this. I will kill her. I will burn her just as this dwelling burns!"

Over his shoulder, Zan watched the line of sweating soldiers passing buckets in a futile attempt to douse the blaze, for the cottage was fast becoming a wall of orange flames. The bonfire was drawing townspeople to the site as the glow reflected in the low-lying clouds. Fearful cries carried the alarm toward the center of Najahmara and confusion reigned.

"Hattusilis, you must compose yourself. Do not cause harm to yourself...."

Even as the words left Zan's mouth, Hattusilis' eyes rolled back in his head and his tongue protruded. The king had but one moment to clutch as his chest before dropping to the ground.

Zan stared in horror at the collapsed body of his king. Rushing to his side, with the other men gathered as witnesses in a circle, Zan checked for breath. There was none.

Hattusilis was dead.

*****

Jahmed waited with Ajah in the dusk of sunset for the ritual to begin. The two women stood just outside the entrance until all within were settled. Each woman was in quiet contemplation of the vast step they were taking into the future. Each faced her own concerns.

For Jahmed, it was the combination of past grief weaving with new dread. Something was in the air, restless and hungry, something that refused to be defined by Jahmed's earthly awareness.

Yes, there was Kulika who was out of control. The reason they must go forward with this sacrament. Kulika must return to his realm before he wreaked further havoc. But there was more - something dark and dangerous held Najahmara within its jaws, ready to crush the life right out of it.

Nose in the air, Jahmed beheld a whiff of something strange. The best she could describe it was as a tangy iron-like taste in her mouth, as if blood had been spilled. When she listened very hard, she thought she heard screaming. It was a faint echo and she was not certain if it existed only in the past. She heard it again - it sounded like children crying in frantic terror.

Pressing her fingers to her ears, Jahmed begged the latent noise to cease. She could not be distracted with the horrors of many yesterdays. She need to focus and to be present with the sacred ceremony that was about to begin.

"What is wrong, Zahava?" Ajah stood behind her. "What do you hear?"

"Nothing." Jahmed forced her hands to her sides and heaved a great breath, pushing away the sounds of bygone times.

Of course this ritual reminded her of those fearful days during the invasion and the loss of their beloved Niala Aaminah. The scent of the herbs burning in the flames, waiting for them to enter, for the ceremony to begin, calmed Jahmed. Just as she took Ajah's arm to guide her into the depths of the cavern, Ajah stiffened.

"Zahava, please understand how much I love you and all my sisters. I want this known, in case something goes awry."

"It will not, Dearest. You will shall tell everyone yourself. After this ritual, you, too, will be a teacher, a healer, a priestess to Gaea, for the Sagittariidae will bring you wisdom beyond belief." Jahmed smoothed the girl's hair, adjusting the flowers woven into the locks. "Be strong."

Ajah exhaled with a groan and her chin dipped forward. "I am not worthy of this."

Jahmed felt the prickle of un-priestess-like irritation rising. *Here, now, again, in this moment of calamity! What is wrong with the young ones that they cannot step up as is their duty without crying? In my day, under Niala, there was never hesitation, only the willingness to surrender to the greater need.*

Jahmed feared that all was coming to an end and there would be no victory over the conditions seeking to destroy Najahmara and her people. And where was Gaea? Why did she not come to save them? Kulika was her mate, why could she not stop him without their intervention? Were they not both of the Spirit Realm? Why did it take mortal sacrifice to bring this horror to an end?

These thoughts brought Jahmed to a complete halt as tears began to leak from her eyes. *'Aaiee, and I, too, cry. What are we coming to? What am I becoming?'*

Filled with forlorn hopelessness that had captured her heart at the death of Niala Aaminah, and now, the loss of her whole body from Gaea's sanctuary, coupled with the deep wounds to her beloved Inni, Jahmed very nearly turned away from the ritual. She could sustain the pain no longer. Perhaps it would be best if she just leapt from the side of the mount.

"Zahava." Ajah took a deep breath and put her arms around Jahmed. "I did not intend to cause you such sorrow. I am ashamed."

"No, no, Dearest." Jahmed also took a steadying breath and returned the embrace. "This is what the Sky God wants, fear and uncertainty. We will not give him the pleasure of seeing us fail."

Straightening her back and shoulders, Jahmed lifted her chin with courageous resolve. "We have all been in this place of fear. Do you believe I ran into the arms of the Leuncolus without first quaking? The spirit beast that put its mark on me was ferocious. Do you not think I wanted to stop the whole thing and go away? Of course, Dearest, all of us who become the bridge between the worlds were first been afraid. It is good to have fear - to still have fear, but never to give up."

Jahmed smiled. "It keeps us honest. And you have seen what dishonesty will do. Instead of fear, find respect and know that you fill a much larger prophecy than this small act. It will be over soon."

"Yes, Zahava." Ajah swallowed hard, nodded once and stepped forward into the cavern. "Let us begin."

The chamber was prepared, as was the special dyes to draw the spirit bird, the Sagittariidae, upon Ajah's skin. It was laid out in small pots, the needle-thin pieces of wood carved for the ceremony were wrapped in leather and placed beside them.

The women of the temple assembled in solemn support, from the youngest to the oldest. They were seated in a half-moon with the fire between them and the pallet Ajah would lie upon.

Pallin stood with her hand outstretched, a beatific smile on her face. She had returned to her true home and peace filled her entire body. Mursilis sat on Inni's lap, dark eyes watching with an intent focus that belied his age.

The fire was lit and sacred herbs waited to be scattered amongst the flame. The smoke would ease Ajah's pain as the dye-covered points of wood entered her body. The smoke would also serve to draw the energies of the women into the plea for the Sagittariidae to bless Ajah and grant her access between the worlds.

The one cause for concern was the artist who would place the holy image upon Ajah. For the first time ever, the artist was a male, and allowed access to the cavern only after a blood-oath of secrecy was sworn. Ajah found the elder man and brought him to Jahmed, just as she promised. He said upon his honor, upon his life, that he could be trusted. Jahmed's eyes darted toward the old man and she prayed this was true.

Seeing this stranger seated in the place of the sacred artist, Jahmed fought the grief once again. Seire had always been the one to perform the rites of passage and create the union between spirit and flesh of a newly initiated priestess.

I cannot think of these things now. I can only bring together the sacred circle and pray Gaea will assist us.

Jahmed led Ajah to the pallet and helped her disrobe. Once the young woman lay on her belly, with her head cradled in her arms, Jahmed placed a light cover across her buttocks and legs. This cover would be pulled up over the likeness of the Sagittariidae to blot the blood.

The man who would draw down the spirit of the Sagittariidae into Ajah smiled at Jahmed, a sweet and loving smile. He who would envision the image and place the reflection of power - the connection between the Great Mother and the Blue Serpent - reassured them all would be well.

Jahmed felt immense relief. She knew this man was not one of the invaders, but found Najahmara through travel with a supply caravan. He was dark of skin, much like her only with a bronze hue. He wore long winding cloths about his body in a manner unseen in Najahmara. Yet, in that moment, he did not seem foreign. He did not hold ego, but rather transcended the differences in physical body with great wisdom and compassion mirrored in his almond-shaped eyes.

Accepting the man whose name was Nishant as part of their priestess tribe became bearable, as if he was meant to be present. Perhaps not only meant to be there, but willed there by something greater than all of them.

A gift from Gaea.

Jahmed returned his smile and nodded.

The drums began.

*****

Kulika swept from the castle, smiling to himself as a few men stood against many. He cared not who survived the skirmish. Even though the traitorous act was against the host body, Kulika held them all in contempt, for they reflected injustice against the Sky god himself.

Those who dismissed Kulika, forgot him, cared nothing of his need to be incarnated - those who saw him only as the mate to their beloved Gaea - those mortals deserved punishment for their disrespect.

In Kulika's mind, humans were all the same. They carried the equal sins whether or not it was dispensed from their own hands.

"Let them bleed," Kulika hissed. "Let them all die."

Drifting in his ethereal form, unseen by human eyes, Kulika made his way up the backbone of raised ground. He had no need to follow a path, only the curve of land as it rose to the tabled ridge. Chuckling to himself, Kulika found the sealed entrance to the caves and remembered how he took refuge within the bosom of his mate after possessing the priestess.

Niala Aaminah, she who could call his spirit into form, opened herself to him when the foreigners attacked and he took her with veracity. His power exceeded even his expectations. As he flooded her body with his will, her human mass shifted and, for once, he was allowed his natural shape - that of a giant blue serpent.

Ahh, how he adored the freedom! All his pent up anger and resentment was expelled as he devoured the mortals who took up weapons against him. He could still taste the blood and flesh and he reveled in it.

After the violence was quelled, the priestess collapsed back into her own body. Kulika planned to hide his spirit within her but War forced him out. Ares stole the woman away from her people and left Kulika without form.

Kulika growled at the memory and craved the blood of the War god even yet for Ares' theft of the woman. There was no other choice but to leave the priestess behind. Kulika slunk away in the chaos and hid within the recesses of the stone. No one was the wiser.

It was within those cavern walls that Kulika found a human

vessel, Hattusilis, pinned beneath a huge urn, legs crushed, unable to run. It was there Kulika tormented the weak mortal until his mind was as broken as his body. Watching his decline brought Kulika true enjoyment - he was certain the mortal would die there, captive of the Sky God.

But, no. War once again intervened.

Deimos found Hattusilis, rescued him and the mortal was healed by the priestess with many braids. The priestess who fought with him. The priestess who called Gaea during ritual but then refused the holy union of Earth and Sky.

And when Kulika finally won out and fully possessed the mortal, the priestess with many braids intervened once again. Though Hattusilis' own man wielded the sword that ended the king's life, it was through the woman's guidance.

She would pay for this travesty. All would be punished.

There was no need to seek an opening into the caves. In his spirit form, Kulika could pass through vegetation, rock, soil and clay without issue. He found himself within the womb of his treasured mate. The utter darkness was of no consequence as Kulika was a child of Day. He could call forth the light. His very being glowed incandescently with captured sunrays.

As he drifted with restless indifference, he felt the disapproval of his beloved seeping through the walls of the cavern.

"You do not understand, Beloved," Kulika whispered. "All around the great sphere of your body, there are those who adore you, who worship you, who love you. They call to you, bring you into human form. I am nothing. They do not know we are mated and would not care if they did. I am left to encircle your body, always present, always protecting but never brought forth to enjoy the delights of mortal kind."

Gaea's displeasure grew. Kulika could feel the stifling edge of her censure closing about him and yet she did not speak.

"I must find another form to inhabit. Do not deny me this existence, even for a short time." As Kulika moved through the cavern, he saw through his serpent's eyes the now-vacant bier. He sniffed the air, picking up the scent of humans. He saw no one. Just an empty tomb.

But there. There was the scent of flesh and blood overriding the grime. Kulika continued forward until he reached the crevice that joined with a tunnel. Sliding through the opening, he followed the aroma. Midway, he felt a vibration that did not belong to the rock surrounding him. When he paused to listen he recognized it.

Drums.

Not loud but a constant rhythm like a beacon to a ship. Kulika followed the echo as if by invitation and he, the honored guest. Not long after, he found the source, a gathering of humans around a fire, huddled within a smaller cavern. On the other side of the circle, Kulika could see an exit, dimly lit by the full moon.

There was something familiar about the drums, the scent of smoke in the air, and the chanting that was no more than a low murmur. He watched as a robed male dipped a pointed stick into a pot and then began to stab it into the skin of a naked female lying on a pallet.

A most inexplicable ritual.

Kulika frowned, uncertain as to what they did. After inhabiting Hattusilis, Kulika saw many rites that appeared awkward and odd to him. There was only one rite he fully embraced, that of their mating ceremony.

This he enjoyed.

The present ceremony made no sense.

While the chanting went on, the man continued to draw upon the reclining female, who lay with her arms folded beneath her head. Her face was turned toward the tunnel, giving Kulika clear vision. Her eyes scrunched up and her lips pinched together with each poke of the stick.

If it hurt, why did she let them do it?

He was puzzled by the behavior. To seek pleasure was beneficial. To seek pain - unless it was someone else's pain -

made no sense.

Gaea's expanding anger buzzed in Kulika's ears but he would have none of it. Yes, he knew these females were special to his mate. They were the ones who called her into form and let her walk amongst them. They were the ones who denied him, unless Gaea commanded his manifestation. They gave everything to Gaea and nothing to Kulika.

He meant nothing to them.

With a hiss, Kulika decided he would inhabit one of them and force retribution for their disrespect. Let them pray to Gaea for their salvation.

Kulika studied the group for a potential host. The male was too well guarded for possession. He carried great light within his body and was at peace with his surroundings.

Kulika needed one who was discontent and unwell, as Hattusilis had been. He scanned each female, though he was hampered by the waking sleep into which they were all engaged. Mesmerized, the females sat with closed eyes, chanting or drumming, oblivious to Kulika's presence.

All but one.

The female with colorless hair glanced toward him. Her eyes widened as she shifted her weight, and the weight of the male child in her lap. She continued to stare in Kulika's direction.

Her mouth fell open and the words of the chant ceased. Her hand passed over her eyes, pausing to rub one as she squinted toward the entrance to the tunnel.

She saw him.

Kulika withdrew, hiding from her sight. How could one of the mortal kind see him, a being of Spirit? He cast back into his memories and the memories of the human he had occupied. The one who stared at him was the frail one locked in bouts of moon madness. She was the one who did not resemble the others with her pale hair, skin and blue eyes.

She was the one who stole the boy from his father, the very boy she held in her lap. Kulika peered around the corner and found

Pallin, the missing mate to Hattusilis.

Kulika had enjoyed her body. The fury at her loss brought about the discarnate position in which he found himself. For that, too, she would suffer, but not just yet, for she was pregnant and not a good choice for him to inhabit.

He saw, too, the priestess with many braids and hatred filled him once more. She caused this. She would be punished most of all.

Gaea railed against him. When that did no good, she begged and pleaded for Kulika, her Dearest, to leave these women alone. They did not deserve the carnage that was in Kulika's thoughts, but he brushed Gaea aside as an insignificant annoyance. For once, he was in control and not the other way around.

With a rattle of his coils and a loud hiss, Kulika descended upon the unsuspecting women. Inni shrieked as the energy was forced inside of her, yet another rape, though of a different ilk.

Mursilis went tumbling from her lap, screaming in terror. The entire group, as one, snapped to attention, eyes flying open, palms lifting to ward off an attack.

Jahmed thought for one fleeting second that it was Hattusilis and his soldiers who invaded the sacred rites. As she blinked, she saw nothing save Inni writhing on the ground as if stung by a nest of flying insects. She beat at her chest, foam dripping from her mouth around the gurgles and gasps.

Although Tulane snatched the babe up, he continued to shriek while straining toward Inni, his little hands batting at the air. Jahmed crawled to Inni's side and tried to bring her to a sitting position. Her body was rigid, frozen into an unmovable dead weight.

"Inni. Inni! Can you hear me? Please, Love, speak to me." Jahmed patted Inni's cheeks and smoothed the wild tumble of hair away from her face. "Someone bring water. Now."

Inni blinked once, eyes glazed. She blinked again and a cunning glint replaced the blankness. Her lips twisted in a semblance of a smile, a wicked knowing smile that made Jahmed draw back in confusion.

"Inni? Are you alright? Speak to me, Dearest."

Instead, Inni rose to her feet in one graceful motion. With a backhand swing, she slapped Jahmed so hard she was sent flying into the cavern wall. A loud crack resounded as her head struck a sharp outcropping of rock and Jahmed slid senseless to the ground. Dark blood ran from her skull and began to pool beneath her.

Kulika reached for the child with malicious intent and was blocked by Pallin, who threw herself in front of Mursilis and Tulane. Kulika laughed aloud with new vocal cords, though in a puny high-pitched laugh and shoved Pallin as hard as the frail body would allow.

Pallin fell into the campfire and began screaming as the pain seared her skin. She tried to roll out of the pit as the end of her braid caught fire but could not. One arm was broken from striking the rocks lining the fire pit.

Danu and the attempted to drag her free of the flames but had not the strength. Instead, she dumped a water flask over her head, hands and arms and into the fire while Pallin sobbed in agony. The male ignored the commotion and instead, continued to create the picture upon the back of the naked priestess with frantic haste.

Nishant knew he faced unholy wickedness and had to finish the cord between Ajah and the Snake Eater. With a few more pricks, the connection would be complete. He whispered prayers to his deities, specifically to Nut, she of the Night Sky, while he worked, beseeching her to intervene. He sensed her presence just as he sensed the Earth Mother, Gaea, who reeled with anguish over the behavior of the Blue Sky.

He did not lift his head to meet the gaze of Kulika. Instead, he bowed over the young woman who now struggled to rise and fight the menace in front of them.

"Stay," Nishant whispered. "Once the cord is tied you will have the strength to stand against this shameful god."

Ajah sobbed as she heard the continued screams of her sisters but held back until the last dot was placed upon her body. With that, the bond was complete. The spirit of the Sagittariidae descended into her and lifted her up, levitating her above the pallet. When Ajah's feet touched the ground, she held her arms above her head and called to Gaea.

"Come! Come to me, Great Mother, and let us put an end to this depravity." Ajah jerked forward, stumbling as the energy took her. When next she opened her eyes, she did not see with her own. Someone else held her in thrall.

It was not Gaea.

"Stop, Blue Sky." The command was laced with heavy warning.

Kulika froze in place. He turned the skinny body of the pale priestess with a slowness born of regret, for he knew who spoke to him.

The female who had lain naked upon the pallet now stood before him bathed in Nut's glory. Kulika saw the essence of the Night Sky behind the unblinking blue eyes. He felt her power radiate outward, capturing him as he was locked in the feeble mortal shell. He found he could go no further.

"Why do you do this?" Nut demanded. "I have sent you numerous warnings to desist this madness. I watched while my sister, Gaea, mourned your misbehavior but was gripped within the weakness of her love for you.

"Many times I urged her to step in, yet she claimed you would tire of this game. That you would leave this people alone of your own free will." Nut took one step forward, arms outstretched.

"I am nothing to them." Kulika spoke with bitterness. "Why should I abandon my games for a boring existence that they ignore?"

"It is not true they disregard your presence. You are the Blue Sky encircling the Earth. They admire your beauty. You protect them."

"They show me no respect."

"They offer you many blessings." Nut flicked her fingers at Kulika. "Come, let us leave them in peace."

Kulika hesitated, his gaze wavering about the cavern. The females huddled around the wounded one, who lay moaning in their midst. The male had risen to his feet, white cloth fluttering about his ankles. He stood vigil with a sharp blade held in one hand, ready to defend the women if Kulika were to advance toward them.

They were all helpless puny mortals who had no defense against him. But Nut - she was in a strong capable body with firm breasts and slim hips that swayed seductively as she moved toward him.

Nut invited him to make love? He licked his lips as his heart was filled with lust, even though he could hear the pleas of his mate, Gaea, begging him to abandon his desires and return to his own realm.

He ignored Gaea and instead smiled at Nut. "I have long wondered what it would be like to take carnal pleasure with you. We have opportunity now to satisfy those erotic dreams."

Nut paused and tilted her head to one side. "I have watched you engage with my sister on many occasions. We could share those delights." She came closer, her lips curved in a sensual smile.

The hunger subsided and suspicion ignited as Kulika stared at her. Gaea often tricked him into sex then sent him back to his own lonely realm. Nut was capable of the same tactic.

This time, he would resist.

"Kulika, come to me." Nut smiled, blue eyes beseeching him to consent. "I have need of you. Would you deny me? There may be no other chance to touch each other."

"No, this is a cruel trick. This time, I refuse." Kulika turned away from Nut. "I will not fall prey."

Kulika ducked out the vine-covered exit from the caverns into the dark night and paused to breathe fresh air.

Freedom at last.

He would leave this valley. He could journey anywhere he wanted. He could find a new stronger body once he was away from the nagging of Gaea and Nut. He could do as he pleased and no one could stop him. He puffed out the scrawny chest of the pallid female and straightened her bony shoulders.

"I will return to my Realm when I wish and not before." His voice echoed in agreement along the ridge, sliding down into the trees of the northern forest.

Rebellion felt good.

He took one step forward and felt a jolt to his back. Searing pain expanded throughout the mortal body. Air whooshed from his mouth and nothing save emptiness returned. Blackness descended across his vision. Weakness stole his balance and he toppled to the ground.

Kulika released the body, separating himself from the unfortunate female. Enraged that, for the second time, he had been forced from his host, Kulika whirled in midair, ready to attack.

His essence appeared as white smoke, invisible to mortal eyes but perceptible to Nut. She stood firm in the form of the naked priestess, feet apart, one hand still raised from her strike, the dagger dripping blood down her arm.

Inni was crumpled at her feet, dead from the blow.

"You see what you have brought about?"

"How dare you steal this from me," raged Kulika. His essence splintered into a vast explosion of colors before coming back together into the white cloud.

"You are deluded. Dangerous." Nut shook her head in sorrow. "Such misbehavior. Has Gaea been so dreadful to you?"

"She controls my every move. I have no existence outside the Earth. I am weary of it."

"My sister offers unconditional love. Shame on you."

Kulika softened, stretched out toward the female who held Nut. "It is true. I do not mean to cause her grief. I merely wish to be celebrated, as you are."

"I am forgotten as well. I do not punish them for it."

"We are not the same. You have all the Stars and the

Moon as your companions. I am alone."

"Not so. You have the Sun." Nut gazed upward to the heavens. "I never seen daylight."

"Are we two of a kind, then? Destined to be solitary and remote from this Mortal Realm?"

"Perhaps it is not fair, yet it is the way our world exists, since time began." Nut nodded, deep in thought. "Even so, you must return to your realm and consider your actions. You have hurt many."

"I refuse."

"Where will you go?" Nut's voice was gentle.

"I will find another body."

"Ahh, Kulika, I cannot allow that."

With a deep exhale, a sigh that sounded like heavy wind in the boughs of the trees, Nut slipped from Ajah's body. She became a hazy swirl of energy smudged against the darkened horizon.

Ajah swayed to the left, staggered a few steps and fell. It was a slow and graceful descent with no harm to her body. One arm went up to cradle her head as she hit and lay still.

Nut's discarnate form coiled around Kulika, and though he struggled and fought and snarled his fury, she held onto him with all her might.

"In time, Kulika, in time, you will understand I do this for you."

With one last surge, Nut took them both away from the Mortal World and into the Sky Realm, where they belonged.

TWENTY-ONE

Niala moved about the quiet chamber hidden within the lower level of Aphrodite's palace with restless inactivity. Too long had she lain upon the soft bed staring at the ceiling, wondering who she was. There was the memory of Niala Aaminah and all that was her life, from her simple beginning as a goatherd to her mortal death as a babe slid from her body.

The memories were present but distant, as clouds on the horizon, seen but uncertain as to what they would bring. Gentle clouds to cover the sun and give relief from the heat? Gray clouds holding much-needed rain to feed the land? Violent clouds bringing lightning and thunder? Purplish clouds dropping ice and snow?

Past lives swirling through her thoughts with great persistence. Niala Aaminah was but one recollection with every detail etched into the fabric of the physical body she inhabited.

The strongest by far, the most recent, it played up and around all the others: once an ancient queen, and again as a tormented slave, a tribal leader and a simple laborer. Mother of none.

The common thread, always a female, never existing in a masculine body. That was curious. In her expanded awareness, there was the question why? Why not cross over to another sexual experience?

Niala touched a pretty fan lying on a lacquered table and traced the delicate pictures painted on the silk. She opened and closed the thin material as she stared at the carved bone ribs holding it together. Waving it in front of her face to feel the slight breeze, she closed her eyes and sought a moment of silence in her mind but the thoughts continued to tumble over and over.

Flashes of what had once been: toiling in hot sun to build a rock shelter, digging in moist soil to harvest a few root vegetables, scraping hides for clothing, baking flat bread over an open fire, catching fish in a cold stream with her bare hands - lives, many lives she had led, all different, all with the sole purpose of what?

Avoidance.

Wrinkling her nose, Niala snapped the fan shut and put it back in its place. She continued circling the room, touching everything in her path. Beautiful wall hangings, glass-blown lamps with many edges, tall candles with etched patterns, a couch with carved animal faces on the armrests, brushes with the patina of many uses glowing on the handles, tiny bottles of scented oils.

One scent in particular caught her attention. She paused to lift it to her nose, inhaling the aroma.

Sandalwood.

Feeling as if she floated in mid-air, Niala was once again in the arms of Ares the Destroyer. She could smell the scent of sandalwood rising from his heated skin as he made love to her. She could feel the roughness of his hands, the weight of his body, hear his harsh breath as it rushed out in completion.

Ares was the key.

He was the reason she was incarnate so many times. She lived and died, hiding from him. Avoiding him.

But why?

Niala's head ached. She put the bottle down and rubbed the

back of her hand beneath her nose, trying to erase the smell, to erase those memories.

From Ares, her mind leapt to Deimos. He whose tender kiss had awakened her, whose face she looked upon when her eyes first opened. Reflected in his black gaze was the blush of mad love, the kind that demanded great sacrifice.

She remembered how Deimos stole her from Athos in spite of the undeniable punishment Ares would exact for the treasonous deed. She remembered Gaea descending into her and calling Kulika, her mate, into Deimos. She remembered their frantic lovemaking behind the stone markers.

The clutch of pain as labor commenced and the birth of a child in a pool of blood. As darkness descended she asked Deimos to take care of the babe, and as light returned to her, she asked for that babe.

Deimos was shamefaced when he could not produce the child. Though she could see he preferred to stay at her side, she bade him find the babe and bring the tiny girl to her mother.

Niala could not hide her relief when Deimos took his leave. Alone, her thoughts went in circles but little emotion followed. It was as if she observed from a distance, these events, these many lives. Questions rose to the forefront like the one before her.

Why had she always incarnated as a female?

Because she sought the one thing that could not come from a male. Niala paused, one finger touching a silk cloth, intricately woven into a scene of round and smiling maidens welcoming home their men from a great oceanic journey.

Children.

She wanted to give birth to children. That had been the promise, had it not?

If she would give permission to Gaea to draw her spirit from the chaotic darkness and thrust her into physical form, children would be her gift. Niala remembered her acceptance of this pact for she longed to have these flesh and blood children.

To be incarnate, to hold them, to love them. Locked in spirit, this seemed impossible, but now there was opportunity.

She agreed to satisfy Gaea's desires and become First Woman on this round ball of dirt, green with fecund growth, veined with clear water and abundant food for such a body. It was with great joy she leapt into that existence, along with her companion destined to be First Man.

Niala rubbed her temples, head aching with these thoughts, wishing them to leave her. None of this was important. It mattered not what once was but what existed in the moment. Yet the chain of events kept repeating until she was forced to examine the finality of that lifetime.

Those bodies, First Woman and First man, were made from the elements and could only exist a short time. This was the knowledge behind the simple creatures they were. The female carried a frantic sense of their temporary existence, wanting no more than to birth a child. To feel something grow within her, to come from her body, to nurture it. This desire was primal and one that all spirit beings watched with interest, for they, too were curious to feel rather than to sense.

Dropping her hand to her side, Niala continued her walk about the small chamber. The sensations of misery and joy, of pain and exultation continued. A memory flashed through her mind of living in a cave, existing in the shadows - a life of great sorrow.

First Man and First Woman were to birth the mortal race so these very spirits, their sisters and brothers, could incarnate and become a living tribute to Gaea, Mother of All.

Niala clasped her fingers together to still the trembling as the memories poured in. Her body froze in place, aching with this distant grief.

She shrieked as the babe was wrenched from her arms by her mate. Scrabbling from the recesses of the cave on her hands and knees, weakened by the birth, unable to stop Anyal from his grim task.

Please, please, please, she howled, a keening wail that went on and on and on but to no avail.

The blood of her babe was no more than a black shadow seeping from the broken head in the twilight. Anyal held in his hand the rock that smashed open the tiny skull, the rock that was now marked with the same black blood. Unheeded, it ran down his fingers and arm and dripped onto his knee as he crouched next to it.

He stared with blind eyes at the small body at his feet. It had no face. A gash where the mouth should be, two holes for a nose, and misshapen eyes sloping to the sides of the head, that was all. No face. The body was twisted, the hairline low, the jaw sunken, the tiny fingers and toes webbed.

It was not human.

Anyal did what he had to do.

She emitted frantic shrieks, pleading with him to give her back the babe, but he did not listen.

With one blow, Anyal had stopped the mewling, and now he watched its blood slow to a trickle and a final end.

He covered his ears, smearing the blood onto his face.

Stop, he roared. What is done is done. We will try again.

No more! She crawled from the cave to the crumpled body of the babe and scooped it into her arms; her wailing grew louder still. No more...ahh...no more.

Niala covered her ears to shut out the screaming only to realize her voice had joined the phantom female's grieving as she clutched the broken body of her babe. Her arms moved to her chest as if she held the same infant and tears streamed from her eyes. Though she begged for breath to gain hold, she knew in her heart the babe was dead.

Killed by his father, Anyal. Murdered before her very eyes after he snatched the child from her breast. She went after him, but it was too late. She saw what he did. She saw what her mate did a dozen times over and she could never forgive him.

Never.

The face of the ancient Anyal merged with the face of Ares the Destroyer. She knew them to be one and the same.

"Why?" Niala railed at Gaea. "Why would you do this to me? And every life after, to never birth a living child? How cruel. What did I do to deserve such punishment?"

Walking faster, Niala circled the chamber again and again, but never once considering the door. Her freedom was on the other side and yet she would not leave.

Deimos had promised to bring her babe to her.

With a deep breath, Niala paused. A child. She had birthed a child in this life and she lived. Not a demon child with no features, but a beautiful girl.

Shaking, Niala sat on a low stool, face buried in her hands, overwhelmed by more reflection on her life as the simple priestess.

Hundreds of years during which she suppressed any possibility of birthing a child - so counter-intuitive to all that had gone before. Why?

Ares the Destroyer had found her and she knew in her heart he was Anyal. She would not let him take another child from her.

A scream lodged in her throat but before it burst loose, another face appeared, a kind sweet face that brought more tears of grief.

Seire.

She had at long last birthed a child and then watched as the tiny babe grew old before her eyes. Seire lived to be an old woman with no hint of illness, but that she was mortal was of no question. And then came her horrifying death at the hands of the invading soldiers, a death she did not deserve.

"You should have gone gently into the Shadowland, my Daughter, not in such an ugly manner."

And yet, Niala knew Seire acted with great courage that night.

Rage rose in a delicate bubble and burst over Niala. There was no frenzied behavior, no madness. There was only a ringing in her ears that echoed deep in her soul and a knowing bloomed from the wrathful carnage of what had once been.

Niala Aaminah no longer existed.

Sleepwalking through eons, through hundreds of lives to avoid the pain of the first one. This time was different. Her body did not deteriorate in death. Lifting a hand, she stared at the fingers, palm, wrist, arm, then dropped it to her side.

She came to her feet again and walked with great care around the quarters, examining every tiny detail until she came across a mirror upon the wall. A shining disc in a frame.

For the first time, she saw her own image. Not distorted in water or warped in polished metal, but clear: luminescent amber eyes, honeyed skin, auburn hair in a tight braid, pulling her features into a severe expression.

A pleasant appearance but unfamiliar.

Shoulders rolling back, belly tightening, she began to scratch at her arms and torso. Her clothing was itchy and she could not stand to wear the gown. She threw it to the floor and stepped on it as if it would bring relief to grind it beneath her feet.

It did not.

A low throaty growl burst forth as she tore at the braid, releasing the wild curls and cascading waves to fall like a blanket all the way to her hips. Still, it stuck to her neck and was too hot, too heavy.

She yanked at the strands, wanting to pull them from her scalp as the tingling became a burning sensation all over her body. Her gaze fell upon the breakfast tray and a knife caught her eye.

Chop it off, throw it away. It is no longer who you are.

Great hunks fell to the floor as she hacked at the autumn hair. Long strands floated in the air around her, drifting away to cling to a piece of fabric or fall upon some surface.

She slashed until it was gone. All that was left were tiny curling tendrils about her ears and on her forehead and cheeks. Wispy strands lay against her neck, revealing a perfectly shaped head and long neck.

Relief flooded over her. She felt light, buoyant and happy.

She was not Niala Aaminah. She would not appear as her.

She crossed the marble floor, now littered with hair, to watch the placid pretty waves roll onto the shore. This, too, she had never seen, always choosing land-locked existence. The only other breakers had been the pounding surf upon the brutal rocks below Athos, or the dirty spray on the boat docks.

So much to understand about these choices, these lives.

This life.

"Who am I?"

Clouds began to gather on the horizon, the promise of a storm charging the air, blotting out the sun. A streak of lightening rent the gloom as the fast-moving bank whipped up the wind. As thunder rattled the leaves and shook the walls, she knew.

She knew who she was.

She was Rebellion.

"My name is Nyx."

The Goddess of Darkness is risen.

EPILOGUE

Najahmara folks buried Inni and Jahmed in the forest behind the little hut they called home. In attendance were those who loved the women, who cherished their lives and mourned their deaths yet took comfort they were now together forever.

Their interment was private, not the spectacle presented for King Hattusilis as all Najahmara was forced to witness. The legion of soldiers and their women feasted for days before the king was placed upon his funeral pyre and set ablaze.

As a female is not allowed to ascend to the crown, Pallin returned to the temple with her son, Mursilis, but that he is too young to rule, she named Zan as the provisionary king. She trusted he would be a compassionate and strong leader during the intervening years.

Ajah took charge of the temple, though young and inexperienced, she held sway over the Great Mother. The Sagittariidae provided resilient and wise support, enabling her to priestess with sage confidence.

Eternal Love's obsession-turned-to-madness finds its way into the Mortal Realm while Anteros lingers with the beautiful Hylas, ignoring his responsibilities. Aphrodite's minions guard her every step, creating diversions and deliberate mayhem while she continues her search for Ares.

Ares is without any power and must rely upon his wits and human endurance to find his way back, but the question upper most in his mind: can he reclaim his immortal body or is he doomed to live out the life of a mortal sailor?

Deimos is unaware of his parent's struggles for he is embroiled in his own plight: where is the babe, Alcippe and why does Eris and Phobos refuse to answer his call?

And Rebellion, the newly-awakened goddess called Nyx, laughs within the shadows at the follies of both Immortal and Mortal Realms.

IMMORTAL & OTHER REALM CHARACTERS

NAME:	**ROLE:**
Aglaia	Love's Brilliance/Dismay, Middle Grace,
Aglauros	Mother of Eris, Wood Nymph
Alcippe	Daughter of Niala and Ares
Amason	Ares' broad sword
Anteros	Love's Response/Manipulation, Deimos' twin
Aphrodite	Eternal Love/Hatred, Wife to Ares, and briefly to Hephaestos,
Ares	Endless War/Creator, Husband to Aphrodite
Arawn	Master of the Wild Hunt
Branwen	Iris of the Rainbows true Sidhe identity
Cedalion	Mountain Dwarf, loyal servant to Hephaestos
Cetacea	Blue Whale Spirit Guide (Pallin)
Clio	Nymph of the Nereid Clan
Corvidae	Raven Spirit Guide (Niala)
Chronos	Titan, father of Zeus
Council of Ages	Ruling body of the Immortal Realm
Danu	Divine Ebb and Flow/Ruler of Tuath De
Deimos	War's Terror/Survival, Son of Ares & Aphrodite, Anteros' twin
Delphinus	Dolphin Spirit Guide
Demeter	Kore/Persephone's Mother
Dryad	Tree Nymph Clan, particularly Oak trees.
Dryops	Hylas' father, King of Oeta
Ellopia	Eris' Sylph Homeland
Enyo	War's Disgrace/Pride, Eater of souls (female)
Eos	Titan goddess of the Dawn – Ares' lover
Eris	War's Strife/Peace, Son of Ares & Aglauros
Erinnyes	War's Punishment/Reward, Ares' minions (also known as the Furies)
Eros	Love's Passion/Fury, Son of Ares & Aphrodite, twin to Phobos
Euphrosyne	Love's Rejoice/Grief, Youngest Grace
Fates	Three immortal females who weave destiny (also known as Moerae)
Fey	Realm of the Tuath De
Furies	The Erinnyes – War's minions
Gaea	Immortal Earth/Abundance, Mother of All, mate to Kulika
Graces	Aglaia, Thaleia, Euphrosyne – servants to Aphrodite

Hades	Perpetual Transformation, Persephone's Husband
Hephaestos	Alchemy/Separation, Second Husband to Aphrodite
Hera	Queen of the Immortals, Ares' mother
Hermes	Communication/Silence, Zeus' messenger
Hypnos	Sleep, son of Hades, twin of Thanatos
Keres	War's Penalty/Return, Female Death Spirits – Ares' minions
Kobaloi	A tribe of fierce warriors living in the Sacred Forest
Kore	**(Persephone)** New Spring/Queen of Souls/Hades' Wife
Kulika	Immortal Sky/Proliferation, Blue serpent, mate to Gaea
Leuce	Daughter of Oceanus, Hades lover
Leuncolus	Great Lion Spirit Guide (Jahmed)
Llywy	Iris of the Rainbows Fey identity
Matholwch	Iris/Branwen's Sidhe husband
Moerae	The Fates – three immoral women who weave destiny
Nemesis	Love's Revenge/Forgiveness
Nereid	Water Nymph Clan
Nyx	Rebellion/Submission – Niala's immortal role
Odyne	Love's Pain/Balm
Oizus	Love's Misery/Joy
Panic	Phobos – son of Ares & Aphrodite
Passion	Eros – son of Aphrodite & Ares
Pegae	Water Nymph Clan
Pehun	Eris' Sylph Grandmother
Pennarddun	Sidhe Queen, mother if Iris/Branwen
Persephone	**(Kore)** Regeneration/Queen of Souls/Hades' Wife
Phobos	War's Panic/Surrender, Son of Ares & Aphrodite, twin to Eros
Priapos	Centaur who trains warriors
Rebellion	Immortal Spirit drawn into Niala Aaminah
Response	Anteros – son of Aphrodite & Ares
Rhea	Titan, Mother of Zeus
Sagittariidae	Snake Eater Crane Spirit Guide (Ajah)
Selene	Moon goddess
Strife	Eris - son of Ares & Aglauros
Sylph	Fey folk of the Sacred Forest – Eris' people
Synod	Winged horse in service to the Immortals
Terror	Deimos – son of Ares & Aphrodite

Thaleia	Love's Bloom/Decay, Middle Grace, (female)
Thanatos	Bitter Death - son of Hades
Tuath De	Sidhe Royalty
Wild Hunt	Tuath De folk who terrorize both Realms
Zelos	Love's Jealousy/Truth (female)
Zelus	Love's Rivalry/Friend
Zeus	King of the Immortals, Ares' father.

MORTAL CHARACTERS

NAME:	ROLE:
Ajah	Sixteen year old girl, Priestess in training
Anyal	First Man in ancient story of creation
Azhar	Hattusilis' first wife
Benor	Trader from the Steppelands
Connal	Zan's brother, soldier in arms
Deniz	Twelve year old girl, priestess in training
Edibe	Helped rescue Niala from Athos, founded Najahmara
Elche	Second Woman in ancient story of creation,
Hattusilis	King of the Steppelands invaders
Ilya	First Woman in ancient story of creation
Inni	Third Priestess of Gaea
Jahmed	Second Priestess of Gaea
Layla	Founded Najahmara with Niala
Mahin	Rescued Niala from Athos, founded Najahmara
Niala Aaminah	First Priestess of Gaea – Ares' obsession
Nishant	Sprit Walker who found his way to Najahmara
Pallin	Fourth Priestess of Gaea
Seire	Fifth Priestess of Gaea, Niala's daughter
Seyyal	Helped rescue Niala from Athos, founded Najahmara
Telio	Nephew of Hattusilis, invader from Steppelands
Tulane	Fourteen year old girl, priestess in training
Warsus	Slayer of Niala's original tribe
Zahava	Teacher/healer, term of respect
Zan	Second in command, invader from Steppelands

LOCATIONS

ANKIRA: City in the Steppelands from which Hattusilis and legions began their journey. (Mortal Realm)

ATHOS: Home of Ares the Destroyer, a gray fortress located on a mountain in Thrace. (Mortal Realm)

BWLCH GIEDD: A gap between the hills leading to Queen Pennarddun's Cairn (lies within both Mortal and Immortal Realms)

COS: Home of Aphrodite, a beautiful, sunny island located in the South Aegean Sea (Mortal Realm)

ELLOPIA: Homeland of Eris, the Sacred Forest of the Sylphs (Mortal Realm)

LEMNOS: Home of Hephaestos, a green, verdant island located in the North Aegean Sea. (Mortal Realm)

LLYN y FAN FAWR: Lake Fan Fawr (lies within both Mortal & Immortal Realms)

NAJAHMARA: A village nestled between the Bayuk and Maendre rivers located in south Cappadocia. Founded by Niala Aaminah and her four companions. (Mortal Realm)

OLYMPUS: Home of the Council, a golden city with Zeus and Hera reigning as king and queen. (Immortal Realm)

PRIAPOS' CAVE: Home of the warrior centaur, the remote and heavily forested island of Kerkyra

SHADOWLAND: Resting place for spirits of the dead. (Hades Immortal Realm)

STEPPELANDS: Far northern reaches of Cappadocia. (Mortal Realm.)

FEY REALM: Homeland of Iris of the Rainbows and the Tuath De/Sidhe Folk

MAP OF THE KNOWN WORLD

ABOUT THE AUTHOR:

Ruth Souther has written three Mythic Fantasy novels (Immortal Journey series) and an intuitive instructional book on Tarot (The Heart of Tarot) all available through Amazon. She is happily married to a wonderful man, has 4 amazing children, along with their spouses, grandchildren and great-grandchildren, pets and grand-pets.

Life is good.

Facebook: Immortal Journey Book Series
www.lifeinthefantasylane.com,
www.astarsjourney.com,
www.theedgeofperception.com
www.aaharaspiritualcommunity.com

AND NOW
FOR A SNEAK
PEEK AT

OBSESSION
OF
LOVE

ONE

Anteros felt the shift of energy as if an earthquake gripped the Isle of Cos. Alarmed, he leaped from the rumpled bed he shared with Hylas, though the young man grabbed at his waist in an attempt to impede his escape.

Laughing, Hylas fell across the silken sheets to lie in a seductive pose. "Come back, Anteros. Do not leave me all alone."

With a shake of his head, Anteros leaned against the door frame and stared out at the frothing sea. It seemed the entire palace tilted onto one edge and he could scarce stand upright without losing his balance.

The walls shuddered and shivered, and the long white draperies blew inward, snapping against his naked body as the wind scuttled across the tiled balcony. Saltwater laced the air along with the underlying scent of flower petals shredded by the wind, and not a bird was winging its way across the sky. The only sounds belonged to the elements.

As he watched, an ominous bank of low-lying clouds shot lightning to the surface of the choppy water. The hair on Anteros' arms stood up in response to the charge and his entire body jerked as if he, too, had been struck by the jagged streak.

"Did you not feel that surge? It was unlike anything I have ever experienced." Anteros ran his hands along his forearms, inhaling deeply to calm himself. He tasted metallic residue on his tongue.

Hylas rose from his resting place and went to stand behind Anteros, slipping his arms around his lean waist. "I am mindful only of my passion for you."

Kissing Anteros' shoulder, Hylas worked his way up to the long neck, moving aside the golden curtain of hair to nibble on his earlobe. One hand crept lower to stroke Anteros' manhood. Always, at his touch, Anteros became aroused and would succumb to another round of lovemaking.

This time, Anteros shrugged Hylas away and stepped onto the walkway, an anxious knot in the pit of his belly. He gripped the iron rail and peered as far to each side of the sprawling structure as he could and then glanced skyward. The knot grew worse as he realized the black swirling thunderheads engulfed the island.

"Something is wrong. There was no hint of a tempest heading our way." A gust of wind blew Anteros' hair about his head in a nimbus of fine strands until he gathered it up and coiled it at the nape of his neck, tucking one end into the center.

"It is just a storm passing through." Hylas joined Anteros at the railing. "Though it does look rather severe. We should return to the comfort of our bed until it moves on."

"This is not a mere squall. Something has happened, I know it here." Anteros tapped his chest with his fist. "I have shirked my duties as Love's Response long enough. I must see to Aphrodite and the children."

"I have responded well to you, have I not?" Hylas pulled Anteros into an embrace and kissed his lips. "There, you see, you have answered the call of your responsibilities through your care of me. However, I desire more of your ministrations."

"No, Dearest." Anteros returned to the interior of their quarters and lifted one hand to bring the oil lamps alight, removing the gloom cast over the pale blue walls. Another wave and he was fully clothed in a white tunic edged in deep blue. "I cannot linger with you for now but I will return as soon as I am able."

"Must I stay here?" Slumping, Hylas sat on the edge of the bed. "I am bored and would like to put my feet upon the earth."

He was such a lovely picture of virility, in spite of the gouges, gashes, scrapes and bruises inflicted upon him by the water nymphs. Anteros was tempted to change his mind and stay.

It had been a mere two weeks since Anteros rescued the young man from the nymphs of Cos, who would surely have killed him if he had not. The moment Anteros laid eyes upon Hylas, he knew he was in love.

He gazed now at Hylas' bounty: brown hair curling just so around a perfect face filled with a straight nose, full lips and wide green eyes. Powerful shoulders, arms and legs, broad chest, squared hips and a well-developed phallus. An intricate pattern of tattoos wound along both arms and across his back to end above the purest heart Anteros had ever found.

Hylas was unassuming, unaware of his beauty.

"You are still mending from the Nereid's attack. It would be best if you did not venture beyond these walls without me."

Smiling kindly, Anteros kissed the downturned mouth of his love. "Soon you may explore Cos to your heart's content."

As long as you do not stray toward the water's edge, Anteros thought.

He did not want to frighten the young man but if the Nereid nymphs laid eyes upon Hylas once again, they would capture him and drag him beneath the waves out of malice. They did not appreciate the loss of their new toy.

I should also send word to Hylas' father that his son is alive and recovering nicely on the Isle of Love, but then King Dryops might well demand his son's return, and that, I will not do.

Anteros did not voice this new thought to Hylas in fear the scattered memories of how he came to be on Cos would return and Hylas, himself, would petition his release.

"But he is not prisoner." Anteros moved along the corridor to mount a stone staircase that led to the uppermost level of

Eternal Love's palace. "I saved him from certain death and now he rests until he is strong enough to make choices."

"Whom did you save from certain death?" Thaleia met him at the entry, hands on hips, her face pinched into an irritated expression. "Yourself? If I could strangle you, I would. Why have you not responded to my call? I went in search of you, yet it seems you have hidden yourself away for reasons I do not understand. Have you any idea what has happened?"

Thaleia paused in her rant to allow Anteros to pass into Aphrodite's quarters.

"Hylas." Embarrassed, Anteros' bronzed cheeks turned a pretty shade of red as he averted his gaze from the angry woman.

Thaleia, one of three Graces - the three sisters who served Aphrodite's every need - stomped past Anteros with the query, "Who is Hylas?"

Throwing one hand in the air with fingers splayed, she added, "Never mind, I do not care who he is or what he is to you."

However, a sharp glance at his blush and she knew very well what the mysterious Hylas meant to Aphrodite's son.

"Disaster has struck and you play games."

"I am certain it is nothing you cannot handle, dear Thaleia, you are quite efficient in the running of this household."

It was true, Thaleia was efficient. She smiled wryly in acknowledgement of Anteros' statement. Being the middle sister had no adverse effect upon her for she adored any opportunity to take charge of Cos and its inhabitants. Yet Aphrodite's bizarre behavior was beyond her abilities.

Ever since Ares was struck down by the dwarf Cedalion's poisoned dagger, her beloved Princess had fallen into a sad decline, most often lying about in a stupor.

Until a few hours before, when Aphrodite flew into madness, consumed with the ignominious side of Love: revenge, jealousy, rivalry, pain and misery. With her minions Nemesis, Zelos, Zelus, Odyne and Oizus at her side, Aphrodite tore away from Cos, heading who knows where.

Most likely, the Mortal Realm to cause havoc amongst the humans.

"A curse on Hephaestos and his servant, Cedalion," Thaleia shrieked. "If not for them this disaster would not have occurred."

Anteros retreated from Thaleia. This fit was unlike her and it did not bode well. The dark clouds above Cos seemed more ominous than before.

"It is not all the Forge god's doing. Mother must take responsibility for her actions." This Anteros offered from a safe distance with a chaise lounge between them.

"Of course it is not all Hephaestos, yet whose feelings were injured enough to attempt to murder Ares? Who would do such a thing over sex?" Thaleia picked up a silver platter and threw it across the room. It clanged against the wall and bounced to the floor.

"Aphrodite's stubborn streak led her to quarrel with Ares over the conception of a child and he refused, over a babe. Imbecile!" A glass vase followed the plate, shattering tiny fragments atop the silver.

"She retaliated by annulling their marriage. It was not the most thought out deed. I wish she had consulted me first." Anteros eyed the debris.

"Aphrodite consults no one. As always, she careens out of control. How foolish of her to expect someone as simple as Hephaestos to understand the inner workings of Eternal Love."

"You have carried the burden well, as have Aglaia and Euphrosyne. I deeply appreciate the way you continue to care for all other proceedings, including my sister, Harmonia. I apologize for my absence, and yet, it was your advice I followed."

With great caution, Anteros approached the enraged Grace who now panted with her exertion. Anxiety creased her forehead and tears of frustration wet her eyes. He placed one hand upon her shoulder in sympathy, hoping to calm her.

"My advice?" Twitching his hand away, Thaleia reached for a flagon of wine and poured a generous amount into a goblet. After draining it, she pointed a finger at Anteros. "I did not advise you to disappear nor to shirk your responsibilities."

"Thaleia, do not speak to me in such a way. The Mantle of Love has not descended upon me but hovers somewhere between myself and Aphrodite. I lack the power to fully govern Love's Realm but I am still your master."

"Humph. If you are indeed Master of this Realm, in whatever potency you might muster, you had best find Aphrodite and restrain her before more damage occurs."

"What do you mean 'find her'? Where is she?"

"Excellent question and I do not have an answer. "She called every shadow of Love to her and then bolted out of here before I could stop her." Filling the goblet for the second time, Thaleia drank it down in one gulp. "I could not prevent this travesty. She is too strong."

"Thaleia, I felt a huge surge of energy and now a storm holds court above our home. Is Aphrodite the cause of this oddity?"

"I know not if my Princess brought this flood into our midst or if it is some other calamity waiting to descend upon our unfortunate heads, but I too felt the shift and it frightens me beyond reason.

"Whatever it is, Anteros, you must find her. You are linked to her, you should feel her presence."

"I am connected to her, as you are, but I do not sense her." Worry pinched his lips in a straight line.

"Nor do I, but here is a thought: who holds her obsession?"

"My father, Ares."

"And where is he?"

They stared at each other in horror before both whispered, "Olympus."

53674843R00180

Made in the USA
Charleston, SC
16 March 2016